International acclaim for

# ADELE PARKS

—who delivers "cleverness to spare"
*(Publishers Weekly)* and shar    savvy portrayals of
relationships, sex, and mar               tional
bestsellin

## LUST FOR LIFE

"Sizzling hot."

*—Marie Claire*

"[A] compulsive, sexy read."

*—The Bookseller* (U.K.)

"Adele Parks has a knack of summing up what we all want in a relationship, answering all of our 'if only' curiosities and bringing us back down to earth gently with a light-hearted take on the real world of romance. . . . Heartfelt and honest."

*—The Express* (U.K.)

"[An] excellent novel . . . well-honed and acutely observed."

*—Daily Mail* (U.K.)

Previously published in the U.K. as
*The Other Woman's Shoes*

# GAME OVER

"A very entertaining read."

*—Heat*

"Parks' style is down to earth and very, very funny."

*—OK*

"Love is found all around. . . . Parks handles it with . . . wit and verve. . . . A guilty pleasure."

*—Entertainment Weekly*

"A saucy twist on twentysomething girl-meets-boy fiction . . . [with] an exhilaratingly unconventional female protagonist. . . . Refreshing. . . . Adele Parks [has] another winner."

*—Jane Honey*

"[A] delightful romp. . . . Fun characters and a hilarious (and not unbelievable) premise."

*—Booklist*

# LARGER THAN LIFE

"Entertaining and sophisticated."

*—Marie Claire*

"Parks has scored another surefire hit with *Larger Than Life*. . . . Expect to see it peeking out of handbags near you soon."

*—Heat*

"A *Bridget Jones* meets motherhood scenario . . . fun and funny."

*—Booklist*

"An engaging read."

—*Independent* (U.K.)

"Entertaining and humorous."

—*Library Journal*

# PLAYING AWAY

"Compulsively addictive!"

—*Elle*

"An affecting first novel . . . a cheeky first-person narrative. . . . A balanced exploration of the rules of marriage."

—*Kirkus Reviews*

"*Playing Away* is a very edgy book. It's also wickedly funny and very sexy."

—*Publishers Weekly*

## Also by Adele Parks:

PLAYING AWAY

LARGER THAN LIFE

GAME OVER

Available from Downtown Press

# Lust for Life

• • • •

## Adele Parks

doWn tOwn press

New York   London   Toronto   Sydney

DOWNTOWN PRESS, published by Pocket Books
1230 Avenue of the Americas
New York, NY 10020

This book is a work of fiction. Names, characters, places
and incidents are products of the author's imagination or are used
fictitiously. Any resemblance to actual events or locales or persons,
living or dead, is entirely coincidental.

ISBN-13: 978-0-7434-9649-0
ISBN-10:    0-7434-9649-3

First Downtown Press trade paperback edition November 2005

10  9  8  7  6  5  4  3  2  1

DOWNTOWN PRESS and colophon are
trademarks of Simon & Schuster, Inc.

Manufactured in the United States of America

For information regarding special discounts for bulk purchases,
please contact Simon & Schuster Special Sales at 1-800-456-6798
or business©simonandschuster.com

# Acknowledgments

I wrote *Lust for Life* in the early months of 2002, which already seems an age ago. Indeed, a lot of water has passed under the bridge since then. Those months were extraordinary ones for me. I would not have got through them, let alone had the strength to write a novel, without the love, laughter and support of some very wonderful people.

Please stand up and take a bow: my son, mum, dad and sister; Louise Buckley, Nicola Williams, Sandie King, Catriona Butler, Emma and Lorcan Woods, Claire Percy-Robb, Louise Moore, Jonny Geller, Deborah Schneider, Carol Jackson, Norma Howard, Lottie Harwood-Mathews, Helen McDermott, Nikki Sung, Amy Apcar, Rene Van Eyssen, Stephen Glendinning and Rashid Akhtar.

I would not have got through a single day without Jim Pride. You amaze me.

For Jim,
a 116,834-word
love letter

If it were not for hope the heart would break.

(ANCIENT PROVERB)

# September

• • • •

# 1

Martha wasn't usually to be found on Earl's Court station in the middle of the afternoon. She rarely travelled by Tube at all; it was so impractical with the children. Not enough of the stations had lifts, and dragging ten-month-old Maisie and two-and-a-half-year-old Mathew (not to mention the related paraphernalia of double buggy, endless bags, several dolls, books, rain covers, etc, etc) up and down escalators or stairs was not Martha's idea of fun. Martha rarely went anywhere without the children so mostly she drove around London in the family car. But today the car was in the garage being serviced.

Lucky bloody car.

Martha looked around, guiltily, as though she'd said her thought aloud. No one was paying her the least bit of notice, which suggested she hadn't.

It's not that she was complaining about Michael's lack of attention, it was just that . . . OK, she *was* complaining.

The children were being looked after by her mother. Martha felt a little bit guilty about this too, although as guilt was the emotion Martha experienced most, she no longer even recognized that she was feeling guilty. Nor did she realize when she felt tense, stressed or even exhausted. She was terrifyingly used to the horrible dull ache in the pit of her stomach, the ache that told her she'd forgotten, or failed, or ruined something somehow, despite all her best efforts.

Martha thought it was unfair to ask her mother to babysit just so she could go to the hairdresser's, however much her mother insisted that it was a pleasure looking after the children. It seemed selfish. She'd visited Toni and Guy's in Knightsbridge to have her hair cut by the amazing Stephen for over five years. Martha normally took the children with her to the salon, which was quite a challenge. One or the other, or both, usually screamed throughout, turning the experience into an ordeal rather than a treat. Martha had considered bringing them along today and taking a cab to avoid the Tube. But then she would have had to fit both car seats into the cab, and the driver always became impatient when she did that. Where would she have put the seats when she arrived at the hairdresser's? They'd have been in the way.

Martha hated being in the way, or causing any sort of scene at all, however minor. She liked to blend, to fit in. Ideally she'd like to be altogether invisible. Besides which, Martha always felt cabs were just a tiny bit self-indulgent, and such extravagance was not her style. Indeed there could hardly be anything less Martha's style than self-indulgence, except perhaps fluorescent-pink hair accessories.

So it had been a toss-up. Luckily, her mother had taken the decision out of Martha's hands, by turning up with balloons and E-additives in the form of sweets and squash.

Martha fingered the already impeccably neat collar of her shirt and straightened it again. She checked her reflection in the shiny chocolate machine that stood, temptingly, on the platform. She brushed a few errant hairs from her shoulders. The cut was perfectly symmetrical. Martha went to the hairdresser's on the first Friday of every month, at 2:15 p.m. Only the very observant would notice that her hair had been cut at all. It was an iota sharper, a fraction tidier. Martha was pleased with it, all the more so because you could hardly tell it had been done.

Martha's hair, like Martha, was neat, sleek, orderly. It was brown with subtle dark-blonde highlights. She loathed bed-hair, scrunched hair, artfully sculpted hair and even curls. Martha liked straight, reliable, controllable hair. Her heart went out to those women who had "bad hair days." Imagine getting out of bed and having random bits of hair sticking out at jaunty, irresponsible angles. Or treacherous hair that went flat when it was supposed to be full, and full when it was supposed to be sleek. Martha breathed in deeply, fearful at the very thought.

Her coat was beige, pure wool, very long. It was tied with a belt, which showed off her neat waist. It wasn't a fashionable coat but it was a classic, and it was flattering. She wore 10-denier skin-tone tights (stockings were ludicrous, stay-ups simply didn't). She wore patent court shoes that she'd bought in Russell and Bromley but somehow, on Martha, they appeared entirely Dr. Scholl. The heel was a sensible inch and a half.

Under her coat she wore a neat tailored navy suit (not black, goodness, she wasn't a barrister and she certainly didn't work in advertising). Her shirt was pale blue and other than her wedding ring and engagement ring (a large cluster of diamonds), she didn't bother with jewellery, although she did wear a beautiful, expensive watch. Whilst women commented that Martha's skin, hair and nails were perfect and would agree to call her attractive, men were more likely to compliment her on her good brain (new man), or quiche lorraine (traditional-variety). She was popular with men who were turned on by school marms and the young Princess Diana. That type of man thought of her as extremely sexy.

It seemed to Martha that just about everybody on the platform at Earl's Court thought just about everybody else on the platform was extremely sexy. She tried, very hard, to keep her eyes on the chocolate-bar machine.

It was about four o'clock, school kicking-out time. The outrage was that all the people finding all the other people sexy were *children*. Martha wanted to keep her face impassive and not allow her mouth to tighten into a tell-tale grimace. But girls, aged anywhere between twelve and sixteen (Martha couldn't tell, who could nowadays?) were blatantly flirting with boys of the same age! Mathew would be this age in the blink of an eye. The thought caused the dull ache in the pit of Martha's stomach to flare into a spasm of searing anguish. It was September, they ought to have been wearing their jackets and there would certainly soon be a need for handkerchiefs, as these girls all insisted on sporting skirts the size of one.

Martha (along with every testosterone-driven youth on the station) found it impossible to avoid staring at one particular girl who stood a few metres along the platform, chewing gum. The girl was leaning against a poster advertising the latest blockbuster movie. It struck Martha that the girl herself had a cinematic quality, as pretty young girls often did. This was probably because they spent a lot of time imagining they were in movies, so every movement was calculated for its effect on an audience. Martha remembered at least that much from her own teenage years. The way the girl wore her jumper tied around her hips and her shirt buttoned up incorrectly was designed to look deliberately casual and to suggest a hasty dressing, the circumstances of which were left to the imagination of the inquisitive voyeur. Martha knew that the look would no doubt have been achieved only after several painstaking rearrangements.

Martha and a gaggle of jostling noisy boys watched as the girl put her finger in her mouth, found the gum, pulled it and stretched it like an umbilical cord from mouth to finger. She twisted it around her finger then popped it back into her mouth again. The action, whilst blatantly flirtatious, was harmless, really, but still it unsettled Martha. It reminded her of something—she couldn't, wouldn't, think what. The tallest boy in the group of jostling noisy boys stepped forward and bravely started talking to the girl. He stared at the girl with obvious longing. It was clear that his only thought was how to get to leave his hand prints all over her body. Martha felt a lump of envy sit heavily on her chest, her hand fluttered to her neck as though she were trying to brush the envy away. Envy was an illegal emotion.

The tall boy wasn't sure how to explain his appetite and possibly wouldn't be eloquent enough for several more years, so the pair stuttered and blushed through a conversation about what Martha presumed was a "pop band" of some sort. How strange that such rampant sexiness was so innocent, so hopeful. Martha's envy dissolved into longing. The girl caught Martha staring and stared back with all the hostility and honesty of youth. Martha blushed and dragged her eyes away. Thank God, the train pulled into the platform. Martha scolded herself; longing was even more dangerous than envy.

# 2

Eliza gazed around Greg's flat. It was a shambolic hole. There was no other way to describe it, and no amount of tie-dye throws or candles in empty wine bottles could disguise the fact; straight up, the opposite was true.

She was thirty. Thirty, not twenty. Because she'd just drunk the best part of a bottle of red wine the number thirty swam around her head, bashing up against her battered brain cells. Thirty. The number hovered like an annoying wasp that she couldn't shoo away. *Thirty.* It was so close to forty that for a moment she stopped breathing. She slowly folded the pizza box in half, taking care not to allow the discarded olives or uneaten crusts to spill on to the carpet. At thirty, she ought to remember when ordering a Fiorentina pizza to say, "But hold the olives."

Then again—at thirty, she should *not* be eating pizza out of a box, in front of a box, on a Friday night. Should she?

Definitely not.

She should be attending, or maybe even hosting, dinner parties for six or eight guests, all of whom ought to be sophisticated, droll and fashionable in equal parts. That's what Martha did. She ought to be wearing Wakely not Warehouse—although these jeans were undoubtedly comfortable. She ought to be on a tropical beach, or in a sauna in a cabin in the snowy foothills of some fashionable ski resort, or dancing in a salsa class at the very least. God, there were countless places that would be more appealing.

Eliza allowed her gaze to drop to Greg. He was smoking pot. Pot, for God's sake! Even his drug selection was embarrassingly unhip and outdated. No one smoked pot any more except for students (who were too young to know any better) and the over-sixties (who were desperate to re-create the days when they were too young to know any better). Eliza hadn't known Greg when he was a student. They'd met four years ago when Greg had already blown out the candles on his thirtieth cake, and yet she'd never known him to behave as though he were anything other.

Initially, she'd been attracted to his "portfolio career" and she'd been extremely irritated when her father had laughed and said, "That's what they're calling too idle or too stupid to get work nowadays, is it?"

Greg played in a band and he was talented, that was certain. But he'd never be "discovered," that was certain too.

The most annoying thing was, he didn't seem to care. Eliza, as a pop-video editor (well, assistant—she too had come to her career rather late in life), was in a position to help him (well, at least introduce him to some guys who might be in a position to help him). But whenever Eliza mooted the idea Greg just shrugged and laughed, and told her she was cute.

He quite enjoyed his day job. He sold hats in Covent Garden, in the Apple Market. The girl who made the hats paid him cash so he always had "spends" for nights at the pub, and he made a bit to finance his gigs, which were also in the local pub.

"Spends." Eliza repeated the word that Greg used to describe his income, and despaired.

Eliza was too old to have a boyfriend whose vocabulary was on a par with her nephew's. Mathew wasn't even three yet.

Aging. Eliza hated it. Or rather, she felt unprepared for it. She had been good at being young, a natural. She had rebelled, yelled, sulked and clubbed. She'd drunk too much, eaten too little, done the drug scene, danced with drag queens. She'd dyed her hair, pierced her nose, tattooed her arms, displayed all her charms (just once, at a rugby match, and the policeman had seen the funny side of it; apparently streakers were more common than you'd imagine). She'd suffered from dysentery in India, eaten fresh fish on Thai beaches, lived on a barge in Camden, and she'd been a beach bum in California. She'd drunk sake with Japanese businessmen, and vodka with some dodgy blokes who claimed to be involved with the Russian Mafia. She'd drunk G&Ts in London town. Plenty of them. It was only in the past few months that she'd started to question whether the nights out were really worth the hangovers.

In the past Eliza had set the pace. Now she wasn't sure if she even wanted to be in the race.

Eliza didn't look her age. Like many Londoners she looked anywhere between eighteen and forty. Age in London was a mindset, although Eliza currently felt it was a minefield. Eliza was five foot eight and very thin. She'd been waiting for boobs to grow since she was ten. Now, twenty years later, she admitted that Jordan must have got the share God had intended for Eliza Evergreen. And whilst she hated the fact men could be categorized by their preference for either leg or breast (as though women were chicken dinners) she was grateful to have long, strong brown legs that seemed to stretch up to her ears. She worked out to maintain her shapely calves and flat stomach and to wage war against the flab that was gathering on her upper arms.

Eliza's hair was cut into a messy bob. Or, rather, whether it was cut that way or not, her hair had a will of its own and always fell that way. Eliza was naturally a brunette, although only her mother knew this. Eliza herself could hardly remember as she dyed her hair as frequently as other girls painted their nails. She had been titian, red, honey, golden, raven, chestnut, scarlet and silver. It was hard to say which colour was most flattering; she always looked good. She had huge brown eyes that dominated her elfin face. She dressed in Kookai, Roxy, Diesel and Miss Sixty. She was one of the few people in this world who manage to look as good as the adverts promise, in such skimpy, trendy kits.

Eliza was a babe.

On two occasions in the 1980s, when Eliza was squandering her youth kicking her heels and smoking Marlboro Lights outside the off-licence, she'd been approached and asked if she'd ever considered modelling. Which just goes to prove it does happen.

"You're having a laugh, aren't you?" she'd replied succinctly and picked up her school bag and dashed off to earn a sackful of GCSEs and A levels with respectable grades.

A bright babe.

Eliza gave the impression that she was an indigenous Londoner, born and bred. Her skinny, tapering limbs, her hip clothes, her high cheekbones and her in-depth knowledge of the music industry all conspired to lend authenticity to the illusion. But she wasn't. She was from a small town in the Midlands, although she'd rather eat ground glass than volunteer that information. But London was in her soul. She was confident, independent, quirky and, when necessary, selfish. The only thing that set her apart from true Londoners was the fact that she could still feel overwhelmed when she saw the Houses of Parliament, Big Ben, or Westminster Bridge. She never understood those people who dashed across the bridge, head down against the wind, holding their briefcases or laptops tightly to their chests, armour to protect them from the cold and bustle.

But, then, Eliza didn't have a briefcase.

Eliza still remembered the thrill of arriving in the city, when she came to study at St. Martin's, aged eighteen. Then her favourite place in all of London had been Covent Garden. The smell of aromatherapy oils wafting up against the smell of coleslaw on jacket potatoes had thrilled her. The stalls selling second-hand Levis or people offering to tell your future for a fiver had struck her as chaotic, avant-garde and creative, everything her hometown was not. Now she hated helping Greg set up at the Apple Market. Covent Garden was changing. Or, rather, it wasn't changing at all, and perhaps that was the problem. Far from being the epitome of cool, it now struck Eliza as a dismal mash of tat and trinkets. The stalls sold stuff that amazed and dismayed Eliza. Who bought it? Who'd want it in their home? Where were the dinky little eateries serving delicious apple strudel and soft nougat? All Eliza could see were homogeneous pizza chains.

Greg loved Covent Garden. He liked having a laugh, meeting people, chatting about the spirituality of amethyst crystals and the like, whilst he earned enough money for his beer, fags and tie-dye throws. He had no desire to have a company expense account, private healthcare or even a Mont Blanc pen. Eliza couldn't help wondering what it would be like to mix with the type of people who bemoaned the lack of a good cleaner.

Eliza sighed and tried to budge her feeling of dissatisfaction, stale air that she harboured deep in her lungs. The dissatisfaction that had slowly crept up on her, taken hold and now threatened to explode. Blowing everything apart. Blowing them apart.

She tried to remember exactly when she had started looking at Greg and seeing failure, when she started to think his come-to-bed, Autumn-sky-blue eyes were more lazy than licentious. She used to like his devil-may-care attitude. She had adored the fact that he'd scribble lyrics on the bathroom wall—now she wanted him to pay attention to Dulux colour charts. She actually ached with the hope he'd mention golf clubs, pension plans and, more specifically, a wedding. She was bored of being an adolescent.

He *was* sexy, though.

Breathtakingly sexy. He had loose hips and firm lips. And whilst she objected to the fact that he ate with his fingers, that he still wore Doc Martens and long overcoats from charity shops—as he had done when he was a nineteen-year-old—and that he earned pretty much the same as he did then, she was extremely grateful that his sex drive had remained adolescent.

Extremely grateful, but no longer eternally grateful.

# 3

**"A**re you coming to bed, darling?" Michael's smile was designed to try to disguise the fact that he was absolutely shattered and it was only the lines at the corners of his mouth that betrayed him; when he was tired they sort of smudged together like tributaries of a river. Martha was at once sympathetic and irritated. A state only possible to achieve if you have been in a solid, positive, long-term relationship for a number of years. One that was just a teensy bit . . . the word "dull" flashed into Martha's mind and then disappeared in an instant. She replaced it with "safe." She did sympathize with the fact that Michael was tired, he worked really hard, as all Captains of Industry had to, doing all sorts of important things for Esso, the exact nature of which she was unsure of. But then it *was* Friday. And Friday night meant sex. Even after ten years, Friday equalled sex. Surely Michael understood that.

Wanted that.

As if reading her mind, Michael paused at the door and added, "We would both benefit from an early night." He smiled again and this one was genuine, saucy, inviting. Martha's body responded: the twinge in her stomach was in answer to the part of her that sympathized with his constant fatigue, and understood his overwhelming ambition. The warmth that she felt between her legs was because another part of her not only respected his drive; she'd married him for it.

The part of her that was irritated that his ever-present fatigue had robbed him of speech for the entire evening—after all, she was tired too, the children had been particularly demanding and uncooperative, yet she had still chattered to him throughout dinner (practically non-stop)—drove her to mutter, "I'll just finish this chapter and then follow you up."

As soon as Michael left the room Martha regretted being sullen. It wasn't very grateful and she ought to be more grateful.

On a more or less daily basis Martha was in the habit of "counting her blessings." It was a hangover from her lower-middle-class upbringing. As a child she'd been grateful that she wasn't an African (no food), a dog (no souls), a geriatric (no bladder control) or one of the Johnsons from down the street (no Raleigh bikes). Nowadays Martha tried to dwell on what she did have (a lot) rather than what she lacked (nothing worth mentioning).

Today, for example, had been a lovely day. It had been very kind of her mother to look after the children. Martha tried not to think of the sweet wrappers she had seen in the bin; instead she concentrated on the fact that her hair was trimmed evenly. And whilst it was irritating that the garage had called to say that the service of the Range Rover had taken longer than they expected and therefore the car wouldn't be ready until after the weekend, she felt very lucky that they had a Range Rover. A very expensive vehicle that, Martha couldn't help thinking, ought more properly to belong to someone else. Martha was always conscious that she'd ended up far richer, aged thirty-two, than her parents had been when they retired. She tried very hard to be grateful for her prosperity, although in truth she found it mildly embarrassing; it was just something else to feel guilty about.

Other blessings? Mathew's face when Martha returned home from the hairdresser's. Martha had been delighted when he'd rushed into the hall and flung his little body at her legs. He'd clung on to her skirt and kissed the nylon of her tights; his urgent, inexpert kisses had touched her heart. And it was even a good thing that he'd shouted, "Yuk, Mummy, your legs are tickerly," reminding her that she needed a leg wax. She must make an appointment, it wasn't like her to let herself go.

"Mathew doesn't normally greet me with such enthusiasm," Martha had commented to her mother. She hoped it didn't sound as though she were accusing her mother of treating Mathew badly—that certainly wasn't what she intended.

"Darling, he doesn't normally have the opportunity to miss you, you never leave him for long enough," Mrs. Evergreen had replied matter-of-factly.

Martha didn't understand how it could be the case but she'd felt mildly chastised. Surely her mother appreciated Martha's devotion to her children and surely she was proud of it. After all, it was exactly as Mrs. Evergreen had acted with Martha and Eliza.

Why was it that all her blessings seemed to be tinged with . . . oh, nagging feelings of . . . Martha left the thought unformed in her mind. She stood up and poured herself half a glass more of white wine. Martha didn't drink much. She never touched spirits (too potent) or red wine (stained her teeth). One and a half glasses of white wine, every third day, was usually Martha's limit; anything more would be totally irresponsible with children in the house. Today she was allowing herself an extra half glass. It was Friday, after all.

Another blessing, both children were in bed and asleep. Generally speaking—and this was *yet* another blessing—the children were becoming easier day by day. Today had been nothing more than a small aberration, she was sure of it. Martha was prepared to admit after her glass and a half of Chardonnay (to herself, and if they'd been there, to her mother and to a couple of her NCT friends) that the theory of having children close together, so as to get the nappy bit over with all at once, was in practice harder than she'd anticipated. Still, Maisie's colic had finally cleared up and she had slept through from 8 p.m. until 6 a.m. four nights in a row; after ten months of waking every three hours this was undoubtedly a godsend.

Sometimes Martha's head, neck, back, eyeballs and even teeth ached with exhaustion. Yet it wasn't so much the lack of sleep that Martha found hard to take—after all, that was a given if you had a baby—it was the screaming. Martha felt ill knowing Maisie was in pain and that she couldn't do anything about it. Martha had spent night after night watching her daughter's tiny body go into spasms, her knees jerk up to her chest. The wailing tore at Martha and left her feeling miserable and inadequate. There was nothing more torturous than a crying child. Martha never understood how Michael was able to sleep through the pitiful wailing. Martha often sent generous cheques to appeals on behalf of children who needed urgent operations, false limbs or simply water and shelter. Martha wanted to hold each and every one of them and shush their crying. How did their mothers face each morning?

And that was why it was silly to get into such a state about something as insignificant as potty-training. And, like she'd told Michael he would, Mathew had finally grasped the concept of pooing in the loo (as opposed to in his bed, the kitchen cupboards, the reception room or—most memorably—Michael's shoe). It had been a long haul. Mathew had been well on the way to being potty-trained at twenty months when Maisie was born, but then suddenly seemed to lose the knack. Martha had tried but failed to ignore the comments from her numerous child-behaviour-expert friends and relatives who felt compelled to constantly comment that the step back in bathroom etiquette was a deliberate act of defiance/anger/terrorism, brought on by sibling jealousy/insecurity/feelings of loneliness.

No kidding.

Remarks like this sent a frisson of tension running up and down Martha's spine. She wanted to point out that she'd had a Caesarean (two, actually), not a lobotomy. She said nothing. She sometimes wondered where she stored her suppressed irritation.

Because it must be adding up.

Martha had read the books and dutifully carved out exclusive "special time" for her and Mathew, with the hope of eradicating the excrement terrorism. They went to the zoo, they made paper boats and floated them on the pond, they fed the ducks and they played in the park. They did this even though it cost a fortune in childcare for Maisie, they did this even when Martha could barely walk with tiredness because she'd been up four times in the night.

But it had been worth it. Mathew was now fully potty-trained.

Martha's blessings included her family. She adored her mum and dad who quietly rumbled through their retirement without making much demand on her time, but were always visibly grateful if she did descend on them for an afternoon with the two children and two dozen bags. Her parents had moved down to a London suburb when they retired as both their daughters and their grandchildren were settled in the capital. They'd hoped to help Martha with the childcare. Secretly they were a little disappointed by her fierce independence and insistence on doing everything on her own. They felt redundant as parents and grandparents, and it didn't take Einstein to work out that Martha could do with some help now and again. Mr. and Mrs. Evergreen feared it would be quite some time before Eliza ever wanted children.

Blessings, blessings. Other than needing spectacles and one of them having a gammy toe, her parents (touch wood) were the picture of health. And they were so *normal.* Martha always felt so sorry for her friends who had alcoholic, neurotic or clingy parents. Hers were so pleasant, so non-intrusive; they were no bother at all. Martha beamed to herself.

And Eliza, her sister, was also a joy. Admittedly, she was unreliable as a conversationalist at dinner parties (she was often deliberately shocking), she was not great at timekeeping, or saving, or choosing men, and she had never done anything quietly in her life; still the very thought of Eliza made Martha smile. What were kid sisters for if not to show you glimpses of the wrong side of the tracks? Martha had always believed that Eliza was predestined to be more glamorous than Martha (therefore more trouble). After all, Martha was called Martha (think mumsy, think nineteenth-century respectable, think good hostess in the Bible), and Eliza was called Eliza, which was a more spirited, passionate, interesting name to live up to. It was Mr. and Mrs. Evergreen's fault that the girls had turned out as they had. Martha often wondered how different her life would have been if she'd been named Eliza.

Then there was Michael, of course. Michael was so much a part of Martha that it was almost easy to overlook the fact that he was a huge blessing. The most fundamental blessing, in fact. Without Michael there would be no Mathew or Maisie. And without Michael's enormous salary there would have been no chance of Martha giving up her work in the Civil Service to bring up the children. They had both agreed that the very best thing for the babies was her undivided attention, that she was the very best person to bring them up. And she barely missed the Civil Service at all.

Barely.

Perhaps she missed the chat with the girls in the morning about the previous night's TV, and the last Friday of the month when they used to have lunches at Pizza Express, which had always been a giggle. She sometimes missed buying suits from Jigsaw and shoes from L. K. Bennett and being able to say she "needed them for the office." She hardly missed the harmless flirting with the blokes from accounts. She certainly did not miss the 45-minute commute twice a day, the tedious meetings, the endless power struggles, or putting money in collections for new babies/twenty-first birthdays/wedding pressies of people she'd never even talked to.

Martha had met Michael ten years ago, not long after she'd graduated and moved down to London to start her first job. They'd met in a pub through a friend of a friend of a friend, the way you do when you're young and up for meeting people. Martha noticed Michael the moment she walked into the pub because he was wearing dark green jeans and a charcoal-grey, tight polo-neck jumper. All the other men in the pub were wearing chinos and pale blue shirts. Michael wasn't particularly tall and Martha liked that; he seemed less intimidating. And he had a good body; broad shoulders, the cutest, neatest bum. His best features were his very dark hair (which was almost blue it was so black) and his shiny, smiley, deep-brown eyes. Michael did not have the gift of the gab, he was not the type of man to talk women into bed; his individual charm was that he listened them into the same place.

Michael was the first man ever to listen to Martha properly. Genuinely listen. He didn't ask questions about her that would inevitably bounce back to a funny story of his own. He didn't spin endless tales about his sexual exploits, in an attempt to make her jealous. Nor did he recount daredevil Action Man exploits, in an attempt to impress her. He didn't interrupt her when she was speaking, nor did his eyes glaze over. If pushed, he would modestly relate a funny anecdote, shyly admit to his ambition to travel the world, and, more honestly, admit to his ambition to be chairman of Esso. Michael told Martha that she had the most beautiful smile in the world, which encouraged her to use it with a new and greater frequency.

Whilst she was smiling at him, drinking her third vodka-orange (because in those days Martha didn't have children and so she could drink three vodka-oranges if she felt like it) Martha noted that Michael had a large chin and nose, which she thought made him look distinguished and masterful. By the end of the evening Martha had decided that Michael was exactly the type of man she ought to marry. Moreover, he was *the* man she wanted to marry. Even their names matched. She decided then and there that their children ought to have names beginning with "M" too. Michael wasn't the type of man that women fell in love or lust with at first meeting, so it surprised them both when Martha fastened on to him so rapidly and tightly. Martha had had two boyfriends before Michael (one throughout the sixth form and one throughout the second and third years at university. She'd had a bash at being wild during the first year but it hadn't been a particularly fruitful experience, she wasn't a natural). Since graduation she'd slept with two other men. Again, she found it didn't suit her: she was a serial monogamist at heart, a heart she wore on her sleeve.

Martha and Michael were married within eighteen months.

And Martha had been right; Michael was *such* a good husband.

He was kind and gentle and trustworthy and very, very hardworking. He was stable, neither a womanizer nor a football fanatic. And she still fancied him, even after ten years. Maybe not in that knickers-dropping, heart-stopping, can't-get-enough-of-you way that she had in her early twenties but, still, he knew which buttons to press.

Every Friday night.

Martha and Michael had plenty of money and plenty of friends and they had the children's names down at some very good schools. And all of these things were undoubtedly blessings.

Martha decided that she didn't want to finish the chapter after all, and went upstairs to the bathroom. She opened the right-hand drawer under the basin and pulled out a cotton-wool ball. Carefully she poured on lotion and then with long, deliberate strokes she cleansed her nose, chin, forehead and then cheeks. She gently removed her make-up—mascara and blusher. This, plus clear lipgloss, was the only make-up Martha ever wore, except at the occasional evening function. If Michael asked her especially, then she could sometimes be spotted sporting eyeshadow as well. She preferred it if everything on her face stayed its original colour. She dropped the used ball into the bin, and repeated the process with toner. Next, she carefully applied her moisturizer in firm, upward, gravity-defying sweeps. Then she checked that the bathroom door was bolted and began to undress. Martha always liked to take a shower before she went to bed and she didn't like Michael walking in on her. She could never understand couples who apparently felt comfortable enough to go to the loo in front of each other. Why would anyone want to do such a thing? Martha tried to imagine who they were—popstars, probably, or method actors.

Martha carefully towelled herself dry and then slipped into a pair of Egyptian-cotton pyjamas and matching slippers. She checked her reflection. Not bad for thirty-two. Should she undo the top button? How many? One? Two?

Finally Martha walked into the bedroom.

"Hey Mickey," she mumbled with only the faintest hint of self-consciousness in her voice. But even before Martha slipped between the sheets she identified the slow, familiar movement of Michael's chest rising and falling, clearly indicating that he was well and truly ensconced in the Land of Nod.

# 4

Eliza sipped her double espresso. It tasted bitter, black. Or maybe that was just her mood on this particular Wednesday morning.

"What's up? You usually love the coffee here." Greg's honeyed tones oozed concern. Eliza dismissed the concern as over-the-top and felt irritated with him for the hundredth time that day. She'd prefer it if he were the type of man who failed to notice that she hadn't touched her coffee but paid his bills by direct debit, and there were loads of that sort of man around. All her friends had married one. Michael, her brother-in-law, was a perfect example. How come she'd missed her chance of one?

I don't like espresso, she thought. It reminds me too much of being a student. I should be drinking Earl Grey and eating passion-fruit gateau in a proper tea shop. That's what women of my age do. That's what Martha would do. I should not be sitting in a smoky café that doesn't even have the decency to be part of a chain but is run and owned by real Italians.

True, its individuality used to appeal to her; in fact, she used to be proud of her amazing find and only introduced her very best friends to Caffè Bianchi. She used to delight in the fact that none of the wooden chairs matched (and most had one leg shorter than the others), and that Signora Bianchi served espresso and cappuccino, and nothing else. No caffè latte, no caffè macchiato, no caffè Americano, no espresso ristretto, no flavours and certainly no decaf. They didn't sell fancy packets of tea or bottles of olive oil for twenty quid. They were true Italians and believed that introducing chairs to the café had already been a huge concession to the oddness of the British people. They did offer a glass of water with each cup of strong pitch-black coffee, "no charja."

Signora Bianchi was extremely fat. Her numerous chins rested on her mammoth bosoms, which often rested on the counter, but if not, rested on her huge stomach. Eliza had never seen her legs because in the seven years that Eliza had visited Caffè Bianchi she had never witnessed Signora Bianchi emerging from behind the counter; yet the Signora dominated the entire bar with her mass and personality. She was a true matriarch: she bossed, fussed and loved all her customers with the passion of a mother. For example, if anyone had the foolish audacity to order a double espresso, she would bang her fist on her ample breast, click her tongue and roll her eyes; thus conveying eloquently that in her opinion two espressos were sure to bring on an instant heart attack.

Signor Bianchi, naturally, had to be a very slight man. There simply wouldn't have been room for him to be anything other. Eliza estimated that he weighed less than nine stone, and that a good part of that weight was made up of his moustache, which was long and waxed. However fragile he looked, he was not a weak man. Although slight and often silent, Signor Bianchi's presence was quintessential to the café and, most particularly, to

Signora Bianchi. She still looked at him in such a way that it was clear to Eliza that the Signora could not see the wizened old man, with his grey hair, ever-increasing bald patch and rasping cough. The Signora saw the nineteen-year-old boy, with a head of ink-black, slicked-back hair, riding a Vespa around the piazza. He'd have had flowers in his hand (for her) and a twinkle in his eye (also for her). A truly handsome boy.

The café was very narrow, not much wider than a corridor, and the bar that ran the entire length was lifted directly from a Hopper picture: a shiny swathe of zinc scratched and scarred by years of use by customers who had become friends. The till consisted of nothing more than three wineglasses: one for small change; one for tender above 50p, and a third for notes. The homogeneous chains had frequently approached Signor and Signora Bianchi in the hope of striking a buy-out deal; the response was always the same. No.

"I should stop drinking coffee," muttered Eliza.

"Why?" asked Greg. He had tipped two packets of sugar on to the table and was drawing a smiley face with his finger.

"Because it decreases iron absorption."

"Are you anaemic?" He looked up, obviously concerned.

"No, but if I were to try for a baby, iron absorption is important."

Greg spluttered into his coffee and then immediately tried to recover his usual composure. "Are you—er—we, presumably we, trying for a baby?" Contraception, like any other form of responsibility in their relationship, fell to Eliza.

"No," she admitted reluctantly.

If Greg was relieved, he had the good sense not to advertise the fact—his facial expression didn't alter a jot. He could be mentally punching the air, as euphoric as Beckham scoring a goal from a free kick against Germany to win the World Cup, and Eliza wouldn't know it. Equally, he could be disappointed. His secrets were mostly safe. The reason for Greg's calculated restraint was that whilst talking to Eliza with whatever part of his brain it was that chit-chatted about iron absorption, he was using another part of his brain to calculate when Eliza's period was due. Because like it or not (and she didn't like it, she didn't even like admitting to it), the truth was Eliza was more than prone to PMT. She didn't fling plates exactly, just insults, jibes and irrational comments.

She wasn't due for another two weeks.

Perhaps she did want a baby. Being a bull-by-the-horns straightforward type of guy, Greg ventured, "Do you want a baby?"

"Eventually, yes." Eliza put down her espresso cup with such force that the black liquid slopped into the doll's-size saucer. She paused, and then added with more accuracy, "Maybe. I'd just like there to be the option."

But there was the option, wasn't there? thought Greg. Her ovaries or womb, or whatever, were all OK, as far as they knew. (Female plumbing beyond the G-spot wasn't his area of expertise—was it any man's?) Of course having a baby was an option if that's what she wanted. She'd just never mentioned it before. He'd never thought about it. But now she had mentioned it, well, why not? Instantly, visions of splashing in the sea with a small grubby person flashed into Greg's mind (and he didn't mean his best mate, Bob, even though Bob was only five foot six, he meant a child. His child). He could see himself and *his child* playing on swings, kicking leaves in a park, hunting for conkers.

"We could have a baby, if that's what you really want." He reached out and took Eliza's hand; she noted with some annoyance that he didn't even have to put down his cigarette to manage the manoeuvre, so practised was he at this art. He had started smoking when he was fourteen, because it made him look hard and cool. He was still doing it now, twenty years later, for the same reasons.

Eliza snatched her hand away and avoided answering the question by saying, "I fancy a cup of tea."

Tea? Christ, cravings already. Eliza never ordered tea. Could she already be up the duff? Was this what these recent mood swings were about? Christ, shit, bloody hell.

Bloody marvellous!

Eliza read Greg's mind.

"I'm not."

"No?"

"No."

"Sure?"

"Certain."

"Oh."

There was a pause. If Eliza had been more tuned into Greg's emotions she'd have noticed that it was a disappointed pause.

"Still, if it's tea you want." Greg stood up and walked to the bar. If only life were that simple: it's tea she wants, she'll be happy once she has a cup of tea. As he walked towards the bar and Signora Bianchi, Greg started to calculate how he should best negotiate procuring a cup of tea in an Italian café, which would be tantamount to treason as far as Signora Bianchi was concerned.

How much caffeine was there in tea then?

# 5

Who on earth chooses to sit in these grubby little cafés, which are really not much better than pubs? wondered Martha as she walked past Caffè Bianchi, pushing a grumbling Maisie in her stroller. The heavy wooden door suddenly opened, coughing forth a cloud of cigarette smoke. A young woman rushed out and fled past Martha and Maisie. Obviously late for something. Signing on, probably, thought Martha, and then immediately regretted the thought. It was very judgemental and censorious, and not necessarily accurate, to jump to the conclusion that the woman was a doley. Just because it was— Martha checked her watch—a quarter to ten in the morning, this didn't necessarily mean that the girl was unemployed. Martha tried to think positively. There are all sorts of things that a woman could do for a living. She might work shifts, or have a shop job. Wednesdays might be her day off, if she works in retail: she's bound to have to work Saturdays and would be due a day in return. Martha noted that the woman's shoes (although they were horrible square-heeled fashion-statement shoes) were at least clean. Martha always noticed people's shoes.

Those shoes were Eliza's shoes. Her own sister's.

"Eliza!" Martha called out, although she didn't like shouting.

Eliza turned round. Her expression of exasperation melted as she recognized her sister and niece. She rushed back towards them and enveloped Martha in a huge hug and planted a fat kiss on Maisie's tear-stained cheek. "Martha, fantastic to see you," she beamed. "Not your neck of the woods, doll."

Though the women lived less than a mile apart (Eliza lived in Shepherd's Bush and Martha lived in Holland Park) their neighbourhoods were worlds apart. Shepherd's Bush was all Poundstretcher and betting shops, with an above average number of newsagents that sold Lottery tickets. Holland Park was a dizzy blur of expensive florists and stunning patisseries. Eliza was right to be surprised to see Martha on her doorstep.

"When we last visited you I noticed the shops that sell Indian saris, and I wanted to take a closer look at the fabrics—you know, for inspiration, colours and things," explained Martha.

"Project Dream House?" asked Eliza. Eliza knew that Project

Dream House was about all that could induce Martha to venture to W12. Martha, Michael and the children had only ever visited Eliza in Greg's flat three times, although she'd lived there for four years. Eliza visited their home at least once a week, sometimes three or four times. Eliza was well aware of Martha's views that Shepherd's Bush wasn't a desirable place to bring the children to. Eliza thought Martha was snobby and overprotective, Martha thought Eliza was irresponsible and imperilled. They loved each other fiercely.

"And how is Project Dream House developing?" continued Eliza.

"We're waiting to hear if the vendors will accept our offer. I expect we'll hear any day now."

Many people have ideas about their dream home. They say, "I'd like a hot tub and a forty-foot swimming pool," they wish for something flashy, flamboyant and often unrealistic. No more expected than their numbers coming up on the Lottery; it could happen but it probably won't. Martha's concept of her dream home was much more sincere than that.

Martha's dream home was the fabric of her self. Since her teens she'd been filling a scrapbook (and when that was full, a box) to be the inspiration for her dream home. She'd collected magazine pictures that had caught her eye, mostly of sunny kitchens and fun-looking children's bedrooms. As she grew more confident in her own creative abilities, she saved a leaf and stored it carefully in her box (because one day she wanted to paint a bathroom that exact same shade of rust), along with a glass marble she'd bought in a toyshop (because she liked the way the colours slipped into one another). She squirrelled away pieces of rich fabrics, textured stones and pebbles, pretty tiles and pottery. Martha spent hours mixing paints when she did craft with Mathew, in an attempt to get the perfect blue (the blue of a troubled sea before a storm), and the exact red (the pinkish red of lazy Spanish walls that just about propped up the terracotta roofs on the sleepy houses). She often went into a haberdasher's and gazed and gazed at the bobbins of cotton: a myriad colours, wonderful rich magentas, soulful greys and lilacs, every nuance of vibrant green. She'd buy the reels and add them to her treasure box.

Her interest was not just about the cosmetic side. Whilst she did buy countless magazines and books about interior design, she also became an expert on the technical aspects of creating a dream home. She knew everything there was to know about renewing roofs, damp-proofing joists, tiling, polishing, converting, dismantling, restoring and maintaining.

Her dream house would be a big house but not ostentatious; the rooms would be light and airy, south-facing. There would be enough bedrooms for the children still to sleep separately, to have lots of friends and family to stay in comfort. Maybe they'd even have a live-in nanny, as Michael often said he wanted.

Every room would be full of love and laughter.

Her dream home would have kids' pictures pinned to the kitchen walls, and there would be lots of pairs of small shoes by the front door. She knew Michael considered their family finished ("a boy and a girl, the set") but she secretly longed for more children; four had always seemed a lovely number. They would have a playroom that would be a fairytale space for adults and children alike: each wall would be painted a different vibrant colour; there would be a library corner where the kids would sit and pore over the books that she'd read as a child (and quite a few modern ones too, which were a damn sight funnier and brighter); and there would be a big wicker basket full of old loo rolls and cereal boxes so that she and the children could make things together—models of space rockets, miniature gardens (and they'd look just like the ones they made on *Blue Peter*). The kids would always have friends round for tea and they'd eat sandwiches and drink big glasses of milk (Mathew's intolerance to wheat and dairy products would have subsided).

It would also be a party house for grown-ups. Martha and Michael had lots of great friends and Martha loved entertaining. There was nothing she liked more than sending home half a dozen, half-cut friends after they'd eaten and drunk well. In her dream home the kitchen would be large enough to have a sofa and a fireplace so that her dinner guests could congregate there as she prepared the food. They'd laugh and chat about the latest celebrity gossip and they'd talk about the serious issues of the day. They'd serve great wines that Martha would be able to recommend with confidence. The children would politely pop downstairs at the start of the evening to say goodnight to the guests (then they'd go back to bed without getting overtired and throwing tantrums). The food would be beautifully presented and delicious (she wouldn't burn a single thing).

After a two-year search Martha and Michael had found the Bridleway: a house without any serious structural faults, within their price bracket, in a fantastic location, with original fireplaces, wooden floors and genuine sash windows—the right blend of potential.

The dream house.

Martha was left breathless just thinking about it.

Eliza knew all there was to know about the Bridleway, and she wanted Martha and Michael's offer to be accepted almost as much as Martha did. Depressed as she was about her own scope for joining the ranks of London's affluent classes, she delighted in living her life vicariously through her sister. Not for a moment was she jealous of Martha's emotional and material success; in fact, it gave her hope.

"Have you time for a cup of tea and then you can update me?" asked Eliza.

"Absolutely, but haven't you just had a hot drink?" asked Martha, gesturing towards Bianchi's.

"They don't serve tea," replied Eliza. "Where are you parked?"

Martha, Maisie and Eliza set off towards the Range Rover. Martha was wondering whether she would still have time to visit the supermarket and pick Mathew up from playschool if she had tea with Eliza. Eliza was contemplating, with amazement, that Martha still thought hot drinks were something to do with needing warmth or quenching thirst, when clearly they were all about being sociable.

Both were desperate to chatter.

# 6

Eliza suspected that Mr. and Mrs. Evergreen had found her on their doorstep, aged (roughly) two days, and had taken her in out of the goodness of their hearts. Because how else could she explain the fact that she was different from her sister in absolutely every way? Mrs. Evergreen was not the type to have conceived a child by the milkman and conned her husband into bringing it up as his own—and yet they couldn't be sisters, could they?

Not only had Martha failed to look impressed when Eliza mentioned she'd spent the night before at a club, drinking with Basement Jaxx, but she looked absolutely bemused. "Did you go to college with her? Have I met her?" Martha inquired politely, desperately searching for a reason why she should be supposed to remember this Bertha Jacks person.

Eliza hadn't bothered to explain, it was too embarrassing.

Besides dressing differently, they talked differently (Martha—entirely the Queen's English; Eliza—all urban hip chick). They walked differently (Martha was stiff and upright, her movements sudden and jerky; Eliza drifted with fluid, languid grace). The first thing Eliza did every morning was put the radio on. She only turned it off to play a CD or watch MTV. She adored the buzz and distraction that background noise supplied. Martha spent her entire day pleading for quiet and her wildest dream was an afternoon of tranquillity. Even before the children had been born Martha only ever tuned in to the radio occasionally; to listen to *Woman's Hour* or a particular concert on Radio 3. They moved in different circles and found it hard to relate to one another's friends. Eliza could quote Simone de Beauvoir at the drop of a hat and thought that the woman should be canonized; Martha (if pushed) expressed the opinion that the women's movement had "confused things." Martha bought all her underwear from Marks and Spencer, as their ranges were "so pretty and extraordinarily good value." The most kinky thing in her knicker drawer was a peach satin balcony bra with matching French panties. Eliza spent half her time and income in Agent Provocateur and daring was going commando.

But they *did* adore each other.

They shared memories that bound them heart and soul. Martha and Eliza knew what each other's childhood had felt, smelt and looked like. They knew which jumpers had itched, which socks had fallen down, they knew the texture of each other's Tiny Tears doll's hair (Martha's had silky hair and Eliza's was matted after an ill-advised game of hairdresser's involving flour and washing-up liquid). Eliza remembered Martha's screams when she got sunburnt in an era before the government's campaigns had encouraged mums to smother their children in factor-50 sun cream. The burns were so severe that even a sheet had been too heavy for Martha's delicate, irritated skin to bear. Eliza had cried as she watched her sister being lowered into a bath of soothing lotion. Just as Martha had cried after a game of circus had gone horribly wrong and Eliza had ended up in hospital and in plaster.

They'd tasted Space Dust for the first time together and Orange Appeal, Nestlé pink milkshake, Angel Delight and Findus Crispy Pancakes. They'd bobbed apples, ridden donkeys, built sandcastles, fought over Pippa Dolls, argued over the TV, screamed over Paul Young and Nik Kershaw together (which was possibly the last time Martha paid any attention to the world of pop). They'd believed and disbelieved in Santa together, which was a bond that could not be broken over something as trivial as ignorance about the current club scene.

Eliza couldn't understand why anyone would want to be a civil servant. Martha didn't even know what a music-video editor did; still Martha loved listening to Eliza's antics. Eliza seemed to mix with such fascinating people, models and DJs, writers and comics. Not that Martha ever recognized their names (a situation not helped by the fact that Eliza rarely mentioned the same name twice). And Eliza went to such interesting venues: she was always at some new club or restaurant. Whilst Martha certainly wouldn't want to swap places, she had to admit that Eliza's life did sound attractive and glamorous. She could see why it worked for Eliza.

And for her part, Eliza admired Martha's neat and tidy life and mind. She loved her niece and nephew, who always smelt clean and radiated hope and innocence (except perhaps now, when Maisie was grizzling angrily as she was teething again). And whilst Eliza's culinary skills were limited to taking a Marks and Spencer ready-made meal out of its packet and putting it in the microwave, she respected Martha's ability to produce delicious meals. In fact, she had sat through a number of tedious dinner parties just on the promise of seared sea bass with roasted vegetables.

Martha drove them to her favourite tea shop in Holland Park, which was actually a bookshop, but at the back of the store there were two or three tables and one large comfortable settee upholstered in tasteful Liberty print. The overall ambience the store manager was trying to create was that of old-world dusty academia; in fact everything in the store was clean and brand new, which meant it looked charming but there was less chance of dust mites. Martha thought it was perfect. The only tea that was available was camomile or Earl Grey. As Eliza had left Caffè Bianchi in a huffy hurry simply because they couldn't offer her so much as PG Tips, she settled into an armchair and prepared herself to be impressed.

Martha insisted on taking Maisie with her as she went to order two Earl Greys. Eliza thought this made Martha's task unnecessarily tricky but couldn't be bothered to say so. Instead, she picked up one of the glossy magazines that were spread across the coffee table for customer perusal, and immediately flicked to the horoscope page. It wasn't her fault she was an Aquarian, it was beyond her control.

Martha carefully lowered the teas on to the table, lowered Maisie into a high chair, passed her a rusk and then sat, or rather collapsed, into the chair opposite her sister.

"Listen to this, Martha," said Eliza with ill-concealed excitement. " 'You certainly could be short of cash if you fail to pay attention to your finances. It would be a good idea to double-check your bank statements.' That is *so* weird, because the cash machine has just refused me any money—I must be overdrawn again."

"There's nothing weird about that, Eliza. You're always overdrawn," said Martha matter-of-factly, glad that she'd picked up the tab for the drinks. "I don't know why you pay any attention to those horoscopes, it's hardly scientific."

"Well, you would say that, you're a Virgo. Virgos are very sceptical."

Martha raised her eyebrows but said nothing. It was a shame that Eliza relied on such mumbo-jumbo to find her direction in life. She seemed so together in other ways. Martha was far luckier. If she had a problem she did not consult horoscopes, tarot cards or tea leaves. She discussed it with Michael, and he was always so good about offering advice.

" 'If you were born between the tenth and the eighteenth of February you may be questioning if the partner who is currently by your side is still the one for you.' Now that's spooky," said Eliza in awe.

"Are you and Greg having problems?" asked Martha, immediately fretful. She didn't like the idea of anyone having problems; it didn't suit her view of life, and she didn't like the idea of her sister having problems most of all.

"Sort of." Eliza sighed and sipped her tea. It tasted like cat's piss and she missed the strong Bianchi espresso, but she wasn't going to admit as much, least of all to herself. "We're not arguing or anything," she confessed. "I'm just bored, I suppose. Do you ever feel bored by Michael?"

"No, never," replied Martha, without thinking about the question.

"And I find him really irritating at the moment. Does Michael ever irritate you?"

"Never." Martha didn't miss a beat. She didn't have the confidence to find anyone irritating, so she certainly couldn't imagine a world where her husband would irritate her. Well, except for the other Friday night, but that didn't count. Martha didn't know why that didn't count but she was sure it didn't.

"See," said Eliza, believing that she'd proved her point. Martha didn't see but didn't know how to say so. "I think I've out-grown him. I think I'll have to call it a day. Cash in my chips," added Eliza, resigned.

"But what will you do without him?" asked Martha, astounded and more than a little disappointed. She'd rather thought that Eliza and Greg were well suited to one another, and she'd been pleased that Eliza had managed to sustain a relationship for four years. Before Greg, Eliza's relationships had only ever lasted a couple of months, at most. Greg and Eliza had always seemed so happy together, they certainly laughed together more than any other couple that Martha knew. And whilst Martha had long given up hope that Eliza would do anything as conventional as marry Greg (and therefore allow Maisie to be flower girl and Mathew a page boy—one of Martha's greatest ambitions) she had thought that they'd last. Martha firmly believed people were better *in* relationships than *out* of them. It was neater that way; as it should be. "Won't you be lonely without him?"

"Well, I'll still have my friends, my work, you. He isn't all-consuming, you know." No man had ever been so to Eliza. She was rarely in one place long enough to establish a relationship, let alone lose her heart. When she'd first started seeing Greg she hadn't expected to stay in London for longer than six months—she was on her way to Australia—but staying just sort of happened. They were always having too much of a laugh for her to apply for a visa, and then she'd got a job in the music industry, the first job that held any real interest for her. She was doing really well. Not much more than a glorified gofer, but she was well liked and well respected. She took her work seriously—well, fairly seriously. She still wasn't great on filing or invoicing or timekeeping, but she tried. She wasn't sure if Greg ever took anything seriously. "He's no longer what I'm looking for."

"So what are you looking for?" asked Martha, wiping Maisie's mouth without taking her eyes off Eliza.

Eliza beamed. She couldn't wait to tell Martha about her recent emotional developments. The fact that she wanted a little more of what Martha had was bound to gain Martha's respect and approval. "I'm looking for a man who wants to be a man, not just a boy. One with a proper job and his own flat. One that I could visualize shopping in Mothercare."

Martha's jaw hit the shiny (fake) wooden floor. "You do?"

"I do. I want a man who buys a monthly Travelcard, rather than one who has to scramble around in his rucksack for loose change every single time he takes the Tube. For that matter, I don't want a man with a rucksack, I want a man with a briefcase and a laptop."

"I see," said Martha, choosing her words carefully, trying not to betray her astonishment. "Well, I'll say one thing for you, Eliza, you never cease to surprise me."

"I knew you'd be pleased." Eliza grinned, oblivious to Martha's reserve. She checked her watch, realized she was in serious danger of being late for work for the third time that week, made her excuses, kissed her sister and niece and left the tea shop, relieved that she didn't have to drink any more cat's piss.

Martha finished her tea and then struggled to put Maisie back into the stroller. Maisie resisted by making her tiny body absolutely rigid, like a steel bar, refusing to sink her bottom into the chair. She wanted her mother to carry her. At only ten months, Maisie was able to communicate her needs and desires with astonishing clarity—something she must have inherited from her father, as Martha couldn't imagine trying to force her will on anyone with such determination, even now. Maisie cried and screamed for a number of minutes, drawing disapproval from other tea-drinkers. Eventually she exhausted herself and collapsed into a sulky sleep. Martha felt the familiar knot of guilt tighten in her stomach. Maisie shouldn't really be asleep at this time of day. She'd never have a lunchtime nap now, and if she didn't have a lunchtime nap she'd be grouchy by the end of the day, and she'd need to go to bed early, which would mean she'd wake up early tomorrow, which would irritate Michael.

Oh dear.

Still, Maisie was asleep now and there was nothing Martha could do about that. Martha decided to try to enjoy the rare luxury of peace and quiet. She would take the opportunity to browse around the bookshop.

Martha rummaged in her bag and pulled out a list of titles from her organizer, then proceeded to locate three of the books. Two were on the Booker prize shortlist that had just been announced, one was a Pulitzer winner. All should prove to be improving and educational. The writing styles would undoubtedly be graceful, confident and intelligent, as described by critics and advertised by the publishers.

Although they might be a little bit gloomy.

Martha shook her head as she thought that she'd got through just five books in nine months. She could remember the time when she'd read five books in a single month. Realistically, it would be unlikely that she would manage to plough through the three she'd just bought by Christmas.

Martha tried to remember what it was like to read a book entirely for pleasure, purely for entertainment. She looked at the huge stacks of books that screeched, "Have a laugh, read me." These were the ones with pink, turquoise or yellow covers, with little cartoon pictures of spangly handbags or overflowing champagne glasses. She allowed her finger to trace the embossed name of the author of one of them, but she couldn't quite bring herself to pick it up. When would she have time to read something so entirely self-indulgent? She knew that the novels she had selected would at least be useful—they would no doubt be discussed at the dinner parties she attended.

Martha moved to the card rack. She fished in her handbag and produced another list. She needed a card for Ed and Bel's wedding anniversary, a "Welcome to your new home" card for Michael's aunt, a birthday card for Michael's father. All tasteful.

No bottoms, no breasts, no gags about wind. Her final purchase was a book for a little friend of Mathew's. Mathew was going to a birthday party and would need to take a gift. Martha chose *The Hungry Caterpillar*, creatively stimulating and educational. Ideal. Martha always bought children books as presents.

Martha left the bookshop undisputedly on a high. She'd stopped fretting about Maisie sleeping at the wrong time of day and she knew that she was in plenty of time to pick up Mathew from playschool. She could go to the supermarket this afternoon. She'd managed to push the thought of Eliza's imminent split from Greg out of her mind. She was very good at ignoring bad news. Retail therapy invariably helped and she was very pleased with today's purchases, all of which were eminently considered. So sensible.

# 7

Eliza was woken up by something licking her face. If it was Greg he really had to see a hygienist. It wasn't Greg, it was Dog. Dog was Greg's spaniel, rescued from a dogs' home two years ago. Dog's life with Greg was anything but a dog's life. Dog was spoilt rotten by both Greg and Eliza. Eliza worried that Dog was her child substitute, and she had no idea where Greg's depth of feelings for Dog came from.

Dog was called Dog because they couldn't agree on a name. Eliza had sighed and thought it was lucky they were never going to have a baby together, as it would probably end up being called Child, or Boy, or Girl.

"OK, OK." Eliza gave in to Dog's affectionate persistence.

She swung her long legs out of bed and stretched her arms above her head.

"Morning, Babe," mumbled Greg. He half opened one eye. "God, you look good, come back to bed."

"Someone has to feed Dog and take him for a walk," huffed Eliza. She wasn't sure what she was most irritated about: missing out on a morning shag or facing the task of unearthing dog food in the filthy kitchen.

Eliza showered and dressed and then warily ventured into the kitchen. It always looked and smelt even worse than she anticipated, hygiene not being a great concern of Greg's. She hunted around for an unpolluted fork and thought despairingly about how depressing it was that one of the only washed items in the kitchen was Dog's bowl and then only because it had been licked clean rather than felt the benefit of Fairy Liquid. Eliza scooped the foul-smelling dead horse into the bowl and gave it to Dog.

"I shouldn't have to do this, I'm a vegetarian," she yelled through to Greg who was, naturally, still in bed.

"Since when?"

"For ages, you just haven't noticed."

"But you had a hotdog when we came out of that club the night before last."

Eliza was momentarily stumped. "There's hardly any meat in those," she called back defiantly.

"And you had fish and chips last night," argued Greg. He now stood in the doorway of the kitchen, stark bollock naked, sleepily rubbing his eyes and lighting a cigarette. A complicated fusion of pleasure and displeasure shone and shot through Eliza's chest. She couldn't deny it—he was an adorable, sexy mix of boy/man. She fancied the hell out of him.

Literally.

If the hell-raiser were out of him, he'd be her perfect man.

Greg was tall and lean. He was in much better shape than he

deserved to be, considering he existed entirely on a diet of take-aways, alcohol and tobacco. He wore his hair longer than was fashionable but somehow it suited him. He always needed a shave, even after he'd just had one.

He was so fuckable.

Although he did need a hair cut and their first-born would be called Child.

"OK, I'm a pescarian then."

"I always thought you were Aquarius."

"Ha ha, very funny," commented Eliza. She reached for the previous evening's *Evening Standard* and turned to the horoscopes. She was never sure if the day described was intended to be the same day the newspaper appeared, because that wouldn't make much sense as everyone read the *Evening Standard* on their commute home from work, and by then there wasn't much of the day left. Therefore the forecasts must be for the following day. To make sure, Eliza always read the newspaper on both days.

*This is a great day for working at relationships. If you have identified areas that you need to pay attention to with a certain person, there's no time like the present for getting going. Clear communication will only be possible if you are entirely honest, particularly with yourself.*

The horoscope's accuracy didn't do much to cheer her up.

"Look, I'm taking Dog for a run; you could make yourself useful by clearing away some of last night's debris."

As usual, Greg's flat was littered with empty cans and chip wrappers. There were breakfast pots that had been accumulating for at least the last four days. Eliza was trying to ignore them but she was aware that the odds were she'd break before Greg noticed them and soon she'd don her rubber gloves. Greg looked around the kitchen in a manner that confirmed to Eliza that he gen-

uinely couldn't see the towering piles of dirty pots, the overflowing black rubbish bag (there was no bin), the sticky gunk that
decorated the lino or the grease on the hob. He did however see
that the cereal box was empty.

"Can you pick up some Crunchy Nut Corn Flakes whilst
you're out? No, get Coco Pops. No, get Frosted Shreddies. Oh
God, I can't decide. Which do you think?"

Eliza let the door bang after her and didn't bother to reply.

# 8

Poor Dog. He'd rather fancied a brief trip to the nearest
lamp-post or, at most, to the local corner shop to pick up
the cereal, but Eliza had something altogether different in mind.
She power-walked him through the streets, all the way along the
bustling Uxbridge Road, dragged him past Shepherd's Bush
Green, not allowing him so much as a sniff of the grass, along
Holland Park Avenue and to her sister's home.

Martha opened the door. She had Maisie on one hip and
Mathew latched to a leg. She was dressed in smart navy slacks, a
white shirt and slip-on suede pumps. Her hair was immaculately
styled, as always, and she was wearing lipgloss. Eliza felt distinctly
scruffy and underdressed in her tracky bottoms and sweatshirt.

Her question seemed redundant. "Hi Martha, is it too early
for a visit?"

"Not at all, the children and I have been up since six."
Martha beamed, delighted to see Eliza. She didn't let on that
she'd had a punishing start to her morning. Maisie had been griz-
zly with teething again, and Mathew was agitated by the atten-

tion Maisie was getting. Martha was beginning to find it difficult to distinguish between their cries as they meshed into a more or less continuous drone. Eliza's arrival was a welcome distraction. Martha shuffled out of the way as best she could with Mathew hooked to her leg, and gestured for Eliza to come in. Eliza carefully wiped her shoes but feared that Dog was going to damage irreparably the plush, immaculate cream hall carpet anyway.

"Is it all right if I bring Dog in?"

"Oh yes, yes, fine. Take him through to the garden; Mathew will be thrilled, something for him to tease other than his sister." Martha tried not to think about worms and made a mental note to check the garden for dog poop when Eliza left.

Eliza followed the instructions whilst Martha tried to set both children up with distractions. The kids rejected the clutch of wooden educational toys, as they clearly would prefer to poke and prod Dog. Eliza felt mildly irresponsible leaving Dog to fend for himself but still she chose to go back to the kitchen and join Martha for a cup of coffee.

"Where's Michael?" asked Eliza as she jumped on to a stool.

"In bed. He's had a very busy week."

I want a husband who's in bed because he's had a very busy week rather than because he's a lazy bugger, thought Eliza, but she didn't say as much; instead she asked if she could have some breakfast.

"Haven't you eaten?" Eliza could hear from the shock in Martha's voice that she disapproved of Eliza leaving the house on less than a full stomach. Eliza's lips tightened, waiting for the reproach.

Perhaps Martha noticed because she didn't articulate her reproach; instead she rolled off the bill of fare available. "Well, I have some freshly squeezed orange juice, some home-made Bircher muesli, which is very nice, even if I say so myself. You could have that with organic yogurt or milk. I've got skimmed, semi-skimmed or the tasty stuff. I have eggs, which I could poach, boil or scramble. I also have bacon and sausages. And I think there are some pastries."

Eliza couldn't help but compare the feast on offer here to the contents of the fridge and cupboards at Greg's. If someone dropped in unexpectedly on her for breakfast on a Saturday morning they'd have to make do with Ryvita, Marmite and black coffee. "I'll have muesli, please, and some orange juice."

Martha scurried around preparing Eliza's breakfast; it was the fourth she'd prepared that morning. The children had eaten first, then she'd had time to grab a slice of toast for herself. After Eliza was sorted out, Martha would have to start on Michael's cooked breakfast—which he liked to have at 11:30. At noon Martha would begin cooking the children's lunch. Eliza looked out of the window.

It was a lovely Indian summer morning. Freakily hot, hot enough to believe that it was August. God or Mother Nature or the guys in the white coats who invented aerosol sprays had got it all muddled again. Throughout the summer you were considered at best irresponsible, at worst an insurance risk, if you ventured out of doors without the protection of knee-high wellies and an umbrella. Now, in mid-September, you wouldn't be thought peculiar if you shimmied along the high street in a shift dress and slapped on sun oil.

The unseasonally hot weather made Martha worry about global warming. It made Eliza smile. This time last year half the population had been barricading their doors with sandbags against flooding rivers. Anything had to be better than that.

Eliza watched her niece and nephew play. They were glowing with sun and excitement. "Look at their rosy cheeks," she sighed adoringly.

"And muddy knees," sighed Martha, her tone noticeably less whimsical. She ran outside and rubbed some more sun cream on to Mathew's face, then scooped Maisie up into her arms. Maisie let out a wail of defiance. She wanted to stay and play with her brother and Dog.

"Is this Bircher muesli difficult to make?" asked Eliza thoughtfully. "It's delicious." She wasn't exactly sure what Bircher muesli was.

Martha flushed with pride, unused to compliments. Not that Michael didn't appreciate her, of course he appreciated her, it's just once you'd been together as long as they had you got out of the way of paying compliments. "It's very easy. Just buy a batch of muesli, get a good-quality one, packed with grains, fruits and nuts. It's worth adding extra nuts to a shop-bought one. Pour a cup of cream and a cup of milk over it and refrigerate it overnight. It's especially nice served with kiwi. I'm sure you'll have most of the ingredients in your cupboard."

No, actually, Eliza had absolutely none of these ingredients in her cupboard. She did most of her grocery shopping on an ad hoc basis at the local garage shop. Eliza rarely visited supermarkets; she hated them with a passion. The frustration began almost as soon as she drove into the car park. She rarely drove anywhere, as her battered, ancient Morris Minor was so unreliable. However, her dread of getting on and off buses with huge shopping bags was greater than her dread of trailing oil up London roads, so she did take the car to the supermarket if she really had to go there. Annoyingly, it was almost impossible for legitimate shoppers to find a space because so many commuters from out of town chose to drive to the supermarket, park their cars and then catch the Tube into the centre of town.

Even if she did find a space, there was the bloody trolley to contend with. She loathed the fact that the trolley couldn't be released from its captivity unless you paid a pound for the privilege. Eliza remembered the time when these things were free. Nothing in life was free now, not even going to the loo. Eliza never had a pound coin, although she did wish that she were the type of woman who always had the correct change. And, of course, after she had run about trying to buy a packet of chewing gum with a twenty-pound note to get a pound coin, and finally secured a trolley, she always discovered that she'd selected the one with the cranky, wobbly wheel. A trolley with suicidal tendencies that wanted to dash across an aisle and throw itself under another trolley.

Then there were the shoppers. Eliza had more or less come to terms with the fact that shopping in supermarkets meant that she was bound to encounter the oddball who insisted on taking six items through the five-items-or-less till. Which didn't necessarily have to be a problem, but did turn into one if the assistant was an oddball too, and insisted on voiding the transaction and sending the customer through another till. The old dears who were slow, the drunks who were smelly, the Filipino housekeepers who were hysterical, the Mediterranean au pairs who were exhausted, were all an inevitable part of Eliza's shopping experience. It all bored her.

Usually.

But now Eliza wanted to make muesli. She was sure that making muesli was where she should be as a person.

So it was with some reluctance and great trepidation that Eliza muttered, "I think I might go to the supermarket."

"Come with us. We always go on a Saturday afternoon, after I've made Michael's breakfast and given the kids their lunch. That way Michael can read the papers in peace, and there's a chance at least one of the children will fall asleep in the car." Martha made the offer with a huge smile on her face, as though she were inviting Eliza somewhere nice. In truth, Martha thought she was. She liked supermarkets. She liked the clean tidy aisles. She admired the armies of people ensuring that the bottles sat side by side, just so. She enjoyed the fact that the jars and tins stood in perfect lines. She loved choosing items, and always imagined the enormous pleasure she'd get as she'd place a special dish on the table and the fresh ingredients, the exotic spices, or the flavoursome cheeses would impress her guests. Her supermarket was her friend and helped her achieve that swell of pride and satisfaction. She liked visiting the supermarket best when Mathew was at playschool and Maisie fell asleep in the trolley. Then she had time to really examine the new lines and products. Reading labels was Martha's idea of "me time."

Eliza couldn't think of anything more depressing than spending her Saturday afternoon in a supermarket—it seemed unnatural. Didn't Martha know that the shops on the King's Road were open?

"Why don't we go now and leave Michael to get his own breakfast?" suggested Eliza.

"Yes, we could—why don't we?" giggled Martha.

"Let's live dangerously," muttered Eliza as she reached for her wallet. "I'll leave Dog here."

An hour and a half later, Martha and Eliza, Mathew and Maisie finally trundled through the doors of the local hypermarket because "now," with two children under the age of two and a half, actually means an age later.

"There's so much choice," mumbled Eliza, somewhat overwhelmed, as she walked through the fruit and vegetable aisle. There were fruits Eliza could hardly pronounce the names of, let alone recognize—tamarillo, guava, feijoa, grenadillo. She wondered what prickly pear, custard apple or star fruit tasted like and whether she ought to keep them in the fridge.

"Where do you usually shop?" asked Martha.

"The newsagent's at the corner of our street, or the garage."

Maisie sat in the trolley that Martha pushed, and Mathew sat in Eliza's.

"It's a joy to have an extra pair of hands," commented Martha. It really was turning out to be such a lovely day for her. "If they're both in the same trolley Mathew often attempts to beat Maisie over the head with a tin of beans or something similar."

Eliza looked at her angelic, smiling nephew and wondered why Martha exaggerated about how difficult it was to look after the children. It sometimes grated on Eliza that Martha didn't know how lucky she was. Mathew and Maisie always behaved beautifully whenever Eliza was with them. It was just a matter of discipline; children would push you as far as they could. If *she* became a mother her children would know the boundaries. Fun time would be great fun, and the other times would be calm, tranquil, relaxed. Perhaps she'd do Zen meditation throughout her pregnancy—that would certainly help the baby's karma.

Eliza looked around the supermarket and noted with some disappointment that most of the parents with children hadn't explained the boundaries clearly enough. She doubted whether any of them had ever benefited from Zen meditation. It seemed that every child, in every trolley, was crying, sulking, begging for sweets or pestering a sibling. Eliza couldn't understand why one mother, standing near the dairy fridge, was arguing with her three-year-old daughter about yogurts. If she really wants the yogurts with the ghastly cartoons of TV characters, then let her have them. That's the fun of being a child.

But Eliza had no concept of sugar content.

She lost interest in the ignominious yogurt battle between the mother and daughter and turned her attention to trolley-reading. That woman over there had digestion problems: her trolley had more prunes and bran cereals than was normal. That other woman was bulimic: two apples, one carrot and a box of Milk Tray. This one was cooking dinner for a lover: salmon, a selection of florets on a microwave tray that cost an entire trust fund per

pound, tubs of Häagen-Dazs. That couple was happy: moz-
zarella, tomatoes, avocados, fresh pasta and pesto sauce. That
couple was waiting for payday: baked beans, sliced loaf, tinned
fruit.

Eliza and Greg never shopped together.

Eliza sighed, wondering if her obsession with other people's
trolleys was healthy. Was it something to do with her intense feelings of jealousy and inadequacy, all brought on by the lack of a
suitable husband? The woman with the trust-fund-microwaveable
florets was certainly not the type of woman to waste four years—
four significant, biological-clock-ticking years—dating a com-
mitment-phobe musician.

Then again, had the floret woman ever had multiple orgasms
or made love on a kitchen unit? Had she ever drunk wine out of
her lover's mouth?

Aghhh. Eliza couldn't, no wouldn't, think about this now. She
picked up a packet of biscuits, then noticed that another brand
had a "two for one" offer. She couldn't choose, and so she eventually put all three packets in her trolley.

Comfort food.

"How do you do it?" marvelled Martha, looking at Eliza's
shopping. Despite Eliza's good intentions to buy fresh fruit and
nutritionally valuable products, her trolley was full of biscuits,
microwave chips, pizzas, sugary cereals and crisps. "How do you
manage to keep your figure? And your skin is terrific."

Martha's trolley was full of nappies for Maisie; for Mathew
there was organic chicken, organic cheese and organic crisps (the
only concession to childhood). There were a number of expensive products labelled "Tastes so special" for Michael. And whilst
Martha knew that these were probably another marketing ploy,
she found the Parmesan cheese—with black and white pictures
on the packaging of Italian kids eating pasta—irresistible.
Michael would love it. Then there were a number of low-fat,

low-taste products for herself. Eliza looked at Martha's groceries and began to doubt her ability to read trolleys like books. Because Martha's trolley said she was repressed and that she undervalued herself, which simply wasn't true. Eliza knew Martha was a happily married woman with a fulfilled life. Martha was always saying as much.

The sisters split up. Eliza wanted to stock her cupboards without Martha seeing the full extent of her neglect, and Martha wanted to buy the food for that night's dinner party and read the headlines of the quality papers.

Martha dawdled in the aisle with magazines and newspapers and started to read the tawdry and tantalizing headlines of the gossipy mags. Were they true, she wondered, or did people make them up so that other people, people like her for instance, felt dissatisfied and provincial? Not that Martha wanted one of those messy lives. She had never broken a rule, let alone a law, in her life. She had never parked in a disabled-driver space, and she paid her TV licence by direct debit. She was a law-abiding, upstanding citizen.

Eliza wondered if there was a single person in the whole world who had never stolen anything at all. She asked herself this question as she watched a well-dressed man in his forties slip a can of furniture polish under his coat. What an odd choice of booty. Eliza decided not to report him to the burly-looking security guard; it was probably a mid-life crisis thing, so why bother? Besides which, the burly-looking security guard elicited absolutely no sympathy in Eliza's heart; he looked bored and aggressive. Whereas the man with the furniture polish now in his inside pocket looked excited and pathetic. Eliza started to list mentally all the things she'd ever stolen: biscuits and pens from work; as well as Tippex, paper clips, Post-it Notes. As a student she'd regularly raided her flatmates' kitchen cupboards. She'd avoided her council tax for three consecutive years. She'd never paid Tube fares when she visited London as a teenager; she could afford them but it was a thrill to jump the barrier, part of the holiday experience. Eliza started to feel a bit like a cross between Ronnie Biggs and Bonnie-and-Clyde, so she pursued a different train of thought.

Chioca, what the fuck was it? Apparently, it was "tasty waxy red tubers, originally cultivated by the ancient Incas"—or so the packet said. Eliza looked for the cooking instructions; she was none the wiser. "Do not need peeling and have a slightly sweet taste; ideal roasted." Eliza shrugged. She put a bottle of organic balsamic vinegar and a bag of wheat-free flour into her trolley. She had a vague idea that you could splash balsamic vinegar on salads, but she wasn't sure if it would work with chips; she would never open the wheat-free flour but the packaging was very attractive and would look good on Greg's shelves.

Bored by her own ignorance, Eliza headed towards the bakery, drawn by the smell of freshly baked bread and sugary doughnuts. She decided to ditch her idea of buying rye bread and honey to be served with prunes. She was going to buy some bacon and eggs, tomatoes, mushrooms. She was going to go back to Greg's flat and cook a massive fry-up and then they could spend the afternoon making love. She'd put all ideas of pension policies and mortgages out of her head for now.

# 9

They did not spend their afternoon making love. When Eliza returned from Martha's she found the flat empty. There was no note to say where he'd gone. Of course not. To think of writing a note, Greg would have had to . . . well, think, for a start. A note would assume a measure of responsibility way beyond Greg's capabilities. Eliza didn't bother cooking up the eggs and bacon; she had no stomach for a brunch for one.

Eliza flung open the windows in an attempt to rid the flat of the various stenches of their lives: from fish and chip wrappers, stale tobacco, sweaty clothes and trainers. She couldn't help but think of the aromas that drifted around Martha's home: freshly brewed coffee, clean clothes, shampooed babies. Eliza felt grubby. She went to the bathroom with the intention of removing some of the grime that seemed to be a permanent symptom of her lifestyle. She pushed the door with some caution—the bathroom was never a pretty sight; even spiders objected to being in there on grounds of health and safety. Wet towels abandoned on the floor had obviously reproduced in her absence and were now forming a barricade. There was a tide mark around the bath that suggested Eliza and Greg worked down t'pit. Various ointments and unguents had mysteriously splurged from their tubes and tubs. They oozed across the sink, mirror, tiles and floor, as though they too were trying to effect an evacuation from this hole of Calcutta to a more sanitary environment. Her feet stuck to the lino, there was no loo roll, the blind didn't open.

Eliza sat on the edge of the bath and cried. When she stopped crying, she started packing.

"Hi, Babe," Greg called from the hall. Well, from the sitting room really, as the front door more or less opened into the sitting room, which smudged into the kitchen, which was barely divided from the bedroom. Only the bathroom was a separate entity in Greg's flat, and even then the door was always open. Eliza was not going to live in a studio flat for the rest of her days.

She flung another pile of Ts into her open suitcase. She heard the front door slam, the TV come on, and the pshushhh of a can of beer being opened. She checked the clock; it was half past four in the afternoon. She knew Greg was now lying on the futon (with his trainers no doubt muddying the throw). His jacket would be on the floor. Greg didn't actually fling it there: his clothes seemed simply to drop off him and land in untidy heaps. Eliza listened to him flick through the channels, horse racing, documentary, rugby, soap omnibus. Greg paused at the *Tweenies* and shouted, "The Tweenie Clock, where will it stop?" He did a great impression of Jake. Eliza would have thought this adorable if they'd had children, but they didn't, so, as it was, she thought it was stupid. Finally Greg settled on MTV. She knew he'd be scratching his stomach and wondering what to wear to the club tonight.

What a man, she sighed.

Eliza continued to pack her clothes. She didn't really know what to take. She'd noticed that whenever anyone ever left anyone on TV they always packed one neat case. How was that possible? Eliza had already filled a rucksack, a suitcase, a vanity case and three bin liners. She hadn't even opened her summer wardrobe. Perhaps she didn't need that black roll neck—she had packed two others, she could come back for it. Eliza sat on the bed and stroked the duvet. Why was she worrying about what to pack when what she should be worrying about was what to say to Greg? She rubbed her hand across their duvet again; it felt cool and smooth, nice. It was just a cotton thing from Debenhams, nothing particularly special, so why did touching it make her stomach lurch? She lay down to smell it. It smelt of Dog and Greg.

"What are you doing?"

Eliza jerked upright at the sound of Greg's voice; he stood in the doorway smoking a cigarette. She hated him smoking in the bedroom.

"Smelling the bed."

"I can see that. I mean, what are these bags about? Are you feng shui-ing your wardrobe?" Greg was trying, and failing, not to sound amused. He was very aware of Eliza's constant (and doomed) quest for a neater, more efficient, more financially successful self. He really didn't get it. He didn't get her compulsion to buy every book on the market that dangled the carrot of an improved self. She didn't need improving. She was pretty damn fly as far as he was concerned. If he were squeezed to name a fault in her, he might say that she was a bit too hung up on appearances, but that only manifested itself in this quirky habit of buying in to feng shui, self-improvement, self-help crap.

"No. I'm not feng shui-ing."

"Car boot sale?"

"No."

"Don't tell me, you're running away with the guy from the corner shop?" laughed Greg. It was an ongoing joke that the guy in their local shop really fancied Eliza; he was ninety if he was a day. Still, occasionally, the infatuation had been useful when Greg had needed something on tick. In one swift movement, Greg threw himself on to the bed and the bags off it. The clothes spilt out on to the floor. Greg cupped Eliza's breast and started to kiss her leg through her sweat pants. He hadn't even bothered to stub out his fag.

"Look at the mess you've made," complained Eliza. "Everything will be creased now." In fact the clothes hadn't been ironed; they both thought ironing was a tedious waste of time and, besides, Eliza had thrown things into the case in a more than haphazard manner. Greg knew all this and so didn't bother to defend himself. Instead he increased the intensity of his kisses and tried to edge Eliza's T-shirt up above her bra.

Eliza broke away. "I'm not in the mood."

"How can that be?" The question was genuine.

"I can't just switch it on like that," lied Eliza. In all honesty, she found it almost impossible to resist Greg and he could always just switch her on like that, by kissing her leg, stroking her hair, staring at her, eating spaghetti—lots of ways, actually. Right now, that annoyed her intensely.

"What's up, chick?" asked Greg as he gently thumbed Eliza's left nipple.

"Where've you been?" This question was asked as a stalling tactic rather than from any genuine curiosity.

"At Bob's, jamming. We've been doing something new—hang on, I'll play it for you." Greg jumped up and went back through to the sitting room to grab his saxophone. He stood his lit cigarette vertically on the dressing table.

Eliza simmered with irritation.

He started to play.

Fucking treacherous toe, tapping away as though she were enjoying his music. And her finger gently counting out the beat on her thigh. Heresy. So he looked good and sounded even better. Eliza had seen Greg perform on countless occasions. She always felt a thrill of pride that he made people stop and listen, that he had that power to entertain. And although she wished he didn't smoke, she had to admit that the smoke looked beautiful reflected back from his eyes and the saxophone.

So?

It was so childish to feel his beat and want to follow him as though he were the Pied fucking Piper. Eliza was so angry with herself that all she wanted to do was storm out of the flat that very moment. She wanted to leave behind her the woeful, soulful notes that were trying to climb inside her brain.

"I'm leaving you, Greg."

Greg stopped playing. "What?"

"I'm leaving you," Eliza repeated. She sounded more together than was actually the case. But then a thousand-piece jigsaw was more together than Eliza was.

"Why?" He felt as though she'd punched him. He put down the saxophone and crouched by Eliza.

"This isn't what I want," she said.

"What isn't?" he asked, genuinely bemused.

"This lifestyle. I feel"—Eliza had been practising this speech all afternoon, but was suddenly stuck for words—"I feel stifled."

"Stifled?" Greg didn't get it. Their life together was very creative. They often wrote lyrics together for his songs. Only the other evening they'd been bathing together and scribbled one on the bathroom wall. He'd thought that was so cool. They read together, and discussed books, gigs, gags, films and clothes. They had great, adventurous sex, and no one had that after four years. What did she mean, stifled? "What do you mean, stifled?"

"I don't think I'm all I could be. I want more."

"Well, what do you want?" he asked reasonably. She probably didn't mean she was leaving. She was probably being over dramatic. It didn't sound like a dumping speech. But then he'd never been dumped before. His past chicks had always just been there and then not been there. It hadn't been a big deal. But he hadn't thought Eliza would ever not be there. Thinking about it now, he couldn't imagine it. If he could, he knew it would be a really big deal.

"It's not you, it's this lifestyle," Eliza tried to explain.

"You're not going out with a lifestyle."

"You can say that again," Eliza sighed. She hadn't wanted to get into a big debate. She hadn't imagined being questioned or made to explain herself, she hadn't thought Greg had that sort of energy. "What's chioca?"

"I have no idea."

"It's a root vegetable. It's the type of ingredient that Martha uses when she's cooking for dinner parties. We don't even know what it is!"

"Aren't we well suited?" Greg's flip comment went down like a lead parachute. Eliza's eyes blazed with anger but he honestly did not know what was making her so furious. "You're dumping me because I don't know about some spice or other?" asked Greg, amazed.

"It's a *vegetable*, and yes . . . well, no, not exactly. We don't have dinner parties," she declared.

"Fran and Andy ate round here just the other night."

"A fish and chip supper without plates is not a dinner party." Eliza was surprised to hear she was shouting.

"OK, OK, we'll have plates next time."

Eliza wasn't placated. She stood up and hauled her case back on to the bed. Frantically, she crammed her clothes back inside. What was wrong with them? They seemed to have metamorphosed into tightly coiled springs. Everything she packed jumped straight out again. With determination she pushed knickers inside of shoes, weighed down slippery, flimsy dresses with heavy jumpers.

"I want matching crockery, I want shiny cutlery, I want private health care and travel insurance. I want a mortgage, not a rent book. I want dinner parties, I want to visit supermarkets and B&Q."

"You can't be serious. B&Q is always full of angry, resentful couples," argued Greg.

"I want to be an angry, resentful couple," yelled Eliza without really thinking what she was asking for.

"Well, you've got that at least, chick." Greg tried to smile—he wanted to appear flip and fearless; he was sure he sounded bitter and sad.

"No. We're not a couple, Greg, that's what I'm trying to say. I want a partner, not a boyfriend."

Greg started to roar. "Now I know you're having a laugh. You've always hated the word *part-ner.*" He said it in the stupid voice they both always used whenever they said the word and with the "carrot-up-the-bum" expression they usually adopted when introduced to someone who insisted on referring to their lover as their partner. "You don't want a *part-ner*. I don't believe you."

Eliza stopped rolling garments into tight angry balls and froze. It was true she didn't want a *part-ner*. She seriously doubted her ability ever to say the word out loud without the aid of fury or a silly expression. But she did want security, stability and respectability. She wanted to own furniture that wasn't so scanky that it had to be covered by tie-dye throws (which in point of fact were also scanky). She wanted to collect Denby pottery, not DVDs. She wanted stacks of Tupperware, smart pans with matching lids, and a fridge without the magnets arranged to spell rude words. She wanted all the things Martha had. And, most of all, she wanted a husband.

"I want to get married," admitted Eliza. She dragged her eyes from the carpet and stared at Greg. Her look was defiant, this wasn't a romantic proposal; it was a challenge.

Greg knew this instantly. He could see the gun that was being held to his head as clearly as he could see his own reflection in the mirror.

Eliza waited. It was possible, just possible, that he'd say, "OK let's do it." She'd even do the Vegas thing and be married by Elvis, if that's what he wanted (although she secretly longed for a replica of her sister's fairytale wedding).

"I see," muttered Greg. "I think I need a drink."

That's not the proper answer, steamed Eliza silently. She angrily tried to force the zip of the case to close. It wouldn't—she had to sit on it. She jumped on top of the case and bounced up and down, and centimetre by centimetre the teeth of the zip locked together.

Greg came back into the bedroom. He was carrying a half-empty bottle of whisky and two glasses. Eliza noticed that the glasses didn't even match—typical. Greg handed her one glass, which she mutely took. He unscrewed the cap of the bottle with his mouth and sloshed generous measures into both glasses.

He had beautiful fingers.

"So tell me again. Why do you want to get married? Because you want matching crockery and cutlery, and private health care and a mortgage?"

"Yes," sighed Eliza. She knew that she wasn't being very clear, but she couldn't find the words. "I want a grown-up life," she offered.

"And we're not that?"

"No. We're not."

"I thought we were, Liza. I thought being helplessly in love was grown up."

Eliza didn't know what to say. She normally loved it when he called her "Liza." It was so intimate because no one else ever shortened her name, never had; today she thought he was being impertinent.

Greg stayed silent for a moment and then said, "We should drink a toast. What do you think we should drink to?" Eliza couldn't bring herself to look at him. "How about, 'to the end of our affair'?" he said and then clinked his glass up against Eliza's.

"Er. To the end," mumbled Eliza, embarrassed at the unconventional nature of the toast.

Greg took a sip and then a chance. "Will you sleep with me one last time? For old times' sake." He smiled a slow, lazy smile, which drew lines around his eyes. Still, he didn't look his age.

Or act it, Eliza reminded herself. "No," she said as firmly as possible.

"No," he repeated quietly, and dropped his head to stare intently at the glass of whisky he was holding. He swirled round the rich, amber liquid, which chased and caught the light of the late afternoon sun that was drifting into the room. The mood could have been romantic. "It's over, isn't it?" he asked, forcing his gaze back upwards.

"Yes," said Eliza. She examined her emotions. She was expecting to feel relieved, even a little bit jubilant. She didn't. She felt horrible. But, she reminded herself, this was her first step on the road to respectability, and everyone knows that the first step is always the hardest.

That's why it hurts.

Not because she'd just thrown away the best thing that had ever happened to her.

# 10

Martha felt wonderful. Absolutely brimming with happiness and, good Lord, excitement even. It had been a while, but now she felt marvellous. Today had been perfect. Today was the type of day when you saw a space in the supermarket car park and you managed to reverse into it, first time, no hesitation. Today was the type of day when you were able to buy absolutely every ingredient on your list for your dinner party. Even chioca. The type of day when the children played happily together (Martha had a convenient memory and had already forgotten the torturous early morning), and your sister called round unexpectedly and you had a really lovely time just doing ordinary things like eating breakfast and buying the weekly groceries.

Today was the day when the estate agent called up to tell you that your offer on your dream home had been accepted. Hurrah!

An absolutely perfect day.

"Michael, isn't it wonderful?" Martha didn't pause for his response because she knew it was wonderful and she knew that Michael would think so too. "It will solve all our problems. A live-in nanny, pure bliss. Somewhere to air the towels and bed linen. A decent-size garden. A Wellington room." Martha pronounced the words "Wellington room" with the same enthusiasm other women reserve for thanking sex gods for multiple orgasms, but Martha didn't know that—she'd never been with a sex god and she'd never benefited from multiple orgasms.

Martha had returned home from the supermarket and immediately called the estate agent, as she had four or five times a day since they'd made the offer on the Bridleway. Martha was used to receiving the polite but uninspiring response, "They're still mulling it over." She wasn't aware of the estate agent's exasperated eye-rolling at his colleagues, or of the fact that they all chorused "Mrs. West again" every time the phone rang. Martha would politely and somewhat hopelessly respond, "Oh well, let me know as soon as you hear anything." Her comment was accompanied by a brave smile and a renewed silent prayer: "Please, please let them accept our offer."

So it was more than a surprise when the estate agent deviated from the established conversation pattern. "Ahh, Mrs. West. I was just about to call you."

"Were you?" Please, please, please God.

"They've accepted your offer."

In those four, or technically five, words, all of Martha's Christmases and birthdays came at once.

Martha had unpacked the shopping, fed the children, played with them all afternoon, taken them to the swings, fed them again, bathed them, read them a story, prepared dinner for six, showered, washed her hair, got dressed and made up, all in an unprecedented state of exhilaration.

It was the perfect day.

Martha allowed her chatter to run on and on as she dashed around the kitchen, completing the final preparations for the dinner party. She asked Michael whether she ought to put champagne in the fridge so that they could celebrate the offer's acceptance. She commented that another plate was chipped. She rooted in the vegetable rack, remarking on the freshness or otherwise of each vegetable; but she wasn't really concentrating on her own chatter. All she was thinking about was the Bridleway. The new house. Their dream home. Martha and Michael's dreams were about to come true. The offer had been accepted. The solicitor had been instructed that it was all systems go, and that they must exchange and complete as fast as humanly possible. Martha had actually rung their solicitor at home, on a Saturday, because she was too excited to wait until Monday—she would never normally have been so bold, even if she and Michael did pay a fortune for her services. Martha was smiling from ear to ear and could not imagine ever stopping smiling.

Michael wasn't concentrating on Martha's chatter either. He had no view on whether Martha should put champagne in the fridge. He couldn't have cared less that another plate was chipped, and the vegetables, for fuck's sake, were, after all, only vegetables.

"I wonder where everyone is? Ed and Bel are normally so prompt. Maybe the traffic is bad? Dom and Tara are always late—that doesn't surprise me in the least. Do you think I should call?" Martha was desperate to tell someone her news. Tara would have such good ideas for the kitchen; she'd recently had hers completely renovated. Martha coveted Tara's taps.

"No."

"No, you're right, it looks a bit rude if I hurry them. I'm sure they'll get here in their own time."

"They're not coming."

"Who aren't? Ed and Bel, or Dom and Tara? Oh Michael, you

could have told me earlier, I've cooked for six. Did they ring? Is it babysitting problems?" Martha continued to dash about the kitchen as she fired these questions. She decanted a bottle of red that needed to breathe, she poured olives into a bowl, she polished the champagne glasses for the second time, and she tried to ignore the surge of irritation that she felt slither up her spine. Lovely as Michael was, he simply didn't understand the logistics of how Martha managed their lives. He should have mentioned that they'd had a cancellation. She hated wasting good food, not to mention precious preparation time. If she hadn't been in such a good mood she might have said something.

But then, she probably wouldn't have.

"So who can't make it?" Martha was already wondering if she had any last-minute stand-ins. Would Eliza and Greg behave if she called them and invited them over? Or would they insist on smoking pot and ranting on about the unfair lack of facilities in state schools?

"None of them are coming."

"None?" Martha didn't understand. She stopped dashing and stared at Michael.

"No."

"Why not?"

"I called them and cancelled."

"You cancelled?" Martha thought she'd misheard, then all at once she understood. "Oh Michael, you sweetie, you want us to celebrate on our own." She moved towards him and went to put her arms around his neck. She pushed aside the thought that he should have told her so that she could have saved a fortune and an awful lot of time. It was a very romantic gesture.

Michael took hold of Martha's arms and slowly, carefully, put them back by her sides. He wasn't looking at her. "I'm leaving, Martha."

"We're going out?" she asked, hesitantly, because there was

something in Michael's voice that didn't say celebration. In fact, his body screamed hostility, frustration, shame and solitude.

Michael sighed very deeply and stared at his mobile phone. He had been fiddling with it for a while and had finally plugged it into the re-charger. "I'm leaving you, Martha. I'm moving out."

The world stopped orbiting.

Martha stopped breathing.

Her heart was pounding so hard she could feel it beating in her skull.

She'd heard his words, or thought she had, but she couldn't have. They were all wrong, they didn't make sense. They swam in front of her but still eluded the part of her brain that might decipher them, the part that could reassure her heart that she must have misheard Michael.

"Isn't it good news about the house?" stuttered Martha. She waited for his beam, his nod. She wanted to tell her heart, "False alarm, just a joke."

"It's over."

"What are you talking about?" The voice didn't sound like Martha's. It was high pitched and very frightened.

"I . . . I . . ." Michael hesitated. He looked around the room and ran his fingers through his hair. "I'm going to a hotel."

"A hotel? But I don't understand." And she really didn't. "What's wrong?"

Cough. "It's . . . it's difficult to say—"

Suddenly Martha didn't want to hear—hard as it might be for him to say, she had the feeling that it would be much, much harder to listen to. She had to stop him. "Well, don't say it. Don't say it. Stop being silly. Let's get on with supper," she said quickly. She picked up a tea towel and started rubbing the already immaculate kitchen surfaces. Silly was one of the words Martha often used when talking to the children; the inadequacy of it suddenly hit her.

Michael ignored her interruption. "It's not you, it's me. I just . . ." He couldn't finish the sentence.

"Just what?" she asked automatically, as a result of years of self-training in taking a polite interest. In fact, she didn't want to know.

"I need some space," he stumbled.

And Martha thought all the clichés were true after all. "You're going to get space. There's plenty of space at the Bridleway. What are you talking about?"

"I can't do this anymore."

"What? What can't you do?" Martha demanded. Her voice was now even quieter than usual. "Live happily with your wife and children?"

"I'm not happy."

Martha swayed. She felt behind her and lowered herself into a chair. *He's not happy. He's not happy.* But she was always asking him if he was happy. "Are you happy, darling?" she'd sing. "Of course I am, which man wouldn't be?" he'd reply, often accompanying his words with a quick peck on the cheek. She tried hard to make him happy. "Aren't we lucky," he'd volunteer. Often. He often said, "Aren't we lucky." Lucky was like happy, wasn't it? Or at least part of it.

"I realize this must be a shock."

Michael's lips moved and Martha watched them, but she didn't know who was talking. Not Michael, that's for certain, not her Micky, not her sweet Mikey. The intruder was wearing Michael's shirt and jeans, admittedly. And he was wearing Michael's watch but not his smile, and his eyes, which occasionally flicked over Martha, were dead. There was no love in them, and Michael's eyes had always oozed love and concern. What was this imposter saying now?

"I'm not in love with you anymore, Martha. Feeling as I do, I think it would be unfair to commit to the new mortgage."

Martha's head exploded. She felt an intense pain inside her brain, and she thought that her head would split wide open, shatter into splinters, and tiny shards of skull would lodge in the kitchen walls. It wouldn't be a loss. It was a useless head, anyway, and a pointless, hopeless mind that hadn't seen this coming, hadn't suspected a thing. Indeed, quite the opposite. Martha had thought, *believed,* that she was safe from such excruciating, searing, clear pain. Because they were happy. Happily *married,* and that was like an insurance policy, wasn't it?

"But you're *already* committed to me. Mortgage or no mortgage. I'm your wife," Martha insisted. She was desperately trying to be logical, but she felt like Alice in Wonderland, confused, shrinking and falling.

"I know that," sighed Michael, and then he too flopped back into a chair. He obviously couldn't get comfortable, or maybe he wanted to make it clear that he really was going, because he immediately leant forward and perched on the edge of the seat. He held his head in his hands.

Martha thought, as she often thought, that he had beautiful hair. Blue black. His eyes were his best point, the eyes that had shone with love and concern, but his hair was lovely too.

They sat in silence.

After an eternity, Michael scraped back his chair and made to stand up.

"Where are you going?" asked Martha quickly.

"A local hotel. I'm booked in for a few days, and then we'll think of something more permanent." He left the room.

"Don't go. Don't," said Martha, but she wasn't even sure if she'd said this out loud or just in her head.

# 11

Nothing was certain any more. Everything she believed in had dissolved. Martha had not slept. She'd spent the night sitting bolt upright in bed. She had not cried either. She had simply stared at the spot where Michael should have been in their bed. She touched the pillow, it was cold. No one had slept there. There had been no tussle over the duvet last night. No one to cuddle her to sleep.

Her husband had disappeared.

He wasn't happy.

Not happy? Well, couldn't he be happy again? Of course he could. He should have just said that he was unhappy and they could have fixed it. She could have fixed it. Why had he left? People, married people with children, didn't leave just because they weren't happy. Did they? What had made him unhappy? What could she do to make him happy again?

Why hadn't she asked him any of this last night?

You can't just say, "I'm unhappy," and then leave. You have to try a bit harder than that. How could he be unhappy and she not have known?

Martha felt stupid.

There had been rows, not that many—although thinking about it, recently the rows had been more frequent. She had been very tired, Maisie's colic had taken it out of them both, as had Mathew's jealousy and tantrums. But Maisie had started to sleep through now, and Mathew was becoming more confident again. They were just children; no one could blame them.

And so Martha and Michael had started to blame each other.

The imminent move had been a bit of a strain too. Spending every weekend searching for the perfect house hadn't exactly been a bundle of laughs. They had nagged, bickered, picked at one another. They were both weary, harried, spent, but they had been working towards a joint future. And that demanded effort. That's why he always worked such long hours. He was ambitious and wanted to build them a future; that's what he always said he wanted more than anything. That couldn't have changed, could it? Not just like that. Was he overworked perhaps? It could be that, yet he always said he loved his job.

But, then, he'd always said he loved her—until last night.

House moving is stressful, everyone knows that. But now they'd found the house they wouldn't have to spend weekends dragging the children around estate agents. They would be OK. They were through the worst. He couldn't leave. He was her husband.

She loved him.

He was not in love with her.

The words whipped her. Scorched and branded her. She was so ashamed. Martha wished she smoked, or drank, or shouted, or had some sort of refuge. Somewhere to hide from her own stupidity and shame.

What did he want? She'd give it to him. Whatever it was, she'd do it. She'd make him happy again. He just had to come home. They just had to forget this silly spat.

Martha reached for the phone and for the hundredth time that night she started to dial the number of Michael's mobile. For the hundredth time, she hung up before she pressed the last digit. She looked at the clock. 5 a.m., too early to call. He was never at his best in the mornings.

It was all a silly mix-up. He would come home today. Best not call him, best not make too big an issue out of it.

"Mama, Mama." The tinkling voice drifted from the nursery.

"I'm coming, Maisie." Martha swung her legs out from under

the duvet; she was still wearing the dress that she'd put on for the dinner party.

"Mummeeee, I need a wee-wee." Mathew's voice this time, more insistent.

"Good boy, Mathew. Well done for telling Mummy, let's get you to the toilet."

See, even toilet-training was working. Everything was getting easier. It would be OK.

Michael didn't call during breakfast. He missed seeing Maisie put her bowl of Coco Pops on her head. Martha had dashed to the garage to buy Coco Pops. They didn't normally have sugary cereals, but Martha thought they were all in need of a treat. She'd never have thought of buying cereal at a garage if it hadn't been for the conversation she'd had with Eliza the day before. She hadn't even taken the time to shower, or change out of her little black dress. She just popped the children into the double buggy and dashed to the garage, without so much as brushing her hair. She didn't stop to consider the possible catastrophe of meeting other mummies from Mathew's playgroup whilst she was in this state of disarray. Odd, because this was normally a major concern of hers.

Mathew couldn't believe his luck that he was allowed Coco Pops—it wasn't even a holiday. Martha also bought doughnuts, and some magazines, like the ones that had intrigued her in the supermarket. Could it be possible that it was only yesterday when Martha had thought that these messy lives were irrelevant? Now the headlines seemed to have been written just for her: "Male Midlife Crisis Happening Earlier and Earlier;" "My Husband Went to the Newsagent's and Never Came Back." There was also another article on Liz Hurley and other celebrity single mums—not that Martha was going to be a single mum, this was just a silly spat. No, that article was definitely not relevant.

Martha quickly put the magazine back on the shelf, as though by holding it she were risking catching a divorce.

Then she picked it up again.

She bought the magazine.

Martha never shouted when the children made a mess eating. She'd read in one of her many books about children's behaviour that if you did so, they started to associate stress and anger with mealtimes, and you'd end up with picky eaters. Michael wanted the children to eat at restaurants and try different delicacies when they were on their foreign holidays; he definitely did not want picky eaters. He didn't like mess, though. He'd have scowled if he'd seen Maisie's hair dripping with chocolatey milk. He'd have told Martha that her laughing was encouraging bad behaviour, that she was too soft.

Mathew didn't ask where his daddy was, although he did ask to go to the park.

"Not today, darling."

"But we always go today," argued Mathew with a child's logic. It was true that Martha took the children to the park every Sunday morning. Church, then park. It wasn't really that she was particularly religious, but church had become somewhere to take the children (before the shops opened) in order to allow Michael some peaceful time to himself. And church was quite a pleasant place to be. The old dears always seemed delighted to see Mathew and Maisie, they often amused one or both of them, giving Martha free hands, if not free time.

But this Sunday she couldn't risk going out in case Michael called. It was unlikely that he would sleep in today. He was bound to call and, no doubt, he would be feeling really silly and would need Martha to be in and to be bright and breezy. If he called and she was out and he had to call again, he might lose his nerve. So although it was a lovely day for a visit to the park, a blustery, bright day and they could have fed the ducks—which they loved to do—they all stayed at home.

In the morning they painted.

"Who's that, Mathew?"

"You."

"And who's that?"

"Me, and that's Maisie."

"Where's Daddy?"

"He's not in my picture. He's at work."

"I think we should draw one for Daddy."

Michael didn't call whilst the children were having their afternoon naps, which would have been a good time because they could have had an uninterrupted discussion. He didn't call at tea time, or bath time or story time.

Michael didn't call.

Martha opened herself a bottle of wine. She chose one of the very best bottles on the rack. She felt in need of another treat—the Coco Pops seemed an age ago—and it certainly felt indulgent opening a bottle of wine just for herself—especially as she knew she wouldn't drink it all—but then what choice did she have, since there was no one to share it with.

It was ten past eight. He'd left twenty-four hours ago. He hadn't called once, not even to ask after the children.

The magazines were perhaps an ill-advised move. Martha wasn't used to their gossipy, irreverent tone and so had read them as gospel. She was now petrified that as nearly half the marriages in Britain ended in divorce, hers was also bound to. Before reading the magazines she'd thought she was in the middle of a tiff; now she was sure she was at the start of an acrimonious custody struggle that would probably culminate in her having to kidnap her own children and run away to stash them in a foreign country. There were numerous articles about struggling or dying relationships: "How to keep the Zap in the Sack;" "The Break-up,

Make-up Cycle: How to Avoid it;" "Why Men are Genetically Inclined to Wander: The Hunter-gatherer Syndrome."

Was there someone else?

It was possible.

Martha didn't want to think it, but she didn't know how to stop thinking it. Michael was always at some function or other in the evenings. To be honest, she'd quite lost track of where he went and who with. She used to know the name and birthday of every person in his department; she used to buy their birthday cards. She still did the same for all Mathew's little playschool friends. Michael's department was too big now. Since he'd been promoted, Martha couldn't keep up.

No, don't be ridiculous. Of course Michael isn't having an affair. This is Michael, for God's sake.

Were they in debt? Would they overstretch themselves with this new house? Perhaps Michael simply didn't dare tell her that they couldn't afford the Bridleway. Silly man, that didn't matter to her. Not really, not now. She didn't need five bedrooms. Not as much as she needed him.

Perhaps he'd been made redundant? Every time she put on the news there was some report about the oil industry and cutbacks management were having to make. Could Michael be one of those men that got dressed for work every day, left with his laptop, and then went to sit in the park until home time? No, he couldn't be; he always worked late, that didn't make sense at all.

None of it made sense.

What should she do? Should she ring him and tell him that it was OK? Whatever it was, it was OK. That they could fix it, that they could work on it and that they could have a better, stronger marriage?

Or should she tell him to piss off?

Martha winced. She never swore, not even in her head. She

looked at her glass. It was already empty, which explained the outburst. She was aware that it was at times of crisis such as this that women turned into alcoholics. You heard about it all the time.

Sod it. She poured another.

Martha's hands felt heavy, her back ached and her legs were dead weights. Eyes open or closed, she couldn't focus. She couldn't move. She had no idea what to do. Her life, which had always been full and busy and purposeful, had lost all its clarity.

# 12

**"T**he doorbell keeps ringing, Mummmmmeeeee," yelled Mathew. He was sat at the kitchen table employed in helping to feed Maisie. A messy, counter-productive exercise, which he largely neglected in favour of running his toy motor-bikes through the pools of chocolatey milk decorating just about every surface in the kitchen.

"I know," said Martha. "I can hear it."

"Answer it. Answer it, Mummy," yelled Mathew again, taking on a persona not unlike the Last Emperor of China. Martha looked at her son and could see a lot of Michael in him. She didn't move towards the door.

Rrrrrrriiiiiiiiiiiinnnnnnngggg.

Someone was persistent. Martha thought it must be the post-man; it couldn't be Michael as he had a key and no reason to ring. She didn't want to see anyone else at all.

Rrrrrrrriiiiiiiiiinnnnnnngggggg.

Martha thought she might cry. Instead she dragged herself

from the table and went to answer the door. She felt she had no choice.

"Sorry for arriving unannounced," said Eliza. "Can I leave that there? There's more in the cab." Without waiting for a reply, Eliza galloped down the front steps, two at a time, and dashed towards a waiting cab. Martha looked at the suitcase in the hall. She hadn't slept for two nights so she was too tired to compute the information.

Eliza paid the cabby, and hauled a number of what appeared to be dead bodies in sacks up towards Martha's doorway.

"I'm so sorry, Martha. But I've been at Mum and Dad's since Saturday tea time. That's what, how many hours?"

"About thirty," said Martha, as she'd been counting her life in hours all weekend.

"Really? Seems a lifetime."

"Doesn't it," agreed Martha.

Eliza bustled past Martha, dragging her luggage behind her. She was too engrossed in her own problems to wonder what Martha meant. "I did spend Sunday afternoon at the estate agent's trying to find somewhere to rent. But what a disaster. They all wanted to knock off at three and I'd had a heavy night the night before, didn't get there until two. There's not much you can achieve by way of renting a flat in an hour."

Eliza had never had to have intimate contact with estate agents in the past. She had travelled too much ever to need a permanent base. And whenever she did need a pad in the U.K. she was the type of girl that people wanted to share a flat with, so friends, or friends of friends, had always had a spare room that she could rent or doss in. Then she'd hooked up with Greg and moved into his place.

"D'you know, I've never met an estate agent before. Not even on a social basis. Not one, not in any of the numerous countries I've visited, or parties I've been to. But then, thinking about it, this isn't such a surprise. It's unlikely that anyone at a party would own up to being an estate agent and still expect to be offered a glass of punch."

"So, erm, what's the problem? Has your washing machine flooded your flat again?" asked Martha politely, interrupting Eliza's prattle. She had no real interest in it. It was clear that this conversation didn't relate to Michael or, most particularly, his whereabouts, but Martha was sensible enough to know she had to ask, if only to momentarily interrupt Eliza's chatter.

"No. I've—bloody hell, Martha, what's happened here? Have you been robbed?"

Whilst they'd been talking, Martha and Eliza had automatically gravitated towards the kitchen. As a rule, Martha's kitchen was a haven of comfort and cleanliness. It was beautifully fitted with Poggenpohl units and stainless-steel surfaces, and neatly stocked with a state-of-the-art cappuccino machine, juicer, bread-maker, pasta-maker, grinder and multi-function food processor. Most unusually, every gadget was regularly used. Martha's kitchen was the best-stocked kitchen in WII. Usually everything had a place and there was a place for everything.

Right now, as far as Eliza could make out, that place was on the floor.

There were at least twelve dirty coffee mugs lurking on the surfaces; there was Lego, paint, Meccano and squashed banana on the floor; there were handprints on the fridge, the windows, the cupboards; there was a sinkful of pans encrusted with baked beans; the usually concealed rubbish bins (of which there were five: paper, biodegradable food waste, tins, bottles, other) were all overflowing; the hamster's cage was rancid and its water bottle was empty.

"Oh God, what's that?" asked Eliza in fear, as she pointed to a brown, sticky mess that stretched right across the floor.

"Coco Pops," sighed Martha.

"Thank God." Eliza dropped all her bags (aware that she was adding to the chaos, but calculating that her contribution would hardly be noticeable). She turned to Martha and noted that she was wearing a little black dress, one she often wore for dinner parties, despite it being just after 9 a.m. on a Monday morning. "What's happened?"

"Michael's left me."

All Sunday Martha had tried to pretend this wasn't the case. Saying the words aloud made them real. Michael had gone. He'd left on Saturday and this was Monday and she hadn't even heard from him.

The enormity of the situation suddenly slapped Martha and shocked the first tears from her. "He's le . . . le . . . left me," she sobbed, as she held up her arms and waited for her sister to scoop her up and make it all better.

Eliza did at least scoop. She held Martha tightly and stroked her hair. "Don't worry, shush, don't worry," she cooed. "It's OK, it's going to be OK." She thought if she said it often enough she had a chance of convincing herself at least.

Maisie and Mathew looked on, wide-eyed. Mummy was funny today.

"It'll be OK. You'll see, it'll be OK," repeated Eliza, firmly, trying hard not to sound as helpless and hopeless as she felt.

# 13

Eliza couldn't hear Martha's crying through the bedroom wall, but she sensed it. She wearily got out of bed and staggered on to the landing. She knocked at the door. Martha mumbled something. It could have been "Come in," it might have been "I want to die." It was impossible to tell because Martha had pulled the duvet over her head to hide her tear-smudged face. Eliza opened the door and asked the dark room, "You OK?" Eliza was very aware of how ludicrous the question was.

"Oh fine," replied Martha, using her Women's Institute voice. Eliza had never thought the voice, or for that matter joining the WI, had suited Martha. "This is nothing, you know. Just a silly spat. It will all blow over," Martha said in her singsong voice; she had repeated the same thing all day and night.

Eliza didn't know much about married life but she didn't think that this was just a tiff. "Can I do anything? Get you anything?" In the shadowy light thrown from the landing, Eliza just about made out Martha shaking her head. It was obvious she couldn't trust herself to say anything more. Eliza quietly closed the door and went back to her bed, or more accurately, Mathew's bed. Mathew had been shoved in with Maisie. Martha, ever the hostess, had tried to make Eliza comfortable. She'd dug out a comfy duvet, Egyptian cotton sheets and numerous duck-feather pillows, but Eliza couldn't fall asleep. The silence of subdued tears kept her awake.

Eliza couldn't understand it. She thought she was pretty good at people, relationships, intuition and stuff. She could, for example, always spot a pregnancy, often even before the expectant mother had skipped. She could identify a philandering husband at a twenty-metre range. In a crowded room of strangers, she could match people with their other halves as easily as if she were playing a game of snap. And yet her own brother-in-law, whom she saw at least once a week, sometimes two or three, had managed to fall out of love with her own sister, without Eliza so much as sniffing that there was anything wrong. How could she have missed the imminent catastrophe looming on the horizon?

Why had he left?

God, if Martha and Michael weren't happy, who the hell was? Martha and Michael had it all. Each other, healthy, beautiful kids (one of each flavour), good prospects, lovely home, plenty of money, fantastic holidays, great family and friends. Did this mean everybody was entitled to be unhappy?

Everybody was *doomed* to be unhappy?

No. She didn't like the direction her mind was drifting in. She couldn't face that possibility. What a ridiculous thought. You have to look on the bright side. No point getting depressed.

But how? How had Michael fallen out of love with Martha? Martha was gorgeous, and kind, and generous, and trusting. It wasn't just that Eliza was biased, everyone thought the same. Martha seemed to have forgotten, but when Martha and Michael got together it was generally conceded that Martha was the real catch and Michael had "done well." Martha was funny, and although it was difficult to believe at the moment, she had a mischievous side to her that made her the life-and-soul of the party. Or used to. She hadn't been much of a life-and-soul of late. Life-and-souls rarely fretted about orange-juice spillage.

Martha was so in love with Michael that she had automatically and honestly sung his praises to anyone who would listen. She was his very own portable PR machine. He obviously believed her hype. Had Martha forgotten herself in her enthusiasm to promote her love? Admittedly, in the last year or so, Martha had become a bit obsessive about the kids' safety, and about cleanliness, and about what the neighbours thought. Which was quite irritating—but, generally, Martha was lovely. Martha was . . . well, Martha. The woman Michael had married. The woman he'd promised to love forever; in sickness and in health; for richer, for poorer; for better, for worse.

Bastard.

The phone rang once and then stopped. Eliza knew that Martha had snatched it up, hoping against hope that it was Michael. The phone had rung four times that day and every time Martha had run, at breakneck speed, to answer it. "Yes," she'd answered breathlessly, expectantly. Each time she was crushed, it was never Michael.

"It's for you." Martha tapped at Eliza's door. Her voice was thick and heavy with disappointment. "It's Greg."

Shit.

Greg.

In all of this chaos Eliza hadn't given a thought to her own domestic crisis.

She jumped out of bed and ran to pick up the phone in the hall downstairs. This was not a conversation she wanted to have in front of Martha.

"It'ssss me."

"You're drunk," she said, grumpily.

"Of course I am. I have feelings, you know."

Eliza smiled. He had a point. She'd been trying to force alcohol on Martha all evening. "What do you want?"

"What do I want?" He was astounded at her stupidity. "I want you to come home and tell me what this is all about."

"I *have* told you," said Eliza. She sounded more impatient than she was, because she felt the sting of guilt. She hadn't really explained anything to Greg. How could she try to get him to understand that his biggest fault was his lack of a pension policy? "Look, this isn't about *you,* it's about *me,*" she added.

Greg let out a laugh that was at once amused and insulted. He could only be amused because he was an extremely easygoing bloke.

"Sorry," said Eliza, kicking herself for resorting to a cliché. "What I mean is you haven't changed or done anything wrong." True, he was the same irresponsible, fun-loving, free spirit that she'd fallen in love with four years ago. "I've changed." She didn't add that the characteristics that had once attracted her now repelled her. "Go to bed, Greg. Sleep off the whisky." Eliza hung up. Her feet were icy. She ran upstairs and threw herself back into bed. She snuggled under the duvet and tried to will away that nagging thought that a pension policy hadn't protected Martha anyway.

# October

# 14

As Eliza put the key in the lock she could hear the now all too familiar sound of Martha's howling. She quickly pushed the door open, not pausing to take off her coat or drop her bag. She charged at Martha and started to wrestle the phone out of her hand. For such a small bird Martha was deceptively strong, and clung tightly to the handset.

"Put the phone down, Martha."

"Please, please, please come home. We need to talk. I love you, Michael," Martha begged.

"I'm going to switch my phone off now, Martha," said Michael calmly.

"No, no, no, you can't switch me off just like that. I'm your wife."

"Look, I'm sorry." He didn't sound sorry. He sounded angry. He just wanted to get her off the line.

"I'm your wife. I'm your wife. I'm—"

"Put the phone down." Eliza snatched the phone from Martha and stabbed the off-button. "Haven't you any self-respect?" she demanded furiously.

"No. Not any more." Martha slumped against the hall wall and started to sob loudly.

Eliza wrapped her arms around her sister and rocked her gently to and fro. God, she'd like to kick the shit out of that bastard Michael. Martha's face was twisted, almost beyond recognition; as she exhaled, she spat the air out: it stung Eliza's cheek like pinpricks. Martha's pain was so visible that Eliza wondered whether she might be able to catch it, box it up and throw it away.

It had been a little over four weeks.

Even Martha was beginning to understand that this was more than "a silly spat."

"Where are the kids?"

"Maisie is taking a nap, Mathew is in the garden."

Eliza was relieved. Martha was at least ensuring that the children didn't witness her collapse.

"I thought we agreed that you weren't going to call him," said Eliza. She knew that Michael wouldn't have called Martha. He never called. He'd walked away from his wife, his children and his home without, as far as Eliza could see, as much as a backward glance. He'd only visited the children four times in the four weeks. All communication (usually frenzied, irrational and often drunken) was precipitated by Martha.

"I had to call him. The estate agent rang."

"So you've told them that you won't be taking the Bridleway?"

"Not exactly."

"Martha, you have to tell them," Eliza insisted with exasperation. She broke away from her sister, walked through to the kitchen and put the kettle on. She'd made hundreds of cups of tea in the last four weeks. She wasn't sure if they helped any, but it was something to do. She felt useless. Having something to do, even something as trivial as putting the kettle on, was necessary. Sometimes Martha drank the tea; sometimes it went cold because Martha ignored it. Eliza made the tea and carried it back to her sister, who hadn't moved an inch; it was beyond her. Eliza was struck again by how small Martha looked. Always a slim woman, she was disappearing before Eliza's eyes. Sometimes Eliza was nervous of holding her too closely in case she snapped.

"Do you want me to call them? You can't keep them hanging on thinking they have a sale, honey. It's not fair on the vendors."

"It's not fair on me," exhorted Martha with a surprising measure of bitterness. "None of this is."

• • •

The last four weeks had been total hell. For four days, Michael wouldn't even speak to Martha. He didn't take or return her calls.

Initially she had left bright and breezy messages:

"Darling, are you there? This is so silly. Call me. Let's sort this out."

"Are you picking up these messages? The children are in bed, it would be a good time to talk because it's peaceful here. Have you eaten? I've made a lamb casserole, your favourite."

The casserole went uneaten and her tone became more concerned:

"Michael, please call me back just to tell me you are safe and well."

She had nightmares of him doing something terrible to himself. She couldn't sleep because she fell into panics, imagining him lying prone in some seedy hotel room, next to empty whisky and aspirin bottles. When by the Wednesday following his walk-out he still hadn't called, she rang all the hospitals in the area. At this point, Eliza suggested trying him from a phone whose number he wouldn't recognize.

He answered immediately. "Michael West here."

"Eliza Evergreen here. Not dead, then," Eliza muttered dryly. She only just resisted adding "yet" as she handed the phone to her sister.

Eliza listened as Martha pleaded, cajoled, reasoned and implored. It took Martha three quarters of an hour to persuade her husband to meet her, just for a talk.

"It'll be fun," Martha had said, rather unrealistically, "like a date."

Their first meeting *was* in some ways like a date. One of Cilla Black's less successful Blind Dates. Martha had barely waited until they were shown to their table in the restaurant before she blurted out, "But what's making you unhappy?"

They were at the local Italian, one of Michael's favourite places to dine. Martha didn't really like it at all. She thought it was overpriced and, anyway, they'd visited it a lot throughout her pregnancy with Maisie. She always associated the yellow walls with feelings of overwhelming nausea, but she'd made the reservation regardless as she hoped to please Michael. She'd bought a new dress for the occasion and, most unusually, she wore full makeup.

But her lipstick couldn't shield her.

"Can't we just order the food first, before we start the big talk?" Michael asked with ill-disguised irritation.

"Oh, of course, if you like." Martha hated herself for sounding so stupidly servile but then again she was used to following his suggestions. How could he think of food right now? But she realized that she had to be very careful, very careful indeed. Michael had left on Saturday evening; it was now Thursday evening. Five days, nearly an entire week. How had the days slipped by like that? How had the clocks managed to tick? Martha certainly hadn't. She was immobilized.

Martha had always believed that two people together were greater than the sum of the parts. That was one of the joys of marriage. It protected you. You were never alone. She and Michael used to say that even when they were apart they were looking out for one another, somehow joined, perhaps by an invisible piece of elastic. If they needed each other, they could call or simply think of the other and their worlds would be better, safer, warmer. They'd said such romantic stuff and Martha, for one, had believed it. With him Martha was enormous, positive, possible. Without him she was microscopic.

Martha still could not believe that this was happening to her. Michael could not mean that he really wanted to leave. Could he? Why would he want that? It was all a terrible misunderstanding. Until Saturday they'd never gone to sleep on a row before. Yes, they'd had rows, but they always made up afterwards. They'd reaffirmed that they would love each other forever and then, if there had been time and the children were both asleep, they'd make love just to prove it.

Even if it wasn't a Friday.

Now they'd lived apart for five days and Martha hadn't got a clue why. She *had* to get Michael home. She had to be very careful.

She stared at the menu for an age but she had no idea what was on offer. Michael ordered calves' liver and seared tuna; as usual, he chose the most expensive things on the menu. As usual, Martha ordered a green salad and pasta, the cheapest things on the menu.

"Mathew drew a picture for you. A farmyard—we went to one on Tuesday." Martha scrabbled about in her bag and pulled out the picture. In fact, it had been given to Eliza, but Martha had taken it off the fridge and brought it to the restaurant. She didn't want Michael to forget he had children. "Maisie walked three steps today—holding on to a chair, admittedly," she gushed.

"That's great. Really good. Send them my love. Give them a big kiss from me."

Martha's heart sank, as it was clear that he wasn't planning on coming home with her that night. She just wanted things to get back to normal. She wanted them to eat this meal together, and at the end of the evening for them to get their coats and him to come home with her. She wanted him to spend ages in the bathroom as she chatted and called through to him from the bedroom. She wanted him to set the alarm on their bedside clock. She wanted him to get into bed next to her. She wanted to put her cold feet on his warm legs.

Michael took the picture from Martha. He was holding it up-side down—but this wasn't necessarily a reflection of his skills as a father; Mathew's pictures were very much at a raw talent stage. "A circus, very good," muttered Michael.

"A farmyard . . . we visited on Tuesday," murmured Martha. The bread stuck in her throat. However much water she drank she couldn't seem to swallow it down. She'd planned to be upbeat and dynamic. She'd wanted to discuss sensibly their posi-tion and, through rational debate, convince Michael to return home. She had everything on her side. He couldn't possibly want to stay away, could he? Not Michael. Michael was kind and sen-sible. Michael was good and reliable. That's why she'd chosen him to marry. He was the marrying kind of man. She'd backed the favourite, not the three-legged outsider, so how could she lose the race? He couldn't really intend to leave her and the children. He couldn't be that vicious, that cruel. He couldn't be thinking of a divorce. Every time the word divorce fought its way into Martha's consciousness it hit her like a stun gun. She was para-lysed and left entirely devoid of upbeat or dynamic conversation. Instead she asked, "How's work?"—as she had asked every night for the last ten years.

"Not too good." Michael winced at the memory of his day. "More culling, I'm afraid."

Martha hated it when Michael referred to redundancies as "culls." She thought it avoided the issue—human lives were being obliterated.

"Is your job under threat? Is this what this is about? Michael, you know I don't care about the Bridleway," surged Martha, hop-ing she'd alighted on a cause of his unhappiness and could there-fore offer a swift solution. It was in Martha's nature to fix things. If she saw a rip, she'd reach for her sewing box. If one of the chil-dren broke an ornament, she'd reach for the Superglue. If some-one was unhappy, she'd buy flowers, send a card or bake a cake in an effort to cheer them up. Martha believed everything could be fixed. Except for death. Her marriage was not dead, she could mend it.

If only she knew what was wrong.

"You do care about the Bridleway," Michael said, slowly.

"Well, yes," she admitted, "but nowhere near as much as I care for you. Are we in debt? Have we over-extended ourselves? Is there something you feel you can't tell me about?"

"We're not in debt, Martha. Well, other than the usual credit cards and mortgage." He didn't offer her any more enlightenment. They fell silent and waited for the starter to arrive.

Michael chewed his calves' liver. Martha played with her green leaf salad.

"Is there another woman?" Martha felt small having to ask. Miniscule.

"For God's sake, Martha, how could you think that of me?"

"I don't know what to think."

Was he having a breakdown? Martha took a sneaky look at him. Oddly, she was a little afraid to meet his eyes. She didn't know what she'd find. He was chewing ravenously. He looked fine. He looked well. He didn't even look worried. Was he a cross-dresser or a closet homosexual? She thought about how much money, time and effort he spent on his wardrobe (entirely Armani, Paul Smith and Boss), and dismissed the idea of him being a cross-dresser. She couldn't imagine him being attracted to Marks and Sparks nylon skirts and costume jewellery. His toe and fingernails were too filthy for him to be a homosexual. God, these thoughts were bizarre. Martha shook her head a tiny fraction, she wasn't thinking clearly; she had to get more sleep.

For the rest of the meal they discussed the décor in the restaurant, the wine list and the other diners. At nine-fifteen they collected their coats and Michael drove Martha home. He pecked her on the cheek. Told her he'd call, although he didn't specify when, and drove away.

From that moment, Martha's initial optimism, that this was a silly spat that could be resolved with a bit of unclouded thought, began to recede. She didn't want to admit it, even to herself, but it had been obvious from the word go that Michael didn't want to be on the date. His reluctance had showed in every gesture, word, stance, even in the tiny muscles above his eyes. Michael didn't want to be with Martha.

Martha cried all night. She didn't understand whose life she was living. Certainly not her own.

Martha and Michael met to "date" once a week. They went for a drink, or a meal, or to the cinema. On each occasion Martha would arrange the day and time, the venue and the babysitter. All Michael had to do was show up.

The dates were predestined to be unmitigated disasters. All Martha wanted was an explanation. Michael thought he'd already given one.

He was no longer in love with her.

A potent mix of cowardliness and kindness forced Michael to agree to the dates. He felt he had little choice; Martha harped on and on, pretty much demanded it. She wouldn't take no for an answer. He wanted to tell her that for months now he'd found himself looking at other women in the street, in the office, in bars. They'd looked back, too. Not many of them were as pretty as Martha, but he wondered if any one of them would love him more than she loved her children. Would any of them nag him any less about his late nights in the office, resist controlling his every movement and still give blow jobs? Would any of them appreciate just how stressful his work was? He thought one of them might; the odds were in his favour. He was sure someone out there could make him happier than he was now. He thought he might already have met her. He knew this wasn't what Martha wanted to hear but he had nothing else to say. He found himself chatting about banalities such as the weather and the journey from work. He adopted a tone of neutrality: cool, polite, firm.

Martha was humiliated by his dispassion and rejection. Invariably she would be unable to hide her pain and confusion; she'd cry, which would embarrass him, or shout, which would repel him. She knew that she had to make herself more attractive to him, not less, but Martha had always been more of a "stand by your man" than a "win back your man" type, so she had no idea how to turn herself into a Venus flytrap.

She took her guidance from anyone who offered it—Eliza, her mother, magazines, old movies, morning chat shows on TV. Initially, Martha tried buying new clothes for the nights out. Her strategy was to be bright and breezy—because it worked for Dusty Springfield's heroines. She bought a beautiful, clingy cashmere dress because she vaguely remembered reading somewhere that getting a man to want to touch you was half the battle, and surely everyone wanted to touch cashmere. Eliza thought the theory (and practice) was bollocks but, because she was a devoted sister, she supported Martha—although she did suggest that a modern take on the theory might be more successful. She suggested Martha buy sexy leather pants.

"Pants?" asked Martha aghast. "I've never been into an Ann Summers shop. I don't know if I'd have the nerve, and anyway, we're not in the type of relationship where he'd get to see my pants at the moment."

"Trousers," Eliza clarified.

"You've never been the same since you visited California," sighed Martha. But she was persuaded, despite the price tag. She'd try anything. Martha rarely spent serious money on her own clothes but as she was rapidly losing weight, she justified the lavish purchases as necessary rather than indulgent.

It didn't matter: Michael didn't notice her new clothes or new figure.

"How do I look?" Martha asked at the beginning of their dates. She hated herself for fishing for compliments, but the days when they were spontaneously given were fast fading into history. She twirled around in front of him, hoping that he believed in her faked vivacity.

"Nice," he'd say, as he'd always said when he'd paid her a compliment in the past. Martha tried to appreciate his answer, but in all truthfulness she'd never really liked being described as "nice." She'd always wanted him to describe her as "stunning" or "beautiful" or "drop dead."

"Shall we eat?" he asked, picking up the menu and dropping his gaze, without waiting for her to agree.

On each date they tried to be "nice" to each other. But trying was trying. Martha arrived late and tired. She always intended to be ready in plenty of time. But, just as she was setting off, one of the children would wake and need resettling, or she'd remember that it was rubbish collection the next day and she'd have to wheel the bins out to the front gate (not easy in kitten heels). It was tricky appearing—what was it that Eliza had suggested—"confident and indifferent" when your whole world had been washed away like an ephemeral sandcastle. It was hard to appear beguiling and bewitching (as suggested by Doris Day, in a film she'd caught a snatch of on Channel 5 the other afternoon) when you felt belittled and bewildered. It was virtually impossible to be interesting and stimulating when your estranged husband's idea of a conversation was muttering monosyllabic replies (often, "No" or "I don't know") to all your deep and probing questions.

As each date passed Michael found it harder and harder to hold eye contact with his wife. Why did she insist on wearing her pathetic pain like a shroud? Why did she insist her life was so difficult? Christ, how hard was it to get to a restaurant on time? He was sure she deliberately arrived late to give her the opportunity to moan about how difficult her life was, her life without him. She would *not* make him feel guilty, which was clearly what she was trying to do. She was trying to manipulate him. Martha's stare soused Michael in a strange cocktail of emotions. He felt ashamed and ignoble, which he didn't like, so he became indignant and resentful in her company. She was no fun. And fun was what he wanted. Didn't she see that? Well fuck her; others saw it. Sleeping in a hotel room wasn't exactly a bundle of laughs, nor was sleeping in his mate's spare room but Michael could, quite clearly, see a time when beds would be fun again. Michael never mentioned his new friends to Martha.

Martha felt that Michael had performed open-heart surgery on her, in boxing gloves, and he had forgotten to sew her back up. She even imagined she was still under anaesthetic because her life had a strange nightmarish unreality to it. She was embarrassed and pained by her open wound and tried to hide it behind excited chatter about the children and her day-to-day life. But her day-to-day life *was* the children; she had nothing else to talk about. Michael had been her only other topic of conversation. If he'd asked after Eliza or her parents, which he didn't anyway, she wouldn't have been able to be honest with him. Martha hated being dishonest, but she couldn't tell him that they were burning his effigy and stabbing the private parts of a voodoo doll. After she'd told Michael that the man from Majestic Wine had called to tell him that he'd received a case of a rather special vintage Michael might be interested in, she had nothing left to say.

Martha realized she was boring him.

At the beginning of each date, Martha would leave the house looking pretty and expectant. She would return looking flattened and woeful. As she put her key in the lock she would muster her resources and manage a smile for Eliza. It was a brave but pointless gesture. Eliza was always watching and waiting for her sister's return, monitoring the progress—or rather lack of progress—as keenly as Martha. As Eliza heard a car draw up, she'd run to the window. She'd watch as Michael planted his cold kisses on Martha's cheek. What sort of date was it when the guy didn't try to plunge his hands inside your knickers? It was hardly polite. She'd note Martha's hunched shoulders and tight mouth as she walked down the garden path. Therefore Eliza was never convinced by the wide smile that Martha tried to pass off as genuine when she walked through the door.

The debrief was an intrinsic part of the date routine, but this was generally as intense and disappointing as the actual date.

Typically, it went something like this. As Martha pushed open the front door Eliza handed her a glass of wine and demanded, "So what the fuck has the Guru had to say for himself tonight?"

Eliza had taken to calling Michael "the Guru" since he had explained to Martha that he was "going through some sort of crisis and needed to find some answers about himself." "No kidding, we bloody knew that already," Eliza had shouted when Martha had related the comment. Martha always regretted telling Eliza what Michael had said. Eliza invariably trivialized it. Perhaps something was lost in the retelling because, when Michael had said as much to Martha, Martha had thought he'd initiated a very positive breakthrough.

"Please don't swear so much in front of the children."

"They're in bed."

"Well, in front of me then," Martha had urged.

"I can't help it, Martha, he makes me mad. You can't just up and off, after ten years, and give no reason for it."

"He has given a reason: he said he was unhappy."

"And why is he unhappy? When did he realize he was unhappy?"

These were, of course, questions Martha had asked herself—

more or less constantly—since Michael left. She was no closer to stumbling on any answers.

Eliza fumed. What was all this talk about being happy, for God's sake? He was married, wasn't he? He couldn't expect to be happy all the time. Didn't he know anything about the real world? And to add insult to injury, since he'd walked away from his wife and children, there was the way he handled the subsequent situation. Or, rather, the fact that he entirely ignored the situation. Martha's every moment was consumed by thinking about their relationship, trying to understand it, rationalize it, excuse it and fix it. Whilst Michael claimed that he was too busy at work to give his floundering marriage any real thought.

"If this had happened to me there wouldn't be any of this 'talking it through' bollocks. It would be straight down to the Citizens Advice Bureau for the name of a good family solicitor," shouted Eliza.

"But we're not alike, and it didn't happen to you, and you aren't me," argued Martha.

Thank God, muttered Eliza to herself. She took a deep breath and tried to be sympathetic. "OK, so tell me what was said tonight."

"Actually, I'm much closer to understanding why he is unhappy."

"And why is that?" (Gritted teeth.)

"Our constant rowing and my being a nag distresses him. Also, he doesn't see enough of his friends." (Brave, bogus smile.)

Eliza was momentarily speechless, and then she resorted to her favoured form of expression. "Jesus, what fucking bullshit, Martha."

"Eliza." Martha pointed frantically to the ceiling. Eliza's profane outburst was surely enough to make their grandparents spin in their graves, so it was certainly more than enough to rouse the curiosity of a light-sleeping toddler.

"You don't believe that, do you?"

"Well, we have argued a lot recently." Martha was in the habit of agreeing with Michael. She'd done so for a long time.

"You argued because he was always out, *and* you'd been left on your own to manage the children, *and* Mathew has been a handful, *and* Maisie has had colic, *and* Michael has insisted you get down to the gym in order to achieve the perfect figure, *and* he sent you around estate agents to find the perfect dream home, *and* it's all been too much for you." Each "and" was delivered in an ever shriller tone of mounting indignation.

"Maybe, but he doesn't like it. He doesn't like my rowing and complaining. That's why he's been going out so much."

"Didn't it cross his mind to stay in and help you?"

"No."

"And what's that nonsense about not seeing enough of his friends? He wouldn't see anything of his friends if it weren't for you. You're the one that invites people over for dinner, you plan picnics at the weekend, you arrange trips to the cinema, you remember your friends' birthdays and the names of their children."

"I know, but he wants to see more of his male friends on his own. He does work very hard, terribly long hours."

"Yeah, most of them in restaurants."

"It's progress," insisted Martha.

"Oh whoopee do," sighed Eliza.

Martha looked hurt and Eliza regretted her flippancy.

"I need to fight for him," Martha insisted.

"Why?"

"Because he's my husband and that's what people do. They fight for their husbands." Although she doubted Eliza would be able to understand. She'd never been married. Surely she was right, as his wife and the mother of his children, surely she should do absolutely anything, anything at all to try to save her marriage. Even if it sometimes felt that she was the only person in the world old-fashioned enough to believe this.

She loved him.

Whilst hating him.

Loved or hated him? It was almost impossible to know.

Eliza was so frustrated. Frustrated with Michael, primarily, for being such a weak, disappointing bastard, and frustrated with her sister for pandering to his behaviour. Eliza hadn't been aware that she resented Michael's lifestyle so much. It had occasionally crossed her mind that her sister had somehow been transported back to the 1950s, but she hadn't questioned Martha's role—in fact she'd sometimes coveted it. Certainly select bits of it. Not having to work had its advantages. Eliza envied Martha for not having to worry about the moods of a premenstrual boss, not having to battle with commuters every morning and evening, not having to raise pesky purchase orders that never tallied with the subsequent invoices. In comparison, pottering around with the children in the park, painting pictures, baking cakes, it all seemed a doddle. Besides which, Martha had always appeared happy. Eliza hadn't wanted, or needed, to interfere. After all, what did Eliza know about marriage, especially someone else's?

But even a blind, deaf, mute alien could now see what her sister apparently couldn't. Michael was now being an unreasonable, irresponsible, arrogant twat.

Oh, she felt better for saying that, even though she'd said it only in her head.

On an almost daily basis, Eliza encouraged Martha to change tack. She argued that Martha had tried being bright and beautiful, rational and reserved, tolerant and stoical, but Michael hadn't responded. So why not try something more confident and seize back some control? (By which Eliza meant Martha must stop acting like a doormat, though she managed to resist saying as much.)

"You should make yourself unavailable. You should go out more. You can't stay tied to the telephone for the rest of your days." Martha shot Eliza a horrified look. "Not that this—err—issue will last the rest of your days but . . . err . . ." Eliza gave up; her grave was deep enough.

"But where would I go and who with? I don't have any real friends."

"That's not true."

"Well, none I can talk to at the moment."

"That's because you've chosen not to tell them about your situation. If you were more honest with them you might find you had more support." And in fact Eliza was slightly fed up of being the only person who Martha turned to, to obsess about her situation. Eliza was Martha's sister and as such her best friend, but as her sister, she was also entitled to dish out the healthiest dose of straight-talking.

"But it would be so humiliating. Michael is bound to come home soon. I couldn't stand a lifetime of condescending looks, of their sympathy and smugness. Imagine if everyone knew I'd taken him back after such a—"

"Brutal rejection." Eliza finished the sentence for her. "I don't think you're being fair to your friends. I think you'll find people are a lot more sympathetic than you imagine."

But Martha couldn't tell anyone. She felt such a failure, such an idiot. She didn't even know why he'd left. She didn't understand it. She knew she wasn't perfect, but who was? She'd always tried her best. Tried so damned hard. They'd said "until death do us part." They'd said "for better, for worse." She'd meant it. Surely if the worst they'd had was a few sleepless nights and a bout of colic they should have been able to get through this. Rows are healthy. You read of couples who stand by each other through appalling situations—illness, redundancy, infertility, death. Some couples weathered storms—how was she going to admit that he'd buggered off at the first sign of drizzle? She worried that if she told people Michael had left simply because he was unhappy, they would assume she was hiding some crucial piece of information. They'd suspect that she'd had a torrid affair, or that she was an alcoholic, or that she was hiding a gambling addiction, or something equally dramatic.

Or worse. They'd mistakenly think that Michael was a spineless, irresponsible coward, because from the outside—if you didn't really know Michael—Martha could see how someone might jump to this conclusion. After all, it wasn't really very nice leaving your wife and kids, was it? It would have been more responsible and more courageous to stay and try to put things right. Martha didn't want people thinking she was married to a spineless, irresponsible coward. Besides which, by not telling anyone Martha could try to pretend it wasn't happening. If she didn't answer the telephone or accept any invites, if she stayed indoors and alone, she might just be able to make time stand still. She just might.

"I don't want to go out with anyone else. I don't want to see anyone else," Martha repeated.

Eliza sighed. She fundamentally disagreed with her sister and wondered when it would become appropriate to say so. Was a marriage worth fighting for just because it was a marriage? She bit her tongue. "Well, OK then. But maybe you shouldn't let him off the hook so easily. Maybe you should demand some answers. Make him think about what he's doing," she suggested.

Martha was desperate and tired. Her patience was slowly beginning to ebb away. Perhaps Eliza was right that Michael would respect her more if she were more exacting. And Michael did need help. Martha was considering the serious possibility that he'd had a breakdown, it sounded more feasible than the body snatchers having got him. It was true that she was getting nowhere fast with this current strategy. Every time Martha ticked off a day in her diary she felt and feared her marriage was slipping from her grasp.

So Martha changed tack. She took the fourth date as an opportunity to quiz, grill and cross-examine Michael relentlessly. She clawed at the open wound that was their separation and found that she'd shown the measure of her hurt and frustration even before the waiter took their order. This new approach didn't help either; if anything it made matters worse. Martha hadn't thought it was possible, but Michael became more and more distant and withdrawn over the evening.

"When did you stop loving me?" she demanded repeatedly. She believed that if she knew this much she'd be able to fix things. She'd be able to go back to the time and the Martha that he did love.

"I haven't." He sighed and he wished Martha would leave off. He hated having a responsibility to this woman. This woman he wasn't *in* love with any more. He hadn't wanted his life to turn out this way. He'd wanted to stay in love with her but he wasn't.

"So you do still love me." Martha couldn't hide her eagerness.

"Yes, in a way. You're my best friend."

"That's enough, isn't it?" Martha begged, hopefully.

Why did she do this to herself? Michael wondered. "No. I don't want to stay with you just because I'm used to you," he sighed reluctantly.

His words punched her in the stomach. Martha was flattened. She was lying face down in the boxing ring, the taste of blood in her mouth, the voice of the referee ringing in her ears. Martha took a deep breath and reminded herself that she was down, but not out. "What did I do wrong?" she cried miserably.

Michael didn't answer.

"Am I a bad mother?"

"You're a perfect mother," he affirmed.

"Am I a bad wife?"

"No, you're a perfect wife."

"So loving me, my being your best friend, my being a perfect mother and wife, and the fact that we have two children together isn't enough for you?" demanded Martha.

"No, it's not. Something's missing."

"You greedy bastard." Martha wasn't sure how it happened. It must have been reflex but she threw her glass of wine at him.

That was their last date.

Martha couldn't see the point in arranging another. She doubted Michael would agree to go out with her again. He hated scenes and wouldn't be able to forgive her for the spectacle in the restaurant. Besides which, when they'd been to the cinema together the previous week, he'd flinched when he accidentally touched his knee against hers, his wife's. Martha thought she might vomit with the pain.

That night she lay in bed alone, no longer even expecting or hoping to sleep. What he'd said about her being a perfect wife and mother but that still not being enough for him was worse than his leaving. It was crueller than his complaints. If he thought she was the perfect wife and mother but still didn't want her, then what he was saying was her best simply wasn't good enough. She'd spent ten years trying her best, wanting to impress Michael, wanting him to feel proud of her, wanting him to validate her—and she'd failed.

The last four weeks had been pure hell.

After the wine-throwing incident, Martha had sworn to Eliza that she wouldn't make contact any more with Michael, and that she'd simply wait until he contacted her. Eliza hoped he would because Martha hoped it, but she wasn't banking on it. Martha had shown remarkable restraint for all of four days (it felt like four years) and then today the estate agent had called Martha asking if she could clarify why there was a delay on the exchange of contracts. Was there a problem he could help with? Martha had wanted to shout, "Yes there is a sodding problem, but no, you can't help. Not unless you can turn back time." Instead she called Michael.

She hadn't planned to be at all emotional. She'd vowed she wouldn't cry. She would try not to berate him about his lack of responsibility (because whilst most of Martha had been shocked and horrified at herself, for flinging wine in a restaurant, a tiny little bit of her found it liberating, she could easily imagine it becoming addictive). She would quell her anger. She'd be aloof, calm, entirely Lauren Bacall. So she was as surprised as Eliza was to find herself regressing to hysterical sobbing and pleading for Michael's return.

She couldn't even trust her own emotions.

Martha took the tea from Eliza and wrapped her hands around the mug. It was a very mild October but Martha felt permanently cold.

"Should I ring the estate agent for you?" asked Eliza. She lowered herself down on to the floor and sat with her back against the wall, next to Martha. "You have so much to sort out even if Michael does come back—"

"What do you mean 'if'? Of course he's coming back," insisted Martha through her gulps of tea and tears.

"Erm, right, yeah. Well, when Michael comes back you aren't going to be in a position to buy a new house. You'll have to rest, and reassure one another before you'll be in a position to galvanize your spirits to tackle a move."

"But the Bridleway would be the perfect fresh start," Martha cried.

"It would be associated with all this confusion. You'll find another house when the time is right," said Eliza. She squeezed Martha's knee reassuringly.

"It's more than a house to me," Martha wailed.

"I know, Babe. But you're going to have to let it go."

Martha felt another shriek of pain sear her body. She was clinging to the idea of the dream home because she was struggling to accept the enormous change that had been thrust upon her. Wasn't it enough that her husband had left her? That he'd deprived the children of the stable family she'd always wanted them to have? That he'd obliterated her past and destroyed her future?

But then, put like that, what did a house matter in the grand scheme of things?

Martha took a deep breath and tried to recapture some of the self-control for which she was (historically) famous. "OK, pass me the telephone. I'll call the estate agent." And whilst the brave smile was frail, it was genuine.

# 15

Eliza's recent dates had not been much more successful than Martha's. Her belief in the happily-ever-after with the man-with-a-pension-plan had taken a severe bruising from Martha and Michael's split, but she wasn't going to admit this.

Eliza had expected to arrive at Martha and Michael's that Monday morning and be guided and helped. She'd expected them to be pleased with her adult decision to move out of a dead-end relationship and find someone who wanted a couple of kids and an endowment policy. She'd even thought that they would introduce her to some of Michael's friends at the golf club. She was looking forward to being mopped up into their happy family environment, which she'd so often admired. She'd wanted

to read the kids stories in the warm orange light of their bedrooms, bedrooms packed with toys and dreams. She'd been looking forward to doing her share of playschool and swimming-class
car runs. She'd wanted to join the dinner parties, she might even
have been eating chioca, for God's sake. But this scene of domestic bliss had disappeared.

Vanished.

Gone.

If *she* felt cheated, God alone must know what Martha was
feeling.

Instead of being the recipient of mugs of hot chocolate and
platefuls of oatmeal cookies, Eliza found herself in the eye of a
confusing, complicated marital storm. Her first thought had
been to turn heel and leg it back to her parents', or even Greg's,
but one look at Martha had wiped such thoughts entirely from
her head. Eliza was needed.

Naturally, as a single thirty-and-some-months woman living in
the twenty-first century, with a large number of friends in a similar position, Eliza was well practised in the "All men are bastards"
line. She also knew that the immediate shockwaves of a break-up
could only be salved with chocolate, wine and weeping. The next
stage was naming and shaming: calling the man in question everything from an arse to a reptile and listing his many, many crimes
against womankind. And the final stage to recovery was shagging
in a random, risqué and raunchy manner. This method to mend a
broken heart had been used by Eliza and her friends after the
breakdown of countless affairs. However, Martha completely rejected Eliza's tried and tested remedy. She did accept the odd glass
of wine and on one or two occasions she even drank just over half
a bottle at one sitting, but she wouldn't touch chocolate. Nor
would she diss Michael. She kept insisting that he must be confused or sad. She wondered what *she'd* done wrong and insisted
that this must be hurting him as much as it was hurting her.

"I doubt that," Eliza yelled in frustration. Eliza had spent days watching her sister on her hands and knees mopping spills, changing nappies, picking up toys, begging the children to eat or sleep at the appropriate times. She'd watched her clean cupboards, floors, windows and the tops of wardrobes. Eliza couldn't decide if Martha thought these tasks essential or whether they were a ploy to keep busy. Eliza tried to help by bathing the children and reading them bedtime stories, but Mathew sensed there was something wrong and clung pathetically to his mother. Eliza often found Martha asleep in Mathew's bed—one night she found her curled up in a tight ball in Maisie's cot. Eliza was shocked, not only at the lengths mothers would go to to placate their children, but also by the size of Martha. Her big sister suddenly looked so tiny.

Vulnerable.

Besides her refusals to get blathered and fat or to berate her ex, Martha also contravened tradition in the third strand of the recovery program. Even Eliza could not imagine Martha shagging her way to restoration.

Eliza, on the other hand, was quite keen to get laid. She hadn't realized how great a sex life she and Greg enjoyed until she'd abandoned it, and now she missed sex. *Not* Greg. She was sure she didn't miss *Greg*. What was there to miss, except noise and chaos? But she did miss something, so it must be the sex. Yet getting laid wasn't proving as easy as she'd imagined.

In the very early days, it would have been insensitive in the extreme for Eliza to mention her imperative need to access Martha's address book. Oddly, Martha had not greeted the news of her sister's split from Greg with quite the enthusiasm Eliza had imagined she would. She'd simply commented, "Poor Greg, poor you." Eliza reasoned that she'd caught Martha at a bad moment.

After a couple of weeks of living together, Martha suddenly found some enthusiasm for Eliza's plan to find a new Mr. Right.

The right Mr. Right. "I know some chaps who might be what you're looking for," she mentioned casually one evening as she was flicking through her address book.

Eliza thought it was quaint that Martha had an address book, not a PalmPilot. All of Eliza's friends had PalmPilots. She also thought it was quaint that Martha called blokes "chaps."

"Who, who?" asked Eliza, without bothering to disguise her enthusiasm.

"Well, you could start with Ted."

"Ted?" Eliza couldn't help thinking of *Play School*. What sort of name for a grown man was Ted? Did this mean he would be particularly hirsute? Still, she shouldn't allow herself to be put off at this embryonic stage, she could always think of a nickname, which was much more street.

Martha was smiling, she knew her sister well enough to guess what was running through her mind. "Should I go on?" she asked playfully.

"Yes. Yes, of course, what does he look like?"

"Surely you ought to be asking what his prospects are if you're so hell-bent on this scheme of finding yourself a respectable husband with a pension plan etc., etc."

"Well, yes, true," Eliza admitted reluctantly, "but I don't want to date the Elephant Man, not even if he is the CEO of every blue-chip company in Britain."

"Oh, I see," said Martha smiling, and betraying the fact that she knew her sister would never settle for anything less than a beautiful man.

"What?"

"Nothing. I'm not saying a thing. Well, Ted is a banker, he's tall, blond and generally considered fairly handsome."

"Blond?"

"Yes."

"Oh."

"What?"

"Nothing."

"Eliza, don't say nothing when there is blatantly something."

"I prefer dark-haired men."

"So Ted's a 'no,' then?"

"He's a 'maybe.' Let's write a list." Eliza jumped up to find pen and paper. She thought it was a very good sign that Martha had managed about a dozen sentences without turning the conversation back to Michael. Maybe this was exactly what Martha needed—something to take her mind off her own problems.

Eliza sat down on the sofa next to Martha and drew three columns. At the top of the columns she wrote, "Hot," "Might Do" and "Not if He were the Last Man Alive." Martha grinned. Underneath "Might Do" Eliza wrote "Ted."

"There's Tarquin. He's dark-haired. He's a solicitor."

"Is that his real name? You really know someone called Tarquin?" asked Eliza, astonished. "No, I'm sorry, I couldn't. I'd laugh every time I said it. I couldn't imagine calling out 'Yes, yes, yes, Tarquin' whilst I'm in the throws of pash. It's simply too tryhard."

"Well, he's not responsible for his name," laughed Martha. "His parents saddled him with it before he could articulate any objection."

"But he does have the option of changing it by deed poll. An option he's obviously chosen not to take advantage of."

"He's very nice."

Eliza sighed and wrote "Tarquin" under "Ted."

Martha went through her entire address book and tried to muster up as many eligible men as she could. Eliza always found grounds for objection: "sounds too posh," "definitely too short," "silly name" featured frequently, as did "can't dance," "sounds dull," "sounds selfish," "divorced—too much baggage." This last comment prompted the exchange:

"Sorry, Martha. I didn't mean anything by that."

"Why are you apologising to me?"

"Well, I'm not saying everyone will think a divorcee has too much baggage," lied Eliza, embarrassed that she'd put her foot in it.

"Why are you apologising to me?" Martha repeated her question, stonily.

"No reason," said Eliza, and returned to the list.

When they had finished, Eliza was disappointed to see that there were no names whatsoever under the *"Hot"* heading, four under *"Might Do,"* and seven under the *"Not if He were the Last Man Alive"* heading.

"Maybe you're being a bit too exacting," offered Martha. She'd thought that the eleven men she'd proffered were all reasonable candidates in answer to Eliza's brief. In fact, she'd done some censoring as she went along, and there were three other names she hadn't even bothered to mention. Knowing this number of single men at this particular age was a rarity, and several of Martha's friends had benefited from the contents of her fat leather address book. None of them had ever been as picky as Eliza. Martha didn't actually think that any of the men in her address book would suit Eliza as well as Greg had, but then Eliza was old enough to make her own mistakes.

"So let's get this right." Martha had been taking notes as Eliza had been making her comments throughout the selection process. She had that kind of mind. She picked up the notebook and in a voice that was entirely "chairperson's summary to the board," she recapped on Eliza's criteria. "So you're looking for a tall, toned—"

"A lean, mean, loving machine," interrupted Eliza, giggling. She'd drunk the lion's share of a bottle of Chardonnay.

"Well, obviously, Eliza, I cannot vouch for their prowess in the bedroom. These are people I have round for dinner not to—"

"*Shag.*" Eliza finished the sentence, as she doubted Martha could.

"Exactly, not to 'shag,'" said Martha as though she were trying out a new word in a foreign language, which in a way she was. Both of the girls threw their heads back and laughed loudly. Eliza thought to herself that this was the first time she'd heard Martha laugh out loud for quite some time. There hadn't been that much laughing out loud, even before Michael had left.

"Now concentrate," continued Martha with mock seriousness. "You're looking for a tall, toned, dark-haired thirtysomething, who earns in excess of 40K, can dance, likes Indian takeaways but also likes to throw his own dinner parties, preferably musical, reads, has a large number of his own friends, but is also keen to mix with your friends. He must not have been married before, no children, no halitosis, and must want to get married next summer."

"That's about the sum of it."

"This is going to be a long haul," said Martha, shaking her head.

"D'you think so?"

"I do."

"Oh, OK, I'll bring the age limit down," conceded Eliza.

"Oh, that should do it," smiled Martha as she reached for the bottle of Chardonnay. It was empty. "Shall we have another?"

# 16

He wasn't Eliza's usual type, that was for certain. She quickly reminded herself that not-my-usual-type was exactly what she was after. He was thin, and his shoulders had slumped and sunk to his stomach. Too many hours at a desk. Had he ever been inside a gym? He wasn't dark (as Martha had promised) but then, nor was he fair: he was mid, nondescript. Nice smile, though, but could that be sufficient compensation for sweaty hands?

"You must be Eliza?" said Tarquin. He leapt to his feet to greet Eliza and as he did so he banged his chair against the next table and upset a glass of wine. It was white wine and it spilt on the floor, not on the diners, but still they made an embarrassing fuss. Tarquin generously bought them a new bottle to compensate for the lost glass. Eliza thought this was very kind. She sat down and wanted to like him.

"You don't look a bit like Martha." Tarquin's ears were still glowing bright red from the blush that had soused him after the wine-spilling incident. Eliza wished she could stop staring at them, but she couldn't. Tarquin turned round to see what was behind him that Eliza was finding so fascinating.

Eliza finally pulled her attention back to his eyes, which were quite nice, certainly friendly. "No, we don't look alike, we're not particularly similar at all."

"I've always thought Martha was such a smashing girl, absolutely lovely, quite perfect," gushed Tarquin. "That Michael's a lucky bugger."

Eliza was torn. Quite a big part of her was thrilled for Martha; it would be lovely to relay the compliment back to her that evening. Martha needed all the ego-boosting she could get at the moment. On the other hand, there was nothing more off-putting in the entire world than your date fancying your older sister.

"God, yes, she's gorgeous," babbled Tarquin.

"Should we order some wine?" asked Eliza. She'd already mentally scrubbed Tarquin off the *"Might Do"* list and downgraded him. She'd never been keen on the name anyway. However, she didn't often get the opportunity to come to restaurants such as Quaglino's and she decided she ought to make the most of it.

"Good idea. Do you like Pouilly Fumé? I know it's Martha's favourite."

Eliza smiled bravely and wondered if she'd make it as far as the sticky toffee pudding.

Eliza's next date was with a rather effete journalist called Sebastian. Eliza had had her doubts even before she'd met him.

"I don't class journalists as reliable boyfriend material," she'd argued with Martha. "They work long hours and always love their work more than their women."

"Oh goodness, Eliza. If you're going to add to the criteria that the chap you're looking for has to love you above everything else, this already difficult task is going to start to compare to the labours of Hercules," teased Martha.

"He doesn't have to love me above everything—well, at least not straight away—but he does have to prefer me to my sister or his job," Eliza joked back. She'd been making much of Tarquin's crush on Martha because she saw it delighted her. Not that Martha was in the least bit interested in any man other than Michael, but her ego did need the promotion.

"Sebastian's really good-looking, I think you should give him a chance."

Sebastian was beautiful. In fact, it disturbed Eliza a little, to note that she and Sebastian looked rather alike. They were both tall, tanned and willowy. They would make a stunning couple—but was that eyeliner he was wearing?

They'd met in a trendy bar, which pleased Eliza. She hadn't known what to wear for her date at Quaglino's (she'd settled for a black trouser suit, something she only ever wore to interviews and funerals—though, interestingly, this proved entirely suitable for the tone of the evening). At least Bar B was the kind of place Eliza normally hung out in. She could confidently don her Diesel clobber.

The bar was tiny, but appeared much larger because the walls and ceiling were covered with minute mosaic mirrored tiles, which was slightly disturbing because Eliza couldn't hold Sebastian's attention—he was too busy checking out his own reflection.

After an hour and a half of competing against the mirrors and the attention of the attractive bartender (male), Eliza made an excuse and went to call Martha. "He's gay."

"I've always wondered."

"Well, now you know."

"Know, know. I mean, has he resisted your advances?"

"No, Martha, I haven't made any, but believe me, this guy is gay."

"Oh well, I'll wait up for you then."

"Yes, do that," sighed Eliza. "I can't imagine I'm going to be late."

Eliza's third date was with a guy called Henry. This once again prompted her to wonder if names defined personalities. Her friends were all called Neil, Mark, Matt, Dave and similar. Martha's friends were called Henry, Piers, Sebastian and Tarquin. How was that possible? Did the Tarquins of this world have a particular affinity for Pierses? Did they hunt one another out? She tried to imagine Greg having a best mate called Gerard. It was possible because Greg was pretty easy going and wouldn't have any preconceptions about someone because of their name (unlike herself), but he'd probably shorten it to something cool like Jed or give him a goofy nickname. Still, Eliza reminded herself that the Henrys, Pierses, Sebastians and Tarquins of this world were much more likely to have mortgages and share options. It was just a matter of focus.

Henry was a management consultant. Eliza didn't have any understanding of what that involved, but she vowed she'd be fascinated. Henry suggested that they meet at the bar at Number 1 Aldwych to drink champagne. Eliza thought this was the right side of flashy and happily agreed.

"How did it go?" asked Martha the moment Eliza walked in the door.

"Oh, he's cool, yeah, fine."

" 'Fine' or 'cool'?" Martha knew Eliza's language—fine was in reality light-years away from cool.

Eliza sat on the big squishy sofa and unbuckled her shoes. She wiggled her toes. Four-inch heels looked fantastic, but they were undoubtedly an instrument of misogynistic torture. She accepted the hot chocolate that Martha handed her, curled her fingers around the cup and curled her legs underneath her bottom.

"Go on then, I want details," demanded Martha.

Eliza was finding the debriefs increasingly difficult. After all, these people were Martha's friends. "He was a bit arrogant. You know, one of those that think men are a superior race because they can open the lids on all their jars."

It didn't seem as though Eliza was going to say anything else, so Martha thought she ought to prompt her. "Didn't you think he was good-looking?"

"Not bad."

"Not bad?" Martha found it difficult to judge the attractiveness or otherwise of men because she'd never looked beyond Michael, not in all the years they'd been together. But she knew that, amongst her friends, Henry was generally considered a dish. Mentioning his name in conversation was guaranteed to raise heartbeats. In fact, Martha had been a little concerned about fixing up this blind date for Eliza, as Henry had a reputation of being a "treat them mean, keep them keen," commitment-phobic Romeo. But then she'd calculated that Eliza was probably fairly well qualified to handle this type of man; Martha had been right: Eliza was a worthy adversary. Henry obviously hadn't got under Eliza's armour; Eliza blatantly hadn't fallen under Henry's spell.

"He was good-looking in an obvious sort of way," added Eliza, but she was just being polite.

"Well, what sort of good-looking are you hoping for?" asked Martha, who was beginning to feel just a tiny bit exasperated by her sister's pickiness.

"Well, he was a bit too clean-cut for me. I like them a bit—"

"Dirtier-looking."

"Exactly."

"More sexy."

"Yes."

"More dangerous."

"Absolutely."

"It's not a look that often comes with being a partner in one of the world's biggest management consultancies. They tend to play it safe when they recruit."

"S'pose. Anyway, he knew he was good-looking and I hate that vanity thing. When they behave as though they're doing you a favour by going out with you. God, isn't it enough that their orgasms are always real?"

"He's a man. What did you expect?"

"I expected him to remember my name."

"Oh, yes, that would be a minimum requirement," agreed Martha.

Both girls fell silent and Martha wondered if Eliza would finally admit to herself that this pursuit was ridiculous. If she'd acknowledge that her perfect man was Greg and go home to him before going home to him ceased to be an option.

The silence stretched between them until Eliza finally said, "So who's next on the list?"

# 17

Martha moved around the almost empty gallery and tried to concentrate on the exhibits. A fortnight after Michael left, her mum and dad absolutely insisted that she have some time to herself and offered to look after the children on Tuesdays and Wednesdays for as long as was necessary. Mr. and Mrs. Evergreen hadn't said much to Martha about Michael's departure, and his name was all the more glaring for its absence. Martha was grateful for their silence, although she wasn't sure whether it was due to calculation or coincidence; it gave her time to scrabble around for a crumb of pride, which had been all but obliterated.

The Evergreens' silence was a result of the fact that they didn't know what to say. They liked Michael, they loved Michael; he'd been like a son to them for so many years. The couple couldn't understand how one daughter had thrown over her soul mate, and the other had been thrown over by her husband, and all in one single evening. It had never been so complicated in their day. There may not have been dishwashers or DVD record players, or whatever they were called, but there weren't the relentless expectations either. People had seemed so much more content, appreciative.

True, Martha and Michael had married young, but then, so

had Mr. and Mrs. Evergreen. True, it wasn't always easy being married; everyone who had ever been married had, at some point or other, asked herself or himself if it was a completely unnatural state to live in. There were always other temptations, other possibilities, other lives to lead, other skirts or trousers to chase. But, on the whole, the advantages outweighed the disadvantages. Surely, nothing in this world could beat the wonderful sense of satisfaction in looking back at a life you'd shared with someone. Someone who had made it better. What was Michael thinking of, leaving his children? Their grandchildren! The poor man must have had a breakdown. And poor Martha was so thin and so bemused. And to be frank, they were too. Neither Mr. nor Mrs. Evergreen could see what could possibly have made Michael leave.

Not happy, Martha had said. Well, why on earth was he not happy?

They felt neutered watching their big girl diminish into a little girl again. They'd always been so proud of how sensible and single-minded Martha was. She'd wanted her ears pierced—but only the once. She'd worked very hard at school and at university, only ever had one boyfriend at a time. They loved and were proud of Eliza too, of course, but she'd always been a bit more of a worry, she never knew what she wanted, never had. Eliza had flounced and floundered from one group of school friends to the next, from one lot of several boyfriends to the next several, from one career to the next, and yet she never seemed satisfied or content.

They'd been quite hopeful when she'd finally found a job editing pop videos, whatever that entailed. It didn't seem very stable and she'd come to it very late in life—twenty-seven was hardly the optimal age to put your first foot on the career ladder—but she did seem to enjoy her work. Not that they could bank on it lasting. After all, she'd always seemed happy with Greg. And whilst Greg was definitely unconventional, he was a well-mannered boy and Mr. and Mrs. Evergreen had liked him.

They were sorry he'd no longer be in their lives. All this coming-and-going. It was so much easier in their day.

Whereas Martha had always been contented. She was happy to be a wife and mother, which was unusual nowadays and such a relief. One daughter frequenting clubs and dodging marriage vows—despite being the wrong side of thirty—was enough for any couple. Who'd have thought that Martha's single-mindedness was going to become such a problem? Martha's entire identity revolved around her husband and children. She'd never wanted to be defined in any other way than as a wife and mother—now when such a big chunk of that identity had been whisked away, she suddenly seemed ghoulishly lacking.

Mr. and Mrs. Evergreen found it hard to discuss Martha's situation with her, as she would barely acknowledge that there was a situation. Her tactic to date had been to carry on as before Michael's departure. Except she wasn't seeing any of her friends. Her self-inflicted solitary confinement was a worry to the Evergreens. And they kept asking her what she wanted, but she didn't have any answers. It appeared that all she was capable of was waiting for Michael's next move. The Evergreens feared he might not make one. So quietly but firmly, they'd insisted on taking over the childcare for a couple of days a week so as to give Martha a reasonable shot at thinking in a logical and uninter-rupted fashion for stretches longer than three minutes.

Or, at the very least, she'd have the luxury of going to the loo unaccompanied.

Mr. and Mrs. Evergreen were right—to an extent. Having time alone did allow Martha to think over her situation with Michael. But then, even when she was knee-deep sorting washing or up to her elbows in baby rice she was thinking about her situation.

She thought of nothing else. She thought so much that her head ached—but she was no closer to understanding any of it.

Martha knew her parents meant well. And it was undoubtedly

a relief to be able to go out of the house, close the door behind her and walk down the garden path without the handicaps of a double buggy, a changing bag, sets of spare clothes, tubs of puréed organic vegetables, a comfy blanket, a cuddly rabbit, and so on.

But once she closed the door she wasn't sure where to go. The only places Martha usually visited were playgroups or supermarkets. The first time she went out on her own, her arms felt strangely weightless; she rushed to the shops to buy things to carry, to fill the void. She bought trousers for Mathew, a hairband and a small, oddly lifelike, cuddly puppy for Maisie. She bought nail varnish for Eliza, some bulbs for her father's garden, the latest Jamie Oliver book for her mother. She was spending her way to a national debt. Sometimes it worked and blunted the pain, and sometimes it didn't—it just made her think that her life was trivial. She wondered how much she would have to spend in a day to validate her existence.

"Weather's been changeable, hasn't it?" said the smiley assistant in BabyGap. She and Martha were on nodding terms with one another, as Martha was a regular customer. "Are you getting a cold—you're looking peaky? How are you?"

Terrible, flattened, annihilated.

Talking to her friends about Michael's departure would somehow concede defeat, but suddenly she saw the attraction of immersing herself in the comfort of strangers. Maybe their distance would provide a perspective that she, so up close, couldn't find. "My husband's left me." Martha said this without an apology, simply with bewilderment.

"That's awful, love, I'm so sorry. When did this happen?"

So Martha told her tale. And it did help. It certainly did. The shop assistant offered uncomplicated, unconditional sympathy. On the back of that success Martha mentioned to the woman in the toyshop that she was living on her own at the moment, and the woman squeezed her hand. She had a soft, dry hand. The chap at the garden centre said he could deliver the heavy stuff, as she didn't have a man to carry it for her.

These kindnesses went some way to soothing the agony. Martha was on a roll; she reasoned that if she told enough strangers, and received enough sympathetic smiles, enough warming hand squeezes, enough help with heavy bags, she would be able to bung the gap in her heart and life. So she talked and talked and talked. She started to tell everyone she met. She told them that it was a shock, that she couldn't understand it, that she was devastated, and that she was going to wait for him to come home, because what else could she do? In this way she embarrassed shop assistants, hairdressers and poor old dears who sat on the bus worrying about their gas bills. Martha didn't notice their embarrassment; she was swamped in her own self-pity.

"How terrible," people said. They shook their heads, mostly saddened by the awful familiarity of Martha's story.

"Why did he leave?" asked the lollipop lady.

Martha felt dense and desolate again. She couldn't say. On top of everything, he'd left her dumbstruck. How stupid to have to answer, "I don't know." How careless.

Martha tried to reason it through. I'm pretty and pleasant, I adore the children, and I'm a good cook. I keep the home immaculate. I don't overspend self-indulgently. Well, at least I didn't until recently.

And I love him.

Loved him?

"Is there another woman?" the helpful lollipop lady asked.

"I don't think so."

"There has to be," she asserted flatly.

Has there? Martha didn't know and she should have known, shouldn't she? She should have had some idea as to whether her husband was having an affair. Other women seemed to have a nose for that sort of thing. Sheila in the butcher's thought that "he must be." The receptionist at the doctors thought that "they're all at it." Even Eliza had hinted that she thought it was possible. But how could Martha believe it? How could she be expected to stop trusting and hoping in an instant? How was she supposed to think so badly of him after ten years of adoring him?

She didn't know how.

Martha liked it best if the strangers patiently listened to her tale, not interrupting with anything more significant than a confused or horrified tut. She didn't like the strangers that insisted on recounting their own stories of disillusionment or failure. And there was a multitude of these. But what help could it possibly be to her to know that everyone had a horror story to match her own? Everyone knew someone who had had exactly the same thing happen to them. How was that a comfort? So irresponsibility and philandering were widespread—great news.

"My brother-in-law left my sister when she was pregnant with twins," said the woman in the dry cleaner's.

"My friend's husband has just left her, and they've been married sixteen years. Turns out he's been having an affair with his secretary all that time; he even slept with her—the secretary, that is—on their wedding night—my friend's wedding night, that is."

"How awful," muttered Martha, and it was. It was.

But other people's awfulness didn't make Michael less awful. Other people's pain didn't alleviate hers; in fact their pain aggravated hers. It was as though a dense cloud of deceit had crept up on her and was now smothering her; when Martha looked around all she saw were grim closed faces, sad disappointed lives, broken dreams and smashed hearts. It didn't help her at all that everyone thought that the only real tragedy about her story was the common-or-garden nature of it. Nobody cared that her marriage was over. They seemed to think it was OK just to dissolve that magic. Martha thought it was a bit like getting her hair cut: no one other than herself seemed to notice. She didn't want to believe that broken promises were an accepted part of the world that she'd brought Mathew and Maisie into. She'd have preferred to believe that she was a freak.

This was her sixth day out alone, and the sense that she'd forgotten something vital (i.e. the children) was beginning to recede. After her first outing of intensive retail therapy, Martha used the free time to do things that she could, if ever given the opportunity, talk to Michael about. (Although she doubted that there was currently much scope for general conversation—not so soon after the wine-throwing fiasco.) The previous Wednesday she'd been to the gym and after her workout she'd read through the *Financial Times*. Yesterday she'd been to the South Bank Centre to listen to a lecture by a war correspondent, who'd spent several very interesting years watching people kill each other. Today she was visiting a small gallery just off the Caledonian Road. The exhibition was very modern and had been given great write-ups in all the Sunday papers. It was entitled *Obliteration*. Perhaps Martha would have been wiser choosing something different, but Michael loved modern art.

Martha wasn't sure if she did.

She had a sneaky suspicion that a lot of it was Emperor's new clothes. A white canvas hung on a white wall? She appreciated the symbolism but . . . to pay £50,000 for an installation when needy kids in countless countries could have their sight saved for seven pounds a throw didn't seem right. How could she be moved by anything so fake?

There weren't many people in the gallery. The big galleries in town attracted tourists every day of the week, but something as specialist as this couldn't hope for, and probably didn't crave, tourist crowds. The gallery curator took his exhibition far too seriously to actually want to meet the masses and gain their approval. Martha wondered if she was missing something (besides her husband). Was she missing something culturally? The three or four other people in the gallery seemed to be entirely engrossed in the exhibition. Maybe she was a philistine. One man had been standing in front of that black canvas *(Gone)* for over twelve minutes—Martha had been timing him. What did he find so fascinating? Why did people slow down when they walked through a gallery? Were they captivated? Was it a sign of respect?

Or had the tedium finally worn down their reserves of energy and they dawdled because their spirits were dampened?

Maybe that man's wife had left him too? If that were the case, then Martha could understand why he appeared to be immobilized by a painting called *Gone.*

God, what a depressing exhibition.

The door of the gallery swung wide open, allowing a whiff of autumnal sunshine to frisk the stuffy room. The traffic and pedestrians zoomed past the gallery, a low oblivious drone of the culturally depraved. How Martha wished she were outside with them, enjoying the sunshine, rather than wading through the dull catalogue detailing the significance of various forms of obliteration. Suddenly, Martha envied the people outside the gallery for their blissful indifference.

What was she doing here? It was Michael who liked modern art, not her. She had four more canvases to see in this room, and a further three in the smaller room next door.

She could just walk out.

Leave.

Join the culturally depraved, happy people on the street. The thought struck Martha as heresy; but at the same time made her smile. She had never left a cinema during a film, although she had sat through some absolute trash—it seemed judgemental on those who were enjoying the film. She had never started reading a book and failed to complete it, however poorly written it was—it seemed rude to the author. If she left the gallery now she'd run the risk of offending the staff and incurring their disapproval. But it did look lovely outside, and Martha really wasn't enjoying the exhibition.

Suddenly Martha found herself striding down the street. The bright autumn sunshine danced on her skin as the coolish breeze played with her hair and caused her long coat to flap about, to dance like the magic clothes in the Disney videos that Mathew was addicted to. His favourite was *Cinderella;* Martha had never told Michael this: somehow she didn't think he'd approve.

Martha found a coffee shop and bought a caffè latte and a large blueberry muffin. She could eat anything she liked at the moment and not put on any weight. She might as well make the most of it. Not that she had eaten that much over the last few weeks. She'd prepared plenty of meals with the intention of tucking in, but every time she took a bite her stomach knotted with stress. Something about deserting the gallery had made her hungry; she ate the entire muffin. Then licked a finger and dabbed at the plate to pick up the crumbs. When she'd finished, she went to find a telephone box.

It was about half past four and the roads were busy. So much life. Such a hullabaloo. So much happening. Face after face. Life after life. People. Martha thought it odd that life insisted on continuing around her as though nothing had happened. So many people firmly declaring that there had not been a cosmic disaster, declaring it brazenly by waiting for buses, eating McDonald's, allowing their dogs to foul the pavement.

There were countless mothers shoving their way with strollers through the cluttered streets, negotiating the too-narrow, too-heavy shop doors. Recently Martha had started checking the left hands of women pushing strollers. Were they married? Martha was the only single mum out of all of her friends. Not that she was really a single mum—she was certain that her position was only temporary—but say she did become a single mum, for real, well then, she'd be the only one she knew. It wasn't a comforting thought. Firstly, Martha didn't like doing anything out of the ordinary. She liked to fit in. Secondly, and this was the big one, why couldn't they make it if everyone else could? What was it about her that Michael had found so repulsive, so impossible? Martha shuddered. The last time she had found herself looking at the left hands of women she came into contact with was when she was in her early twenties and wanted to get engaged. Then, like now, everyone seemed to be sporting a ring. She looked at her own rings, beautiful and classic. A plain gold band and a diamond cluster. They still shone brightly, tauntingly.

Deceitfully.

Martha looked closer. Without exception, the mothers still looked harassed. Busy and anxious. So the rings didn't protect them from that, or alleviate their exhaustion. Martha nodded and half-smiled at one or two of them. They took a second out from worrying about what to buy for tea to hurriedly smile back.

Since Michael had left, Martha had failed to lend any import to what she or the children would be eating for tea. Suddenly Martha wanted to climb back inside this world of trivia; she'd always insisted that life was lived through details. Details such as finding the correct *Teletubbies* plastic cup for Mathew to drink his juice from (Laa-Laa). The small stuff was something she set a lot of store by, and Michael had set none. Martha wondered if she'd ever have the energy to truly engage again. She hoped so. She took a deep breath. The air did smell good. Sharp and blue. She made a conscious effort to relax her shoulders, which she had worn hunched around her ears recently.

She watched one young mum and her little girl choose a pumpkin. Martha ought to buy one. She could cut out a face, nothing too scary, perhaps a cat's face. Maisie was a little young for a monster pumpkin, it might frighten her. If she bought a pumpkin she could carve it out tonight, it would be something to do. Martha handed over her money for a hefty pumpkin and felt a faint sense of involvement, of belonging. The loneliness, that had more or less permanently engulfed her since Michael had left, receded slightly.

Could she belong to something other than Michael?

Besides the women with the strollers, there were countless groups of schoolchildren hanging around the street, delaying the inevitable moment when they would have to go home and be nagged about homework. Did they all have mothers and fathers who lived together? They couldn't have, not when one considered the statistics, reasoned Martha. Martha thought of Dawn, one of her oldest and best friends. Dawn was a mother of three, including twins, and was one of the warmest, funniest, most grounded women Martha knew. Dawn's parents had divorced when she was young. She might give Dawn a call tonight and, well, update her.

And thinking about her post-natal group, who were a great bunch of women, three of them came from a family where there had been a divorce. Martha was sure that if she called any one of them and admitted to her situation, they'd be supportive. She might be the first of her contemporaries to be getting divorced, but she certainly wasn't the first person ever. It didn't follow that parents who were separated were worse parents than those who stayed together, or that the children were more likely to turn out dysfunctional. Martha knew lots of emotionally crippled, dysfunctional psychotics who came from families where parents had stayed together. Michael was a clear example.

Not that Martha was going to end up divorced.

But, say, if she did.

Martha remembered she was looking for a phone box and asked one young boy for directions to the nearest one. From his scrawny size, Martha imagined he was about twelve; he was smoking and he had a pierced ear. He seemed to think it a little bit odd that this posh bint was asking for his help, but in polite,

grammatically incorrect, embarrassed stutters he gave her directions. He only said "shit" once.

Martha scrabbled around in her bag. She always carried a
purse full of change for phone boxes, meters and tips. First she
rang her mother to check if the children were OK—naturally
they were fine.

In fact, Mrs. Evergreen didn't seem to want to talk about the
children much at all. "We're having so much fun here," she reassured Martha, "no need for you to worry about rushing home.
Your dad and I will give them their tea and bathe them. We can
stay until late if you want. Why don't you call someone and meet
up for a drink? Now, have you bought anything nice?"

"A blueberry muffin."

"Is that all? No clothes or LPs?" Her mother would never get
used to CDs.

"No, you're not talking to Eliza, you know."

"You haven't always been so different," said Mrs. Evergreen.
"When you were girls, teenagers, you both liked the same
things—admittedly, you always approached things a little more
quietly, but you both used to buy records and clothes."

"Did we?" Martha couldn't really remember being a teenager.
She didn't remember much before Michael. Thinking about it now,
she had a vague recollection of having a pleasant time. Having fun.

"Oh yes. You both loved loud pop music, clothes, make-up,
boys." Mrs. Evergreen tried to sound disapproving but she
wasn't. In truth, some of the happiest years of her life had been
watching her girls on the brink of womanhood. They'd been so
spirited, so full of gossip and fun and chat and hope. It was
harder to watch them as they got older: Martha so disappointed
and Eliza so restless. "Don't you remember?"

"Not really, not clearly," admitted Martha.

"All three of us used to go shopping every Saturday to buy
both of you something new for your dates that evening."

"We did, didn't we?"

Suddenly Martha could remember the hours she and Eliza had dragged their mother in and out of endless, tiny changing rooms.

"How do I look?" they'd demanded.

"Gorgeous," Mrs. Evergreen had always gushed (and believed).

"No, I don't, my stomach looks fat!"

"This makes my legs look short!"

"It's molly!" (That had been the ultimate censure.)

"God, we were horrible," sighed Martha, remembering how ungrateful they were.

"No, you were just normal teenagers. You were often a lot of fun."

They had laughed a great deal in those days. Laughed at the recounting of awful dates, laughed at new dance routines, laughed at determined teenage pursuers, laughed at puffball skirts, leg warmers.

Martha let the thoughts drift away and came back to her more miserable present. "Don't forget that Maisie needs—"

"Chest rub after her bath. No, I won't forget."

"And Mathew can be very picky. There's a chicken leg in the fridge, but he'll only eat it if you take the skin off and cut it up into very small pieces."

"Oh no, Martha, you would have smiled this lunchtime. Mathew tucked into the leg with your dad. He ate it all up, skin included, straight off the bone. He loves playing the little man. The chicken's gone, I'm planning on doing them pasta for tea."

"And Maisie?"

"Pasta for Maisie too, I'll chop it up. Don't worry. I've done this before, you know," added Mrs. Evergreen cheerfully. She was clearly in her element. She adored spending time with her grandchildren, but more than that, which perhaps Martha hadn't quite tuned into, Mrs. Evergreen was desperate to help her daughter, to give her a break.

Martha insisted that she would be home for bath-time and then hung up. She looked through the dirty window of the telephone box. The school kids had dispersed, and she couldn't see any young mums either—although now there were dozens of smiling couples striding down the street. It wasn't actual hatred Martha felt for them, but it was something close. There were also lots of tired-looking pensioners pottering about. Martha noted that pensioners tended to carry large shopping bags, but they only ever seemed to purchase one or two products at a time. A tin of cat food, a quarter of ham, a very small cauliflower. This way they'd have to come out again the next day and buy something else. It was something to do, she supposed.

Oh God, who would she grow old with?

She called Eliza. "Eliza, it's me."

"Hi Me, what are you up to?"

"Nothing much. You know Mum and Dad are looking after the children today."

"So you're young, free and single, you lucky thing."

The happy words had bounced out of Eliza's mouth before she'd had a chance to really think them through. The problem was that Martha had called her right in the middle of a very important meeting about tonality and treatment of a very important vid. Eliza couldn't be expected to put Martha's disintegrating marriage at the top of her agenda 24/7, could she? Of course Martha didn't want to be young, free and single, and therefore she didn't feel in the least bit lucky. Eliza wanted to grab the words back, but she couldn't. Martha was exhaustingly sensitive nowadays. Eliza missed the calm, reliable Martha of old.

"I've just called Mum, and the kids seem fine without me," said Martha. Her voice sounded small and forced, as if she were actually trying to throttle the words before they came into existence.

"That's good then, isn't it?" asked Eliza. She thought it was, but already sensed that Martha didn't.

"Not really," Martha muttered.

"Why, Babe?" Eliza signalled to her boss that she had to take the handset out of the room. Her boss waved her hand impatiently. It was a divorce, not a death. Still Eliza didn't cut the conversation short.

"I know Mum and Dad mean well by coming to babysit two days a week, and of course it is very kind of them to offer to babysit tonight but . . ." The tenuous bubble of happiness that Martha had been blowing—by abandoning a dull exhibition, eating a muffin and buying a pumpkin—had burst. There had been a few minutes when life had seemed bearable. But suddenly, Martha felt lonely and cold again. The sun chose that second to dodge behind a cloud. Martha shivered. "No one needs me. I can't get Mathew to eat chicken with skin, I'm a failure." Martha was a sentence away from sobbing. The children being happy in her absence was in fact a tribute to her mothering skills; she wanted them to be confident with other people. And after all she hadn't abandoned them in a station with a begging note tied around their necks, they were with their grandparents. But Martha had never felt more forlorn and alone.

"What?" Eliza was lost. She used lots of criteria to measure her success or otherwise as a person. Her achievements at work, whether or not she was in a happy relationship, if she remembered to send her parents an anniversary card—but getting Mathew to eat chicken with its skin on was a new one on her. "Look, we'll talk about this when I get home tonight. I have to go now, my boss is looking for me." Eliza felt terrible but she had work to do.

"Yeah, OK. My money is about to run out anyway." Martha was desperately trying to swallow back her sobs; Eliza could hear it in her voice.

"Your money? Where are you calling from?"

"A call box on the Caledonian Road."

"A call box?" How quaint. "Don't you have a mobile?"

"No, Michael had one."

The sisters paused. Eliza was fighting back the urge to blast Martha with the words, "Well, that's no frigging use to you now, is it?" Martha was still fighting back tears.

"Well, you'll have to get a mobile now you're a single girl about town. They're essential," said Eliza with a joviality that was entirely forced.

"I don't want to be a single girl about town." Martha's needs and wants were very tame. She wanted a clean, warm and safe home. Something someone of her age, class and social position was surely pretty much guaranteed. She wanted her children to be healthy, happy and not absolute rogues in the playground. She wanted her husband to have a good income but—and this was the bit that was most important to her—she wanted him to earn it doing a job he liked. She wanted her parents to live to a comfortable old age. And she wanted to remember her friends' birthdays.

She did not want to be divorced.

She did not want to be looking around garden centres on her own, aged fifty-five.

She did not want to be a single girl around town.

"I know, Martha." Eliza's resolve stiffened. "But you are."

Like it or not.

# 18

Eliza got home just after nine that evening, which wasn't late, considering she'd been working on the final edit of a video for a fairly prominent band. Often the way bands liked to work was that they'd arrive in the editing suite at about 11 p.m. and then insist on ordering takeaways, alcohol and drugs. Sometimes the real work didn't even begin until after 1 a.m. Often the final approval wasn't secured until dawn. Eliza, as the most junior member of the editing team, was always required to stay until the bitter end. Sometimes it seemed that the most important aspect of her job was scooping the band members into taxis, as discreetly as possible, at the end of the session. However, this band had been consummate professionals. They'd arrived in the studio at 2 p.m. as agreed, there were no surprises in the video treatment from the editors, nor were there any last-minute requests for changes from the band. The vid was very trippy, very cool; Eliza was proud to be involved in it, even in a small capacity. By seven-thirty everything was signed, sealed and delivered, and though Eliza had been invited out for a well-earned celebratory drink, she'd declined. She needed to make a quick detour to Tottenham Court Road, and then she wanted to dash home as quickly as possible.

She'd been worrying about Martha ever since she'd received the phone call about chicken skin a couple of hours earlier.

Bloody Michael.

When Eliza got home, the children were asleep in bed and her parents had gone home.

"Where are Mum and Dad? Did you scare them off?"

Martha had the decency to look a tiny bit guilty and shifty. "I perhaps didn't express my gratitude as clearly as I should have."

In fact, Martha had bitten their heads off. Mr. Evergreen had fixed the dripping tap in the downstairs cloakroom. He'd also changed two light bulbs and put up a shelf in Mathew's bedroom. He was clearly commenting on Michael's inadequacy in the field of DIY, and Martha took exception. Besides her triumph with the chicken, her mother had also had time to restock the fridge, cupboards and freezer. She'd vacuumed, and she'd

changed the sheets on the bed. It was true Martha had let her
standards slip a little since Michael had left. The house used to
look like a show home, and now it looked more like a pigsty.

Martha really couldn't see the point of tidying up; the house
seemed to untidy itself the next day. In the past she had made it a
point of principle that all the children's toys were cleared away before 7 p.m. As were the clothes that had dried on the radiators
during the day. (Michael hated to see that, it was so working class;
what was the point of having a dryer if you were going to hang
clothes on the radiators?) Now toys lay scattered on the floor, day
in, day out, and it was surprising how much time that saved
Martha. She didn't use the time to pair up socks or slice vegetables, the way she'd always used any spare moments when Michael
lived at home. Now she tended to squander her extra time watching soap operas and reading magazines. She took some comfort
from the fact that the lives of the characters were even messier
than her own. She couldn't remember when she last washed out
the inside of the fridge. Her mother's industry today left Martha
feeling inadequate and exposed. She was a lapsed housewife.

"I thought they might have waited to say hello to me," commented Eliza, a little grumpily.

Martha decided not to mention that she'd led her parents to
believe that Eliza wouldn't be back until very late. She changed
the subject. "You've had a telephone call."

"Who from?"

"Hubert."

"Oh yeah, we met at your friend Chloe's dinner party last
weekend. I was sloshed, so gave him my number," sighed Eliza.

"Give him a call," urged Martha.

Eliza did as she was told. She was losing interest in the search
for Mr. Pension Policy but felt she had to continue with it—
because what other option was there? "Hi, Hubert, it's Eliza Evergreen here."

"Eliza. Great to hear from you. How are you keeping?"

"Oh, I'm fine." Eliza wasn't prepared to be interesting.

"Well, that's good. I'm well too. In fact a funny thing happened today."

Blah, blah, blah. Eliza doubted that anything really funny could possibly ever happen to someone called Hubert, so she tuned out of the conversation.

She only tuned back in again when she heard him say, "We should meet up."

"Why not," said Eliza.

It was all the encouragement he needed. "I'll cycle over, if you like, we could have tea."

Tea! Christ, she was about to accept a date with Rupert Bear. "That sounds great," said Eliza with fake enthusiasm. Luckily, Rupert Bear was not too alert to conversational nuances. He lived in a world where meeting for tea really *was* a great idea. Eliza fixed a time and day and then put the phone down. She looked despondent. Tea was so cheap. He wasn't even trying to impress her. He might have been thirty and single, but he was male, therefore nobody noticed. It was a crucial difference.

"Mum left a beef casserole. Should I serve it up?" offered Martha in an effort to cheer her up.

"OK," agreed Eliza, instantly brightening. "But before that I have a surprise for you."

Eliza left the room and Martha could hear her grunting as she shifted something in the hall. Martha crossed her fingers and prayed it wasn't a puppy.

Eliza staggered back into the room carrying a large box. "Clear a space."

"A computer?" asked Martha, not attempting to hide her disgust.

"Not just a computer, but the key to your chastity belt, fair maiden."

"What?"

"No mobile: therefore no text messages. No computer: therefore no email. How do you hope to flirt in the twenty-first century?"

"I don't propose to flirt at all."

"Awful defeatist attitude," snapped Eliza bossily, and for a moment Martha felt like the little sister. "Here." Eliza tossed a smaller box over to Martha; it was a mobile phone.

It took them four and a half hours to set it up. Neither woman could honestly list "instruction comprehension" as a skill on her CV, but both had to admit to a huge sense of satisfaction when it finally whirled into action, and the little icons declaring "email facility," "Internet Explorer," "my briefcase," "recycle bin" littered the screen.

Eliza was thrilled. The phone and computer had been the most expensive gifts she had ever bought anyone, and she had enjoyed being generous. Martha wouldn't accept any rent, and so for the first time since moving to London Eliza felt a bit flush.

Martha was dubious. "But what use will it be?"

"Well, you *need* access to the Internet."

"Why?"

"Because it's lonely living in the Dark Ages."

Martha looked concerned and cautious.

"Email is great fun," encouraged Eliza.

Martha still wasn't convinced. She feared that email might just turn out to be like her answering machine, another reminder that no one cared.

As if reading her mind, Eliza said consolingly, "Look, at the very least you can shop."

# November

# 19

Maisie would be a year old in mid November. Martha had set herself a target to get Michael to return home by the time Maisie was due to blow out the candle. She had ten more days to succeed. Surely this silliness wasn't going to last longer than that.

Was it?

Martha wasn't certain.

Since Martha had thrown the glass of wine over Michael they had not seen each other without the restraining presence of the children. Michael used them as a shield to avoid any difficult questions or discussions, so she had no idea what his current thinking on their situation was. Martha's head hurt from beating it against the invisible brick wall that had grown up between them. If only she had the confidence to admit, even to herself, that she was becoming heartily sick of his sanctimonious mutterings—"Not in front of the children, Martha, we'll talk about it later." When? When was bloody "later"? The whole situation was beginning to have a horrible sense of "already too late."

Michael's visits to see the children had been less than satisfactory. He often arrived late, he always left early. His excuse was invariably the same: he was tired; he was so busy at work. Somehow Michael had managed to claw his way up to the moral high ground. He repeatedly insisted that Martha was hysterical and impossible to talk to.

Which was true, and therefore it was rude of him to draw attention to the fact.

Martha was frustrated, angry and bewildered—which tended

to manifest itself in hysteria. She bounced from tears, to remorse, to fury, as though she were a pre-menstrual, pre-exam, mid-acne-outbreak adolescent. Despite this rainbow of emotions, she still could not bring herself to regret the wine-throwing incident.

Michael thought this was proof of her hysteria.

Eliza thought this was progress.

Martha didn't know what to think.

"I see you've bought a computer," commented Michael on this particular evening. He and Martha were standing in the kitchen, but to know that she had a computer he must have been into the dining room. Martha wasn't hosting any dinner parties at the moment, and the family had taken to eating in the kitchen—it was cosier—so the computer was set up in the dining room. Eliza had wanted to put it in Michael's den, but Martha wouldn't hear of it. She preserved the den as though it were a shrine, even though dusting the collection of over 100 Matchbox cars was a fiddly job. So, then, it was yet another contradiction that Martha felt ever so slightly irritated that Michael had been poking around the house. Which was silly, of course. It was, after all, still Michael's house, it was still their home and Martha wanted it to be so.

It was just that recently it had seemed more hers than theirs.

Of course he could snoop wherever he chose, including in the dining room. After all, Martha had no secrets.

Except for the stack of washing that needed to be ironed, which—as luck would have it—she had hurriedly stashed in the dining room; it was a bit shame-making that Michael would know that she was behind on her ironing. She had never let things slip so dramatically when he lived at home but, recently, doing the ironing no longer struck her as a genuine priority. Martha blushed on the inside; she didn't like him thinking of her as less than perfect.

Suddenly, somehow, his presence seemed a little intrusive.

"No, actually, I didn't buy it. Eliza bought it for me. Don't you think that was generous?" smiled Martha, trying to put the vision of crumpled washing out of her mind.

"Well, she is living here rent-free."

"Would you like my email address? I'm finding surfing on the Internet fascinating, and there are some great educational sites for Mathew." Education was Michael's big thing as far as the children were concerned. She didn't bother to explain that she wouldn't dream of taking money for rent off her own sister. "And I have a mobile." Martha held up her handset.

Michael took it from her and swiftly appraised it with an expert eye trained in assessing gizmos and gadgets. "Top of the range. Has Eliza won the Lottery?"

Martha was hurt. She'd secretly hoped that Michael would be impressed with her modernity. He spent hours on the Internet and she'd thought, hoped, he'd be pleased with her for taking an interest in something new. He'd often suggested that she needed a hobby. Although Lord knows how Martha had been supposed to find time for a hobby when Michael lived at home. But he didn't congratulate her, or ask for her mobile number, nor did he seem to notice that she was wearing make-up. Which was a shame, because he'd often encouraged her to make more of herself, and now that she had made an effort . . . he was oblivious to it.

Martha shoved the thought from her mind and tried to tune into what he was saying, tried to find it interesting.

Michael had talked a lot about money recently. He'd asked how much Mathew's new shoes had cost, and muttered that it seemed to be only five minutes since they'd bought the last pair. Which was almost true; that was growing children for you. He'd checked the phone bill and observed that maybe Martha should make an effort to call her parents after 6 p.m. When she told him what she was buying Maisie for her birthday he remarked that their daughter would be happier with a cardboard box, and it would be a lot cheaper. It was a comment that's often made about children, but in Maisie's case it wasn't true: she really didn't like cardboard boxes; she really liked plastic toys with bells and buttons.

"I've sent out the invites for Maisie's party next week," said Martha. "We made them ourselves—Maisie, Mathew and, well, me. Me mostly, but it was very jolly." Martha showed Michael an invite. It was a piece of pink card cut into the shape of a balloon; Mathew had added glitter and stickers, Maisie had added finger-prints and saliva. They'd had a lovely, squabble-free afternoon making them and Martha was really proud of the results. But looking at them now, as Michael was looking at them, they looked tatty and amateur.

"Very nice," murmured Michael, just as he had muttered that the weather was "very nice," the biscuits Martha had baked were "very nice," the colour she'd painted the hall was "very nice." Martha wasn't sure how it was possible that the words "very nice" could sound so bored, so critical.

Martha had been thinking a lot about Maisie's birthday. Every little baby's first birthday was obviously a very significant date, but to Martha this particular birthday was monumental. How was it possible that only a year ago Michael had counted the sec-onds between Martha's contractions, told her she was a clever girl, told her he was proud of her, cried with pleasure when the midwife put Maisie into his arms . . . and now he lived alone in a hotel? How was it possible? Martha didn't know the answer but she was determined to correct the situation. She was determined to get Michael to come home. To put a stop to this silliness.

She had planned a surprise for Michael. Three years ago her grandmother had died and left her and Eliza a small inheritance. Michael had insisted that Martha open a post-office account and put the money there. He'd insisted that she didn't squander it on kids' toys or clothes. He'd wanted her to buy something important and meaningful with it. Something of her own to remember her grandmother by. Which was lovely of him and proved that he'd once loved her very much.

Which surely meant he could love her again, didn't it?

Martha had thought that she'd spend the money on a special piece of furniture once they'd bought their dream home; she'd thought a family dining table and set of chairs would be appropriate. However, Martha was beginning to get nervous that if she didn't do something radical they might never live in a dream home, not the Bridleway, not any sort of way.

So that morning Martha had been to the post office and withdrawn all the money. Then she'd visited a travel agent and booked a one-week holiday for all four of them at Disneyland Paris. She'd spared no expense. She bought first-class train tickets. She chose the best hotel, bought day passes for the park, and secured a babysitter for two of the evenings so that she and Michael could dine alone. She'd booked the train for the day after Maisie's party, so they'd travel on her actual birthday.

Surely Michael would be moved. It was exactly what they both needed, all needed. Michael just needed to remember how wonderful it was being a family. The last few months had been cruel and angry and not representative. They needed to have some good times to restore the family equilibrium, jog the memory away from past troubles. They'd often talked about taking the kids to Disneyland. They'd agreed that the flight to America was far too long for young children, and so they'd planned to go to Paris when Maisie was two and a half and Mathew four. Martha and Michael had agreed on this plan because the children would appreciate the trip more at that age; Mathew might even remember it when he got older. They were great planners.

But now Martha had decided to throw caution to the wind. She was certain that this trip was her ace card in winning the game of bringing Michael home.

The tickets sat behind the mug stand, on a unit, in the kitchen. Martha felt her eye being irresistibly drawn to them; she was so excited. She couldn't wait to present him with the tickets. She'd spent the day in a state of heightened anticipation, simply imagining the pleasure on his face.

Michael had come round to read the children a bedtime story. Martha's plan was to offer him a glass of wine and then spring the surprise gift on him. She knew he'd be delighted with the gesture and the actual holiday. It was odd how the household responsibilities seemed to have naturally divided over the years. Michael always booked the holidays; it was his job. Martha was sure that he'd be thrilled to be treated in this way, for someone else to take over his responsibility. The same as she would be thrilled if he ever cooked a meal for her. Or emptied the dishwasher. Or put petrol in the car.

In fact one of Martha's biggest fantasies was Michael bathing the kids, drying them, putting on the creams and nappies, massaging in the vapour rub, battling to clean their teeth, warming their milk, putting them into their pyjamas, feeding them milk, reading them a bedtime story and getting them to settle in bed. Since he'd left home, he had on three occasions arrived in time to read a story, but in almost three years of parenthood Martha had never known him to complete the full routine from bath to bed.

"Would you like a glass of wine?" she offered.

"Yes, that would be very nice," replied Michael.

Martha wished his brain would tell his face that he thought the idea was *very nice* because, to be honest, he looked as miserable as ill-fitting shoes.

God, where does this impatience come from? thought Martha. I haven't even had a glass of Chardonnay yet.

She carried on with her plan. "I've been wanting to talk to you about Maisie's birthday," she said. She felt a flutter of nervous excitement; she loved giving gifts, she really did. She liked choosing the gift, wrapping it up, adored attaching bows and ribbons and always used far too many. Her gifts often ended up looking like Easter bonnets made by eight-year-olds. She loved springing surprises, and she had an overwhelming conviction that this was going to be the best gift, a real cracker, a gift that was going to draw her family back together.

"Yes, I want to talk about that too," Michael said, and then he fell silent, not showing any inclination to talk about anything at all.

Martha took this as her cue. "I've planned a—" she gushed.

"I want a divorce," he interrupted.

"Surprise," she completed. The word hung uselessly in the air.

"After the party," he added finally.

He said he hated having failed at his marriage, but it was better than failing at life, because you only get one life, and his just wasn't any fun any more.

The wedding photo was a lie. The house was a lie. Their holidays together were lies. The children and hamster probably didn't exist. What was this man saying now?

He was telling her that it was expensive to stay in a hotel; he was saying that he thought he ought to rent a flat, which seemed horrible, final. He was telling her that he'd been unhappy before he'd left and that the rows since he'd left had exasperated him further. He couldn't imagine how they'd ever find a way to a reconciliation.

She heard herself tell him about Disneyland Paris. He spat out a peculiar sound, like a sea lion, a shocked indignant sound, and he replied that he couldn't bring himself to spend seven hours with her, let alone seven days, not now. She heard herself shout that he had to spend seven days with her because she was his wife, his wife, his wife.

He repeated that he wanted a divorce. That she hadn't been listening to him, not for months now. She repeated that she was his wife, his wife. He shrugged and looked pitying.

Finally she stopped repeating the word. It sounded ridiculous, she'd said it so often. Wife was apparently a defunct currency.

He was right; Martha hadn't been listening to him. She was sure that this separation was just a silly spat. An early mid-life crisis thing. A tiff that had got out of hand. An issue that they could, and would, solve. They were married. *Married.* People didn't just stop being married. Well of course they did, but not people like Martha. Not Martha. Martha had always believed marriage was forever. That's what she'd believed and she'd believed it with her heart. Her *heart.* Until that moment Martha hadn't given that much thought to her heart, beyond keeping it in good repair by choosing low-cholesterol spreads and knowing she should be drinking red wine rather than white (but still drinking white anyway—it didn't stain her teeth). As for the notion that the heart was more than an organ that pumped blood around her body, that it was a source of great romantic emotion, well, it wasn't scientific, was it?

She hadn't understood what people meant when they said they were heartbroken, particularly as the phrase was often used of a minor disappointment. "They didn't have the shoes I liked in my size, I was heartbroken"; "Someone scratched his car, he was heartbroken"; "Man U are two-one down to Leeds, it's heartbreaking." The constant repetition had absolutely silenced the expression. And anyway it wasn't *scientific.*

She heard her heart shatter. She felt it crumble to dust. At that moment Martha wondered how she'd ever be able to tell the children that the world was a good place, that telling the truth was best, that being kind was essential, that a happily-ever-after was possible. As unfashionable as it sounded, she'd always believed in goodness, truth and kindness. She thought she was living in the happily-ever-after. But what was the point of giving to charity, helping old ladies in supermarkets, always having time to listen to your friends, cooking, cleaning, caring and cherishing your husband if things could still turn out so ugly? Her belief in people, in goodness, in truth, in kindness, in her life was entirely based on the fact that she and Michael were happy.

And now he'd pissed on it. The whole show. He'd pissed on it.

Martha concentrated very hard. Through the ringing in her ears she managed to decipher "the children . . . our priority"; "sell house, no rush, springtime good time for house sales"; "solicitors . . . not likely to be necessary"; "surely still be friends;" "simply impossible to live with"; "one life, no fun."

"Is there someone else?"

"Christ, Martha, this again?"

"Everyone thinks there is."

"You mix with some very small-minded people, Martha."

She ignored his arrogance and focused on what she wanted, an answer. "Is there?"

"I'm not dignifying that question with a reply."

"So there is."

"Grow up."

"Just tell me, tell me! Are you having an affair? Or maybe not an affair, not yet, but . . . but you think you're in love with someone else, or just fancy them, or . . ." Martha gasped for air through her tears and agony. "Just tell me. Help me understand why you've ruined everything. *Are* you having an affair?" She wanted him to say he wasn't. She would believe him, despite the mounting evidence suggesting he was. She hadn't told anyone, not even Eliza, but she'd come across a statement from Michael's gym. He'd taken a guest there. Who? And why had he worked so late, so often, recently? Was he really at work? And the weekend break he'd just taken—does anyone really go to Paris alone?

Martha wanted to believe that there could be innocent explanations. She still trusted him more than anyone. But if he was having an affair she wanted to hear that too. She just wanted some honesty. He owed her that at least. Surely he realized that she needed to have some respect for the father of her children. Even if it was galling, reluctant respect, because he'd told a truth she didn't want to hear. "Just talk to me," she sobbed.

"I can't talk to you, Martha. Don't you understand? You're silencing me. I know I've disappointed you. You've made that very clear, but I'm sorry, I just don't love you any more. And as uncomfortable as that is for you to accept, you're going to have to, because I'm not spending the rest of my life with someone I don't love. Not to save you this hurt, not for the sake of the children, not because our friends and parents want it. It's my life and I don't want you."

"Just fuck off, Michael. Get the pissing hell out of here, you spineless, faithless bastard."

Martha was beginning to feel rather affectionate towards expletives.

# 20

Eliza considered this date a success. She was deciding whether to have pudding and coffee or just coffee. Best just have coffee. She didn't want to look down at a bulging stomach whilst lying flat on her back, and she did want to get flat on her back (and on top as well, for that matter). She was debating whether she would take him back to her place or go to his. Obviously, dating law dictated that it was safer at her own place, but as her own place was actually Martha's place, Eliza thought it would probably be best going to Charlie's. He was unlikely to prove to be an axe-wielding psycho because he was a friend of Martha's; besides which, Martha was trying to seduce Michael tonight with tickets to Disneyland Paris. If she succeeded, it was likely they'd soon be in the throes of passion; and if the ruse failed, she'd be sobbing into her handkerchief.

Again.

Eliza didn't really expect the plan to be successful. She thought that Martha was reading Michael wrongly. As Eliza read the situation, he'd buggered off because he was fed up of having the responsibility of being a father. He'd tried ditching as many responsibilities as possible (Eliza could hardly believe it when Martha confided that Michael had never once got up in the night, not for either of the children). However, ditching the responsibilities of being a father had, unexpectedly to him, incurred the wrath of Martha, and Michael had obviously found being constantly reminded of his shortcomings about as comfortable as washing his bollocks in bleach. His only option was to take himself out of the picture altogether. Even thinking about it made Eliza want to puke.

She felt guilty knowing that Martha would in all likelihood be crying right now; on the other hand, she didn't half fancy a shag. It had been weeks and this man was the nearest thing to a possibility Eliza had come across since Greg.

Charlie was a dot-com millionaire. He'd had the sense to sell his shares early on before people became too greedy. He'd walked away with enough to retire on at the age of twenty-eight. But he hadn't retired; instead he'd set up his own company, something to do with DVD licensing. Eliza didn't really listen while he explained it, although she was very impressed with the fact that he was still working when he didn't have to. She knew for a fact that if Greg were ever to make enough money to retire, he would do just that. And he'd be penniless again in next to no time. Not that he ever would make enough money to retire.

It surprised Eliza how often she thought about Greg.

Of course it was never favourably. Well, except when she'd

been out with Tarquin and thought how much she preferred Greg's name. And when she'd been out with Sebastian and thought how much she preferred Greg's heterosexuality. And when she'd been out with Henry and she'd preferred Greg's humility. And when she'd been out with Will and preferred Greg's sense of humour. And when she had been out with Giles and he was nice enough but when they'd got to the tongue action, she preferred Greg's kisses.

But Charlie had a reasonable name, he was heterosexual, he seemed amusing, charming, he remembered her name, he was good-looking. She would have to do something about his clothes; the woolly jumper would have to go. Greg would never be seen dead in something like that. But he did pay for dinner and besides which, she was gagging for it.

It wasn't for want of trying. It wasn't for lack of effort or will, but something went wrong. Charlie took Eliza back to his place. They'd both happily hopped in to the cab. They were both clear about what her accepting a coffee really meant, so there were no embarrassed silences. In fact, Charlie immediately got down to snogging her, although actually Eliza would have preferred it if he'd waited until they'd got to his flat. Yes, she was keen for a bit of action, but it always seemed so sordid to snog in a cab. It usually meant that the couple were adulterous, or minors.

His flat was fine. Clean, comfortable. Clearly, everything in it was expensive, but the general impression was not showy. There were no horrors in the bathroom, no stray pubes on the sheets. He had a cleaner because Eliza noted that the windowsills were dust-free and no man dusted windowsills. Or at least Eliza hoped they didn't because she didn't, and whilst her housekeeping standards weren't great, she liked to think they were better than the average single man's.

He poured her a glass of wine. He had an impressive wine se-

lection but didn't talk about it endlessly or highlight her ignorance by asking her to select. He made a suggestion, told her it
was full-bodied, that she'd like it, then opened the bottle.

When she thought she was drunk enough to get on with it
and yet not too drunk so as she wouldn't remember it, she suggested they move into the bedroom.

Technically it was OK, she supposed. She'd had worse. But
the problem was she'd had much, much better. It wasn't his fault.
He knew that a certain amount of foreplay was polite and he
obliged. He was neither squeamish nor prudish, neither kinky
nor lazy. But he wasn't familiar with her body, he wasn't right.

She wasn't a tease, and as she was lying in his bed wearing
nothing but a G-string (he was totally naked, men loved taking
their clothes off) she felt she couldn't back out. So she bumped
and ground her pelvis into his fingers, hoping that things would
improve when he got up. They didn't. The deeper he got the
more disappointed she felt. He couldn't seem to find the spot
that worked for her. Eliza tried to push his hand in the right direction; he took the hint but still nothing, even though his fingers were so far inside her she expected him to soon tickle her
tonsils. How odd. When Greg finger-fucked her she went wild.
The neighbours once knocked on the adjoining wall and asked
them to keep the noise down. What was it? Were Charlie's fingers
too small? She'd never thought of herself as particularly roomy;
she did lots of pelvic-floor exercises and she hadn't even had a
baby.

Perhaps if they just got down to it. He had a reasonable-size
penis. Normal size. In Eliza's experience they all looked pretty
similar and only incited comment if they were especially small or
excitingly large. He popped it in and started to groan. He seemed
to be having a good enough time at least. Wasn't it bizarre, she'd
been gagging for it for weeks? Now, here she was, flat on her back
in between Egyptian cotton sheets, with a cute-enough dude—

and all she wanted to do was roll over and go to sleep. Of course she couldn't. It would be rude and he was doing his best. Eliza manoeuvred so that she could climb astride, it was usually a faster way to orgasm for her, and she had the feeling that Charlie wasn't going to come until she did. That's how you spotted the gentlemen of the twenty-first century. Normally she was appreciative of such consideration; tonight it was a nuisance.

He grabbed her boobs, and started to knead them. The pressure he applied was the right side of rough but it still wasn't happening for her. Irrespective of this, Eliza started to rotate her head and moan. It had been a while since she'd had to fake orgasm, but in her day she could have earned an Oscar. The good thing about faking it with a new man was that he didn't know the difference between "show time" and "real time." The bad thing was that he thought he'd done something well and would be inclined to repeat the same non-sexy stuff next time you slept with him. But Eliza already knew that wouldn't matter: there wouldn't be a next time with Charlie.

# 21

Eliza pushed open the front door; the house was unusually, eerily silent. Maybe Martha had taken the children to the park. She picked up the post. Two bills, a mailshot for expensive, French children's clothes and another postcard from Greg. It was the third Eliza had received. It was odd, but only a week after Eliza had left Greg, his group had been asked to back quite a big, up and coming boy band, on a tour around the U.K. and Germany. He'd dismissed their music as crap and it wasn't exactly a big break, more of a slight crack—most of the gigs were in clubs, not mega venues—but it was regular work for six weeks. The first six weeks that Greg would ever have received a regular income in all his adult life. Eliza was pleased for him.

His postcards were oddly unsettling.

Not because they declared undying love and begged her to take him back.

But because they didn't.

Eliza had done her fair share of ditching in her days. In fact, more than her fair share. She knew the form. She'd tell them that it wasn't them but her (which was partly true, she knew it). They'd beg her to explain what they'd done wrong (she never could), sometimes they cried, sometimes they sent flowers, sometimes poems and once something in a box from Tiffany's. They always wanted her back. Greg hadn't done any of the above. Besides his drunken call a couple of nights after they'd split up, Greg hadn't put any pressure on her to return. His postcards were light chatty notes detailing the funny antics of the band. They were the type of postcard that he could have sent to any one of his many friends. They never alluded to the fact that they had been lovers. He'd obviously forgotten about her already. Four years meant absolutely nothing to him.

He was so shallow.

"Aunty Iza, Aunty Iza," yelled Mathew from the kitchen or, possibly, the back garden.

Eliza tucked her postcard into a deep pocket in her bag and her mind, and followed her nephew's voice. "Mum, Dad, nice surprise," she said, kissing both her parents. "I hadn't realized you were looking after the children today."

"Mummy's drunk," said Mathew, "drunk-as-a-skunk, drunk-as-a-skunk. Drunk." He yelled with delight, "Drunk-as-a-skunk, skunk, skunk!"

"Shush, Mathew, why don't you go with Grandad and try and find some worms," encouraged Mrs. Evergreen. Mathew weighed up his options and decided that torturing worms just about had the edge over exposing his mother's frailties to the neighbourhood, so he happily took his grandfather's hand.

"What's going on?" asked Eliza. "Why are you all outside?"

"Recovery is what's going on. And we've brought the children outside because we're trying to keep the noise down."

"Recovery from a hangover?"

"That and recovery from a broken marriage," sighed Mrs. Evergreen. "Don't you recognize it, Eliza? This is your famous Stage One. Next, she'll be eating Mars Bars and calling him the things he deserves to be called."

Eliza looked up at the window of Martha's bedroom; the curtains were still drawn. "So she's finally accepted this is serious."

"He asked for a divorce last night," said Mrs. Evergreen.

"A divorce? Already? Isn't it a bit sudden? Martha thought they were blissfully happy up until seven weeks ago. Shouldn't they try counselling or something first?"

"Martha might have thought that they were blissfully happy but Michael blatantly didn't. Who knows how long he's been working out that he wants out. Martha's got quite a lot of catching up to do. What was that noise?"

"It sounded like the door," replied Eliza. "I'll go and see."

Martha hurriedly walked out of the front gate and down the street. She heard Eliza shout to her but she ignored it. She didn't want to talk to Eliza, or anyone for that matter. Not her parents, not her children, not even Michael. She needed to think. And she needed fried eggs. She didn't have a hangover, but she couldn't kid herself that this was because she hadn't got very drunk yesterday. She had got very, very drunk. In fact she was still drunk—and that was the only reason that she didn't have a hangover yet.

She felt surreally disconnected from the world around her. She couldn't decide whether to attribute this to the fact that she'd drunk two and a half bottles of wine last night, or to the fact that her husband had asked for a divorce. A divorce—what was that about? She felt as though she were operating in slow motion and everything around her—people, that dog weeing up a lamp-post, the traffic whizzing by—was working at double speed. Michael was certainly working faster than she could comprehend. She had been extremely slow, retarded in fact, in her detection of the extent of his rejection.

Two and a half bottles of wine. The last time she'd drunk quantities like that was when she'd just met Michael. They used to have Friday nights where their friends would just turn up at Michael's flat with half-a-dozen tinnies and bottles of wine, foul stuff, screw tops, lethal. But fun. Such fun. The nearest they got to Michelin-star cooking was putting Phileas Fogg crisps in a bowl. They'd play ridiculous drinking games and everyone would get plastered. In those days they were all too young to worry about hangovers, too irresponsible, too damn lucky. Was that the fun Michael missed? When did they start introducing filo pastry and cutting back on the units? When did they become sanitized? Dull? Because they must have slipped into dull at some point. Had the fire been dampened in Michael's belly by an overload of seating plans and olive ciabatta?

Martha hadn't planned to drink so much last night. After Michael had slammed out of the house and she'd kicked and kicked the front door (wishing it were him, and hurting her foot), she'd known exactly what *not* to do. It wouldn't be a good idea to listen to sloppy love songs. Definitely a really bad idea. How could playing the songs that they'd danced to at their wedding reception do anything other than upset her?

It wouldn't help.

She'd put them on anyway.

And cried. She bawled and sobbed and howled. So hard that her T-shirt was wet, right to the navel. By the time she'd listened to *All Women*—volumes one and two—Martha had drunk a full bottle of white wine. For the past four years she had been either trying to conceive, pregnant or breastfeeding and her tolerance was down. She'd gulped the wine. She knew she ought to stop drinking—but she also knew she wasn't going to. She was thirsty and needy, and besides, it tasted nice. The cool sting of a dry wine hit her throat and then her stomach. When she shook her head in time to the music, it hurt; she knew she was working towards a terrific hangover. She didn't care. She was almost looking forward to it. She could always take a tablet to alleviate that pain.

The worst thing to do would be to look through old photos. It would probably destroy her. The second bottle was half empty by the time she picked up the first big fat leather album. It was full of photos of their early holidays together, their engagement party, her pregnant with Mathew, Mathew's first bath. There were a large number of photos of Martha and Michael together. Neither of them were particularly good photographers so they'd invested in an idiot-proof camera. Michael often used to put his left arm around Martha, hold the camera in his right hand and extend his arm, point and press. A number of the photos were mainly of walls, ceilings or wardrobes. Martha and Michael would be squashed to one side of the frame, partially decapitated, or simply distorted because of the odd angle at which they'd been immortalized.

But they were always beaming broadly. Grinning insanely, looking like people who believe in forever. God, it was bad enough losing the bastard (which she certainly had, which he certainly was), but now she'd reminded herself that he once was a very special, decent, worthwhile man. She wanted to eat her own soul. Another glass of wine and it struck Martha that she didn't recognize the young, cheerful, kind man on these shots; she hadn't seen him for months. He'd vanished. The man she'd fallen in love with had already left the scene of the crime: all that remained was his sorry apology for an alibi.

She was drinking the dregs of the second bottle by the time she picked up the very last packet of photos. They'd been taken that August at Center Parcs. Martha hadn't found the time or, more accurately, the will to put them into albums yet. She examined the photos carefully. That was a lovely one of Mathew hugging Maisie, very cute. There was a good one of Mathew jumping on the bouncy castle, and a sweet one of Maisie's delighted expressions as she tried ice cream for the first time. Despite it being during Martha's birthday tea, Martha and Michael had had a row about that. Michael was right of course, she was a plump baby and she probably shouldn't be encouraged to have a sweet tooth. But it was just the smallest bit of ice cream and it was hardly likely she'd go and blow all her pocket money in the sweet shop behind their backs; she couldn't walk yet. Besides, Martha had been a fat baby and she was skin and bone now. Babies were supposed to be chubby.

Martha flicked through the photos to try and find one of Michael and her together. There weren't any. Her skirt was in the one of the children sat on a picnic rug, and there were three of Michael, which Martha had taken. They were posed; she'd handed him Maisie and asked him to sit next to Mathew, as she'd wanted some nice family shots to send to his parents. They weren't good photos. It could have been that Michael was squinting at the sun but he looked sullen, a reluctant sitter.

By the time Martha opened her third bottle she could hardly see. Her T-shirt endured its second soaking of the evening when she spilt the wine as she lifted the glass to her mouth. The alcohol zapped her brain cells but couldn't anaesthetise her heart. It ached, literally screamed in her chest. Martha just wanted to understand Michael, which at the moment was impossible because she didn't even know him. Not any more. He didn't want her. Not being wanted was the worst bit. No, it wasn't. It was the fact that he didn't want his children, *that* was the worst bit. No, actually, it was the fact that he'd destroyed her history. These people on the photographs were utter strangers. And he'd obliterated her future. The big family, the big family home, the happily-ever-after were washed away. What a horrible waste.

He'd been the person she'd turned to, to chat, to confer, to confide, to confess, for ten years, most of her adult life. He'd been her next-of-kin; it said so on countless official documents. He'd been there at the births of her two children. His two children. He'd seen inside her stomach and between her legs. He'd watched as they sewed her up and threw away the placentas. He'd been her best friend, her ally and her lover.

Now he was to be nothing to her.

She'd already found herself describing him as the children's father.

At one-thirty in the morning she'd finally fallen asleep. She'd left her clothes and the lights on, the empty bottles had rolled around the kitchen floor and come to rest near the cupboards and back door, the kids' toys stayed scattered throughout the house, as did the shreds of the photos. At six-thirty Martha had woken up as usual. She'd changed Maisie's nappy and given her some milk and breakfast. Then she'd got Mathew up and dressed, and tried to force-feed him some wheat-free toast. At seven-thirty she called her parents and sent out a mayday.

When she woke for the second time she could hear her family in the garden. She looked out of the window and saw her father and Mathew bent over a vegetable patch, earnestly looking for worms. Her father's slight bald spot and Mathew's tiny frame brought a lump to her throat. They both looked so vulnerable. She saw her mother and Eliza huddled over Maisie. They were encouraging her to try to walk between them, helping her find her independence. They were talking in low voices; Martha could guess the subject matter. She felt ashamed that she was such a worry to them all.

She looked in the mirror; her face was puffy, swollen with alcohol, sleep deprivation and tears. The excessive crying had reduced her eyes to skinny slits. Martha was too tired to feel regret at her lonely drinking bout. And too tired to try to be cheerful for her family. Without bothering to change her clothes, or put on socks, or brush her hair or teeth, Martha set off towards the local greasy spoon. A place which she'd often walked past on the way to the swings, but had never frequented.

She *needed* fried eggs.

The tea tasted of washing-up liquid. Martha tried to find some comfort in the fact that this did at least prove that the cup had been washed. Martha marvelled at how easy it had been to walk into a café (full of burly builders and devoid of any women customers) and order a strong tea and one ("no, go on then, make it two") fried eggs. The builders were reading tabloids. Their bottoms spread over the tiny wooden chairs, their stomachs rolled over their belts. They didn't seem to care; Martha envied them their serenity.

It was a bright November morning. Martha wasn't as cold as perhaps she should have been, but then she was insulated with booze-induced hot flushes. She picked a seat near the window.

The autumnal sun splattered its rays on to the frosty road, creating the illusion that the streets of London were paved not with gold but diamonds. It bounced in through the window and played with the chrome salt and pepper pots, the sugar bowl, her knife and fork and the grease on her fried eggs, making everything look precious. If Martha hadn't been so preoccupied she might have thought the little greasy spoon was quite heavenly.

Martha sat and thought. Thinking was scary. Painful. But necessary.

Was he serious?

Yes.

This was serious.

Could she ever change his mind? Martha thought back over the last couple of months. She had pleaded, cajoled, wept, begged, threatened, sent love letters, reasoned, yelled, stormed, sulked, and Michael had been unmoved.

She could not change his mind.

He was no longer in love with her. To be specific, he'd said she was boring and a nag. That she had no interest in him, that she took him for granted.

This and much, much more had been said last night. Despite Martha's best efforts to blank the scene of parting, she remembered that they'd both spat out cruel insults and exchanged vicious criticisms. He'd said that the thrill of being with her had gone, that it was entirely lost. She'd told him that he was shallow, and "not a sticker." He'd commented that was typical of her, always throwing about abuse. He'd then added, "You'd never forgive me, Martha, you'd never be able to forget this." Which had confused her. Did he want her forgiveness? Did he want to come home?

Immediately, Martha had insisted, "You're wrong, we would be OK. I love you. We *are* a family. We should be together. We should be visiting Kew Gardens, having picnics. Come home. Come home. Just stop this nonsense, Michael, and come home, please."

But all Michael had said was, "I hate picnics."

Martha loathed herself for begging him to come home, for subduing herself so entirely. She loathed herself for giving him countless opportunities.

Opportunities he didn't take.

She'd told him that she was exhausted and felt neglected. He'd told her he'd rather be at work, at the gym, in the arms of another woman, anywhere except with her. She'd yelled at him to fuck right off and find another woman if he could, but she doubted he'd find anyone else fool enough to put up with his selfish, myopic ways, he'd been lucky enough to find one in a lifetime. He'd shouted he might just do exactly that and more sinisterly he added, maybe he already had. Then he'd said that swearing didn't become her, that he'd never liked women who swore, it was undignified, disgusting. The words sliced through her tautly stretched patience. She'd then hurled every four-lettered word she could think of. Which just showed that there was definitely a fault in the hardware of her brain. She was thinking, You disappointing, arrogant, hapless man, and yet her voice box had interpreted that into words of four letters of Anglo-Saxon origin.

She wasn't exactly proud of herself, but she couldn't think of any other way to hurt him. And she did want to hurt him.

How had it deteriorated so quickly?

They had fought and ranted and screamed and bickered and nagged and cried and flung glasses of wine and now it was over.

Finished.

The end.

It was his certainty that hurt Martha the most. He'd never once (to her knowledge) questioned whether he was doing the right thing in walking away from her, Mathew, Maisie and the Bridleway. He'd known his own mind. Oh God, how she'd loved that quality in him once, and now how she despised it.

Martha ordered more tea and another fried egg. This was possibly the finest meal she had ever eaten. Far better than anything she'd eaten in the numerous fancy restaurants she'd frequented in the past. Far tastier than any international cuisine she'd sampled. She ate the egg thinking that the white looked like an opal and the yolk like liquid gold. Such an elaborate description of an egg proved she was still drunk. She couldn't imagine going to fancy restaurants without Michael. But would she miss them?

The time she'd spent alone had been terrifying, shocking, humiliating.

But it hadn't been all bad.

Martha liked having a mobile phone and the Internet was genuinely fascinating. Admittedly, her initial interest had been inspired by a desire to impress Michael, but when he appeared resolutely nonplussed at her foray into the world of technology, she realized that the enjoyment she'd derived wasn't diminished; it had nothing to do with him.

She liked not putting the toys away every night. She actually felt quite liberated watching the ironing stack up. The other day she had dressed herself and the children from the pile of non-ironed clothes—and the world hadn't screeched to a stop. Her grocery bill had halved, as had the time she spent in supermarkets. She had more wardrobe space and she adored her new leather pants.

No, it wasn't all bad, thought Martha. Which was the scariest thought she'd had that day.

She measured out the meal so that she finished the last bite of toast at exactly the same moment as she finished the last piece of egg and scooped the last splurge of tomato sauce into her mouth. After the fried breakfast, she drank four more cups of tea and ate two chocolate croissants.

A triumph.

Did she really want him back at all? The thought erupted into Martha's consciousness and shocked her. It was definitely the alcohol. Decent fried eggs and a sunny café shouldn't make you think of giving up on your marriage.

She looked up and noticed that the builders had left. The two fat ladies behind the counter sat gossiping. It was obvious from their countenances that gossiping was routine, necessary but no longer fascinating.

Martha missed Eliza; she wanted to talk to her. She scrambled in her bag and found her mobile. "Hi, it's me."

"Hi Me. Where are you?"

"I'm in that café opposite the Esso garage." Martha glared at the branding. She used to feel a little glimmer of pride every time she passed an Esso garage. She used to think, That's who my husband works for, that's how he spends his days. Michael thought that Esso was important, so Martha did too. Now the branding simply looked grubby, an eyesore.

"Order me a full fried, I'll be there in less than ten. Onions, mushrooms, the works. OK?"

"OK."

# 22

Eliza saw the remnants of Martha's breakfast. "Feel better?"

"Feel rotten."

"Hangover, or life?"

"Not sure I know yet," muttered Martha. "S'pose Mum's filled you in with the details?"

"Yeah, Babes, she has," sighed Eliza as she plonked herself into the seat opposite Martha.

"He wants a divorce."

"I know."

"Why? Why is he doing this?"

"I don't know."

"I don't know either." Martha fell silent and stared at her empty teacup. She wanted to be brave. She really didn't want to embarrass Eliza, whose breakfast had just arrived; she didn't want to put her sister off her food by crying and making the toast soggy, but being brave wasn't easy. "I feel so ridiculous, so stupid. As though I've been caught sleeping on duty."

"What do you mean?" asked Eliza.

"I thought we had a good marriage. I thought we were happy. He said he was happy."

"When?"

"When I asked him."

"Oh, you had to ask him." Eliza took a hungry bite of her sausage, chewed it thoughtfully, then probed, "D'you think there's someone else?"

"Yes. No. I don't know. I keep asking him."

"Any ideas?"

"There is one woman in his office who he used to mention all the time; Karen."

"What's she like?"

"Well, that's the odd thing, I haven't met her. He was always doing things with Karen and her mates but I was never invited along. Do you think he's having an affair with this Karen?"

Eliza thought it was more likely to be one of Karen's friends. Karen was an alibi but she didn't say anything. It was just a gut feeling, she had no proof. Instead she asked, "When did he last make *you* happy?"

"Well . . ." Martha wasn't sure what to say.

"What was the last nice thing he did for you?" pushed Eliza.

"He's always doing nice things."

"Really?"

"Yes. He took the children to the park last week so I could get to the gym."

"They *are* his children. He did that for them and for himself, not you." Eliza enthusiastically cut into her egg. Martha felt tempted to order yet another. "When was the last time he asked you how you were?"

"Don't be silly, he always asks." She leaned over and stole a sausage from Eliza's plate. Where had her appetite come from?

"And listened to your reply?"

Martha didn't answer and Eliza took this as her conceding the point.

"Why are you being cruel about him?" asked Martha with genuine bewilderment.

"Because he's treated you so badly over the last few months. He's been mind-blowingly selfish. He's not so much a product of the 'Generation X,' more of the 'Generation I.' And he's been lazy and irresponsible. He's hurt you and you're my sister. I could rip his head off."

"Oh, I see," commented Martha.

Both the women fell silent and looked out of the window. London was, as ever, teeming with life. The traffic was already heavy. Café owners stood in the doorways of their premises, smoking cigarettes, assessing the weather, wondering if it was worth unstacking the metal bistro chairs for lunch. The streets were full of pedestrians walking their dogs and hurrying their children, scooters, people on skates, boards, bikes. Everyone was in a hurry.

Martha loved this time of year; it was possibly her favourite. As a child she remembered it as one exciting event followed by another. Half-term, Hallowe'en, Guy Fawkes Night; before you knew it, it was Christmas. Martha still found autumn exciting. She loved the cold, crisp days. The shockingly bright, cobalt-blue skies. It was fun to walk in London parks kicking leaves and hearing them crunch underfoot. She never worried about dog muck. Unearthing a shiny, fat conker still seemed like finding treasure to her. She liked the gaudy displays of witches and fireworks that littered shop windows; she liked bobbing for apples on Hallowe'en, and the smell of fried onions and burgers and hotdogs, smouldering fires, and burnt-out fireworks five days later. For Martha, autumn was the season of new beginnings, even more so than spring. It was probably something to do with a new school year. Autumn was full of small pleasures. These small pleasures added up to something much bigger. They were all pleasures that were independent of Michael.

Eliza reached across the table and squeezed her sister's hand. Was it the right moment? Did she dare? Maybe it was what Martha needed to hear. "He wasn't perfect, you know."

The words sat between them. Eliza waited to see if she'd just chucked a hand grenade into their relationship.

"Didn't you think so?" sighed Martha. It was odd how they'd both started talking about Michael in the past tense.

"Did you think so?"

Martha opened her mouth to say "yes," but the word never emerged. She was so used to singing Michael's praises, finding the good things to say about him. Telling everyone—including herself—how lucky she was to be married to him. But was she?

For ten years she'd let the platitudes roll off her tongue. "I couldn't be happier, he's everything I ever dreamed of, and more, and he is so kind, so responsible, such a good husband." And he was. He really was.

Or rather, he had been.

She tried to think of the last time he'd behaved like an Action Man. She couldn't remember. Lately, he hadn't even been helping her carry the shopping into the house from the car. He was always tired, always napping. She was the one that behaved like a superhero—juggling endless tasks, tantrums, jobs and jinxes.

He never made her feel fascinating any more; he made her feel boring. And sometimes she was a little bored of him.

They'd both changed.

She believed in marriage. She really did, and she hadn't expected it to be easy. Nothing that was worth anything was easy, but she'd thought that they'd make it. He'd promised to love her and be with her for better, for worse, in sickness and in health. It wasn't even such a bad worse. A couple of lovely kids that ate up her time and energy, how bad was that?

Martha had always thought that Michael was the ambitious one. The one that hated failure. But no, it was her. She hated the fact that their marriage hadn't worked. Recently she'd wanted to tell him to pull himself together, to make more of an effort, to have some backbone.

She hated his lack of backbone.

Maybe she didn't want him around any more?

She'd sacrificed a lot to make this marriage work. She'd curbed her career and agreed to live in London, when really she'd have preferred to be the other side of the green belt. And whilst Michael's view was that no one sacrifices anything if they are truly in love, she'd thought that immature. As she'd thought his inability to forgive *her* tiredness, her distracted state of mind, her frustrations and her anger, was immature. No one came without baggage. You would have to be shallow and dull to have travelled to adulthood without acquiring a few battle scars.

Michael had turned out to be more ordinary than Martha had thought. She felt duped.

"He wasn't always perfect," she admitted. Immediately a spasm of guilt swept over her. She felt miserably disloyal so quickly added, "But no one is. Marriage is about compromise."

Not that Martha could remember the last time Michael compromised on anything.

Besides the extra wardrobe space and the liberation from the ironing pile, there was something else that suggested to Martha that there was a distinct possibility that Michael wasn't perfect, at least not for her or with her. Over the last few weeks Martha had felt just a little bit more comfortable, a little bit more at ease with herself. Not all the time, obviously. A lot of the time she'd behaved like Attila the Hun, and she'd often felt like the broken-hearted bird in *Swan Lake*. She'd been nearly paralysed by the chilling loneliness ebbing into her body. She'd felt small and vulnerable and completely alone. But there had been the odd moment, the odd glimpse of a more confident and engaging Martha emerging. Like when she was buying the pumpkin, or the first time she went into a chat room, or when she'd eaten fish fingers and chips for tea—then she had felt fine.

Really rather good.

And sometimes she felt horrible. Indescribably vile. Ruined.

"You'll meet someone else," said Eliza.

Martha looked up sharply. She was aghast. "I don't want anyone else. How can you talk about meeting someone else less than twenty-four hours after talking about the probable success of Project Disney?"

"No, not right now, obviously," Eliza rushed. She wished their mother was here. Eliza seemed to have a gift for saying the wrong thing at the moment.

"God, Eliza, next thing you'll be telling me to wear bright colours. Red or pink—cheerful happy colours—and to think sunny thoughts. Look in a mirror and tell myself I'm wonderful."

"I've heard that works."

Martha glared at Eliza across her teacup and hoped her look of anger would be enough to silence her sister.

It wasn't. Eliza continued, "I'm just saying that *eventually* you *will* meet someone else, you're lovely and—"

"But *Cinderella* doesn't end with: 'And they lived happily for a certain period of time, until they each moved on to a new partner,'" snapped Martha.

"Yes, but *Cinderella* is a fairytale. Life isn't a fairytale," argued Eliza. "You don't believe in glass slippers, they'd be lethal. Or

Fairy Godmothers, or choosing your wife after three dances, or virgins marrying."

Martha allowed herself to grin at the last example. "True," she admitted and then added, "but I did believe in the happily-ever-after."

Both girls sat quietly for a moment.

"Me too," confessed Eliza.

More silence.

"I still think that there is a happily-ever-after out there for you. I know it," urged Eliza.

"What, with two kids?" asked doubting Martha.

"Ideal if the chap is infertile," encouraged Eliza.

"And a stack of baggage?" worried Martha.

"Don't talk about it—be silent, deep and interesting." Eliza caught and held Martha's eye. It hurt both of them to look at each other. Martha felt so ashamed, such a failure. Eliza felt miserable on her behalf.

"But Michael was the culmination of all my dreams since Bodie, through John Travolta and Paul Young."

"What are you talking about?"

"I just wanted to be loved. How hard can that be? I'm not so bad, am I?"

"You're cool, Babes."

"Then why didn't it work?"

"I don't know. Life—"

"Sucks." Martha sighed again but she couldn't expel the sadness that lingered inside. "Eliza, who will I chat to about stuff? About the silly things? Like what I've bought for tea? And what the window cleaner charged?"

"Me."

"What will I do if I have a flat battery?"

"Ring a garage."

"But he's a man, car mechanics tell him the truth."

"Join the AA, or the RAC."

"What about sports days?"

"D'you really think he'd ever take time off to go to one?"

"Well no, but . . . Who will I show Mathew's paintings to?"

"Me. Like you always have."

"Right," agreed Martha.

She took a deep breath and thought of Mathew and Maisie. She pictured them on the swings at the local park. Red-cheeked and chubby. Cocooned in half a dozen layers, smiling, laughing and kicking their legs. Her two children were such a responsibility. But then she'd always believed that responsibility was a good thing.

They loved her and needed her and depended on her. There was no time for self-pity or self-indulgence. Even if she longed to fling herself into bed and bury herself in the duvet (quite literally) it was not an option. Nor was crying in a greasy spoon café.

Last night when Michael had asked for a divorce, Martha had felt her heart crumble to dust. She was scared. It was possible— she'd seen countless examples—that her heart would be replaced by a ball of miserable, aching cynicism. A cynicism that, over the years, would be inflamed by countless unfairnesses, unfairnesses that until now she had let slip from her like water from a duck's back. Now she feared she would become vicious and twisted. How was she going to be able to shrug it off when short-changed by fifty pence? Now it was possible she'd storm back to the shop to rip the thieving bastard's head off. She might become the type of woman who hooted her horn repeatedly and stuck up two fingers when another driver pinched the space she'd been patiently waiting for. She might end up hating traffic wardens like everyone else, instead of defending them and saying, "Well, someone has to do it."

She wondered whether she'd ever find the energy to be kind or optimistic again. Whether she'd find it in her heart to invite the boring neighbours in for drinks. Would she become one of those women who made tasteless gags at friends' weddings? Jokes about it being good whilst it lasts, but in her experience that wasn't very long.

She didn't want to be this angry.

It was time to stop blaming, complaining and regretting. It was time to reclaim her life and decide what she wanted. Who she wanted to be, where she wanted to go, how she wanted to live.

Martha was going to let go. More, she was going to be as elegant, charitable and generous as she possibly could be.

Martha was going to get on with her life.

It might even be fabulous.

# 23

Eliza had been right: Martha did feel better once she started talking openly to her friends about her split from Michael and, well, the possibility—no, the probability—of an imminent divorce. No one gloated. No one sighed audibly with relief, grateful that Martha and Michael had fulfilled the statistical quota for this group of friends. No one thought that her divorce made them safe. Martha was reassured to note that all of them were as stunned by the news as she had been. Everyone assumed that a reconciliation was on the cards, as Martha had. When Martha gently but firmly explained that this was no longer an option, not what she wanted any more, her statement was quietly accepted.

It was an enormous relief.

Admitting your life wasn't perfect.

In fact, admitting your life had gone—what was Eliza's expression? *Tits up,* that was it. Admitting your life had gone tits up was an enormous relief.

Martha suddenly found that she was entirely released from the tyranny of housework, timetables, cookbooks, starch bottles, the gym, educational and development books about children—and from Michael's expectations.

Expectations that she'd always had the feeling she'd failed.

Martha would no longer host elaborate dinner parties. Instead she started having impromptu sleepovers, when her friends were too smashed to drive home. Martha couldn't imagine there being a similar scenario when Michael had lived with her; the idea had never crossed her mind. Slowly Martha had come to the conclusion that it was ludicrous to run around in a frenzy, wiping sticky hand prints off surfaces at night time; they were always back again by 8:30 the following morning. She soon found out that, after the children had gone to bed, it was a pleasure to stick a simple meal in the microwave. There was less washing up and shopping and cleaning to do.

There were fewer rows. There was less tension, anxiety and irritability.

But there was no less love in the house, which made Martha wonder when the love had left. Obviously way before Michael had.

Martha began writing herself lists of the things she hoped to achieve over the next few days. That way, if she had any free time and was in danger of thinking—which inevitably led to crying—she could consult the list and find something to do with herself. Sometimes the lists included the smallest of tasks (buy cards, write cards, buy stamps, post cards). Simply writing "send cards" would have earned only a single tick, and it was satisfying to see four small ticks on the list. A tick signalled a sense of self-approval, which Martha wanted to believe in.

The problem with self-worth was that no one else could do the job—although, in fairness, everyone tried. Her friends and family amazed her with their level of support; they called and talked and listened and encouraged and affirmed. They didn't comment when she insisted that as the father of her children he deserved her respect and kindness. Nor did they comment when she vowed to sniff him out, track him down, and cut off his bollocks.

A surprising number of people suggested that Martha hire a private detective, because no one understood why he'd left. Everyone agreed that "not happy" was an inadequate explanation for deserting your family. Martha was tempted. It would almost be a relief if a detective handed over a set of black and white photographs showing Michael leaving a flat and a woman at the door, who was clasping her frilly dressing gown to her heaving bosom and looking both delighted and dishevelled. Martha just wanted to understand Michael, which at the moment was impossible because she didn't even know him. Not any more.

The birthday party was an enormous success. There were balloons and bubbles and prizes and music and laughter. Nothing was missing. Michael wasn't there and yet nothing was missing.

After the final party bag had been given away, all the discarded tissue and wrapping paper collected into large black sacks, and exhausted Maisie and Mathew tucked into their beds, Eliza and Martha kicked off their shoes and prepared to enjoy the silence.

"Leave the washing up, it'll keep," said Martha, who really was making a huge effort to try to relax more. She'd been surprised to discover that this wasn't as much of a contradiction as it might sound.

Eliza didn't need to be asked twice. She happily abandoned the sink and reached for a bottle of wine.

"Fancy a glass?"

"I do." Martha nodded enthusiastically. "I think it was a success, don't you?"

"Yeah. Jelly and ice cream up the walls, crisps underfoot, not an organic morsel in sight—my idea of a good party," joked Eliza. "Was there a single child who didn't have a crying fit?"

"Unlikely."

"Thought not."

The women wandered through to the sitting room. Martha picked out a CD and put it on. Billie Holiday crooned her way into the room.

"You need some new tunes," commented Eliza.

"Do I? Don't you like this?"

"I'm not saying that. It's a classic, but you've been playing it forever."

"Actually, that's not true. I played it at university, but I can't remember playing it in the last ten years."

"Really?" Eliza recognized the ten-years indicator to mean "pre-Michael." She was relieved to note that Martha had resisted saying his name.

"You always had such lovely rooms at university," said Eliza.

"I did, didn't I?" Martha's rooms had been a heady mix of romance, expectation and possibility. Innumerable Pre-Raphaelite posters and postcards blotted out the ugly woodchip wallpaper. The images weren't Eliza's cup of cha—far too many fair maidens drowning or crying or simply waiting for a knight in shining armour—but they were very Martha, the eternal romantic. The grubby, threadbare carpet was covered with a shaggy rug bought in a junk shop. Martha had studied English and art history, so her room was always packed with books. She had enormous respect for them, and the black spines of the Penguin Classics stood to attention like soldiers on her shelves, in strict alphabetical order. Eliza had always found it easier to drop her books on the floor; after all, the only inconvenience was when you tripped over the unwieldy piles, after having one or two glasses too many.

"Martha, do you remember how much you loved those ugly green and gold mugs?"

"Thank you very much. There was nothing ugly about them," laughed Martha.

"And you had that horrible purple Paisley bedspread!"

"It was the height of fashion," defended Martha, giggling.

"To be fair, you were very fashionable in your time."

Why didn't that sound like a compliment? Eliza had intended it to be one. Martha would have liked it to be one.

"You wore short skirts in those days, and DMs."

"Corduroy jackets," added Martha.

"With leather-patched elbows."

"Ripped second-hand jeans."

The sisters screeched their surprise at the recollection.

"Whatever happened to—"

"Me?"

"I was going to say, your leather beret."

They fell silent. The pertinent question was: what had happened to Martha? When had the romantic individualist drowned in rubber gloves and suffocated in furniture polish?

"I've been thinking about my college days a lot recently," mused Martha. "It was the last time I was entirely selfish. It was the last time I had to think only about me. Realistically, I'm never going to be in that position again."

"Well, at least not until you're in your fifties."

Martha laughed. To both women "your fifties" seemed far enough away to be "never again."

"Don't get me wrong, I don't regret any of it. I don't regret marrying Michael and I certainly don't regret having the children. I'm just saying that I'd like the opportunity to put myself first."

As she put a lot of work into every aspect of making the children's lives as happy as possible, Martha had put a lot of work into making the party a success. The paper plates, balloons and streamers had been colour coordinated, which was more than could be said for Martha's wardrobe. She'd spent an age dressing the children for the party, but only seconds putting on her own lipstick. She'd agonized over choosing Maisie's presents. She'd striven for a mix of unusual, thoughtful, educational and good-value toys. She'd been particularly pleased with the multi-coloured, heart-shaped fairy lights and the wooden tricycle. Yet Martha hadn't had a long soak in a bath in months; she always said there was no time.

As if reading her mind, Eliza said, "You could put yourself first now and again. Not all the time, admittedly. But you don't have to be a martyr to be a good mum."

True.

"Martha, you should go out more. Accept some of these invitations you're getting."

"I *do* accept invitations."

"No, you *don't*. I heard you today, you accepted all the invitations that relate to the children. You're going to the ball park at Syon House and the Monkey Music class, but I heard you turn down the invite to Claire's thirtieth birthday."

"I couldn't possibly go to that."

"Why not?"

"Everyone will be in a couple."

"Not true, I checked with her. Martha, you have to claw your way out of your comfort zone."

"She's holding it at a Salsa bar and restaurant. I don't know how to Salsa."

"Don't be pathetic, you just have to shake your hips."

"It isn't just shaking your hips, though, is it? It's all very raunchy. There's a whole lot of gyrating."

Eliza tried not to laugh. "Live dangerously for once. What's the worst that can happen? You can't live your life thinking that risqué is not following a Delia recipe to the letter, substituting some flat-leafed parsley for basil."

"Don't be silly. I do risqué things."

"Name one."

"One?"

"Yes. One. One risqué thing you've done in the last ten years."

Martha was cross. Partly with her sister, but mostly with herself because Eliza had a point.

"What will I wear?" There was something in Martha's tone that suggested her resistance was lowering. She wanted to be persuaded.

"Good question, we'll have to do something with your look."

"My look?"

Eliza jumped up from the sofa and dashed for a pile of fashion magazines that she'd stashed earlier. It was clear she'd been waiting for this opportunity. She quickly started to flick through the mags and point out pictures of leggy models looking sensational in jeans and skimpy tops.

"I couldn't wear that," cried Martha, aghast. "Anyway, I did buy some new clothes."

"A couple of things, and it was weeks ago. You've really got a great figure, you ought to make more of it."

"Great figure." The compliment barely had time to compute before the scary implications of "you ought to make more of it" hit home.

"A make-over?" Martha asked, wide-eyed with fear.

"An image change," Eliza stated confidently. "We need to shop!"

# December

# 24

They don't like me. I can tell they hate me, thought Martha, as she eyed the other guests at the birthday dinner. I have "scarlet woman" written all over me. In bright red. Every woman is thinking, I'm not letting my husband anywhere near her. Every man is thinking that there must be some intrinsic flaw; it may not be obvious what, but it's a certainty. Why else would my husband have left me? They'll be surmising that I'm lousy in bed, or that I have a foul temper, or that I'm jealous and nagging. Because they'll know there must be something fundamentally wrong with me.

They just don't know *what*.

Nor did Martha. The agony of not being wanted by someone who had said they would want you forever was bloody. The disappointment, the disbelief, the disgust. Martha was unable to believe that anyone would want to spend five minutes with her, without the distraction of cable TV.

"What you drinking, Martha?" asked one of the gang, kindly. (Kindly, because her friends *were* kind. Kind, because they didn't hate her. They liked her. And she was right, they didn't understand why she was on her own, but they couldn't imagine it would be for long.)

She considered ordering an orange juice, but decided that she'd need more than vitamin C to help her through this evening. She hated this question. She never knew what to answer. Whilst recently she'd indulged in some blow-outs with Eliza, she'd always reached oblivion with a decent Chardonnay. She detested beer and spirits, and only really enjoyed the occasional glass of good wine, and then only with a meal; the wines sold in pubs and bars such as this were generally lousy.

"A white-wine spritzer," she offered finally, although she knew her choice was viewed as a wimpy drink. Her friend brought back a large white wine with a splash of soda.

Martha gulped it back and then offered to buy a round. She couldn't stand the sort of women who thought they didn't have to buy any drinks just because they were single. She definitely didn't want to be that type of woman, so she bought a round and then organized a kitty. A very generous kitty. It was quite nice in here, thought Martha. Fun, relaxed. Not that she had an awful lot of venues to compare it with; she couldn't remember the last time she and Michael had gone to a club. Eight years ago? Could it be that long?

She had of course been to a club more recently than that—she used to go with the guys and girls from the office fairly regularly. Michael was invited along as well, but he always seemed to have a previous engagement or simply too hefty a workload to join her. But then she'd left her job three years ago. Could it be possible that she hadn't danced for three years? Of course, there had been weddings. She liked a bop, but recently her dancing partners had often been under two foot (Mathew and his chums). The hokey-cokey simply didn't count. When did she stop dancing with Michael? When did she stop dancing? Martha suddenly realized that she couldn't see her glass clearly, it was swimming. She blinked away the hot, angry, sentimental tears, brought her glass into focus again and poured another drink. No good came from thinking of Michael, she knew that. She couldn't spend any more time thinking about why he didn't want her. Icy fact was, he didn't.

His loss.

The food was taking an age to arrive but, despite Martha's fears, the conversation was flowing. A number of the women had

children and so Martha felt on safe ground as she discussed with
them the pros and cons of the MMR vaccination. Although, she
couldn't understand why she twice slipped up and referred to it as
the MRR. It was a hot room and Martha was very thirsty.

And flirty.

God, she couldn't believe she'd just thought that. But she *was*
feeling excitable; there was no denying it. Who'd bought the
champagne? She did enjoy a glass of champagne; there was never
a reason to say no. Lord, were they still talking about the MRR,
didn't they have anything else to discuss? Martha instantly felt
guilty. What a mean thought. It wasn't so long ago that she'd
happily have discussed her children all night. Indeed, she'd
thought about nothing else for three years but suddenly tonight
she wanted to think about something else. Tonight she wanted a
night off. Maybe it was her new suede skirt and black gypsy-style
top.

Although she couldn't explain why her suede skirt and black
gypsy-style top would make her notice those guys sat at that
other table over there. Notice how handsome a group they were,
and one of them in particular.

Martha blushed and was grateful no one could read minds.
Goodness, what was she thinking? She was spending far too
much time with Eliza. She reached for the one bottle that still
had some wine in it and poured it all into her glass. She put the
bottle down next to the other numerous empties that her table
had accumulated.

"Shall we order some more?" she suggested.

"Good idea, keep us going until the food comes," someone
else agreed, and then suddenly there were two more white and
two more red, apparently out of nowhere. Odd, but the house
wine tasted fine once you got used to it.

The food finally arrived and by all accounts it was very good.
Although Martha never found out. She tried to shovel it into her

mouth, but all the little bits kept falling off her fork. It was rather undignified. In the end she gave up, it was so much easier just to keep topping up her wineglass. Again and again. The music from the dance floor downstairs was pounding through her body, she was finding it increasingly difficult to sit still.

"Let's go downstairs for a boogie." Martha looked around to see who had made that suggestion and was surprised to realize it was her. It must be the Salsa music. Suddenly she felt that dancing to Salsa music was going to be OK. No one would be any good at it, and what was it Eliza had said? Just keep shaking your hips. She could do that.

No one was dancing. There were a large number of dodgy-looking Latino types standing around the edges of the floor. Normally Martha would have clutched her handbag and stood at a distance from the floor until it was packed full. Then she might have been prepared discreetly to bob around her bag. But tonight, stoked with South Californian courage, she wanted to strut her funky stuff and she wanted to do it *now.*

"Come on," she ordered.

The guys in her party turned down the invitation but one or two of the braver, and equally drunk, women joined her. It was all the encouragement the dodgy Latinos needed. Like leopards they pounced, like leeches they stuck. Suddenly about eight, inanely grinning men surrounded Martha. She was torn between total embarrassment (their shirts were louder than the music and there was an above-average score on facial hair) and being fairly impressed (they could dance; but was it really necessary to get so close?). Martha remembered her mother instructing her to accept a dance if ever it was offered, as it took a lot of courage for men to ask women to dance, and—after all—men were only human.

Which showed what her mother knew.

However, Martha was far too used to following rules than to

suddenly decide to rebel, so she politely danced one dance with each man who asked her. It amazed her that her stony, sullen silence was seen as positive encouragement, and dance followed dance followed dance.

Martha was spun from short man to short man until she was sure her head and the room were orbiting her body.

There he was again.

The handsome one.

Eliza would call him hot.

Damn hot.

Even if he was wearing a 'lace around his neck.

"Would you like to dance with me, rescue me from these awful shirts?" Martha stood in front of the hot, damn hot, man and his two friends and wondered how the hell she'd spun there and how would she deal with the humiliation if he turned her down. Why had she just done that? Probably because her sister had said the most adventurous thing she'd ever done was adapt a Delia Smith recipe. Well, watch this space Eliza dear. She hoped to God that the mother of the hot, damn hot, man had taught him the same rule her mother had taught her. She couldn't remember the last time she'd asked a man to dance like that, a complete stranger. Before she met Michael, certainly. But thinking about it, before Michael, she'd always been first up on the dance floor and she'd never minded asking people to dance. It was only dancing, after all.

"All right." He passed his glass to his mate and followed her back on to the floor. "So are you prepared to dance with the devil, although I suppose it's hardly pale moonlight?"

"What?"

"You know, Jack Nicolson, the Joker in *Batman*. He asks his victims if . . ." The hot, damn hot, man trailed off. He could see Martha wasn't getting it.

"Right," said Martha. She wasn't sure what else to say.

It was always a risk. What if he danced like an uncle? Martha took a braver, longer look at him and tried to focus. He *was* gorgeous. She decided it wouldn't matter if he danced like her greatuncle. He wasn't tall but as Martha was barely five foot four she didn't like men over six foot. She didn't want to look like Lucy Ewing. He was probably brushing five eleven, lean, with wide shoulders, short-cropped hair, good clothes, and, err, that was about all she could make out. The features were fuzzy, more to do with her alcoholic intake than his genes.

He could dance; in fact he was seriously good. And funny. He kept doing silly little wiggle things, which made him look at once ridiculous and, well, sexy. Sending yourself up demands a certain amount of self-confidence, and a certain amount of self-confidence is sexy. She watched him and felt a strange churn, a definite pang of longing, somewhere between her thighs and stomach. She wasn't entirely naive, despite what Eliza thought; she recognized the churn as a delicious swell of lust.

The Salsa music suddenly seemed seductive, not stupid, and the idea of having a daft dance of no import suddenly receded— and Martha knew she fancied the life out of him. It was so long since she'd felt this way that it seemed illicit. But right. Illicit and right. Fascinating. The track changed and Martha realized there was a risk that he would now smile politely then merge back into the crowd forever, to join his friends.

He didn't.

He stayed and they danced five or six or more dances. Martha noted the admiring glances from the other women at the club, who were staring at her with ill-concealed jealousy, and Martha felt top.

"Fancy a drink?" he asked. She nodded. "What would you like?"

"White wine." Without hesitation. She didn't even consider trying to be more hip than she was by requesting a trendy beer or spirits.

"What's your name?" she yelled above the crowd and music.

"Muad'Dib, a name can be a weapon." Martha looked blank. What an unusual name. "Muad'Dib, he's in the film *Dune.*"

"I don't think I've seen it," said Martha, feeling like the dull housewife she was.

"Sting was in it," he added and raised his voice at the end of the sentence the way people do when they expect you to know what they're talking about.

Martha shook her head to convey that she was none the wiser. It wasn't unusual for Martha not to recognize references to popular culture, unless they related to *Bob the Builder* or the *Tweenies.* "What's your real name?"

"Jack, Jack Hope." Martha nodded and tried desperately to commit it to memory. She knew she was hopelessly drunk but she didn't want to offend him by forgetting his name, at least not in the next twenty minutes. "And you are?"

This was when Martha wished her parents had called her Scarlet.

"Martha."

"That's unusual," he said, without missing a beat.

"Awful, isn't it?" giggled Martha. "I hate it."

"Well, Babe. What's your second name?"

"Evergreen." Martha gave her maiden name without even thinking about the fact that, technically, she was still West.

"Well, I shall call you Little Miss E."

Little Missy, thought Martha. She liked it.

Little Miss E. and Jack talked all night. They told each other their life stories. They veered wildly through the trivial: favourite colours, music they liked to listen to, shops they bought clothes from, the fact that when he was a little boy Jack carved *Rambo* into his arm with a compass. And, just because she knew Eliza would ask, Martha got him to tell her his birth sign.

"Which did you prefer: *Starsky and Hutch* or *The Dukes of Hazzard?*" she asked.

"*Dukes of Hazzard.*"

"Really?"

"Yeah, lots more tits and ass."

"Right."

Martha told him that she listened to Billie Holiday even though Eliza had given her strict instructions to drop the Chemical Brothers and Freestylers into conversation if asked. Martha told him that she'd fancied Paul Young when it was clearly more acceptable to admit to a crush on any one of Spandau Ballet. She said that currently her favourite colour was green, because it represented independence and healing, but normally she'd choose silver or blue. Martha told him she was a mother of two, waiting for a divorce. She thought that about summed her up. She waited for him to say he was going to the loo. It had been a nice flirtation, but now that she'd blurted out the truth it had to be over. Over before it had begun. She waited for him to disappear.

He didn't. He just said, "So—*Blue Peter* or *Magpie?*"

"*Blue Peter.*"

"Me too. *Morecambe and Wise* or *The Two Ronnies?*"

"Oh, that's tough," sighed Martha. "They were both good, though slightly different eras. It's a close call, but I think it'll have to be *Morecambe and Wise.*"

"I feel exactly the same," grinned Jack Hope. He played with an imaginary (presumably skewed) pair of glasses. Martha grinned back. She couldn't remember when she'd last been asked her opinion or when anyone had listened to the answers. She felt fantastic, uncorked. She felt as though she was talking to one of her good girl friends or Eliza, not to a man at all. It seemed OK to tell him all of this and it was easy to slip from the trivial to the amazingly intimate. He told her about his family, his disappointing mother, his admirable father. He talked about his first love and his last. She wondered if he was as intimate and honest with everyone—she hoped not. She hoped that somehow she'd unlocked something. She asked him if she had. She hadn't. He was this honest and open indiscriminately. "Why not?" Honesty was a big thing for Jack.

The conversation began to swim in front of Martha's mind. She wasn't too sure what she was saying but apparently it was fascinating. Or at least interesting. Jack seemed interested. And everything he said was amusing, intelligent, sharp, fun. She wasn't sure how they started kissing. It was more than possible that she asked him to kiss her.

As simple as that.

As bold as that.

He was a fabulous kisser.

His lips were firm and tender. Slick, clear, they fitted.

She wasn't sure when he picked her up. Literally. But at one point he lifted her up and she wrapped her legs around him like Julia Roberts in some film or other. He made her feel so delicate, so girl-like. They fitted. They were in a club, kissing and fitting. He made her feel like a film star.

"Aren't you drinking?" asked Martha, more than aware that she was drinking enough for them both.

"No."

"Are you driving?"

"Yes, but that's not why I'm not drinking. I never drink."

He's an alcoholic, thought Martha, and she immediately started to calculate if she had the emotional resources to deal with it, because if this man was an alcoholic and he needed someone with the emotional resources to deal with it, she would like it to be her.

"Are you an alcoholic?" Martha asked, too drunk to beat about the bush or consider how impertinent she was being.

"Everyone asks that." Martha was stung; she didn't want to be like everyone. Still, at least he didn't seem offended. "No, I'm not. I just don't like the taste."

Since when had the word "taste" been so sexy?

Everything Martha had ever known advised against the next move. Her upbringing, her current circumstances, the local news, the rules. She shouldn't accept a lift home. She certainly shouldn't suggest that there was a place they could park up. She definitely shouldn't give him a blow job. But what could she do? She couldn't let her days drift by—a tribute to missed opportunities.

Maybe it was the alcohol that was buoying her up. Or maybe it was the realization that she'd always played by the rules and look where that had landed her. Whatever.

His dick smelt clean. He smelt clean. And it was beautiful. Large, magnificent, straight, strong, symmetrical. Martha had always thought penises were rather silly. Odd shapes and ugly colours—but his was a joy. He was a joy.

She sat up, cum and saliva on her cheek, and she felt clean. Not smutty, which surely should have been the order of the day, considering she was more than necking, parked up half a mile from home, age thirty-two.

She trusted him.

He dropped her off. The house was silent and Martha felt strangely relieved that Eliza was in bed. She didn't want to talk to anyone. She just wanted to go to bed and dream.

She forced her eyes open and was surprised to find the sun slamming through the curtains. It was December, shouldn't it be grey? She moved her head; it didn't hurt, shouldn't she have a hangover? Shouldn't her first thought be absolute horror, swiftly served up with a large dollop of shame and regret?

No sign.

Martha stretched her legs and arms. My God, she'd gone to

bed naked. She reached for her pyjamas and just managed to pull the top over her head and slither into the bottoms before Eliza, Mathew and Maisie burst into her bedroom.

"Rise and shine. I've brought you a cup of tea, I certainly hope you're feeling terrible." Eliza handed Maisie to Martha and put the tea on the bedside table. Mathew jumped on the bed, nearly knocking the tea over, and then he snuggled under the covers with his mother and sister. Although Eliza was already dressed she couldn't resist the intimacy and also climbed into the bed, on what Martha still thought of as Michael's side.

"So, did you have a good night?"

"Very, thanks."

"Thought you must have. See, I knew you'd enjoy it when you got there. What time did you get in? It must have been late because I stayed up watching some film on Sky until three."

"Er, yeah, I think I got in nearer four."

"What were you doing until that time? Did you go back to Claire's for more drinks?"

"No."

"What then?"

"You wouldn't believe me."

"Try me."

"I was in Holland Park giving a B-L-O-W-J-O-B." Martha spelt the words out, although it was impossible that Mathew would know what it meant.

"You what?" Eliza sat bolt upright, and this time the tea did go flying. There was a quick scrabble around for tissues, the duvet was mopped clean, but nothing could budge the look of shock from Eliza's face. "Tell me you're joking."

"I'm not."

"Who was he? Do I know him?"

"No. I just met him."

"Bloody hell, Martha." Eliza considered what to say next. She

was sure her sister would be immersed in remorse and humiliation, and so she didn't want to be too harsh, however knocked
sideways she herself felt. "Look, don't worry Martha. Lots of people do silly things when they're drunk. Just put it down as a life
experience and don't dwell on the humiliation too much."

"I don't feel humiliated."

"Well, self-loathing, then. That's just as negative, more so,
don't dwell or self-loathe."

"I'm not."

"You're not?"

"No, I had a brilliant time," asserted Martha and she grinned
to herself as a flashback sprung to mind: Jack picking her up and
her clinging to him—"Cheeky monkey," he'd said. He was impressive, beautiful, large, in fact *huge*. He'd seemed to really like
her blow job. He'd been throbbing hard. And it was so sexy to be
wanted in such a crude, candid way. Martha scratched her nose
and wondered how she could possibly be turning into the type of
woman who was interested in beautiful cocks.

Eliza stared at her sister. She couldn't decide what line to take.
Her expression was a bewildered mix of amazement, delight and
fury. Martha wasn't supposed to do that kind of thing. Eliza
never thought of herself as someone who was resistant to change.
But Martha behaving like this was odd. Eliza wanted everything
to go back to how it was—and this was never how it was. Or was
it? Thinking right back to their school days, Martha did get her
share of snogs at the church hall disco. They used to hide in their
bedrooms on Saturday morning, eating toast, drinking tea, ignoring their parents and talking tongues.

But tongues, not cocks.

"What's he like then?" Eliza muttered.

"Very nice."

"Very nice? Sounds terrible. Give me details."

Martha stalled by lifting Mathew out of bed and setting him

on the floor with a jigsaw. She was stuck. Not only was she out of practice with the official debriefing scenario and didn't remember that she was supposed to describe the guy and their meeting in tiny, gruesome detail, but also she didn't have the vocabulary to describe him—and if she had, no one would have believed her anyway.

He was divine.

Absolutely perfect.

The kind of bloke you only ever came across in books or films. Not real at all.

She looked at Eliza and wondered how she would even start to explain. Eliza waited, her face now eager and aglow.

"Well, it's hard to say exactly."

"Well, start with the physical stuff: what does he look like?"

"Divine, perfect. Like the hero in a book or film." Martha grinned, broadly; she couldn't help herself. Eliza's eager face fell; she nodded and tried to smile her encouragement, but Martha saw the caution cloud her sister's eyes. "What?" she demanded crossly.

"Nothing, nothing. Go on."

"*Why* are you looking so concerned?"

"I'm not."

"You are." Martha kissed Maisie's head and absentmindedly traced "Round and Round the Garden like a Teddy Bear" on her foot. Maisie giggled.

"Well, it's just that there aren't any men like in books and films. Not really. That's why we buy the books and go to see the films, to fulfil our fantasy life," said Eliza. She was sorry to be the one who had to break this news to Martha; on the other hand, someone had to. Martha was a lamb wearing a big sign saying "Eat Me Alive," and she had just wandered into a den of lions.

"Well, Jack is. He's gorgeous-looking, 's got a bod to live for, he's straightforward, dresses well and is very kind," maintained Martha.

Bod? thought Eliza. "A bod to live for": had her sister really just said that? "How can you know that if you've just met him?"

"I don't know how I know, but I do."

"Can he dance?" she probed.

"Yes, brilliantly, and he doesn't drink."

"See, there's always a flaw. Why doesn't he drink? Is he an alcoholic?"

"Says not." Martha was ruffled, not least because this thought had crossed her mind too. "So what if he is?" she asked defiantly.

Eliza simply raised her eyebrows. "So he's a 'my body is a temple' type, is he? Won't drink because it's loaded with calories. A control freak."

"He simply doesn't like the taste," sighed Martha, wishing Eliza wasn't hell-bent on pouring icy water. "Look, it was a great night. That's all. I'm just saying I'm not wracked with shame or guilt. I don't feel smutty or slutty. It was a lovely experience. It was you who told me to take some risks."

"Buy a suede skirt, not give blow jobs in public places, to total strangers."

"He doesn't feel like a stranger."

"But he is. He could have been a murderer."

"But he wasn't."

"He won't respect you."

"I think he does."

"You are *so* naive."

"And *you* are a cynic."

"He won't call you."

"Ha ha, that's where you're wrong." Martha stretched her arm and felt under her bed. She located her mobile and held it up triumphantly to Eliza. The text message read "Hello, Gorgeous. Want to hook up later?"

Eliza was stunned. Not least because Martha had successfully swapped telephone numbers and negotiated her way around the mobile menu.

"I'm not proposing to marry him, just hang out with him," defended Martha.

"Hang out with him"—Martha never hung out anything other than the washing. "Well, you're a fast learner, I'll give you that," said Eliza. "Come on, Mathew, Maisie, let's leave your mother alone, we'll go and have breakfast." Eliza flounced out of the room and, really, it was a shame she wasn't wearing a big, long skirt with a bustle to complete the effect.

Martha hadn't expected her sister to be so censorious. After all, Martha had listened to Eliza's countless accounts of similar exploits, and she had never passed judgement, although at the time she'd wanted to. Eliza had always maintained that a few well-placed one-night stands give you cred; she was not the type of girl who believed that they left you tarnished. The infuriating thing was, Martha knew this wasn't about whether Eliza morally approved or disapproved of her behaviour; she knew that Eliza's objection was spurred by concern. Eliza didn't think Martha could cope with this, didn't think she was experienced enough, because sex was Eliza's area of expertise, not Martha's. How patronizing, thought Martha, I've given birth twice, of course I can give head. Besides, my husband has just left me, I haven't got a heart to break; it's disintegrated. I'm safe.

# 25

"Will you babysit tonight?" Martha asked Eliza. She'd been working up the courage to ask this question for about an hour. She'd given the children their tea and bath, so babysitting wouldn't be hard work, and Eliza generally didn't mind helping out. In fact, wasn't it Eliza who'd said Martha should go out more? But Martha had a sneaky suspicion that Eliza wouldn't approve of her plans.

"Why? Where you going?" Eliza replied, without looking up from her magazine.

Martha knew her sister well enough to know that she was entirely focused on Martha's social life, and not on the article about detoxing. "Out with Jack, if that's OK, *Mum.*" Martha tried to make light of her little sister's officious, meddlesome attitude, but actually she was irritated by it. She drew the curtains, locking out the winter night and holding in the happy domestic scene. Mathew was playing quietly with his train set. Maisie was drinking her milk. Martha stooped to pick up her daughter and to give her a cuddle. She breathed in the smell of her newly washed hair, the most precious perfume. Calvin Klein could never bottle this.

"You've already agreed, have you?" asked Eliza irritably.

"No. I said yes, provisionally, but I explained that I'd have to check if you could sit for me," replied Martha patiently.

And dishonestly.

She'd already agreed to hook up with Jack. She'd calculated that her sister was unlikely to be going anywhere on a Monday night and therefore would be free to sit.

"So, have you told him you have children?" challenged Eliza.

"Yes."

"And what did he make of that?"

"He was cool with it."

"Cool with it," "cool with it." Eliza repeated the phrase in her head. A perfectly ordinary phrase made extraordinary because her sister had uttered it. She looked at Martha to see if her new and affected language embarrassed her. Martha seemed unconcerned. In fact, the only odd thing about Martha was that she seemed so content, so natural.

"Well, he's keen, I'll give you that. He texted you straight away, and less than forty-eight hours after meeting you, he's already taking you out," commented Eliza.

"Do you think he's keen?" Martha threw Maisie in the air and caught her again, a bundle of chuckles and gurgles. Martha giggled too; Eliza wasn't sure if she was giggling at Maisie or with delight at the idea of Jack's keenness.

"Yeah, of course he's keen."

"Really?" Martha couldn't hide her joy.

"Yeah, you haven't slept with him yet."

"Will you babysit, or do I need to call an agency?" asked Martha calmly, refusing to take the bait.

"I'll do it," sighed Eliza.

"Thank you." Martha turned to walk out of the room.

Just as Martha was leaving the sitting room Eliza added, "Look, Martha, it's not that I mind babysitting, you know."

"I know." She closed the door.

Not much had actually been said, but the sisters had spoken volumes.

Martha thought it was unnecessary for Eliza to worry as much as she was doing. It wasn't as though Martha had spent the entire two days mooning around thinking about Jack. She hadn't been dwelling on flashbacks of the things he said, the way he smiled, the way he moved. She hadn't been planning what to wear and say on their first date. She hadn't chalked his name on Mathew's blackboard. She hadn't punched the air when he called, or danced around the house when he suggested meeting up.

All right, she had.

Still, being this excited, feeling this alive, was a good thing, surely.

Martha didn't have time for a long soak in a bath scented with Body Shop sensuous oil, or to exfoliate, rub on anti-cellulite cream, moisturize body and face and apply full make-up, like girls do when they have a hot date. She didn't pay any attention to her underwear, or even her outerwear. Mathew was running a slight temperature. Nothing to worry about, but enough to make him grumpy and clingy. She ran in and out of his bedroom trying to pacify him with stories, cuddly toys and Calpol. She'd just tried on two almost identical black tops, and two very similar white tops, when Maisie threw up in bed, necessitating a change of sheets.

"Is she very sick?" asked Eliza.

"No, just over-fed and over-excited," replied Martha as she whipped off the sodden sheet.

Eliza hovered in the doorway trying not to balk actively.

"Mathew, have you been feeding Maisie Smarties?"

"You said, nice to share." Mathew turned his huge blue eyes on his mother, totally disarming her.

"I did, Darling, and it is." Martha crouched down to her son's height and hugged him. Maisie launched herself on to her mother and brother for a spontaneous group hug. "Maybe I shouldn't go out," said Martha, suddenly pickled in guilt.

"Don't go, Mummy. Stay with Mathew and Maisie," begged Mathew. It was amazing how he could spring from rapture to despair in the blink of an eye.

Martha looked at Eliza and waited for direction. She was late anyway and hardly looked her best. If the children really were ill she'd never forgive herself.

Eliza was sure that this Jack Hope spelt trouble. Martha was so obviously out of her depth. She could push the advantage and persuade Martha to stay in. They could open a bottle of Chardonnay and a box of chocs. They could have a lovely evening.

She sighed. "Come on, Mathew, let your mummy go and get ready. Leave that, Martha, I'll change the sheets. If you don't get a move on you're going to be really late."

The thing is, Martha looked so happy.
Happier than Eliza could recall.

Martha couldn't remember what he looked like. Not exactly. She remembered that he was gorgeous but, God, what if that had been beer goggles, and he was grotesque rather than gorgeous? What if she didn't recognize him? What if he was a prat? What if he thought she was a slut? She had acted like a slut. Would he be able to tell that she wasn't really, and would he care? What if he was tedious or arrogant? Maybe he only appeared interesting because Michael was the benchmark. Martha giggled at her mental dig at Michael; there was something very attractive about cruelty.

Her hair was still damp, and she was wearing a bit of mascara and lipgloss, jeans and a black shirt. Martha groaned—she could hardly be accused of going over the top. What was she doing? It was only three months since she and her husband had split up, what was she doing meeting other men? Wasn't she rushing things? And normally she was so cautious. Surely it should feel odd.

But it didn't.

She pushed against the heavy wooden door. Funny he'd chosen here to meet. All Bar One. She'd expected him to select some funky bar in the West End. One with a dress code that she would fail. This All Bar One was an old-time favourite of Martha's; she used to come here a lot before the children were born. It was somewhere she felt comfortable.

Well, normally she felt comfortable. Not today. Today her heart was in her throat.

Then she saw him.

And now her heart was in her knickers. Which Martha thought was very odd indeed.

He was standing by the bar. He'd obviously just arrived because he was paying for his orange juice. He grinned. "Can I get

you a drink? You look beautiful." He kissed her on the lips as
though that was the most natural thing in the world.

He was stunning. How could she have doubted it? Why
hadn't she mentioned to Eliza how fantastic his body was? In-
credible shoulders, and look at those forearms. How could she
have forgotten those eyes? A distinctive fusion of greens and yellows. They reminded her of walking in a forest on a summer's
day. They were the same colours as the leaves on tall oak trees,
when dappled with sunshine. How was it possible to have eyes
like a summer's day?

It turned out that he really was interesting, it hadn't just been
the wine. He was intelligent, concerned, inquisitive and experienced. Like the first time they'd met, they talked and talked.
They talked about his work (he was a Web designer, fairly senior
from what she could glean), and his friends (who were his life
blood), and his father (who'd brought him up), and the rest of his
family (who he'd left behind).

He was frighteningly trendy. He talked about being "down on
the street" and although he was being a little figurative, it was
clear that he was achingly hip. He wore Diesel clothes; he didn't
fasten his shoelaces, but tucked them into his trainers because
this, apparently, was cooler. Martha knew Mathew would be
thrilled to hear this and she wondered how long she could keep
this nugget of information from him. Jack listened to bands that
Martha hadn't a hope of knowing. He had a vocabulary that she
was unfamiliar with, but just about understood. He "got into the
zone." She was a "hot babe." His friends were "dudes." A really
cool jacket was "bitchin." He played video games and was in love
with Ulala; Lara Croft was a has-been. He was happenin'. And
she wanted to be happenin' with him.

And yet the strangest thing was that he was 100 per cent
gentleman. Almost otherwordly in his courteous, gallant approach towards her. He wasn't smooth. Although he was prac-

tised. He hadn't learnt to open doors for women at prep school; in fact, the only thing he'd learnt at his state school was how to force open car doors. He opened doors for women because he liked women. He wasn't shy. He entertained her with stories about how he'd lost his virginity at fourteen (or, rather, flung it away, but she was touched to note that he'd taken his jacket off so that his girl could lie on it). He had few formal qualifications and yet his mind raced and challenged as though he'd been a member of the Oxford Union for years. He listened with sincerity. He questioned with regard. He talked with animation.

She was falling in love with him.

No, that last bit couldn't be true.

It would be far too fast. It would be ridiculous. She couldn't be falling in love.

But it did feel like falling in love.

He was funny, very funny. Sharp. And chatty and informed. He looked at her and his eyes seared her soul, scorching it with an exquisite mix of pleasure and pain.

He was *sooooo* bloody sexy.

"The blokes you were with in the bar the other night, who are they again?" asked Martha, trying to keep her mind and eyes away from the contents of Jack's trousers.

"Dave and Drew. I work with them."

"I think you told me that," said Martha, and a small bell rang in the depths of her hazy memories of the Saturday night.

"I did."

"Sorry, I was drunk."

"I know."

They both grinned and Martha felt relieved not to have to be apologetic. Somehow everything she did or said seemed OK with Jack.

"How are Mathew and Maisie?" he asked.

Martha was flattered that he'd remembered her children's names.

"Fine, gorgeous. Well, a bit sickly and a bit grumpy but, you know, fine, gorgeous."

"Actually, I don't know. I've never had any contact with kids, not really."

"Don't any of your friends have children?" asked Martha, amazed. Her world was chock-a-block with small people.

"Not many of my friends have girlfriends, let alone children."

Good, perfect. Martha didn't want to sit around all day talking about kids; she could do that with all her other friends. Martha just wanted a bit of fun, a distraction.

"We're all resolutely single," he added.

Resolutely. That didn't sound good. Not that she wanted a real relationship, just a bit of fun, a distraction. Sometimes it felt as though the organist was only just packing up the music from her wedding march.

"I'm not looking for a father for the children. They have one. And I'm not looking for a husband because, technically, I still have one of those too."

Where did that come from? The glass of Chardonnay probably.

"Are you looking for a boyfriend?"

"No." Martha hadn't been looking at all, not actively.

"That's good, because I'm just out of a relationship and I want to be single for a while."

Martha was a bit confused. If he wanted to be single, why did he have his hand on her leg? Why had he kissed her when she walked into the bar? Where did she fit in? "Just out?"

"Err, we split up in the summer."

Sounded like a positively respectable length of time to her. "Did she leave you? Do you miss her?"

"Err, no, I was the one who finished it. No, I'm not heartbro-

ken or anything. Not bitter and twisted. I'm just having too
much fun with my naked friends so I don't want a girlfriend."

" 'Naked friends'?"

"Like I was telling you on Saturday night."

Martha looked blank.

Jack looked aghast. "You can't remember, can you?"

"What can't I remember?"

"About naked friends?"

"Remind me."

He explained the concept. In a nutshell, he wanted affectionate
sex with any one of a number of women at any one time, but he
didn't want to have to lie about it. He didn't like lying. It confused things. He wanted to make it clear that naked friends were
different from lays, because he, like most men given the opportunity, would lay just about any chick with a bod and a pulse. He
was only "naked friends" with girls he liked, ones he could talk to
and have a laugh with, not bunny-boilers.

Martha was surprised to realize that she didn't find the naked
friends concept a complete turn-off. He managed to tell her that
this was what he wanted in such a gentle, non-presumptuous
manner that she really believed it was a great idea. In fact, it
turned her on. She was flattered to be invited to be one. She
didn't want a boyfriend. She didn't want to find anyone to replace Michael; she didn't think it was possible. A husband, the father of your children, couldn't be replaced. But how do you open
up anything other than your legs after having loved and lost?
How do you open your heart and mind? But she did want to be
held. She did want to be touched, because when he stroked her
cheek, or moved a stray lock of hair from in front of her eyes and
tucked it behind her ear, it felt lovely. And when he kissed the tip
of each of her fingers it felt very lovely. When he kissed her lips it
felt very, very lovely.

•     •     •

They'd come back to her place and were doing all the usual things, which was all very unusual for Martha.

"Err, tea or coffee?" she offered, smiling brightly, hoping the brightness would eclipse the nervousness.

And she *was* nervous, because they were back at her place for hot sex, not a hot drink. They'd discussed it at length in the bar and agreed the exact terms, almost as though they were making a business transaction. Jack said he found Martha fantastically cute, and would happily shag her until the early hours. Martha was thrilled. She needed to feel wanted again. She wanted to feel needed. They each realized and acknowledged that there were other people competing for a share of their minds and hearts. They would respect and recognize the importance of these other people. Martha's "other people" were Mathew and Maisie. Jack's "other people" were an inexact number of other "naked friends."

It might not have sounded like the most romantic proposal Martha had ever received—it was far too modern to be romantic—but then Martha was fed up to her back fillings with romance. Wedding vows were very romantic, but had proved to be fairly tenuous when it came down to it. Martha liked this bargain. It sounded simple. It sounded uncomplicated, a win-win situation. It sounded as good as it gets when you are a hand-me-down, when you are spoiled goods. Her own husband hadn't wanted her, who the hell could be expected to pick up the pieces? The intimacy Martha had been used to had been ripped apart and she missed it. She wanted to re-create it, even if it was just for a short time. She wanted her bed to be warmed by something other than a hot-water bottle. Even if it was just for the one night. Martha couldn't look beyond that.

"I don't really like hot drinks, have you got any juice?"

"No alcohol, no caffeine, you freak." Martha wanted to eat her tongue. Her comment had been intended to be funny but had come out sounding offensive. She looked at Jack; he was still smiling. His gentle, non-assuming smile. Martha, somewhat rashly, tried to make amends by breaking into song, the old Adam Ant song about a guy who didn't drink and didn't smoke. The question was, what did he do? She wriggled her body in a way that was supposed to be, at best, sexy or at least funny; she feared it was ludicrous. Her Adam Ant impression wasn't bad, but it wasn't good either, and Martha doubted it was original. Jack's smile widened a fraction, but she got the feeling that he was just being polite and that her impression was so lousy that he didn't really know who she was trying to imitate. She dived into the fridge and started to yell out the options that she offered Mathew and his tiny friends. "I have orange juice, Ribena, strawberry Crush or milk." She was at least a great hostess.

"Milk, please."

Martha felt everything inside her body tighten with delight. He sounded like a little boy. So polite, and such a childlike choice. Suddenly the glorious beauty of Jack didn't intimidate her in the slightest; he was just a guy whose preferred beverage was milk. Impulsively, Martha dipped her finger into a tub of yogurt and drew a white line across the bridge of her nose, Adam Ant-style. She turned to Jack and yelled, "Stand and deliver!" She couldn't remember the words of this old Adam Ant song, so she la-la-laed the melody, almost in tune.

This time, Jack's smile cracked across his entire face and lit his eyes. It was possibly the biggest smile of the many that he had flashed all night. He looked around the kitchen and, as if by magic (and Martha would always believe it really was by magic), he located the mask from Mathew's Batman costume and put it on.

"Hey, you're a dandy highwayman," said Martha.

Jack started singing. Naturally, he did know the words. He bounced around the kitchen, making his thumbs and forefingers into guns. He blew on the tip of the finger on his right hand.

Martha joined in where she could. "Isn't the next line something about spending cash and looking good?"

" 'Looking flash,' " sang Jack excitedly.

"Yes, that must be right, it rhymes. Then isn't it about grabbing attention?" added Martha.

"You've got that, Babe." And it should have sounded like a line, but it didn't.

Their kisses worked. Some people can kiss; others—and this is the shocker—can't. It's a gift. Martha could. Jack could. They could together. It worked. They kissed forever. He kissed her lips and her jaw, her cheeks, her eyelids, her ears, her neck. He really seemed to be enjoying kissing her. He didn't seem to have any concept of time and just meandered. There was no sense that he wanted to move on to the next stage, which was lucky because Martha wasn't sure how you moved on to the next stage.

Not exactly.

She couldn't quite remember.

Well, it was a long time ago.

She tried not to think about it. Chances were, Jack had a fair idea. His kisses varied in intensity, rushing from romance to raunch and back again, leaving her head spinning.

And, err, her knickers.

God, what type of knickers was she wearing? It was quite possible that they were Mothercare maternity-wear ones. She'd never got round to throwing them out and white cotton was, after all, the ultimate in comfort. Although not necessarily great in the seduction stakes.

Although, arguably, by the time they got to the knickers stage, Jack was unlikely to back out.

All the time he was kissing her he stroked her, as though he

knew that he had to wipe away her loneliness. With each caress
he carefully eased the isolation out of her body and the desola-
tion from her mind. His touch repaired her, comforted her and
soon—for brief seconds at a time—when Martha forgot to
worry, his touch excited her. He expertly eased her from one position to the next, leaving her feeling tiny and doll-like, whilst
making him appear powerful; the cliché made her want to sing
and skip and dance. He touched her ribs and set them on fire.
He traced his thumb across her hip bone towards the zip of her
jeans and she arched her back, silently willing him to tug the zip
down.

My God, did she really intend to go through with this?

He dragged his T-shirt over his head in one, swift, practised
move. His torso was gorgeous, stunning. She'd never seen anything like it, not in real life, not on any of her friends' dates, not
on any stranger passing in the street, not even on adverts. He had
broad shoulders, golden skin, defined abs, not a blemish. He had
a small tattoo in the centre of his back. It looked fantastic.
Martha hadn't realized that she was the type of woman to be so
turned on by physical beauty.

Too right she was going through with this.

Hell, she'd always fancied men because of their brains, not
brawn. Then again, the evening she'd spent with Jack suggested
she could benefit from both attributes. Was that possible? Was
that fair? For Jack to exist, did it mean that there was someone
hideously ugly and damned stupid trying (but failing) to pull in
All Bar One tonight? Probably, maybe even more than one. Bugger fair.

She couldn't remember at which point he edged her trousers
down, inch by inch, but certainly not before time. She was lying
on the carpet in the living room, that much she could remember.
It might have been the fact that she was lying on a carpet in the
living room and trying not to make too much noise so as not to

wake Eliza and the children, but Martha felt exactly as she'd felt in her late teens when she'd fooled around in silence with her boyfriend on her parents' couch, conscious that even one over-enthusiastic groan would excite their unwanted attention.

His cool fingers wandered towards her freckled shoulders and traced a line from one freckle to the next, as though he were play-ing a game of dot-to-dot. In a rapid, almost unperceivable, ma-noeuvre he removed the shirt that was clinging to her wrists and unfastened and removed her bra. He cupped her breast. He seemed to anticipate where she would like to be touched next and the pressure she'd like him to apply. Groaning quietly, mov-ing slowly, so slowly, as though he had all the time in the world to spend on her, his cool fingertips teased and plucked her ner-vous system into overdrive.

They'd never be breasts again. Martha had tits. Sexy, desir-able, pleasing tits. She felt wanted, almost hunted. Thrilled and thrilling.

He lowered her back on to the carpet.

And back into herself.

They rode hard and fast and long and slow. The sweat ran down Martha's back and slipped between her buttocks, making her skin appear sparkling and precious. He sucked, stroked and eventually stabbed with the precision to leave her breathless, speechless, helpless, hopeful. She felt him consume every ridge. His big and beautiful cock had taken ownership; she came again and again and again. With each wave of cum that spilt between her legs, her history was wiped away. His kisses burnt her lips, like acid removing fingerprints. She had been no one before him.

She could smell her own sex. It smelt fantastic. Fabulous. Her legs were longer, her tits were more pert, her waist was smaller. He felt like chances, and dreams, and possibility. It was supposed to feel odd. That's what she had expected, after years of making love with one man, a new man should feel odd.

But it didn't.

It felt like his clean, neat, smooth, hard body had been built solely to pleasure her clean, neat, smooth, hard body. She felt as though she had been constructed, actually created, to accommodate him. Hold him. Encompass him.

Everything went white and then black.

She thought she'd opened her eyes but she wasn't sure, she couldn't see anything clearly. Slowly her vision began to sharpen and she was faced with his half-closed eyes. He smiled nervously: had he done OK? Was she happy? Did she feel like he did? Did he feel like she did? She stared at him, studying everything, even the delicate, almost transparent skin of his eyelids. The exact texture of his firm, solid lips. She wanted to remember it, consume it, eat it all up, she wanted to be it. She wanted to get so close as to be under his skin, she wanted to be his skin.

They lay in the dark sitting room, lit only by the street light that flooded in through the window. Martha nuzzled into his shoulder, smudging her existence into his. He pulled her a fraction closer still.

It was possible that he'd kissed every inch of her body and mind. He'd reached her. She realized she should have closed off. She should have been more cautious. Every sensible bone in her body was screaming out for reserve, discretion, wariness, watchfulness. But Martha plunged. Dived. Fell. Disregarding any prudence that ought to be employed.

She'd been kicked when she was down, but now she had hope.

She'd loved and she'd lost, but she still believed.

# 26

"So let me get this straight," demanded Eliza. "All night?"

"Yup."

"I don't believe you."

"I've never believed it when I've heard people going on about it, but it's true."

"So numbers then, give me numbers."

"Four."

"So now you're in love with him, right?"

"Ha ha, I never said that." Martha was no longer sure what being in love was; but she thought it was safest to change the subject. "He's got great eyebrows."

"Eyebrows." Eliza was stunned. "God, he must be evil-looking if you have to resort to complimenting his eyebrows."

Martha smiled and hummed to herself. "Actually the reverse. He's soooooo perfect that even his eyebrows are perfect. They look like he visits Amy every week." Amy was their marvellous beautician; both women knew the extent of Martha's compliment. "You know when you see someone famous on the street? Someone from your favourite soap opera you've always had a bit of a crush on?"

"Yeah."

"And they're always a disappointment. You're struck by how short they are, or their bad skin."

"Yes."

"Well, he wasn't disappointing. He was even more delicious than I'd remembered. His eyelashes are so long, they rest on his cheekbones. His cheekbones are chiselled. His skin is iridescent. He has heroic stubble. You know what, Eliza, he looks like the type of man you imagine would be a gladiator. He even looks good when he's had no sleep." Eliza raised one of her own eyebrows in a way that clearly communicated more than a little scepticism mixed with a healthy dose of irritation. Martha realized she hadn't done such a fantastic job of changing the subject.

"Martha, girlfriend, you are in lust."

The debrief was taking place the next day, in the sitting room. The two women were putting up the Christmas tree. Their hope was to finish this task before Mathew returned home from playschool and before Maisie woke up from her afternoon nap. They were at the stage where they had retrieved the huge box of decorations from the loft, and had managed to stand the tree in its pot and it was—more or less—vertical. They had even done the insufferably boring bit of testing the fairy lights. Only to discover that, naturally, as was always the case, lights that had been in perfect working order when put away at the end of the previous Christmas no longer flashed or fluttered. They were as dead as a string of dodos could be; no amount of tightening bulbs could resuscitate them. Martha had given up on them and been out to buy a new box. As she had bought them from her local artsy-craftsy shop, she had paid way over the odds. Still, they were beautiful. Martha thought, What the hell, she was having fun and she was very touched that Eliza had taken an afternoon's holiday to help her put up the tree.

Eliza had decided to spend some of her scant and precious holiday allowance to help Martha with this task as she was sure that it would be a terrible emotional ordeal for Martha to tackle on her own: surely every single bauble was imbued with history and memories.

"Throw that awful star in the bin. I'm having a fairy guarding my Christmas tree this year," instructed Martha.

"What?"

"Well, it's certainly past its prime. Look, the glitter is coming off on your hands."

"That's the point," argued Eliza, shocked. "That's the point of Christmas decorations, they're meant to be past their prime."

"I've never had you down as overly syrupy," commented Martha. "No, throw it out, and that tinsel, and all those Santas that are missing their beards."

"Your tree will be bare."

"No. I'll buy new."

Eliza felt grumpy. She wasn't expecting this from Martha, not at all. Shouldn't she be more distracted? More sentimental? Shouldn't she be just a smidgen more nostalgic? Not that Eliza wanted Martha to mourn Michael any longer, but surely this Jack character couldn't have blown Michael so entirely and cleanly out of the picture, could he? Martha was so naïve, Eliza fumed. She had no idea. Of course this Jack bloke had left Martha feeling wonderful; he was well practised; he was bound to be an orgasm generator. He'd probably left dozens of women feeling wonderful in his time. Poor Martha. How was it possible to be such an unapologetic romantic in this day and age?

Eliza decided it was right to inject some caution into Martha's fledgling relationship. "So let me get this 'naked friends' thing right. He has a number of friends, and I say this holding the first two fingers on each hand in the air, and making wanky speech marks around the word 'friends.'" Martha sighed; Eliza ignored her and carried on. "He has a number of 'friends' with whom he sleeps, but they're not girlfriends."

"Yes."

"But he takes them out for meals, to the cinema, to bars, he sees them regularly."

"Yes."

"So why aren't they girlfriends?"

"He says a girlfriend is a person you argue with in supermarkets."

"How romantic. That's fucking inspired. God, these blokes have some nerve. I hope you told him to piss off." Eliza was squeezing a plastic beardless Santa. The pressure became too much for him to bear and his head caved in under her thumb. It was clear she was imagining it was Jack's face. Or maybe Michael's. Or maybe Tarquin's, Piers's, Charlie's or Sebastian's. Or maybe they were all on her list.

"Not exactly," confessed Martha taking the broken beardless Santa away from Eliza and dropping the remnants into the bin. She made a mental note to buy Eliza a stress ball for her desk at work. She wasn't nearly as chilled since she and Greg split up; Greg had been such a great influence.

"How 'not exactly'?" demanded Eliza.

"So he doesn't want an exclusive relationship, it's no big deal," shrugged Martha.

"It is, Martha. You're not up to this."

"How do you know?" Martha concentrated on finding the exact place to hang a wooden robin.

"You're not the type to handle this, you're a serial monogamist."

"It suits me right now. I don't want to walk straight into another relationship myself. Besides, I can do the naked friends thing with other men too."

Eliza nearly choked and only stopped herself through an amazing act of will. It would be awful to choke to death before she'd had the chance to splutter, "Who? I've been trying to get naked for weeks now and it's virtually impossible in the circles you mix in. The men in your Filofax would rather take a girl out for tea than take her sexually."

Martha stooped down to pick up another ornament. She chose a toy soldier with a ramrod posture. "Leave me alone, Eliza."

But Eliza couldn't. "Martha, it won't work. Will you stop that bloody humming," she demanded, becoming increasingly perturbed. "The thing is, this is typical of you. Cast your mind back. You always fall in love with the men you sleep with."

Martha stopped humming for a second but only because a dazzling flashback had just prised its way into her consciousness: the moment when Jack's fabulous cock had eased its way into her hot, expectant body. He'd held her gaze throughout, as though casting a spell, and his eyes had bored into her mind with the same intensity as his cock drove into her body.

"Michael called last night," said Eliza.

"Did he?"

"Aren't you going to ask what he said?"

"What did he say?" asked Martha dutifully, but it was clear to Eliza that her mind was elsewhere. Eliza briefly considered the possibility that Martha had tried drugs for the first time. Then dismissed it. But there had to be some explanation above and beyond this chancer's sexual expertise, didn't there?

"He said he wants to talk to you about dividing furniture," Eliza reported.

"How very seasonal of him," muttered Martha, before returning to the topic of conversation that really interested her. "Jack asked me what I was thinking. Afterwards, when we were just lying together."

"I don't believe you. No man has ever asked a woman what she's thinking. They don't care. You've made that up."

"No, honestly, he really did ask me."

Eliza was incredulous, but because she was talking to Martha—who didn't tell lies—she decided to take her word. "So, what were you thinking?"

"I don't know," said Martha, "it hardly matters."

"No, I suppose not."

Both women fell silent and concentrated on the tree for a little while. As Eliza carefully lowered a plastic dove of peace on to one of the prickly branches she said, "Martha, there's something you should know. Every woman who has dated a womanizer has the same fantasy."

"Really? And what would that be?"

"To be the one that makes the cute bastard settle down."

"Really?"

"Yes. And do you know what?"

"No, what?"

"No woman has ever succeeded."

"Really?"

"I suppose he told you he'd phone."

"Yes, he did."

"Well, he won't."

"He already has." Eliza tried not to show her surprise and Martha tried not to show her glee. "He's coming round tonight."

"This is a rebound thing."

"Who cares if I'm bouncing?"

"You're making a mistake," warned Eliza.

"Well, at least they are *new* mistakes," countered Martha.

# 27

Eliza felt rotten, as was the usual state of affairs for her throughout December. Her days were merging into a shambolic haze of parties and long lunches and the obligatory accompanying hangovers. All her promises to be more mature this year in her approach to the season of goodwill had flown out of the window. If anything, she had accepted more invites than in previous years. It wasn't as though she had anywhere better to go. It was no fun staying in at Martha's any more, and she didn't have a home of her own.

Eliza felt angry. She wasn't exactly sure who or what her anger was directed at; there were a number of possible suspects. Moving from the micro to the macro. She was angry at Fred and Ella, with whom she had spent most of last night propping up the bar at the Atlantic. Why had Fred suggested that third round of tequilas? And why hadn't either of them suggested buying any food to line their stomachs? It was hardly responsible to keep buying bottles of Chardonnay just because the previous bottle had run out. OK, she'd had a laugh at the time and Ella had spooned her into a cab. To be fair, she'd also called this morning to check Eliza was still in one piece (she could just about answer in the affirmative), but that still didn't make up for the irresponsible behaviour last night.

Besides all of this, Eliza was heartily fed up with the Christmas shoppers. Why had they left it until December 22nd to do their entire Christmas shop for every single one of their friends and family and colleagues and acquaintances? Obviously she herself had had no choice, she'd been so very busy at the various parties, receptions, lunches and dinners that the media industry swamped this time of year with. Oh God, she felt far too hungover to try to tackle this seriously.

Eliza was also a bit fed up with Martha at the moment. It simply wasn't the same staying with her since she'd met this Jack Hope. Martha was never free for girly chats any more. Well, admittedly, she would ask if such and such a pair of trousers looked good with such and such a top, and she might want to talk about new tunes, but she didn't seem to need Eliza in the same way as she had back in the early autumn. Eliza was no longer called upon to hand out tissues, dab eyes and soothe hearts, although Martha now asked her to babysit with indecent regularity. And the other day she'd dashed into Eliza's room and asked if Eliza had a spare condom. Bloody hell. To be honest, Eliza was finding it all a bit embarrassing. Knowing her older sister was having sex was only one step removed from knowing that her parents were. Horrible thought. Traumatic.

Speaking of her parents, Eliza was also fairly miffed with Mr. and Mrs. Evergreen. The fact was that it was patently clear that Martha was OK. She was getting more sex than a particularly randy adolescent bunny, and she'd never looked better in her life—her new shaggy crop really did suit her, as did the new clothes and jewellery. But were Mr. and Mrs. Evergreen convinced? They were not. They insisted on calling Martha every day to ask how she was. Martha went to great lengths to reassure them that she was "very happy," but they couldn't accept this. So they added insult to injury by ringing Eliza at work just so that she could confirm that Martha "really was OK and not trying to protect us. Because she's very considerate like that."

Bloody hell, what about Eliza? No one asked if she was OK. She wasn't getting stacks of sex; in fact she wasn't getting any sex. She wasn't blowing a small fortune on clothes every single Saturday. Her hair wasn't growing into an oh-so-wonderful-suits-you-why-didn't-you-always-wear-it-like-that style. In fact the reverse was true. Whilst Martha was experimenting with a wilder, unbridled look, Eliza was battling to tame her feral locks. She'd rashly had her hair cut into a severe crop. It was supposed to draw attention to her elfin features, but she looked as though she'd just done a six-month stint in Holloway. It didn't work and she wanted to cry every time she looked in the mirror.

Just because she'd left Greg, it didn't follow that she was over him. They were together for four years, after all. And they may not have been married but they were as good as. To all intents and purposes he was the first proper love of her life. And if the men she had dated since were a representative selection—and she feared they were—there was a serious possibility that he would be the only love of her life.

"Hello."

"Hello."

There he was. Just standing at the checkout in Boots, buying shaving cream as though that was a normal thing to do. But it wasn't normal. Not when him standing there stole her breath away; her lungs collapsed as though they were deflating balloons. Eliza had been on eight dinner dates and six lunches. She'd visited the cinema four times, she'd seen three concerts, she'd been bowling twice, and she'd even played a game of squash; not one of the eligible men that Martha had introduced her to had caused a fanfare to explode in her heart, or even done as much as put a swing in her step. She was not passionate about any of them.

And she was putting on weight.

"Wow, Greg." She leaned in to hug him because it was more natural to touch him than not to. Greg looked and smelt and felt familiar, yet strange. Familiar, like home. Strange, like a beautiful new piece of furniture in the home.

"How are you?" He smiled his signature big, sloppy, relaxed smile. "You look different."

"Oh yeah, the hair." Eliza's hand shot up to finger what was left of her hair. Did it make her look more grown up?

"New coat?"

"Yeah, erm, do you think it says young thrusting executive?"

"Not really, Liza. It says—now, look, don't be offended, but did your mum help you pick it out?"

Eliza laughed and nodded her head.

"So besides the terrible haircut and awful fashion faux pas, how are you?"

She should have been offended but she wasn't. "Fine. Fine. Cool, cool, really good, cool," she twittered. He smiled again and his smile massaged her shoulders.

"Well, that's good."

"And you?" she asked.

"Not too bad, you know?"

No, she didn't know. What did that mean? Was he missing her? Was he heartbroken? Was he indifferent? Was he shacked up with a six-foot-two, size-eight nymphomaniac and her willing best friend?

Why did she care?

"The tour, was it . . . ?"

"A hoot, yeah. A real laugh. Back to the real world now, though."

"The real world? Selling hats?" Eliza sniggered. She sounded unkind, which had not been her intention; she'd wanted to sound amusing.

Greg shrugged. "I like it."

Eliza felt chastised and just wanted to leave. Her reaction to uncomfortable situations was always to leave. How many of the men she'd dated so far had said they liked their work? None of them. The most positive thing she'd heard them say was that "it paid well," or that it was "a way of keeping busy."

Eliza would have made her excuses and run away but Greg asked, "How's Martha?"

"Oh, you know."

"Yes, I do."

"She's great."

Greg looked puzzled. "I've called her a couple of times just to see if there's anything I can help out on."

"Yeah, she mentioned it, but there's no need to worry, Martha's great. Really good, she's shagging and it suits her." Once again Eliza wanted to kick herself—why did she say such stupid things? "I've missed you." Like that, for instance, that was a stupid thing to say.

Because it could only lead to:

"I've missed you too."

And what do you say to that? Eliza looked at the pile of Boots carrier bags that had been customized especially for the season of goodwill. They wished her "a Happy Christmas and a Peaceful New Year." These didn't seem like even remote possibilities.

"How are the Bianchis?"

"They miss you too."

"I miss them."

God, this was a stupid conversation. Why was she rooted to the spot? Why didn't she just turn and walk away?

Why didn't he just kiss her? He hadn't looked away from her for a second, and although she was bouncing her eyes around the store as though she had a particularly dreadful astigmatism, looking to the floor, the ceiling, the make-up counter—anywhere but at Greg—still he managed to more or less hold her gaze. At least it was a valiant attempt.

"Don't you miss it, Liza?"

"What?"

"It. Us. The things we used to do." Eliza immediately assumed he meant the things they used to do in bed and so was surprised when he said, "Things like send silly postcards to each other."

"Forget birthdays," she added snidely.

"Wear nothing but each other's sweat."

"Forget to pay credit-card bills."

"Feed each other with our fingers; use each other's bodies as plates."

"Do the weekly shop at Cullen's, instead of a supermarket, which would have been eminently more sensible."

"Oh sensible, yeah." He smiled to himself and Eliza knew without him having to say it that it wasn't as though either of them was particularly famed for their ability to be sensible. "Read by candlelight," he added.

"Let wax melt into the carpet," she countered.

But she sounded angrier than she was.

Greg gave up. "I better get going, I've still got loads of shopping to do. I s'pose, as you're really sensible now, you did all yours in November."

"Absolutely," lied Eliza. She was wearing mittens, which was lucky because she could cross her fingers without him seeing; she was superstitious about telling lies without crossing her fingers. That seemed *really* dishonest.

"Right well, err, have a nice Christmas then."

"Yeah, and you."

Greg leaned in to kiss Eliza. Was he planning to kiss her cheek or her lips? She moved her head swiftly to remove any doubt. She thought that the disappointment might incite spontaneous tears if her cheek were his target. That had to be the hangover, didn't it? That's why she felt so overly emotional. The kiss landed on her ear lobe. It lasted about a nano-second and was the most erotic kiss Eliza had received in three months. Greg whispered into her ear, "You can change your clothes and your hair, Eliza, but you can't change your heart."

Eliza sprung away. "You can change your mind," she asserted.

"Yes, but not your heart." He turned and slipped back into the crowds of Christmas shoppers.

Eliza watched him disappear. Greg was a man and therefore wouldn't give a rat's arse if someone noticed his new haircut, but . . . He paused, turned round and shouted, "By the way, Liza, the hair, I think it's cute."

Yessssssssss!

Bugger.

# 28

Martha spent her December doing exactly what she did every December. She bought Christmas cards and posted them way in advance of the deadline, as recommended by her Majesty's postal service. She shoved her way through crowds of frantic shoppers with long lists and little time. She chose thoughtful gifts for her family and friends. She wrapped them in an extravagant number of sheets of tissue paper and attached a ridiculous amount of bows and ribbons. She threw a party for the children and their friends. She bought a turkey, baked a cake and made a pudding. She went to the carol service at Westminster Abbey. She made Mathew an innkeeper's costume for his nativity play. She hung stockings.

Keeping busy in this way made her life bearable.

The only differences between this December and every previous December of Martha's life were that this year she fought a great deal with Michael (because being elegant, charitable and generous was proving to be quite difficult in practice), and she had lots and lots of sex with Jack (because being desirable, cute and fascinating was proving to be a doddle).

She fought with Michael because he turned down Martha's offer to spend Christmas Day with them. Whilst Martha was accepting of Michael's rejection of her, she was still reeling from the shock of his being able to walk away from their children. Didn't he want to see their faces as they destroyed her handiwork of paper and ribbons? They fought because Michael wanted to take some of *her* Christmas decorations to decorate *his* flat. They fought because he bought her an extremely expensive gift for

Christmas, when normally they gave each other tiny tokens. What was the meaning of the gift? Was he paying her off? Was it reconciliatory? He said not. Was it to salve his conscience? They fought because he said he was enjoying the season and Martha thought that was demonic.

The horrible tinny renditions of "Rudolf the Red-Nosed Reindeer" that were pumped out in every department store depressed her. The angelic voices and faces of the children's choir in Westminster Abbey failed to lift her. She received a number of cards still addressed to her and Michael, as many of their friends didn't even know that they were divorcing, and this embarrassed her. All of the cards wished Martha "a Merry Christmas and a Happy New Year," as was traditional; it just seemed spiteful.

They didn't fight about Jack. Martha called Michael and told him about Jack. Her motives for doing so were complicated. She told Eliza that she wanted to be honest and straightforward; she wasn't one for skulking. After all, Michael had said he didn't want her. He'd told her she was free to do as she pleased. But a little bit of Martha—just a tiny bit—was sure that Michael would find the reality of her dating different to the theory. Martha didn't reveal to Eliza her more ignoble motives for her call—that she wanted him to be jealous. Michael was not in the slightest bit concerned that she'd met someone so quickly; in fact, his response was one of relief and encouragement.

Martha had found that particularly insulting.

Throughout December Martha continued to look after her children and, naturally, she did an admirable job, better than admirable. She read to them, played with them, dressed them, taught them, guarded them. She cooked and cleaned and entertained. These things ensured her life was meaningful. But it was only when she was with Jack that Martha relaxed. Her life was bearable, even meaningful, without Jack, but with him it was pleasurable too. There was joy in her day if he texted, or rang, or, best yet, visited. Jack was the excitement. He was the bit that was about her. And if there were half a dozen other women thinking the same thing about him, well, that was a risk Martha would have to take. She needed him.

They had a great deal of sex.

They had great sex—that was the deal.

Martha hoped that somehow his beautiful cock would plug her enough to stop her optimism leaking away. She felt lonely a lot of the time, but when she was with him she felt a lot less lonely, and when they made love she felt nothing but wonderful. It was a relief.

"Is this just about lust?" Eliza demanded.

"Lust and fun," twinkled Martha, giggling.

Eliza wasn't sure if Martha was making the distinction. She was acting like a porn star. She was wearing clingy tops and low-cut or see-through shirts. OK, they were the same sort of stuff that Eliza and all her mates wore, and OK, admittedly, they didn't look too whorish because Martha was as lacking in the cleavage department as Eliza was, but it still made Eliza uncomfortable. Besides which, Martha kept talking about sex. "Have you ever taken photos?" "Have you ever made a film?" Jesus, Eliza was beginning to feel prudish.

"Tell me about the fun," Eliza asked sceptically. She'd heard more than enough details on the lust and wasn't sure if she could stomach much more before she imploded with jealousy.

"We've watched some great movies on DVD." *Naked.* They watched films naked, films that Martha had never even heard of. The best bit was that they ate popcorn off each other's bodies. This from a woman who used to lock the bathroom door when she took a shower and used to sleep in pyjamas. Now all she slept in was sweat. "At night he lulls me to sleep reciting Spike Milligan's 'Silly Old Baboon.' Do you remember? We read it as children."

"Yes, I remember it," Eliza said impatiently.

Jack usually recited Spike after he'd shagged Martha's brains out, at least twice, but Martha sensed Eliza's unwillingness to hear that type of detail.

"I've played video games with him." Martha now knew what a console was and whilst it was unlikely that she'd ever remember the name of the speedy, spiky hedgehog, let alone help him save the world, she had played Rez, which was as near as she'd ever get to going to a trippy, ravey gig. They'd been naked for that too. But again, Martha thought this was a fact best kept to herself. "We put a bet on it being a white Christmas, in a betting shop. Have you ever been in a betting shop?" They'd been dressed that time; after all, it was December.

"What's so special about Jack?" demanded Eliza.

"Haven't I told you?"

"No. Well, you mentioned that you turn to goo when you think of him, he has a large and expert penis, he kisses a lot, and it's convenient that he works in Holland Park. Oh yeah, you said he dresses well and it's good news that he doesn't drink because he can give you lifts home, but no, beyond that I'm not sure if I know anything about him."

"How odd of me," said Martha. She was genuinely surprised. "Well, where to start? He's a fantastic friend. Nothing is too much trouble for his mates. He's never, ever been unfaithful. Not even kissed anyone else when he's had a girlfriend."

"That's rare."

"Rare? I thought it was extinct until I met Jack."

"But, he does have this naked-friends thing going on, so he has a free pass when he hasn't got a steady girlfriend."

Martha chose to ignore the interruption. "He had a less than easy upbringing. He could have ended up tough and cruel, he could have been a crook, but he took a more honourable path. He's worked for everything he has; nothing's been handed to him by adoring and rich parents. The only thing his parents could bequeath him was examples of right and wrong, which his father and mother personify respectively. He left school at sixteen, but he's doing the same job as friends of mine who are Oxbridge graduates. He sold fruit and veg when he was a teenager to save up for a bike. He loves his cats, and he plays with my children with a tenderness that could split my heart. He's special because when he walks into a room he holds his head up high and he has every right to do so."

"It's pitiful, Martha, that you don't see; there has to be a catch."

"It's pitiful that you never see anything other."

"It just seems very quick to me."

"I realize what it looks like from the outside. But I don't care. I don't care what anyone thinks." Martha hadn't realized this was the case until she said so, but having said it, she was sure.

"Look, you're scaring me. One moment you're a Stepford wife, and the next you could be teaching Pammie A a thing or two about bedroom tricks. I'm not saying you suited being a Stepford wife—you didn't—but you're not behaving like yourself at all. I think you're in shock."

Martha turned to Eliza and slowly said, "I feel like I am being more myself than ever before."

Eliza was disconcerted that such a little voice and little sentence could hold such force and conviction. She made a mental note to look up Post-Traumatic Stress on the web. Maybe Martha was suffering from that. "What about his other naked friends?" she asked desperately. "Does he ever talk about them?"

"I never ask."

Jack didn't tell lies to Martha. Sometimes she wished he could lie to her, it would be much easier. She'd once made the mistake of asking him if he'd slept with a friend of his. She'd liked the girl until she heard his reply, which was yes. Jack had kissed Martha as he told her the truth, and Martha couldn't work out if the kiss was to silence her or comfort her. It did both. Jack had pulled Martha to her feet and then picked her up in the way that you carry a bride over a threshold. He rocked her to and fro. Martha had closed her eyes and held her tongue. Maybe they could get over the threshold. If she didn't ask too many questions. If she didn't demand too many replies.

"It's simple, Eliza. It's straightforward. We're having fun and the way I see it, we can continue to have fun indefinitely. There's no reason why not." Martha was parroting the conversation she'd had with Jack the night before; in fact it had been Jack who'd suggested that they have fun indefinitely.

Martha had asked, "Is indefinitely the same as forever?"

And he'd replied, "Maybe, Baby."

The "maybe not" had been left unspoken.

They had lots of fun, and Martha reminded herself that this was probably because neither of them wanted to fall in love. Sometimes Martha thought she might want that. She'd try to imagine what it would be like if she could magically fast-forward her life to a point where he asked her to marry him, and they would all live happily ever after; it would be a neater life. Then she'd remember it didn't make any difference. Marriage wasn't a guarantee. Husbands could still up and off. The bit of paper that she'd always believed was an unrepeatable lifelong commitment—the only available magic in a secular world driven by technology, profitability and bottom lines—was, after all, a bit of paper. How do you trust in this century? The century of mobile-phone theft and Internet porn? How do you believe that there is someone out there who transcends all that is mechanical, all that is diabolical, all that is robotic, and is love?

Martha knew there weren't any guarantees, just lots of get-out clauses. Naked friends was just one. Forever was a long time; maybe indefinitely was a good offer. Indefinite fun. It sounded OK. Why over-complicate it?

Martha held her arms wide open and Maisie stumbled from her aunt towards her mother, one unsure foot in front of the other.

"That's a girl. Steady as you go," Martha encouraged Maisie. "Look up, not down."

Maisie and Martha were both learning to walk. One foot in front of the other. One day at a time, there was no other way. It was best not to think about anything else other than the here-and-now. Martha just had to concentrate on being happy.

It was because of Jack that Martha noticed posters on the Tube advertising new bands or restaurants. She read new books and talked about them. She even re-read her old favourites, which meant that she never had time to hoover in the cupboard under the stairs any more. Because Jack was in her life she found the courage to visit stores that she'd never even dared look in the window of, and they turned out to be anything other than horrible. The girls in Miss Sixty seemed to think that she was entitled to try on the funky "distressed" jeans. In fact, they envied Martha's size 26 waist and asked her which diet she followed. She told them the cabbage soup one; she thought it would sound churlish to say the deserted-wife diet. In Diesel, the male assistants positively flirted with her—well, at least the straight ones did—and she smiled back in a sort of flirtatious way. No one seemed to think Martha's status as a mother and soon-to-be-ex-wife disqualified her from looking cool. In fact, when she did say the children were hers the response was always amazement. "Really, I thought you were their aunt or nanny or something," followed by admiration: "Wow, how did you get your figure back?"

And Martha knew they were sales assistants, paid to flatter and make her feel good so that she'd whip out her plastic. They probably worked on commission, but still it was nice. The snobby sales assistants in the designer sections of the large department stores had never made her feel good.

Since Michael's departure, Martha had skipped her monthly hair appointment; sometimes it had been all she could do to get dressed in the morning, and the level of commitment necessary for grooming—visits to the beautician, hair appointments and the like—was beyond Martha's resources. But just before Christmas she decided that she did need to do something about her hair. When she mentioned, just in passing to Jack, that she was going to the hairdresser's, he asked, "What are you having done?"

"Oh, probably the usual, a trim. I've worn my hair this way—well, a bit neater and shorter than this but more or less this way—for ages now. Forever actually. I am thinking of growing it." Martha hadn't realized she was thinking of growing it until she heard herself say so.

"Cool," smiled Jack, "you'd suit it shaggy and a bit messier. Then again, I bet you'd look gorgeous however you wore your hair." Then he kissed her, and then they had sex on the kitchen table.

The kitchen table!

Martha contemplated that the most fun she'd had on the kitchen table in the past was making the invites for Maisie's party. There was no competition.

Jack always wanted to know what she'd bought in the shops that day, what she and the kids had for lunch. He asked her what her plans were for the weekend, what she'd bought as Christmas presents for her parents. He asked her what he should read, whether she liked the Fun Lovin' Criminals CD, their second album, *100% Colombian*. He assumed she'd have a viewpoint, and she was surprised to find that she did. He was the only person she knew who didn't think of her as Michael's, which somehow (and she couldn't explain this either) allowed her to talk about anything from the mystery of why there was an increase in peanut allergies (Martha and Jack agreed that they hadn't known anyone with a peanut allergy when they were at school), to whether she thought it would be erotic to wear a blindfold during sex (yeah, probably, just the once, just to try). The sheets they loved on soaked up her pain and past like blotting paper.

And whilst they talked about everything, Eliza warned Martha not to talk to Jack about her relationship with Michael. She said he'd tire of it. And Martha did try to keep that sad, messy side of her life quite separate from the fun, indulgent bit. She didn't want to pollute the fairytale world they were constructing, but it was hard not to talk about it after, say, she'd just had a conversation with Michael that went along the lines:

"We need to talk about money, Martha."

"Oh." Martha rarely thought about money.

"Yes. As you know, I'm renting and that's certainly not cheap." Whose fault was that? "And this place is far too big for just the three of you."

"There's four of us including Eliza."

"Well, Eliza isn't a permanent fixture, is she?" Who was? "We have to put the house on the market."

Martha called Jack, and he told her that he'd had a dream about Kylie the night before, and at the critical moment of penetration, Kylie had turned into Martha.

It cheered her up.

"Don't worry about him, Little Miss E. He's the same old show."

"That's a song title—Basement Jaxx." Martha grinned; she was getting the hang of this, she had the measure of him.

"No, it was me. I meant it for real."

And Martha would call Jack if she'd completed all the tasks on her day's list and was lapsing into grim feelings of purposelessness because she was reminded of how her role as a wife had been wiped away. If, like at Mathew's playschool nativity play, she ached with loneliness and an unbearable, overwhelming feeling of emptiness because Mathew was the only one there without a daddy and Martha the only one there without a husband, she would ring up Jack.

"God, life sucks, doesn't it? 'Your father was a hamster, your mother stinks of elderberries,'" said Jack.

"Sorry?"

"Monty Python, Babe, don't you recognize it?"

"What have the Romans ever done for us?" giggled Martha, and for a moment she forgot that her life had veered away from her plan. For a moment she just enjoyed herself.

"The roads, the sanitation," replied Jack, and then he suggested all sorts of other roles Martha could play besides housewife: nurse, schoolgirl, straightforward tart.

He wanted her. He lusted after her. She made him laugh. He thought she was sexy. He thought she was clever. He thought she was interesting. And if he thought it, this beautiful, intelligent Sex God, then maybe, just maybe, it might be true.

He always called when he said he would, which was often several times a day. He always visited when he said he would, which was frequently, and he'd arrive bearing dinner, instead of expecting Martha to cook for him. It was the party season so it was nearly impossible to secure a babysitter, but Jack didn't seem to mind. He didn't think staying in with Martha was boring. He didn't rush to do other jobs, to call friends, to go on line, he didn't read trade journals and ignore her. At first Martha found these stretches of time that they spent together—doing, well, nothing really, nothing very constructive—intimidating. She wanted to dash about the kitchen and bake cakes, or wrap Christmas presents or clean cupboards. She liked doing things that proved, categorically, that she was useful, purposeful. But Jack seemed happy just hanging, as he called it. Chatting, laughing, telling stories, just being. Sometimes, if they were feeling

really energetic, she might get out an old photo album and entertain him with photos of herself at college.

"You haven't changed at all, have you?" He smiled.

Martha looked at the photo that Jack was holding. A slim giggling girl beamed back at her. The girl was wearing a clingy white
T-shirt and a pair of ripped and faded jeans, she was sporting
huge hoop earrings, which had been fashionable in the early
nineties, she wasn't wearing socks, just trainers. The girl was in a
bar with a group of friends. Martha knew when the photograph
had been taken: just minutes after she'd finished the last exam in
her finals. That girl believed all of life's tests were over; that's why
she was giggling with such confidence and abandon.

Little did she know that her life was going to be a series of
tests. And that she'd fail the biggest one before she was even
thirty-three. Martha hadn't been able to hold her marriage together despite trying so hard, despite wanting it so much. Martha
felt a huge wave of nausea wash over her body. She felt like she'd
let down the girl in the photo. Her life was a catastrophe, she'd
flunked.

As though Jack were reading her mind, he carefully repeated,
"You haven't changed at all, have you? You look just like you did
then."

Martha was wearing jeans and T-shirt. She wasn't wearing any
socks or shoes but her nails were beautifully manicured with a
deep scarlet polish. She did look a bit like the girl in the photograph. "Do I ever look that carefree? That optimistic?" she asked
him. She knew he'd tell her the truth. They'd promised never to
tell each other any lies. Martha believed in Jack's honesty not
least because he said honesty made his life easier and he was a big
fan of easy lives.

"Yeah, Little Miss E., you're always laughing. You're one of the
smiliest people I've ever met. You're very chilled and, considering
what you're going through, I think you're amazing the way you're

managing to remain relaxed and relatively carefree. But there's only you who can say if you honestly feel optimistic. Do you?"

She paused and considered the question, and then answered carefully. "Sometimes."

She felt optimistic when he slid his hand under her top. His hands were huge and her body was slight so they wrapped all the way around her ribs. He started to kiss her, gently chewing and sucking and pulling on her lips. And then not so gently. Her body responded immediately, arching towards his. They were lying on the floor; they rarely sat on the sofa or chairs but preferred to loll about like teenagers. He pulled her closer, rolled on to his back and in one swift movement she was lying on top of him and then he pushed her body away so she was astride him. His hand was still flat on her ribs. He moved his thumb a fraction so it touched the curve of her breast. A bolt of excitement shot up from between her legs through her body, she grinned her encouragement, and leant in to try to kiss him again, but he held her at a distance, making them both wait. His hands started to move, they were everywhere, grabbing her arse, teasing her nipples, caressing her neck. She pulled her top off and sat facing him, half-naked.

"I love your fantastic pert tits, they are so sexy," he said as he leant in to suck them. And whilst Martha had never been a fan of her tiny boobs, suddenly she was proud of them. She looked down at her magenta nipples erect under his attention and had to agree: they were sexy, she was sexy. They slipped out of their clothes, neither of them paying much attention to who was undressing who; the important thing was to feel their skin against the other's as quickly as possible. He flung her about, but in a way that made her feel safe and protected, not abused or endangered. They ran their fingers and tongues over one another, hers along the shaft of his penis, over his balls, grabbing his buttocks. His hands were between her legs, inside, outside, inside again.

When their fingers couldn't touch enough of each other, couldn't cup, grasp, grab enough, they used the flat of their palms, then the soft underside of their forearms, then their whole bodies to rub up and down each other. Riding, writhing, climbing to breathtaking, awe-making, fan-fucking-tastic orgasms.

At times like those Martha felt optimistic.

# 29

Jack had asked Martha if she wanted to come out with him, Dave, Drew and Drew's girlfriend, Sara. They were going clubbing. Martha agreed before she'd had time to consider the implications of agreeing. She thought that was best. If she'd given it any real thought she'd have been so entirely over-whelmed with primal terror that she would most certainly have opted for another night in front of the TV watching repeats of *The Bill.*

A club.

With his friends.

For Martha, this was like telling an agoraphobic that a nice trip to the Sahara would be a fun experience. A club was a mine-field. A real club was much more risky than a tacky Salsa bar. Martha had a feeling that a bit of random hip-swaying would not be enough. And what if his friends didn't like her? That sort of thing could ruin a relationship. Jack was exceptionally open-minded and accepting; Martha was suddenly struck by a fear that he was in fact simply being charitable and that, after all, she was a geek, a freak. His friends would certainly notice this. How do people dance nowadays? Martha used to be quite a good dancer, for someone who was tone deaf. But that was a long time ago. In her day (and she was well aware that starting a sentence with the words "in my day" put her on a par with her grandmother, but *in her day*), it had been enough to blow a whistle and wave your hands in the air—in a way that was reminiscent of someone frantically trying to put out a chip-pan fire. It had worked. She wasn't sure if it would be adequate now. She asked Eliza, "Have you heard of a club called Fabric?"

"Oh yeah, it's v. cool."

Her comment hardly encouraged Martha. "Erm, what sort of music do they play?"

"It's a mixed bag. There are a number of different rooms all playing different tunes, house, hip-hop, breakbeats."

"Oh." Well, that's cleared that up.

"It's huge, it's really easy to get lost."

Martha might have to resort to that. Was it worth asking? "And—erm—what sort of clothes do people wear?"

"Anything goes."

Very helpful.

Martha assumed, even with her limited knowledge, that "anything" did not include a smart navy twin set or a nice pair of suede pumps. Martha looked in her wardrobe in disgust. She couldn't remember or even imagine how she'd ever found any of her old gear acceptable. And Jack had seen all the new stuff. What to wear?

Unfortunately, one of Jack's many qualities was that he was very prompt. He arrived when he said he would, which was about an hour before Martha was expecting him.

"Are you going in that? I'm not complaining, you look stunning."

Martha had answered the door in her underwear and she still had a towel wrapped around her wet hair.

"Very funny. Come in before I catch my death of cold or,

worse still, Mrs. Benton at number four calls the vice squad. She's very hot on Neighbourhood Watch. I can see her nets twitching already."

Jack laughed, as though he thought Martha really was funny.

"Actually, I don't know what to wear." Martha immediately regretted confessing this and wanted to rip out her own vocal chords. Such an admission exposed her as uncool, not very together.

However, Jack just smiled. "Naturally, you're a girl. Come on, show me the choices." Jack followed Martha upstairs and she punched the air because not only had he called her a girl (which was only insulting when you were one, once you were a woman you hankered after this politically incorrect endearment), but also he cared what she was going to wear.

Naturally, as Martha had been married for several years, she was very used to the process of getting ready in front of someone. It went like this. She would try on several nearly identical outfits (black, knee-length, cap-sleeved dresses if they were going out to dinner, or Gap jeans and crisp white shirts if they were going to the cinema). After trying on all the nearly identical outfits several times, Martha would naturally select the one she had tried on first. She'd look in the mirror and be happy with the choice.

For about ten seconds.

Then she would turn to Michael and expect him to bolster her flagging self-esteem.

"How do I look?" she'd tentatively ask.

"Nice," he'd reply, and sometimes he'd even look at her.

Martha was never convinced. If she looked nice she wouldn't have to ask.

Martha knew the routine so she was stunned when Jack actually flicked through the hangers in her wardrobe whilst saying things like "That's very sexy, have you tried that on?" or "You always look stunning in that one, and I love it when you wear it

with boots." He didn't mind that she tried on numerous combi-
nations and on more than one occasion made suggestions like
"Try that top on again but with the skirt." He said she looked
drop-dead gorgeous in the outfit they finally agreed on. Martha
was beginning to worry that Eliza was right after all; he was too
good to be true. Obviously he was gay.

But then he cupped her boob, kissed her neck and made
them late because they shagged each other senseless in front of
the mirror.

As they approached the club, Martha was instantly reminded of
the many reasons she'd given up clubbing. It was December, she
was scantily clad and there was a queue stretching all the way to
Newcastle. The bouncers were textbook. Huge, about six feet in
both directions, wearing black, and they'd taught Vinny Jones
how to enunciate. Obviously they were not letting the freezing
would-be-clubbers in, even though chances were the club was
empty inside; its rep entirely depended on the length of the
queue and the difficulty of gaining access. The only thing that
pleased a bouncer more than making the punters queue unnecessarily was seeing their aggrieved faces as members or those on the
guest list hopped to the front. Martha had thought this practice
insulting and unfair, until she discovered Jack was a member and
she enjoyed a fleeting feeling of importance as her gang swept up
to the red rope and were quickly ushered inside.

Jack's mates were nice. They seemed to think that Martha was
perfectly entitled to be there. No one suggested that she go home
and start scouring the grill. They laughed at her jokes and not her
dancing, they didn't mind that she drank white wine, or anything
else she liked, as long as she stood her round, and they took it as
read that she was "with Jack." Jack led Martha around the club
by the hand. Not obviously, not stamping his ownership of her,
but in a quiet, private manner. He'd hold his hand out behind

him and wave his fingers until she caught it, then he'd squeeze it tightly. He chatted to her whilst pointing out B celebs, introducing her to people he knew, discussing the tunes. He kissed her neck and lips, told her she was stunning, he made sure she had a good time.

Dancing turned out to be fine.

Fun.

Fantastic, actually.

Martha was gratified to note that the aciiiiiiiiiiiddddddddd hand-waving popular in her day had made a sort of comeback (if it had ever gone away, perhaps it had just kept going, she'd never be sure). A bit of waving your arms in the air and shaking your booty appeared to be all that was required.

Jack was such a good dancer that Martha wondered if she should be intimidated; surely she should be, and surely she would be—if she didn't keep having such spine-tingling, hair-raising, eye-popping flashbacks. It was impossible to forget that less than a couple of hours ago this man had slid himself inside her as he'd looked at her with outrageous, tormenting intensity. After that intimacy it would seem a little inappropriate to worry about the modernity or otherwise of her moves on the dance floor. They moved together, coolly swaying their hips as though they were joined. They incited looks of both admiration and envy and Martha knew they looked good together. They looked as though they belonged together, as though they were together.

Martha was startled when she looked at her watch and realized it was way past midnight. Jack saw her checking the time and said, "You're right. We've the babysitter to think of, we should start making tracks." Such consideration. Martha could have kissed him.

So she did.

Drew and Sara came too as they wanted to cadge a lift off Jack; Dave stayed on at the club as he was on the promise of a totally different kind of ride. Drew and Sara took immediate advantage of the back seat and giggled and chatted with each other in the way couples do when they want to block out the rest of the world. Martha smiled happily. Their exclusivity gave her and Jack time to talk. She collapsed back into her seat and turned to Jack.

"I've had a really excellent night, Jack."

"It was cool, wasn't it, Babe?" smiled Jack, resting his hand on Martha's thigh.

Martha revelled in the moment. She checked her body. She started with one foot, carefully rotating it, nothing. She lifted both feet a couple of inches off the ground and then lowered them again. Her legs didn't ache. She rotated her neck, it didn't click, and it didn't sting. Finally she leaned forward to stretch her back, it wasn't throbbing.

"What's up, Babe, too much exercise?" asked Jack cheekily.

"No, the opposite," smiled Martha. She'd been wondering where all that suppressed irritation that she used to live with was now hidden. There was no sign of a tense headache, or a pain in her lower back; she didn't have heavy legs. "I feel so comfortable, really happy," she beamed.

"Yeah, these are great seats. Recaro sports seats are an improvement to the Subaru Impreza WRX. The old Impreza turbos didn't used to have seats as good as this." He adored his car, but . . . Martha considered punching him. He should have understood her. She meant emotionally comfortable, not his bloody car seats. She turned to glare at him. He was grinning again.

"Oh, I see, a joke."

"Joke, Babe," he confirmed. Then he added, "We're cool, Babe."

Cool. Jack-speak for comfortable.

It was a perfect night. It wasn't stressful or complicated. No one rowed or bickered. It wasn't demanding. No one needed escorting to the loo—well, except for Sara, but that was so they could talk about make-up, not because she needed her bottom wiping. No one demanded anything of her or expected anything of her. No one was disappointed in her. Everyone seemed to want to be with her. Especially Jack.

On the journey home it started to snow.

"We might win our white Christmas bet," said Martha with excitement.

"We might, Babe. Stranger things have happened."

Flurries of flakes danced in the car's headlights, as though they were driving in a Hollywood film. Next we'll be having sex in front of the open fire, thought Martha (which actually proved a correct prediction). Martha thought that the flakes looked like dancing fireflies. Jack said they reminded him of that moment in *Star Wars*.

"Sorry?"

"The *Millennium Falcon* as it jumps into hyperspace."

"Oh, right." Still, it was romantic watching the snow. Martha was being romanced and she loved it. They fell silent again; the only sound was the swish of the windscreen wipers and the crunch of the car tyres packing the snow into the road. Martha hoped the snow would last long enough for the children to see it in the morning. She considered waking them up when she got home so they could have their first-ever glimpse.

"You are not a job, or money in the bank, you're not even a beautiful snowflake," said Martha.

*"Fight Club?"*

"Yes."

"You just quoted from *Fight Club*, Martha. Or to be exact *mis*quoted," said Jack, grinning. He was obviously astounded and impressed.

"I did, Jack," laughed Martha. She felt as though she belonged in an elite club.

It was a perfect night. All of it. Well, except the bit when Jack was getting petrol and Drew asked her, "So, are you two an item yet?"

"No. I'd definitely know if we were," said Martha, smiling, rather pleased with her quick answer. She knew that it was the kind of cool answer that Eliza would be proud of.

"So what's the difference between you two and a couple?" chipped in Sara. They'd only just met, but they were both female and therefore knew, absolutely *knew* that they liked each other, really liked each other, and therefore could cut the small talk. If they'd been male, it would have taken another fifteen years before they moved the conversation on from designer beers and the hilarity of Yoda twirling his light sabre in *Attack of the Clones*. "I mean, you seem really good together. You go out together, you have a laugh, you chat, you obviously care for each other."

"Well, we're exactly like a proper couple in every way except that we can sleep with other people if we want to," explained Martha.

"Do you sleep with other people?" asked Sara, not sure whether to be impressed or horrified.

"Not really. Well, no. Actually, I don't."

"Does he?"

"I think so."

"Oh."

So it was a perfect night, apart from that.

# 30

Martha woke up on Christmas Day and wished it was all over. She wished it was the end of the day, and that she was falling asleep with a hideously distended stomach and a woozy head. It wasn't the children's tantrums that she was dreading. It wasn't the threat of family bickering. It wasn't the near-certainty that she was about to unwrap an unimaginable number of bottles of bath salts and packets of pot-pourri, even though she still had a drawer stuffed with last year's supply. These minor irritations were all part of Christmas and, in a way, Martha rather welcomed them because they were certainties. The thing that made her wish the day was over was the horrible expectancy.

She blamed Hollywood.

Because it was Christmas Day, she knew that her mother and her son, and to a lesser extent her father and even her sister, had expectations of Michael. In truth, so did she. If they were in a film, he'd arrive with a huge bag of gifts for everyone, really thoughtful gifts. He'd tell her it was a terrible mistake, that things had got out of hand, that he couldn't live without her. They'd forget all the awful things they'd said to each other because both of them were sensible enough to know that things said in anger were never meant. He'd fling his arms around her and say he was never going to let her go again. Martha couldn't help but think of the Christmases gone by. They'd been so happy. Martha couldn't remember them ever having a single row on Christmas Day. How many couples could say that? Last year had been wonderful, hadn't it? Martha thought so. But maybe Michael didn't.

It sickened Martha to think that even now, if it were possible, she would scrub it all out. Erase the last three months. She'd forgo the new wardrobe, the hilarious nights spent with her girl-friends, the size-eight figure, and even the fantastic sex with Jack. She'd swap it all to be just where she was before. In Michael's arms. In Michael's esteem.

She'd rewind to put her family back together.

That's what Christmas did to you.

And bloody Hollywood.

God, this was confusing. Why couldn't she think badly of him, or well of him, for longer than five consecutive minutes? How was it possible that sometimes Jack disappeared from her mind completely, and yet in another way she felt he was with her all the time?

Michael had visited Mathew and Maisie on Christmas Eve morning, before Mr. and Mrs. Evergreen had arrived. Eliza had called him a coward and said that it was pretty crap that a grown man couldn't face a pair of oldies square on, which, as Martha pointed out, was hardly likely to encourage him to join them on Christmas Day. He'd made his plans very clear; he was going to his own parents for Christmas Day. Martha sent her love and carefully chosen, elaborately wrapped gifts.

But, despite the facts, there was still the expectancy.

Mrs. Evergreen knocked on Martha's bedroom door and walked straight in. "Happy Christmas, Darling. Mathew has al-ready opened his stocking. I tried to convince him it's too early to get up but—"

"Mummy, Mummy, look what Father Christmas has brought me." Mathew's excited voice cut across his grandmother's. He charged into Martha's bedroom and jumped on to the bed.

Martha swung her legs out of bed and pulled her face into an expression of curiosity, although in reality she had picked out all of the children's presents, alone. And neither Father Christmas nor the biological father had contributed to the process. "Where's Maisie?"

"Eliza is giving her breakfast. Come on, Love, put your dressing gown on and let's go downstairs, your dad is making a fried breakfast and heating croissants."

This year it had seemed sensible for Mr. and Mrs. Evergreen to stay at Martha's for Christmas—Eliza was already there, as were the children's toys. Despite not being on their own turf, they were still clearly in charge. Martha was grateful and surrendered herself to their care.

As usual, the Evergreens had a hearty cooked breakfast, then champagne and croissants. One of the advantages of all the family staying at Martha's was that nobody had to worry about staying sober to drive home, so the alcohol started to flow even before daylight. They opened their stockings. Father Christmas had been particularly creative this year. He'd opted for lager-and-lime flavoured condoms, a fake tattoo and a copy of the *Kama Sutra* for Martha ("Thanks, Eliza"), a desk tidy and a new leather wallet for Eliza ("Thanks, Martha"), rather than the more traditional chocolate coins and satsumas of years gone by. However, Mr. Evergreen did still receive socks and golf tees, and Mrs. Evergreen padded coat-hangers and little sachets of lavender.

Mathew fought to open everyone's presents, whilst Maisie didn't want to open even her own. She sat under the Christmas tree playing with her oldest toys and seemed to be showing a sudden but particular affection for those that were cast-offs from Mathew. They all went for a walk to the local park and pushed the children on the swings whilst the turkey cooked. When they got home Martha found she couldn't hold out any longer; she called Michael.

"Merry Christmas," said Martha, with all the sincerity of a satan-worshipper promising a Jehovah's witness that yes, she would read the little pamphlet.

"Merry Christmas."

"You bastard."

"That's lovely, Martha. Quite a twist on the traditional greeting, which, if I'm not mistaken, goes something along the lines of 'and a Happy New Year.'"

"Yes, and it concludes *'To you and yours.'* Well, you bastard, for your information, *yours* are having a wonderful time."

"Clearly."

"Were you ever going to ring to wish your children a happy day?"

"Yes, I was, Martha. But it's only eleven-thirty."

Martha was a little surprised to hear this. Of course, Mathew had been up since five and the rest of the family had had to succumb to the pressure of his jubilation at about ten past five. Everyone had finished breakfast by eight. Martha had assumed it was later in the day, and that was why she was so furious with Michael for not calling. Aunty Flo from Australia had called. Her friends Claire and Dawn had called.

"The children have been up since the crack of dawn, and if you had any idea about your children you'd know that. You bastard."

"Marvellous, Martha, yet more of your tirades of abuse. I'd really prefer it if you didn't swear."

"I do know that you'd prefer me not to swear, Michael, you selfish wanker, but sometimes I find it helps me through the day."

"Look, Martha, I'm not having the best Christmas either. My parents are arguing over the temperature they ought to set the oven at, my grandmother is insisting on retelling her stories of Christmas during the Blitz for what really must be the tenth time today, and Harry and Becky have just arrived with their kids. I miss mine."

"Not enough to call, though." Martha hung up because she

didn't want Michael to hear her cry. What bit of evolution dictates that being elegant, charitable and generous was impossible on Christmas Day? Martha didn't get to church because she sat on the sofa sobbing, wondering how, if he was so unhappy, he could still prefer being there rather than here with her and her wonderful children.

Fuck, this was cruel.

By the time Eliza, her parents and the children came back from church Martha had reapplied her make-up and pinned her smile back on.

"Those are the last tears I'm going to cry over him," she whispered to her mum. Her mum hugged her and had the good sense not to comment how unlikely that was.

Greg visited to drop off presents for everyone, which clearly delighted Eliza, although she tried to appear annoyed and intimate that his presence was intrusive. She claimed that she was furious with her mother for insisting that he join them for dinner.

"Where's your Christian spirit, Eliza?" hissed Mrs. Evergreen. Eliza didn't reply; she was far from religious and the only spirit she had at Christmas, or at any other time, was the liquid bottled variety. "We can't let him go home alone on Christmas Day. You, more than anyone, must know that there'll be nothing in his fridge."

Eliza popped her head around the sitting-room door. Greg was lolling on the floor with Mathew. It looked like Greg had worked out how to play the electric guitar Mathew had been given. Everyone else had tried to make music with it earlier that morning but with zero success. Maisie was sat propped against his legs, gurgling happily. Mr. Evergreen was forcing a beer on Greg, clearly delighted to have another male to even up the numbers. He was feeling vulnerable—so much hysteria, so many tears, and they hadn't even listened to the Queen's speech yet, which was guaranteed to set off Mrs. Evergreen. Even Martha was smiling as she answered Greg's questions. The first proper smile she'd treated them to all day.

Eliza knew when she was outnumbered.

Besides, she wanted to see what Greg would make of the mince pies; she'd made them herself. No, really, even the pastry. Well, she had at least rolled out that pre-packed stuff she'd bought at the supermarket. There was no need to create unnecessary work.

Martha was pleased to see Eliza laugh and joke with Greg; it was a little bit like the old days. It was funny to see Eliza evict Mathew from his preferred seat next to Greg so that she could sit there. She'd had to bribe him with pulling all the crackers on the table. Martha was very happy for Eliza, who was obviously going to get her Hollywood ending this Christmas. Providing, of course, she didn't do anything really silly again, and with Eliza there was never any guarantee that she wouldn't do something really silly. It was crystal clear that Greg made Eliza happier than anyone else had ever been able to. And from what Martha could glean, Greg was still entirely smitten with Eliza. She supposed it was better that one of the sisters was happy.

"Is that your mobile?" asked Eliza.

"Oh, must be." Martha jumped up.

"Hello, Babe."

"Jack!" Her nipples sprang up at the sound of his voice, which she felt a little bit bad about. It was Christmas Day, and she was within her parents' earshot.

"Are you having a good Christmas, Little Miss E.?"

"Yes." Now.

"Just wanted to call and see how you were getting on. How are the little dudes? Are they having fun?" Martha took the rest of the call outside the dining room. When she returned, her mother was serving up the Christmas pudding and no one alluded to the call.

"Ouch, I think I've swallowed a filling," yelled Martha.

"No, that will be the sixpence," said Mrs. Evergreen. "You have to make a wish."

Martha suspected a certain amount of fixing the odds so that the "lucky sixpence" ended up in her serving. The rest of the family all smiled politely, but obviously suspected the same. Martha made a silent wish. She wished that Eliza would "see sense," because she didn't have a clue as to what to wish for herself.

# January

# 31

"Well, it wasn't exactly a roaring success as a method for you, was it?"

"No, I can't say it was. Mar, I don't think I can go on much further with my search," groaned Eliza.

"You've dated some of the most scintillating and eligible men in London, Eliza," insisted Martha.

"I know. That's what worries me." The girls giggled and then paused to sip their coffees.

"So, if making a list of your criteria for a desirable man is failing so dismally for you, why do you think it will be any more productive as an exercise for me?" asked Martha.

"The productive bit is knowing and asserting what you want. The tricky bit is actually getting a man to meet the brief."

"I'm fine as I am. I'm having loads of fun with Jack, and I'm not looking for anything more than loads of fun."

"Is that so?"

"Yes."

Eliza sank into one of her silences that definitely meant she disagreed. She didn't disagree that Martha was having fun with Jack—that much was obvious. What worried her was that when it stopped being fun, which undoubtedly it would—and probably sooner rather than later—Martha didn't have a back-up plan, and everyone should have a back-up plan. It was clear to Eliza, and to every adult in the Western world other than Martha, that this party with Jack wouldn't, couldn't, last. Martha was bound to fall in love; worse still, she'd show it; worst of all, she'd tell him; and then he'd run a mile. Eliza agreed with Martha, he was gorgeous. He was witty and winning and hot; that was the problem. A man like that was not going to take on a ready-made family, he had too many options, too many possibilities.

It *was* possible that his role in life was as a Sex God destined to service the women of west London. But why put such a small geographical limit on it? He'd service women north, south, east and west of London, and all over Europe, and also the States. He'd give pleasure where he could. He had no concept that each time he gave pleasure he gave pain too. Because, from what Martha said, after they'd done Hope, they did hope he'd be around for longer than the time it took to have breakfast. It was human nature that hope slipped into expectation, and where was Martha in all this? Heading for meltdown, that's where. Eliza just thought it would be a good idea to have a back-up plan. Maybe if Martha made a list of the criteria for her perfect man she would have to notice and concede how far away from that ideal Jack was.

"You said that you might take other naked friends when all this started," Eliza insisted.

True, Martha had said that, but she'd never believed it. She wasn't the type. She was a serial monogamist, as unfashionable as it clearly was. She'd said she might take up the naked-friend option just as a way to excuse Jack for doing the same.

Martha felt distinctly uncomfortable; she hated unpleasant silences. Eliza knew this. Eliza hated not getting her own way. Martha knew this. It was just a matter of who broke first.

"OK, then. Have you got a pen?" asked Martha.

"Here," beamed Eliza, waving a pen and a notebook in the air, her mood instantly brightening, reminding Martha of Mathew when he'd won some hard-fought victory such as not having to eat up his peas.

"Right. Well, I want a man who will de-scale the kettle and change the water filter."

"That's your top priority?" asked Eliza in dismay.

"Well, it's symbolic. If he'll do those ho-hum household jobs, he'll definitely be the type to stick a pile of whites into the washing machine."

"So you're looking for someone particularly effeminate?"

"Ha ha. No. Actually, I want him to be hung like a donkey and to know how to use his equipment with indecent frequency," said Martha.

Eliza laughed. She liked this new funny, funky sister. She was so much more entertaining than the sister whose biggest concern had been that Flora had changed their packaging. "OK, what else?"

"Well, obviously, he'd love me. All of me." Martha smiled at the thought. "You know when you're really upset about something and you're asked, 'What's wrong?' and you stubbornly reply 'Nothing'?"

"Yeah."

"And you wait to be asked, 'No, really, what is wrong?' because you want to be pushed. More, you want *him* to want to discover you."

"Yeah. But no man ever does that," sighed Eliza.

"Well, my perfect man would push me. He'd peel me like, like . . ." Martha hesitated, as she searched for the correct words. "Like an onion."

"Nice analogy."

"You know what I mean."

Martha was ready for the striptease. She wanted to be known. Recently she'd started to believe that she was worth knowing and her ideal man would think so too.

"Right," said Eliza, sighing. She thought it was a pity that Martha was such a romantic. Such a typical Virgo.

Martha was also thinking that her ideal man would love it when she took hold of him and wanked him so expertly that he came quickly, spilling over her body. She didn't think this was the kind of thing she could share with Eliza or indeed anyone.

Other than Jack.

Martha was holding this conversation as she stood in the doorway between the kitchen and the back garden. Mathew and Maisie were feeding the sparrows; there was rarely anything more exotic in London gardens; occasionally a pigeon was spotted, but only if the tourists in Trafalgar Square were being particularly mean. A weak winter sun bounced on their smiling faces. January was normally such a bleak and grey month, full of tatty merchandise on sale racks, and offering nothing more exciting than a free membership to Weight Watchers, but this year January had seemed unseasonably illustrious.

"Come on in and wash your hands, you two," called Martha. She didn't really hold much hope of Mathew listening to her or Maisie understanding her. Without skipping a beat she turned back to Eliza and continued, "But besides that, he would really be worth knowing. He'd be strong. Physically, emotionally and morally."

"Phew, you're not asking for much, are you?"

"Yes, I am. I know that I am. But I give, too."

Eliza thought how good it was to hear Martha value herself, really refreshing, it gave her a buzz just listening.

Of course she was utterly doomed.

This search for the perfect man was a non-starter.

Eliza attempted to redirect Martha towards something a little more conventional. "What about things like good with children, or earns a decent salary?"

"That's so last season," commented Martha. She winked and then more seriously added, "That's husband criteria. I'm not looking for a husband. I've had one of those. I'm looking for excitement, and that definitely demands an entirely different wish list."

"Is that responsible?"

"I've been responsible all my life and look where it got me. I think I'm overdue a bit of irresponsibility. You could lend me yours."

"Unfair! I'm trying to be really responsible right now. I have a desk tidy and I back up my PalmPilot every night. I've had my hair cut, bought a suit. I'm looking for a husband with a serious income and a serious wardrobe and a serious job."

"You honestly believe it was responsible to leave Greg, don't you?"

"Yes," said Eliza firmly.

"Amazing."

Eliza scowled. "We're talking about *you* here, not me."

"OK, I'd also want all the usual stuff, you know. Good-looking, nice smile, good teeth, dark hair, preferably green eyes, no body odour, no dandruff, someone who ferociously loathes football—I simply cannot go through another World Cup and be expected to keep my sanity—wide shoulders, tight butt, single, no baggage, GSOH."

Eliza reread the list of criteria. "Jesus, Martha, I thought you said I was the demanding one. This list is totally unrealistic. This man is beyond fantasy. You're looking for a single, stunning, sensitive, smiley Sex God who is prepared to don washing-up gloves. This man doesn't exist."

"He does," smiled Martha. She leaned back against the kitchen counter, wearing an indecently smug smile and she thought, Jack's all of these things. He is.

# 32

They'd decided to manage the divorce without the intervention of solicitors. Martha thought this was the route that was most likely to fall in with her mantra of behaving with elegance, charity and generosity, although Eliza thought Martha was mad.

"I don't need a solicitor, I trust Michael. He'd never leave me without money for the children."

"Martha, a couple of months ago you thought he'd never leave you, period."

Period? Oh, another Americanism. God, sometimes Martha despised Eliza's straight-talking. It was as though she were pulling out toenails.

"Why are you doing it this way, Martha?"

"Which way?"

"This über-sensible, let's-all-be-friends way. Don't you ever want to fling crockery about, or cut the crotch out of all his suits?"

Frequently.

Martha, who was, after all, only human, had thought of pouring sugar into the petrol tank of his Boxster. She'd considered emailing embarrassing photos to his work colleagues; she had a selection to choose from. There was the one of him wearing a basque and suspenders. OK, he was going to a *Rocky Horror Show* party, but his colleagues wouldn't know that. There were the ones of him on his stag weekend, and not just the ones of him in the commando suit, which were silly in Martha's opinion (but she knew that other men wouldn't think so). But there was

the one his best man had taken when Michael had passed out
after drinking the obligatory twelve pints. They'd shaved his entire body except for his eyebrows. Martha had been furious. The
regrowth proved more than uncomfortable for both of them during their honeymoon, but she was grateful they'd left his eyebrows alone—at least the ambush hadn't ruined the wedding
photos.

Not that it mattered now how either of them looked in their
wedding photos. Their wedding photos were being slowly removed from a number of sideboards and walls up and down the
country.

Such petty acts of revenge were inane, insane. Small gestures
that wouldn't, couldn't, counter the hurt Martha felt; therefore
they seemed pointless.

"What would be the sense in my going out of my way to be
nasty?" Martha was annoyed at herself for lapsing into fury; she
hated the rows with Michael, although sometimes she really
couldn't seem to stop herself. She certainly didn't need to go and
look for aggro. "What would it achieve?"

"Peace of mind."

"Sorry?"

"You'd feel better," asserted Eliza.

"Actually, I'm not sure I would."

Managing the divorce yourself involved buying petitions for
£2.50 from a particular stationer's on Chancery Lane. Martha
knew this because there was an extremely useful Internet site that
guided people like her through the divorce procedure.

Handy, the things you find on the Net.

Martha had limited experience of Chancery Lane, even
though she'd lived in London all her adult life. There were no
shops, no supermarkets, few restaurants—in short, nothing to induce her to visit there at all. She did know that Chancery Lane

was near the Strand, where she would find the Royal Courts of Justice; she knew that because she watched the six o'clock news and there were often TV cameras gathered outside trying to capture the comments of the latest acquitted defendant, or at least of their lawyers.

Martha pushed open the door to the stationer's and a loud bell chimed, announcing her presence. This was completely cringe-making; she'd rather hoped to creep in to buy the petition and then creep out again, without attracting anyone's attention. She milled around the shelves, looking at the selection of hole punches and various-size packets of Blu-Tack. Martha was astounded to note that you couldn't even purchase a lever-arch file for the price of a divorce petition. A lever-arch file cost £2.75, unless you bought them in bulk. The whole process was cheap and sickeningly undignified. After moseying around the shop for what seemed like a month, Martha realized she was unlikely to find the documentation she required without asking for assistance.

As coincidence would have it, the shop assistants came to exactly the same conclusion at exactly the same time. "Can I help you?" asked the younger of the two available (male) assistants.

And it shouldn't have mattered that he was a man, but it did. In Martha's bleaker moments, she found herself believing (illogically) that they were "all in cahoots." They were all deserters and philanderers and they all had an inability to keep promises, especially promises they made in church whilst wearing a suit hired from Moss Bros. It hurt her to think this, but not as much as it hurt to admit that actually she'd simply made a duff choice.

The assistant was plump and scruffy, and he looked vaguely dusty like an elderly academic, but Martha guessed that he was only in his late twenties. His stomach folded over his trousers, completely hiding his belt. Martha wouldn't normally notice this kind of thing, but she was having difficulty dragging her eyes up from waist level—she didn't really want to meet his stare. When she finally managed to do so, she didn't like what she saw. Somehow this man had guessed what she needed and he was enjoying it, she was sure. He was actively taking pleasure from her obvious pain and embarrassment.

"I'd like a copy of a divorce petition, please," said Martha. She pronounced every word carefully, as though elocution could protect her.

"Is either of the parties an adulterer?" asked the chubby shop assistant.

Martha noticed that he bit his nails and his fingers looked like sausages. She bet he wore nylon trousers, although she couldn't quite see because his legs were behind the counter. She didn't like him at all. "No," she said, trying her best to sound like the queen. She'd like to have replied, "Yes, my husband is sleeping with your wife—how do you feel about that? But perhaps she was getting things a little out of proportion. Martha was divorcing Michael on the grounds of unreasonable behaviour, and she had to cite three examples. Just three.

"Silly me, it doesn't matter now, it's the same form anyway," smirked the assistant.

Martha would have liked to say he smiled but it was definitely a smirk. She suspected that he got off on asking women like her if she, or her husband, was having it away with a cute third party, but she had no proof. All she could do was hand over her £2.50, and try and ignore his damp, sweaty paw.

Martha was about to leave the shop when she thought again. "I'd better take two," she said. She was notoriously bad at filling out forms, she was bound to make a mistake.

"Bigamy is a crime, you know," laughed the assistant. He had no idea how criminal it was that four lives that had been inextricably woven together had been hacked apart. Martha treated him to a steely glare and left the shop.

The next stage was filling out the blasted form. She was required to give examples of Michael's unreasonable behaviour. Apparently "He doesn't love me" didn't count. They quietly agreed the words between them, settling on inoffensive, bloodless reasons for a divorce. Martha found that insulting too. Surely the reasons for a divorce ought to be great and dramatic.

Next, she went to the post office and made lots of photocopies of the petition and of their wedding certificate. Then she sent the package to the austere Courts of Justice, remembering to use registered post. She understood that the whole process could take as little as twelve weeks. It had taken her longer to choose the table decorations for her wedding reception.

It ought to have been grander, more serious, thought Martha as she negotiated Maisie's stroller through the narrow post-office doorway and out on to the street. She looked around. There wasn't a hat in sight, nor even the smallest handful of confetti.

Martha thought this was a good day to take her rings off. She wasn't sure why she'd kept them on for so long. Sentimentality? To show the world that she'd been respectably married before she conceived her two children? Ha. Jack didn't like her wearing her engagement and wedding rings. He hadn't actually said, "I don't like you wearing your rings," but he had asked her why she continued wearing them in a way that implied "I don't like you wearing your rings." It was a fair question, to which the reply—"habit"—seemed inadequate. There was something sweet and old-fashioned, if not a bit inconsistent, in the fact that Jack would happily bed a married woman, but not one who was wearing her rings.

Martha didn't feel like a married woman. She felt like a single girl, so the rings had to go. She wasn't even deceiving herself any more. Her fingers were so skinny at the moment that the rings swung helplessly around; it was easy to slip them off.

Her hand would feel bare, and for weeks afterwards she

would keep rubbing her thumb against her fourth finger where her rings used to be. Every time she did so, it surprised her to find that her finger was bare. She was once so proud of her rings. The engagement ring was her favourite. She remembered the first time she'd made love as an engaged woman. She'd thought that she'd never make love to any other man again. She'd thought she was safe, complete. But that was a long time ago. Now her finger was nude.

Michael came to move out the rest of his clothes and possessions. It was as she had promised herself it would be—all very civilized.

At least until the part where she sobbed and howled like a banshee, "The worst of this, Michael, is that in years to come, when Mathew and Maisie ask why we aren't a family, I'll have to confess that I don't know." He held her tightly and remained silent.

Michael had hired a white van for the day; he'd rung her a week in advance to say that he'd arrive at about 11 a.m. and expected to leave at about 4:30 p.m. Martha, in her wisdom and superior position as the person who'd managed their lives for the last ten years, knew that this would not be enough time for Michael to pack up his belongings and shift them. Michael didn't know this because Martha had always done the lion's share of that kind of thing as they'd moved from flat to flat, and eventually to this house. Their home. Martha found it hard to break a habit of a lifetime, and so helpfully packed up Michael's suits, jumpers, shirts, T-shirts, pants, socks and shoes. She even packed up his navy towelling dressing gown that was the same as hers. She washed it before she did so, because there was nothing nicer than a clean, fluffy towelling dressing gown.

Except perhaps two clean, fluffy, towelling dressing gowns hanging side by side on the back of the bathroom door.

Martha carefully packed all Michael's books, videos and

DVDs. She gave him *Billy Elliot* even though she loved the film, because, strictly speaking, it was his. Mathew and Maisie had "bought" it for him for Father's Day. The gaps on the bookshelves and video rack reminded Martha of the gaps the tooth fairy leaves in a seven-year-old's mouth. They divided up the furniture, the crockery, the cutlery and the bedding. He took the shoe polish, the non-stick frying pan, the mountain bike. There were gaps everywhere. Physical, emotional, historical and moral. They separated their lives. They were separating.

"How'd it go, Little Miss E.?" asked Jack when he phoned later that afternoon.

"OK," said Martha. She'd never lied to Jack, and she didn't want to start now, not even with a white lie, so she added, "Considering."

"Must be a bitch."

"Yes." Martha stared around her home. It looked ravaged, incomplete. It didn't look like her home. It didn't look like a home at all. "I keep going to get things and realizing they're not here any more, that they went with Michael."

"What sort of things?"

"Tupperware boxes."

"What?"

Martha could hear the astonishment in Jack's voice. She was glad he wasn't in the room; he'd be able to see she was crying and he'd probably think it was odd to cry over Tupperware boxes.

"Tupperware boxes," she repeated down the phone.

"What are they?"

"You know, plastic boxes, air-tight lids; I put the kids' food in them. I cleared up after their tea today, went to put the ham in a Tupperware box and realized that I don't have any Tupperware boxes any more."

"What did you do?" asked Jack, making out that he was horrified.

Martha thought about the conversation and started to smile to herself. "I wrapped the ham in tinfoil." Martha was now in serious danger of laughing.

"Good thinking, Dude. That saved the day," said Jack, then he added, "Should I come round?"

Jack arrived at Martha's house thirty minutes later. He brought dinner, his smile and his sex appeal. She opened the door to him but he didn't bother with small talk. There was nothing he could say to comfort her. Instead he cupped her face in his hands and kissed her. Really kissed her. His hands enveloped her head. She was almost scared that she might drown in his hands. She opened her eyes to see that he hadn't closed his, he was watching her as though she was important. Vital. He nibbled her ear, which sent an electrical storm directly down her spine, through her buttocks, under, and up into her. He inched his hand down from her chin to rest flat on her breast, he firmly but gently massaged her nipple between his finger and thumb.

His lips never left hers until he'd teased, then bruised her with tiny, pleasurably painful bites. Without removing any of her clothes and without moving from that position, he pulled her into orgasm; her breath was shallow, her heartbeat fast, her chest was flushed, her pants were wet. She came once, then again, then again. And it helped. Her mind was full of the smell of sex and the feel of blood pulsing around her genitals, which helped cloud out the lost Tupperware, the lost husband and the lost family. He inched her out of her jeans and sweatshirt. She moved quickly and shamelessly, stripped him bare, then threw away her own lacy briefs. They stood naked in the kitchen and in each other's arms and kissed. Then kissed and kissed some more.

People had said to her that divorce was like death; that you had to grieve, that it was natural to feel lost and angry and sad. Martha didn't know about that, all she wanted was to feel alive.

With each joyous thrust she felt lit up, stirred, awake. He picked her up and she wrapped her legs around his waist. She directed him to the kitchen table so she could rest her buttocks rather than have him take all her weight—not that he cared, she seemed weightless to him. He pulled her closer and closer into him, entering her a little deeper, faster and harder each time. They behaved like animals that couldn't, wouldn't ever get enough of each other. They fucked hard, often, and with great hope and affection. She'd been a girl, then a woman, now she was a girl again.

# February

• • • •

# 33

Martha would always remember February as sunny. Which was peculiar, as February was normally so dull and soulless. This year, every morning she was greeted by bright blue skies split by sharp winter sun. She wore a great deal of yellow, and she smiled an awful lot, despite Eliza asking questions like, "You do know there's no such thing as a perfect man, don't you?" Martha didn't think she was actually required to reply, so she didn't. Her silence provoked Eliza to demand, "You think he's perfect, don't you?" in a tone that made it clear the correct answer, as far as she was concerned, would not be "yes."

"Near as damn it," breezed Martha as she buttered a slice of toast for Maisie. Maisie took the toast, held it for about two seconds, then threw it on the floor. Naturally, sod's law was in force and the toast landed buttered side down.

"Oh dear," laughed Martha. She buttered a second slice and handed it over. Stupid little things like smudging butter into the carpet didn't upset Martha any more. For the first few weeks after Michael had left, Martha found that she cried if she spilt milk, despite the old saying that there was no point in doing so. The children's tantrums had almost overwhelmed her; if one of them fell and grazed a knee, it had been a close call who cried the most— Martha or the child. The care of Mathew and Maisie had appeared as a huge challenge that she was not up to. Now, nurturing, comforting, loving and protecting them was once again effortless.

Or at least possible.

Getting jiggy with Jack was good for Martha. She felt validated.

Eliza's constant harping didn't even get to Martha, although it sometimes seemed that Eliza's *raison d'être* was to urinate on Martha's parade.

"Jack has so much energy. I wonder if you could cope with it 24/7?" asked Eliza. She crammed the final spoon of her cereal down her throat and then immediately started flying about the kitchen, packing up the things she needed to take to work.

Was it possible that one day Martha would come to think his constant chatter as irritating as Michael's silence was alienating? No, she couldn't imagine it. Eliza was mistaken.

"It was you who said perfect men didn't exist. If so, Jack has to have some flaw, and if his biggest fault is being energetic then things can't be too bad," reasoned Martha. "Besides, which, I'm not proposing 24/7." Oddly, Martha didn't feel as ridiculous as she perhaps should have in using a phrase that belonged in a teen movie.

"Have you introduced him to anyone yet?"

"What do you mean, 'introduced him'? You've met him." Martha started to clear the breakfast plates from the table and stack them in the dishwasher.

"I've *met* him, you didn't *introduce* him to me." The difference, which was obviously apparent to Eliza, eluded Martha; she looked puzzled. Eliza tried to be clear. "I was here, he came here, you told me his name. It's not the same as going out of your way to introduce him to someone. Have you introduced him to Mum and Dad yet?" Eliza stopped her frantic search for her mobile, her credit card and her Tube pass and turned to face her sister, hands on her hips.

Martha recognized a challenge when she saw one. "Err, no, the opportunity hasn't arisen," she admitted.

"Or Claire, or Dawn, or Dom and Tara, or any of your friends, or Michael?"

"Michael? For God's sake, Eliza, why would I want to introduce Jack to Michael?"

"No one's met him, have they?"

"I've told everyone who's important about him."

"But none of them have met him?"

"No."

"Odd that," said Eliza; she was finding it difficult to resist adding "Ha."

"Not so odd."

"He's a shag then, not a boyfriend."

"He's a tender shag."

"But not a boyfriend," Eliza said flatly.

"He does care," argued Martha.

"You know that all the women he's tenderly shagging will think that," said Eliza emphatically, then she asked if Martha had seen her Tube pass.

Martha would not think about it. It couldn't be helped; therefore thinking about it wouldn't help. So Jack saw other women. So what? Slept with other women—so what? A vision of Jack kissing another woman flashed into Martha's head. The woman's face was blurred, indistinct. Martha pushed the cruel picture out of her mind, but not before it stabbed. She felt the pain in her chest. This was silly. She'd been through this in her head a million times. So, he still wanted variety. So, he wasn't ready to settle down. Nor was she. He cared about her. She was having fun. That was all that mattered. There was no need at all to think beyond that. It was as good as it got.

In her position.

Eliza bounced upstairs. Martha could hear her turn the tap on to full as she cleaned her teeth. Eliza bounced back downstairs again: she was always late, always in a hurry. Martha handed her her Tube pass.

"Oh, thanks."

"The thing is, Eliza, the odd mix of affection and coolness suits me; I'm not sure I'm ready for anything more."

"You're just saying that because he's not offering you anything more," argued Eliza as she zipped up her knee-high boots.

"I'm having fun, hanging with a style guru who doesn't do coke, how much harm can be done?"

"Lots."

"He's sexy and beautiful and—"

"And you're asking me what harm can be done? Look, he's not your type. He has a tattoo, wears a necklace and rides a motorbike." Put like that, it almost seemed as though Eliza had a point. Martha wasn't usually attracted to men with tattoos, or bikers or jewellery-wearers but, oddly, Jack had made all three things the epitome of horniness.

"He has form. He's slept with a stripper, and ticks off women he's done by country of birth. Variety is his thing," insisted Eliza.

"So he has a past—don't we all?" Martha made a mental note not to share quite as much info with Eliza. It was evidence that was later used against her.

Eliza slid into her huge winter coat. She wasn't exactly cheerful as it was, but putting on the ugly coat always catapulted her into a dire mood. The coat didn't suit her. It had been a duff purchase. "It's not even his past that worries me, it's the fact that he wants a future."

Martha sighed inwardly. She knew Eliza was right. The other day she'd asked Jack if he'd ever done three-in-a-bed. She'd sort of been joking, but he'd taken her question seriously and said, "No, not yet." Martha didn't dare confess this to Eliza; she knew she'd be outraged. She'd also asked him if she was the first married woman he'd ever slept with. A fairly ignominious question, but she was struggling for a first, and she so wanted to be unique to him in some way. Unfortunately, it turned out that a few years back he'd casually dated some woman who was also waiting for her divorce to come through.

At least he was honest.

Cold comfort.

Martha only brightened when she realized that she hadn't asked him if she was the first mother he'd slept with; she made a mental note to do so.

As if Eliza were reading her mind, she sighed theatrically and warned, "Oh Martha. You're heading for such trouble. Even white mice in laboratories learn faster than this."

Martha raged inwardly. She wanted to ask what Eliza wanted her to learn. How to close down? How to be cold and untrusting? How to shield herself against falling in love again? That wasn't a life as far as Martha was concerned. She didn't say any of this; all she said was, "At least I won't be in tidying the kids' toy boxes on Valentine's night."

"What makes you so sure?"

"Well . . ." Martha couldn't think of anything else to say. She'd assumed that Jack would spend Valentine's with her but, thinking about it, there weren't any guarantees.

"How do you know he won't want to spend Valentine's night with one of his many other naked friends?" inquired Eliza.

How indeed?

"Look, Martha, I don't want to seem unnecessarily cruel but"—but she was going to be unnecessarily cruel, Martha just knew it—"you're looking really great at the moment, and you've always had the sweetest nature, but, Babe, there are a lot of great-looking girls out there—hundreds of them—and, well, men rarely fall for sweet natures."

Oh.

Martha didn't want to ask but she knew she had to. "What *do* men fall for?"

"Great tits. A challenge. Kylie Minogue."

Martha looked down at her average tits; small-but-perfectly-formed was the best description she could ever hope for.

Martha thought Eliza had been entirely clear, but Eliza obviously saw a need to be more explicit. "I mean, I know they say that more than a handful is a waste, but neither of us has even a sufficiency. And you're not Kylie—you can't even sing—and as for being a challenge . . ." She stopped mid-sentence, as though there was nothing more to be said.

"What?" demanded Martha. "Why aren't I a challenge?"

"Martha, you're available, caring and predictable. Does that sound like a challenge to you?"

"I'm not going to play games. It's just not me. Besides, I'd lose."

Eliza looked at her sister and once again thought how utterly horrific this situation was. Martha should not be getting divorced, she wasn't brutal enough to forge her way through the dating jungle. It was obvious that Jack was going to make mincemeat of her, it was only a matter of time. Although Martha had repeatedly insisted that Jack was just for fun, it was clear that she was falling for him. Falling hard.

It was also clear that Eliza was wasting her time trying to preach caution.

She wasn't trying to be a killjoy; she was honestly worried for Martha. "Right then, if you are insisting on continuing with this *relationship*"—she said the word in the same way most women say *pornography*—"then at least make an effort to understand him, give yourself a fair chance." Martha was all ears. "Men like Jack—"

"What do you mean, 'men like Jack'?" interrupted Martha.

"Men who are too good-looking for their own good."

Although Eliza didn't intend it to, her comment increased Martha's ardour; Martha fizzed with pride.

"Men like Jack aren't planners," pursued Eliza, "so what you need to do is something, everything, to put yourself in the forefront of his mind. Easy access, so to speak. It's an ever-increasingly competitive environment out there, Martha. You have to cut through the clutter."

Martha got the impression that Eliza was practising a pitch for raising the budget on a music video. "What do you mean?"

"You have to be the first and last woman he thinks of every day."

"How do I do that?"

"Oh, I don't know, think creatively." She glanced at the kitchen clock. "I'm late for work, we'll talk about it tonight." Eliza kissed her niece and nephew and blew a kiss to her sister. "Give it some thought, think out of the box."

The door banged shut behind Eliza.

# 34

"You did *what?*" asked Eliza. She was absolutely aghast and couldn't for the life of her hide it.

"Well, it was you who said I had to cut through the clutter, put myself at the front of his mind," defended Martha.

"But, Martha, you sent out all the wrong signals."

"Did I?"

"Oh God, you are a case." Eliza stared at the spreadsheet on the screen in front of her. The numbers were beginning to blur into one another. She almost wished that she hadn't picked up the phone; she didn't need this. "Yes. They're not children, Martha. Chocolate, for fuck's sake? Why didn't you just take a copy of the *Beano* and some Johnson's baby wipes and be done with it? You don't want to be seen as a mother. You want to be seen as fun."

"But I am a mother, and moreover, I thought it was fun. You know that Friday Crunchie feeling. It is a Friday."

"Well, you've blown it. You're buggered. You're *never* going to see him or hear from him again."

Martha's enormous and overwhelming crime was that she had dropped in at Jack's office and left three Crunchie bars in reception. One for him, and one each for his colleagues Drew and Dave. Martha had wrapped the chocolate bars in brown paper, tied the parcel with black ribbon and marked it "urgent." She hadn't included a note. She was quite pleased. It had taken quite some restraint not to include a note; she thought it gave the impression that she was cool and mysterious.

The delivery of chocolate was not a totally unmeditated gesture. For one, it *was* Friday afternoon, and in a matter of hours Jack would be coming round to see Martha. She was so excited, she'd had that Friday Crunchie feeling all day. (To be accurate, she'd had it all month.) The odd thing was she wasn't alone in thinking this. Jack had texted her and said he had that Friday feeling. *And* Jack had a surprisingly, scandalously, sweet tooth.

Another motivation was that Eliza had said Martha was predictable; Martha had been stung.

It all added up to a Crunchie bar.

She'd delivered the package at three-fifteen after a particularly intense day of swapping flirty text messages. However, it was now six-thirty and she hadn't heard anything from him yet. She'd expected him to call straight away. She was stuck in that miserable no-man's-land of an embryonic relationship. She was tortured.

There were of course a number of factors that could explain his silence. Perhaps he hadn't received the package: maybe it was still lingering, unnoticed, in an in-tray somewhere. He might not get his post until Monday morning now, which would ruin the joke entirely. Or maybe he *had* received it but thought it was from someone else (she should definitely have included a note; it was stupid, arrogant not to). Or possibly he'd received it and thought it was a ridiculous, infantile thing for Martha to have done. Had she embarrassed him? Martha generally felt very confident in Jack's company, but perhaps she didn't know him as well as she thought—It wasn't as though they were proper girlfriend and boyfriend. He had other naked friends. Were Crunchie bars presumptuous?

Martha called Eliza at work for guidance and succour. Eliza did take away Martha's horrible feelings of uncertainty but she was not at all cheering. Eliza firmly believed that the third explanation was a certainty.

"When were you supposed to be seeing him next?" demanded Eliza.

"Tonight."

"Tonight? So *why* did you get in touch at all? There was no reason to speak or contact him today if you're seeing him tonight."

"I got in touch because I was thinking about him and I wanted him to be thinking about me. You said the first and—"

"Last woman he thought of. Yes, I know, I know, but bloody hell, Martha, you are *so* ignorant. Don't you have any understanding of the dating rules?"

"No, not really," admitted Martha. She was inches away from reminding Eliza that she was newly dumped and had been out of the "game" for over ten years. She had bugger all idea about what to say, or do, to influence. She had no clue how to lure. She used to have. She was sure she had had some idea in her youth—but now? It was all text-messaging and mobiles, and they gave the game away by saying how often you'd called, what time and where from; it wasn't easy to be subtle. Also, because of the sophisticated missed-call feature on every phone, you couldn't kid yourself that he must have called when he clearly hadn't. If he hadn't called it was a cold truth. She was out of her depth. But she thought that giving a Crunchie bar was quite innocuous. A fun gesture. She hadn't realized that it was breaking the rules and would lead to the certainty of being dumped.

"We'd been texting. He'd even said he had that Crunchie feeling, and I'd texted back that I knew exactly what he meant and that I'd had that exact feeling for a while now."

"What?" Eliza was obviously disappointed with Martha's attempt to explain and justify her actions. "Well, to start with, you should definitely not have texted him today at all. There was no need if you were expecting to see him. You have to play it cool."

"Do I?"

"Yes!" "Duh" wasn't articulated; it didn't need to be. "How many times did you text him today?"

"I don't know. I lost count. About four."

"Martha! Bloody hell, you should *never, ever* text more than once in a day."

"But he texted me too," said Martha in self-defence.

Eliza ignored this. "And then you sent chocolate. Well, forget it, it's over. Start checking out your Filofax for alternatives, Babe, you've left yourself wide open. There is *no* way he's going to get back to you now you've opened yourself up."

With that happy prediction, Eliza swiftly changed the subject and started talking about a pair of brown cord jeans she'd seen in Karen Millen at lunchtime, and thought she might buy the next day. Then she said to Martha that she had to go, she had to finish her spreadsheet on the budget for some video or other.

Eliza said she had a date and wouldn't be back until late; Martha needn't wait up.

Martha was barely listening.

•     •     •

Martha fed the children, bathed them and started to read to them. Maisie, as usual, paid no attention whatsoever to the progress of the story, the concept of turning pages in sequence, or indeed which way up the book should be held. She irritated Mathew by chewing its corners and snatching at the pages. This induced an almighty row that Martha found she had little patience for. Instead of carefully negotiating her way through *Peter Rabbit*—by offering Maisie distractions and pleading with Mathew for his understanding—she smartly popped Maisie into her cot and tucked Mathew into his bed. She turned out the lights.

Martha pulled the sitting-room curtains closed. Stupid of her to imagine that February was anything other than bleak. She stood with her bottom resting on the radiator, which she'd hiked up to full heat, and folded her arms across her body—but she still couldn't get warm. She picked up the remote and flicked through the channels; nothing could hold her attention, not even the tawdry goings-on in *Eastenders*. On automatic pilot, Martha wandered through to the kitchen and opened the fridge. She stared inside and tried to decide what to eat. The problem was, she wasn't hungry. None of it looked tempting. She had no appetite.

He hadn't called.

How exactly had a Crunchie bar opened her mind and her heart?

She pulled out a bottle of chilled white wine, and opened it. She carefully poured herself a large glass; she no longer guiltily looked around the house, waiting for someone to shout at her for doing this. She supposed that was some progress. But then she thought how frequently she was opening a bottle of wine and immediately doubted that it was. She could clear away the children's tea plates, she could wash up. She could put on a load of washing, or do some ironing; there was always plenty of that. She could tidy the drawer where she kept plastic carrier bags. These were the kind of tasks that she used to do when she was waiting for Michael to come home and he was caught in a long meeting. None of it appealed.

She flicked through her CD collection. She had a number of recent acquisitions: Chemical Brothers, Nelly Furtado, Röyksopp. She was proud of her growing collection but, sadly, none of them suited her mood right now. She didn't have any Smiths. "Heaven Knows I'm Miserable Now" would have been perfect.

She couldn't believe it. Eliza was right. She was wrong. He was a faithless, fickle and, and, and . . . Martha searched around for a word that was damning enough. A faithless, fickle, ordinary man, she seethed.

Why hadn't he called? He was supposed to be coming to see her tonight, but he hadn't called to confirm the arrangements. Martha didn't know if she should make her own supper. The thought of a lifetime of lonely suppers was too distressing; she knew she wouldn't be able to swallow a bite.

He'd found someone new.

He was probably kissing her collarbone this very second.

It was clear that he would be spending Valentine's Day, and for that matter every other day, with a new woman. Who was she kidding, but herself? Probably several new women. She was forgotten. What was so wrong with a Crunchie bar? Because things had been fine up until then. Did men really hate it so much when you showed them you cared?

Martha thought about Michael. Her caring hadn't done much good there, either. She took a slug of wine.

But Jack had even made plans. He'd talked about the summer. He'd actually said things like "can't wait to see you with a tan." What was that, if it wasn't planning ahead? Of course, she knew Michael had said that they'd be married forever and he'd lied about that. Of course, after that she should have taken everything any man said to her with a mountain of salt. But she'd believed in Jack. She didn't know why. It defied logic and reason, but she had. Martha pounced on her mobile and reread the text messages that he'd sent her that day. They were, without exception, flirtatious, witty, friendly.

Martha didn't get it.

She poured herself another glass of wine, and noticed that she was shaking with rage. She couldn't imagine ever feeling serene again. The world was a disappointing place. He was just as disappointing as her husband, and the next man in her life would be just as disappointing too. Her arms felt like lead. She couldn't raise them even to waist height to continue pouring her drink. She put the bottle down before it slipped out of her grasp. The glass that was in her other hand wasn't as lucky: it fell to the floor and smashed. She didn't bother picking it up. The glassware that she once loved meant nothing to her.

They all let you down in the end. They all hurt and tear and spoil. They all leave. She could feel her heart pounding against her chest. She wanted to ring him so that she could give him what she used to refer to as "a piece of her mind." Now she wanted to give him "a right-royal bollocking."

Didn't he see? Couldn't he tell? Hadn't he guessed how much he'd wormed his way under her skin? He'd seemed like another layer of her skin, somewhere between all the messy bits, the innards, the heart, the soul and her toughened outer skin. Although it was not tough enough, as things had turned out.

He could at least have called. But to leave her just sitting here. Imagining . . .

He had never treated her so disrespectfully in December, and December was the party season, wall-to-wall totty. If he'd wanted to exercise his right to have other women, indulge in this naked-friend thing, then that would have been the time. The ideal opportunity.

Martha wasn't being bullish. She genuinely hadn't minded that there were other women. Jack helped her get through the endless renditions of "We Wish You a Merry Christmas." Something to help her swallow the endless, syrupy films, programmes and adverts that appeared throughout the season. The ones that persisted in showing the ideal family unit: husband, wife, two kids and a dog; they were, if not actually sitting around a piano, then certainly gathered around a TV. Every one of them, even the dog, smiling contentedly, oozing self-satisfaction and perfect happiness. The same dream she'd been living, the dream she'd watched Michael flush down the loo, as though her marriage were a dead goldfish. And Jack had helped her through all that sentimental claptrap. Like a very large glass of wine, he'd anaesthetized the voracious, relentless pain that ripped at her heart, the pain of not being wanted by her husband. At least Jack wanted her. Even if the way he wanted her wasn't the noblest. Maybe, as Eliza had repeatedly insisted, it was just sex, but it had never felt like that to Martha; it had always seemed friendlier, kinder, and gentler.

Then there'd been January. He'd been a friend to her. He'd always been at the other end of the phone. When Michael wouldn't take her calls, Jack would. And Jack listened to her endless frets about the children's colds and ear infections; but more than that, he took her out to bars and clubs and shops. He acted as though she were fun. He acted as though he wanted her around. But now it appeared he didn't want her—either nobly or ignobly.

Maybe "acted" was the operative word. Suddenly Martha was faced with the double shock of dealing, really dealing, with not being wanted as a life partner or even as a casual, friendly shag.

She thought she was going to implode.

Martha waited until nine forty-five when it was absolutely certain that he wasn't simply working late at the office. Jack always arrived at her house by seven-thirty, latest. He wasn't coming. The bottle of wine was empty and Martha couldn't think of anything more constructive to do than sink into bed alone.

Except.

She punched his mobile number into her phone. It rang two or three times before he picked it up. The tiniest smidgen of hope she'd still been harbouring—that somehow he was stuck in the office, unable to get to either his mobile or a land line—was dashed; she could hear the definite sounds of a good time in the background. A bar, possibly a club.

"Hello." He didn't exactly sound thrilled to hear from her. Yet he'd answered. He'd have known the call was from her because her name would have popped up on the screen.

The only thing Martha could deduce was that he wanted her to know that he was out with someone else. This was the coward's way of giving her the brush-off. Well, she wasn't going to give him the satisfaction. "I'm calling to tell you not to come round tonight," she said. It was pretty clear that he had no intention of coming round. Well, possibly, if he didn't get lucky, he might have been planning to come round after the club closed to roger her senseless. She had to make it perfectly clear that this was not an option.

"Oh, right," he said.

"I'm too tired," she said, meaning, of course, It's very late for a date. "And I don't want to see you. Tonight—or ever again for that matter. Whatever we had, which was irritatingly ill-defined, is over. OK? Forget it."

"If you like."

The phone went dead.

Martha fell back into her bed and cried herself to sleep.

# 35

Martha couldn't remember feeling worse. In fact, the hangover was a blessing. She deserved it; it couldn't cause enough pain, no matter what. Thank God Eliza was still sleeping; Martha really couldn't face a dose of "I told you so," even if Eliza had told her so.

*Especially* as Eliza had told her so.

But what could she have done differently? How could she have resisted Jack?

Martha poured the children large bowls of Coco Pops. Recently she worried less about their teeth; she spent more time wondering how she'd protect their hearts. The children ate their Coco Pops with unsuitable cheeriness, oblivious to their mother's disappointment.

Of course all good sense had dictated that Martha's fling with Jack would be meaningless and short-lived. Everything was against it. She hardly knew him (although it had felt as though they'd known each other forever). She'd slept with him far too quickly (although at the time it had felt right, good, proper). They had great sex, which meant he'd had zillions of lovers (although when he made love to her it didn't feel like *Kama Sutra*, page 124—it felt like affection). He'd insisted on a non-exclusive relationship (a fact that was indefensible, and as such, Martha wasn't going to try to defend it; she'd planned on continuing to ignore it). If ever she'd given the naked-friend situation any thought, she'd assumed that he was simply articulating a right; she hadn't really expected him to exercise that right. She wasn't sure when he'd have the time to do so. He was always with her.

She'd sort of assumed that the time he spent with her, which was high in quality and quantity, meant that he couldn't possibly be seeing anyone else. It would require too much energy. She hadn't given any real thought to how she'd feel learning that he was kissing other women's lips and necks, nibbling other ears, cupping other breasts. But now she was thinking about it, and the thought was horrific. Of course there were others, he'd said there was going to be, hadn't he? It was clear that sooner or later he'd meet a more attractive naked friend. He'd moved on. She could have asked him last night. His horrible honesty policy meant that he would have told her the truth, she was sure of that. But, Christ, Martha had sharpened the knife, put it in his hand, even guided the plunge, with her ridiculous naivety and hopefulness; she wasn't going to twist it too.

OK, maybe she hadn't been very realistic. Why would the one remaining single, exceptionally good-looking, fit, wealthy, witty, hung-like-a-donkey Sex God left in London—or possibly the whole of the U.K.—choose her, Martha Evergreen? And, more unlikely still, why would he choose the whole package? A mum aged thirty-two, a toddler and a baby.

Martha glanced over at her children and her heart melted with love as she watched Maisie spoon Coco Pops into her ear, and Mathew, who really should have known better, squash a banana on to the seat of the chair next to him. Both children had green slime running out of their noses, because it was the season that children got colds—in other words, it was any month apart from July or August (of course their noses ran then too, but that was from hay fever, not a cold). There was an awful smell coming from Maisie's nappy, and an awful whine coming from Mathew's mouth. Situation normal, then, thought Martha. Irresistible? Hardly. Even their bloody father had resisted. How could she hope that Jack would want it?

Martha showered and brushed her hair. She forced the children into clean clothes and then into the car. She drove to Sel-fridges. Surely looking at an abundance of overpriced luxury items would make her feel better. Normally the Food Hall did the trick, or at least the cosmetics area. But Selfridges failed to cheer her up. Martha sighed. She remembered when a trip around the local su-permarket was a treat, and that wasn't so long ago. Was her life better or worse now that she expected more from it?

She couldn't understand it. She didn't believe it. Michael and she had been together for ten years and he'd shocked and failed her—there was no denying that. But she thought she'd been doing quite well; she'd thought that if she wasn't quite getting over it, then she was, at least, getting *on* with it. Admittedly, she still rowed with Michael on occasion—well, fairly frequently, ac-tually. But she hadn't rubbished him to anyone. She'd worked hard at maintaining the relationship he had with the children by arranging days together for them, even though she hated being without the children on Sunday afternoons. She'd agreed to his idea that they handle the divorce themselves and not introduce solicitors into the proceedings, even though most people thought acquiescing made her a sandwich short of a picnic.

And, recently, and she knew this sounded mad, she'd started to get a feeling that Jack was some sort of reward.

Obviously, she didn't mean a reward from Heaven or any-thing like that—she wasn't certifiable. It just seemed to her that, as horrible as it was for her to lose Michael and have to go through a divorce, maybe there was a consolation, or possibly more than that: maybe there was a reason.

Because Jack seemed different from any other man she'd ever met.

Special.

Of course, it didn't make sense to believe that they could really make a go of it. Of course, they were just having a fling. A rebound thing.

But a girl can hope, can't she?

And that was another thing; his surname was Hope. That had to be more than a coincidence; that was a sign. When she'd thought she'd never believe in human nature again. When everyone had thought Martha was wrong to expect loyalty, morality, decency in this world, Hope had come along.

It was such a shock that Jack had turned out to be a Jack-the-lad, and had treated her with such foul disrespect. She had, despite everything—experience, evidence, expectations—believed in him. She couldn't help it. She had trusted him and this wasn't simply to do with her "un-fucking-believable naivety, gullibility and propensity to choose toss-pots," as her sister maintained; it was because he really seemed decent.

She knew it, believed it.

Or, at least, thought she had.

She wasn't expecting a marriage proposal. She knew what game he was in because he'd told her. Her mistake had been to think she could play that game. Her mistake had been to trust him, but she did trust him.

*Had* trusted him.

And since they'd met, there had been no reason not to trust him. They'd been having a great time together. She'd made dates with him, gently suggesting when they could meet. She tried to sound casual and spontaneous, but the truth was that any night in or out with him demanded that she balance childcare, Michael's access rights and Eliza's social life. It wasn't easy. Jack always immediately agreed to the dates or, at worst, said that he might have a previous arrangement to check. In those cases he gave her a time when he'd get back to confirm. He always confirmed, one way or another, at the agreed time. He was rarely late, and if he were going to be, he'd call to say so.

Jack opened doors for her, he made her cups of tea even though he didn't drink tea himself, he fixed things around the house without her having to ask or even hint, he changed the batteries in the kids' toys. She could have done these things for herself, but he always wanted to do them for her. He'd treated her with respect and kindness. But Eliza had been right after all. You can't trust them. They are all the same, fallible and unreliable.

And it hurt. The disappointment was quite astounding. Martha felt incredibly, indescribably and unrelentingly sad. She missed him. She scrabbled around in her handbag to find her phone (how had she ever managed without one?) and called Eliza.

"Hey, Doll, where are you?" asked Eliza, sleepily.

"Selfridges."

"Cool, keep an eye out for brown cords, and if you see any you think I'd like, I'll come and meet you."

"OK. I didn't see Jack last night."

"Surprise, surprise." And then more thoughtfully she added, "I'm sorry. I wish it hadn't had to turn out like this." She was a woman of the world, she'd already assumed the worst.

"I think I'm going to call him."

"For fuck's sake, Martha, don't call him." Martha could almost see Eliza jumping out of bed in alarm; she was probably grabbing her travel pass and running for the number 94 bus in a frantic effort to intervene.

"I have to," insisted Martha.

"Why do you have to?"

Martha thought about how her biggest ambition had been seeing Eliza married so that Maisie could be a flower girl and Mathew a page. That wasn't her ambition now. Her ambition had changed. She'd like to learn how to snowboard. She'd like to see an Elvis-impersonator, preferably in Vegas. She'd like to see the tulip fields in Holland. Her idea of a good time on a Saturday had been weeding the garden, then finding time to de-scale the showerhead before she did the weekly shop. Now she took the children for lunch in the Bluebird restaurant and blew a fortune in Miss Sixty. She now wore a toe-ring and was considering having her belly button pierced. Jack wasn't responsible for all of that, but he was part of it. Since meeting Jack, Martha hadn't become a better person or a different person, she'd become herself. It felt right wearing hipster jeans and steel-heel boots. Better than neat suits and court shoes had ever felt. She thought she was just at the beginning of something, and she didn't want it to finish yet. "Because my life is better with him in it than out of it."

"You're going to make a fool of yourself. He doesn't want to know, and he's going to find your pursuing him embarrassing."

"Maybe, Baby."

Maybe, Baby, maybe, Baby. Eliza repeated the phrase in her head, "What kind of talk is that?" she demanded. "Jack-shit-talk?"

But Martha didn't reply, she'd already rung off.

Martha called Jack's mobile. It went through to voicemail, but she didn't leave a message. She feared that she was only going to get one shot at this, and she didn't want to blow it by mumbling something stupid to his answering service. And experience showed that there was no chance of her saying anything sensible or accurate to the answering service—she didn't even do that if she was leaving a meter reading with the gas board.

Five minutes later her phone trilled; the reverberation thrilled like a vibrator. "Jack Mobile" flashed up on her screen.

"Hi," she said.

"Hi." He sounded hound dog.

Guilt, probably, thought Martha. "Hi," she said again because she couldn't think what else to say.

"Hi." Evidently neither could he.

"You said that."

"So did you."

"Well, about last night, I was really pissed off." Martha was finding it extremely easy to use expletives these days.

"So I gathered."

"You made me feel cheap, unwanted and used. Like a shag, not a naked friend, not any kind of friend at all."

"I have no idea how I did that," said Jack slowly.

"Because I'm not a shag, you can't just come round after the pubs kick you out. I'm over that. I'm older than that. I deserve more than that. And, OK, so I sent you a Crunchie bar, and that may mean more than the fact that I know you have a sweet tooth, but you could at least have called and said you thought things were going too quickly. Just ignoring me and hoping I'd go away was the coward's way out." Martha finally paused for breath.

"Crunchie bar. Way out? What are you talking about? I explained about Philip's birthday party. I said I wouldn't be round until later."

"What?"

"I said that I was previously committed and wouldn't be able to make it for ages. I said it was a duff idea to hook up, but you insisted that I still come round."

"Did I?"

"If my memory serves me correctly, you were very insistent."

Somewhere grey, Martha began to remember the conversation they had had on Wednesday evening.

"Oh fuck, bloody, bloody, bloody fuck," said Martha. She thought that summed up the situation. She had said that she was fine with it. "Go to the party, we'll meet later on," she'd said. She started to giggle, part relief, part embarrassment.

"I think maybe we had that discussion when you'd had one or two vinos," suggested Jack.

Martha could hear relief in his voice too; which made her want to punch the air. She didn't bother denying the vinos, it was true, she was so useless at drinking.

Fuck, fuck. What female fuckwittage.

"I am so, so sorry," said Martha, because she was. She really,

really was. All that torment for nothing. "I'd totally forgotten that was what we'd agreed. I thought it was because of the Crunchie bars."

"What?"

"I thought you were—sort of—put off. That I'd . . ." Martha didn't really know what to say. It seemed so silly. She seemed so silly.

"Oh yeah, the Crunchie bars. Very funny. Thanks."

"You liked them?"

"I loved them. You make me laugh, Little Miss E."

She knew it. She knew it. This world was a good world. She didn't have to be frightened. There were all sorts of possibilities out there. She should have trusted him. She should have believed, and hoped, and trusted, and cared, and not tarred him with the same brush, because he wasn't the same canvas, and he did deserve that respect and chance. So did the world. Martha wasn't going to be bitter.

"You're right, I remember now. God, I'm mortified. I am *so* sorry."

"I was upset, girl. What was all that about last night? Why did you dump me? What did I do wrong?"

"I'd forgotten. Oh God, I'm sorry." He thought *she'd* dumped him.

"I'm glad you're back. Lovely Little Miss E." Jack was smiling; Martha could hear it in his voice as he instantly forgave her. As he understood her frailties and insecurities. "Martha, there's something you need to remember. There's only one thing you need to remember. I'm not going to do anything to hurt you. In fact, I'm going to do my best to make you happy and make sure you have as much fun as possible. I'm very straightforward. If I change my mind, I'll tell you. I wouldn't just not turn up."

And Martha believed him. Despite the popular fiction of her day advising her otherwise.

"The thing is, I like you in my life. My life is better with you in it than out of it," he said.

"That's what I've been thinking all day, too," said Martha.

# 36

For the first time in years, Martha felt excited about Valentine's Day. Giggly to her core. Would he send her a card? He probably would, he'd mentioned Valentine's Day to her a couple of times, so he must be planning on celebrating it. She couldn't believe that either, that there were men in Britain who actually remembered February 14th and didn't need prompting. In all the shops where Martha had browsed through the cards, chocolate kisses and chocolate willies, where she'd bought heart-shape sparklers and seriously considered buying a velvet eye mask, she'd seen other women browsing, not men. It was women who pondered, considered and finally purchased the cards. Women who fingered the pretty little boxes that held candies but offered dreams.

Whilst selecting her Valentine's gift Martha had fun chatting to the other female shoppers. They compared merchandise and swapped stories as they looked at the displays of red crêpe paper and pink tissue roses; the women had nothing in common other than the fun and expectancy. Would he buy her a present? She doubted it would be flowers or chocolates; in fact, she'd be a bit disappointed if it was. It would be a bit predictable, which would make the fact that she'd had her pubes shaved into a heart shape and dyed red a tiny bit embarrassing.

What a laugh she'd had at the beautician's. She remembered

the first time she'd heard of anyone having their pubic hair waxed into a shape. An arrow, if she remembered correctly. Martha had been horrified. "How silly! How frivolous!" She'd said so to Eliza, but Eliza had surprised her and said, "Oh, I don't know, I once had mine shaped into a heart and that was quite fun."

At the time, Martha had seen this simply as further evidence of her sister's status as a changeling. Now Martha thought a heart, just as Eliza had described it, sounded quite fun.

"New twist on wearing your heart on your sleeve," commented Amy, Martha's beautician. She hardly smirked at all, which was good of her, since prior to this, the most outrageous thing Martha had ever requested was a colour on her toe nails. It was Amy who suggested the red dye.

Martha had huge fun choosing Valentine cards and gifts. She couldn't quite remember Valentine's last year. She was sure that Michael must have given her a card. They always gave cards. They handed them over with the cornflakes at the breakfast table. But when was the last time they'd done something really special for Valentine's Day? She couldn't remember the last time they'd shared champagne, or a meal, or a bed, especially because it was Valentine's Day. Michael had always thought that the whole event was very commercial; the only winners were the card and chocolate manufacturers. And Martha had always agreed with him.

Publicly.

But she did remember the thrill when, as a girl of about fourteen, she'd received six Valentine cards, more than anyone else in her class. She'd walked on air for a month.

In a Stalinesque manner, Martha had now rewritten history. With a week's perspective, "the Crunchie Debacle" was now fondly looked back upon as a roaring success. Jack and Martha's first misunderstanding had, conversely, brought them closer. Without being conscious of it, they were building a bank of shared experiences. They had happy days going to the cinema, playing with the children, chatting, reading, listening to music, and wonderful nights sharing a bed, a pizza and a pot of bio yogurt; now they even had a shared misunderstanding. The misunderstanding wasn't consequential enough for either party to hold an actual gripe, but it was important enough for both to realize that they could hurt each other—seriously—therefore they had to be careful not to. *Couples* had misunderstandings.

The rewriting of history was so complete that Martha convinced herself that the indisputable success of delivering the Crunchie package to Jack's office demanded that she do something similar for Valentine's Day. Similar, but on a grander scale. She didn't share her plan with Eliza, as she knew that Eliza would make disparaging remarks and Martha could do without the discouragement. Recently Martha had started to question whether Eliza really did know so much about men, romance and all the associated matters of the heart. From where Martha was standing, Eliza seemed to get as much wrong and as much right as the next woman. In Martha's considered opinion, not that Eliza ever asked for Martha's considered opinion, Eliza had made a mistake in leaving Greg. A grave mistake. She hadn't seemed happy since. So Martha didn't tell anyone her plans for Valentine's Day. She simply did what seemed right to her.

The reception area of Jack's office was intimidating. It was one of those places that needed and used nothing but space to tell you just how trendy it was: white walls, white marble floors, white lilies in a white vase perched on a walnut reception desk. The desk was high, almost at Martha's chest level.

"I need your help." Martha smiled her broadest smile at the burly-looking guy on reception. She was grateful that the receptionist wasn't a beautiful, skinny, starlet type. That would have been crippling. It was lucky that she had come at lunchtime when the regular receptionist would be on her break and the security guard was in charge.

"Erm, how into Valentine's Day are you?" she asked, giggling and blushing at once. Being careful to flutter her eyelashes extravagantly. What was it that Eliza had said? "Practice flirting with everyone. It will make you a better flirt and everyone will be your friend."

The burly guy was smiling, at least with his eyes. He was enjoying Martha's embarrassment and her flirtatiousness.

"I'd like you to send up this card and pressie, and then send up these cards, drip-fed through the after—"

The beautiful receptionist emerged from nowhere. She was carrying two cups of steaming coffee. She passed one to the security guard and then looked at Martha. "Can I help you?" she sang pleasantly.

"Erm . . ." Now the embarrassment was tenfold. Martha wondered if she should make a run for it, or whether she had already been recorded on CCTV somewhere.

She took a deep breath. "I need your help," Martha repeated. She managed the smile, but really couldn't bring herself to bat the lashes. She explained once again that she wanted one card and pressie to be delivered first, with strict instructions that the card must be opened before the present, and then the other three cards needed to be delivered at intervals throughout the day. The first card read "I wanted to take the opportunity of this special day to say something meaningful . . ." Then the pressie was a Thorntons chocolate heart, upon which she'd had iced an anagram of "something meaningful": "I shag fun men longtime." She hoped he'd get it. The other three cards were all in different styles, and she'd written different messages with different pens. The messages ranged from the raunchy to the romantic. Martha was really pleased with herself.

The receptionist warmed to Martha and beamed.

"Er, they're for—" started Martha.

"Jack Hope," smiled the receptionist, revealing that although it was an office of over 300 employees, most of whom were male, as far as the gagging-for-it female population of West London was concerned, there was only one real option. "Are you the one who rang earlier this morning?" she asked pleasantly.

"No." Martha managed to continue wearing her smile whilst she begged God to strike her down with a flash of lightning right there and then. The receptionist looked mortified; the burly security guard looked amused. He was too old to be Jack Hope, but, hell, he wished he had at least sired him.

"No, that wasn't me. I'm one of a number." Martha tried to ease the receptionist's discomfort, she was very used to making everyone else feel OK. "Don't worry, I know the score." She tried to sound more hip than she was feeling. It was becoming increasingly difficult to blank out the other naked friends. "That's why I've bought so many cards. I want to give him the thrill of loads of women, without actually having to have loads of women." Suddenly her romantic plan seemed desperate and ludicrous. "I *am* going out with him tonight," she added gormlessly.

The receptionist nodded pityingly. Martha realized it was probably wisest to shut up. She didn't owe these people an explanation, even if they were lovely people.

"Err, so who was this other caller this morning? D'you have any ideas?" Martha then inquired, blowing her cool 100 per cent.

"She didn't sound very nice," said the receptionist kindly, immediately forgetting that she'd initially thought the caller and Martha were one and the same. "She didn't know his schedule. She wanted to know if he'd be in the office today, or whether he'd be in the West End. He's—"

"In the office," said Martha. She knew. She knew he was in the office because he'd already called her several times that day. This mystery Valentine caller was nothing to worry about. Martha was so used to trying to reassure people that she wanted to put the receptionist and security guard at their ease, but then sensibly decided against it. "Have a nice day," she said instead.

"You too," smiled the receptionist.

# 37

It was a long day. The longest. Martha took the children to the park and the shops, and they had lunch out.

At two minutes past two, Jack called. "Thanks for the chocolate heart, Little Miss E."

"What chocolate heart?" Martha feigned ignorance, as convention demanded.

"I know it was from you," he insisted.

"Why? Can't any of the other women you sleep with spell?" teased Martha.

Jack laughed. "You're very funny. That anagram thing, very witty. You're the most fabulous woman I've ever met."

And then he hung up.

Hung up!

He'd said she was fabulous—the most fabulous—and then he'd hung up, before she had a chance to reply or react.

OhmyGodOhmyGodOhmyGodOhmyGod.

He thought she was "the most fabulous" woman he'd ever met.

Martha walked on air for the rest of the day, which she spent in the lingerie department of John Lewis. Jack had texted her and asked if she would "indulge him as it was Valentine's Day and wear cute underwear." Martha was thrilled, flattered and petrified in equal parts. Thrilled and flattered that Jack believed that she was the type of woman to have cute underwear, and petrified because she wasn't that type of woman at all, and so obviously she'd have to go and buy something new.

Martha assumed cute underwear meant stockings, suspenders, a lacy bra and knickers. She wasn't going to entertain the idea of crotchless or anything kinky like that; she wouldn't manage to keep a straight face. Besides, she wasn't absolutely certain as to whether crotchless knickers really existed, or whether they were just a figment of the imagination of the type of man who read the *Sun*. She supposed a visit to Ann Summers would put her mind at rest one way or the other, but she couldn't pluck up the courage, not on such short notice. Martha had never worn stockings before. No one had ever taken the time to ask her to bother. Possibly because she had always voiced the opinion that stockings were ludicrous. She was the type of woman who slept in pyjamas, for goodness sake; it was a significant jump from that to Agent Provocateur lingerie.

She decided to buy black. Red was out of the question. Well, at least first time round. Martha didn't think it was an unrealistic idea to introduce red at a later date. How much lace before she looked like a saloon girl? And did you wear the belt around your waist or hips? Under or over your panties? The picture on the packet showed the belt over, but then would you be able to go to the loo? Then what to wear over the top of "cute underwear"? Trousers were out of the question; a little black dress seemed too dressy. In the end, Martha chose a black T-shirt and a beige leather skirt, not too tight, but tight enough, with black knee-high boots.

At seven o'clock Mrs. Evergreen knocked on Martha's door. Martha had arranged for her mother to babysit because obviously Eliza had a date.

"Lord, Mum, that's a big bag, are you moving in?"

"No, dear, I've brought my knitting," smiled Mrs. Evergreen.

Martha thought her mother was being optimistic. Mathew had lined up an arsenal of games to play with his adored granny. Martha doubted her mother would get the time to make a cup of tea, let alone knit up a pair of bedsocks or whatever.

"I won't be late," she assured.

"Don't worry. You just enjoy yourself, you deserve it," smiled Mrs. Evergreen. "I don't suppose—"

"No, nothing." Martha cut her off before she could ask whether Michael had sent a card or flowers. Her mother looked disappointed. Martha wondered if she should tell her that she was "the most fabulous girl" Jack knew. After all, it had made Martha's day.

They'd agreed to meet at the bar in the Sanderson Hotel. The hotel was funky and well, yes, pretentious too. Martha knew that Michael would have loved it. They'd visited a number of Ian Schrager hotels before the children had been born. The modernity and beauty had blown them away, as had the cost. The fact that they (or their firms) had been able to afford for them to stay in such stylish places had been a thrill. They'd made love in the big, white beds under the large, imposing mirrors and amazing, challenging art. Martha remembered how excited and impressed they'd been on their first visit. She couldn't remember when it became commonplace to stay in fabulous hotels where even the bellboys wore Armani. She couldn't remember when Michael had first started to complain that the service was slow, "especially considering what we're paying." She couldn't remember exactly when the complaining overwhelmed the pleasure, but she knew it was wrong.

The bar was full of beautiful people: women who were too thin, and men who were too wealthy. Martha wondered whether there would ever be a world where the roles were reversed. Where the women were wealthy enough to arrogantly carry beer bellies and the men had eating disorders and silicon implants. Martha rarely mixed with this type of person, although Eliza did, and often came home with funny anecdotes about women who could tell you the number of calories in the olive in their Martinis and men who could give you the numbers on the banknotes in their wallet. To Eliza's credit, she was able to enjoy the glitz of visiting bars and hotels such as these, rubbing shoulders with the beautiful young things of the twenty-first century, without taking it too seriously. She wasn't a wannabe, and therefore people assumed she already was. Martha decided to adopt the same policy so that she could relax and enjoy the hotel bar, the chic women and chiselled-jawed men.

There was Jack. He was standing at the end of the bar, drinking apple juice. Martha felt a surge of pride; she firmly believed he was the most beautiful man in the bar. He wasn't the tallest and everyone was dressed well, but he definitely had the kindest eyes. She threaded her way through the crowds. He watched her being watched.

"God, you look hot," he said, kissing her on the lips. He lingered there.

Martha wondered if it was hip to kiss in a bar like this. She wasn't sure what the current fashionable thinking was on public displays of affection. Whatever—it made her feel as amazing as holding the winning Lottery ticket.

She had never looked "hot." She had been pretty, lovely, and on her wedding day one or two people had described her as beautiful (old aunties and Michael).

But here she was being hot.

Her lips were glossed. Her lashes were long. Her hipbone jutted out at a sexy angle and, really, she couldn't wait for him to find that out.

"What can I get you to drink?" he asked.

"I'll have a Red Bull."

"Sure?"

"Yeah, I don't want to get drunk." Martha had been drinking far more than was good for her recently. Well, since Michael had asked for a divorce. She knew it was weak and self-destructive and she didn't want to get maudlin or forget anything important tonight. Although it seemed such a shame to come to a bar like this and not try one of the many champagne cocktails on offer. She did enjoy a glass of crisp, cold champagne.

"Don't you fancy a glass of crisp, cold champagne?" asked Jack. "It seems a shame to come to a cool gig like this and not have something special."

Martha gave in to the ESP and asked for champers. The service was embarrassingly slow, but without the embarrassment. Whilst it was nearly impossible to catch the eye of the barman, Martha was surprised when she noticed that *she* caught the eye of two or three strangers. They were flirting, registering their interest in her. And they were good-looking, really good-looking. They were the type of men who would never have given Martha a second glance when she wore her neat shirts and M&S slacks, but were now more than ready and willing to whip off her Ted Baker T and leather skirt. As such they were less interesting to her than even Michael. For all his faults, at least he had once fancied her in clothes from Monsoon. OK, as it turned out, she didn't like herself in clothes from Monsoon, but that was hardly the point. The good-looking men were obviously shallow. Martha looked at Jack and once again marvelled at how peculiar it was that he was this odd mix of *über* cool, and yet totally unfazed by her very-recent geekiness.

Martha hunted out a quiet table, Jack following her. She took a seat and as he sat down opposite, her whole body redirected itself towards him. Outwardly she didn't move an inch; inwardly she felt her lungs fill with fresh oxygen, her heart lean towards him. The hairs on her body stood up in deference. Her smile was a fraction wider for him. Her teeth slightly whiter, her lips slightly wetter. Her sex that bit hotter.

"Remarkable that there's a free table," commented Jack.

"Not really, it's too out of the way for the see-and-be-seen. Most of the people here would rather hover uncomfortably at a crowded bar than miss spotting Stella McCartney's eyebrow."

Jack laughed. "I love it that you're not impressed by that shit, Martha, that you know your own mind."

"Well, if it was Madonna's eyebrow, that would be a different story." She paused. "Don't you think I'm molly?"

"Molly? What's 'molly'?"

"Girl geek-like," explained Martha.

"No way, Martha, the opposite. I've told you, I think you're fabulous."

"Why do you think I'm fabulous?"

"Because you pay attention to everything that's going on around you, you seem to be fascinated with life and that in turn makes you fascinating. Because you're beautiful and strong and because you try hard to be kind and decent."

Martha basked under the praise for a second or two.

"And most of all because you're a fantastic shag," added Jack.

So, the same reasons that Martha thought Jack was fabulous, then.

After they'd had a drink Jack asked Martha if she wanted dinner or a room. He assured her that he'd be equally happy with either choice. Martha pointed out that she couldn't stay over because she had to get back for the children. Jack admitted having arranged with Mrs. Evergreen for her to stop the night to look after Mathew and Maisie, which explained the outsize bag. Martha was horrified.

"Do you think that was presumptuous?" he asked, concerned. "I mean, it's not like we haven't had sex before."

"I know that," said Martha, aghast, "but my mother doesn't.

She thinks Mathew and Maisie were immaculate conceptions, or at least test tube. If she could have, she'd have blindfolded the midwife who delivered my babies."

Jack was obviously amused by Martha's panic. "On the contrary, she made it very clear that she wanted you to have a good time. She repeatedly insisted that you needed it and deserved it. I only cut her short on her lecture on responsible attitudes towards contraception."

Martha was bemused but somewhat reassured. She went outside the bar to ring home. She wanted to check that her mum really was OK with babysitting overnight, and hadn't been browbeaten into it by Jack. Her mother scattered the appropriate assurances, and insisted with such force that Martha did her very best to enjoy herself that Martha truly believed it was her filial duty to have multiple orgasms.

When Martha returned to the table, Jack was nowhere to be seen. The waiter handed her an envelope. "Apparently it's an anagram," he said without an iota of interest. The waiter was very beautiful, probably too beautiful to have a pulse, let alone a heart or a sense of humour, thought Martha.

The envelope was blue. She opened it up and was not too surprised to find it was a funny card with a cartoon picture and a fairly obvious joke about the importance of the size of a man's equipment. Well, she hadn't been expecting a Shakespearean sonnet. Inside the card Jack had written "Mum in on shafting glee." She studied it for some time—"Mum in on shafting glee," what did he mean? Martha began to giggle. Of course, it was another anagram of "something meaningful." There was also a room number.

Martha ran up to join Jack.

Literally ran.

She could skip dinner.

# 38

He slammed her against the wall and urgently and repeatedly kissed her. She wrapped her legs around him and started exploring his body, probably for the hundredth time, although it always seemed like the first.

It was a perfect night. Jack had bought her a present, a pair of blue glittery trainers from Diesel. They were stylish, unconventional, the right size and coveted by Martha. She was thrilled. The perfect Valentine's present. Jack opened the gifts Martha had bought him. She'd bought a selection. Two good books she'd read. A small yellow shaped animal toy that laughed when you picked it up. The hooting bag seemed appropriate because Jack was a big pack of laughs. She'd also bought him a purple cushion that in 1950s retro style had a black picture of a bus and the words "Hop on Baby" emblazoned across it. The double entendre wasn't lost on either of them. There wasn't a heart or piece of red tissue in sight. Martha thought her pressies were cool yet thoughtful. Jack was clearly delighted. She was glad that she'd ignored Eliza's advice, which was not to bother with gifts ("They show you care." "But I do care." "Exactly, that's why you definitely shouldn't show it.").

"Christ, this place is a giggle," said Jack. He'd first flung himself full length on to the bed and was now bouncing up and down; he looked like a child. He was unashamedly impressed. He pored over the menus, checked out the minimalist packed toiletries, fed her the complimentary slices of pineapple. He showed her the contents of the mini bar, and they both expressed their amazement that it sold everything from Durex to jelly beans, disposable cameras to baseball hats. Martha wasn't really surprised; the contents of the mini bar were the same in all the Schrager hotels, she'd seen it all before.

"D'you think the camera and the Durex are meant to be used together?" he joked. He opened the bathroom cabinet, switched on the hairdryer, rang room service and requested that CDs were brought to their room, as well as beans on toast. They chose beans on toast because it wasn't on the menu; besides which, Martha had never drunk champagne with beans on toast. Martha found Jack's enthusiasm infectious. She suddenly found that it was OK to be impressed. Overwhelmed.

She lay on the bed next to him. He started to kiss her with his pure, extreme, potent, probing kisses. However, despite the fun they were having and the champagne she was drinking, Martha was riddled with trepidation. How would she ever approach the subject of her "cute underwear"? It was peculiar, considering she'd sat stripped bare and spreadlegged in front, on top and behind him, that she felt ridiculous for having complied with his request. Maybe he'd only been joking when he suggested it and would think that she was a total tart once she undressed. And the un-dressing would have to be sooner rather than later, because at the moment she couldn't take her boots off. Little as she knew about seductive apparel, she did know that the toe seams of nylons were not sexy—but the heels on her boots were high enough to be lethal. Surely he thought it was odd that she hadn't taken off her boots, usually shoes and socks off was the first thing she did at home, the moment she walked through the door. It was the only way to relax. Was she supposed to wait and let him discover the saloon girl get-up during the course of the evening? Or was she supposed to go into the bathroom and strip down to the essen-tials and emerge with a flamboyant "Tah-dah"? Why didn't sexy lingerie come with a set of handy hints on how to conduct one-self, she wondered.

In the end, Martha opted for the fast strip in the bathroom. At least that way she could get the moment over with and start to relax, enjoy what the evening had in store for her. She checked her reflection one last time.

Who was that sexy woman smiling back at her? The woman with glossy, blowjob lips and an MTV figure, the woman in black bra, knickers, suspenders and knee-high boots? The sexy woman didn't care a bit if the four-inch steel heels ripped the sheets (although she didn't want to injure Jack).

Martha barely recognized her.

But she did like her.

She liked her much more than the woman who had stood on the Tube platform envying lusty teenage girls chewing gum and attracting the attention of hormonal teenage boys.

"You look fabulous. Absolutely amazing," he said. His voice licked her mind, causing her to quiver like an animal shaking water from its fur. She was amazing. She was a goddess. And not just because he said so. Martha didn't reply. She said nothing at all as she climbed on to the bed and started to lick his magnificent cock. She was excited to the very centre of her being, she smelt his skin, his sex, his sweat. The sweat of his bollocks, the sweat of his pits. Did she dare? Did people ever? It seemed so whorish. But then she was wearing suspenders. She nuzzled him and stealthily edged her knickers to one side so he could enter her without her removing them. He fingered the silky material of the suspender belt, gently twanging it against her thigh. Then he slipped his fingers inside her, finding her soused in her own excitement. Wintry fingers on scalding flesh. She came instantly, pouring out on to his hands. The acute release caused her to quake and convulse. But she bit her tongue and remained silent as she rolled the condom over his hardness, straddled him and then rode him hard until they were both spent.

●     ●     ●

She put her hand on his sleeping chest that gently rose and fell. It was hot, and the smooth, soft skin scorched her. It was nearly five in the morning. Was this it? Was this what everyone was always thinking of, writing songs about, hoping for? Was this love? This amazing combination of fun, happiness, contentment and stunning sex?

# 39

"Mostly, being a child is a tedious waiting game. Don't you think?" asked Eliza, who was born a teenager.

Tom didn't know what to reply. He'd enjoyed his childhood. It had been idyllic, in a '70s middle-class way, more Angel Delight and Mr. Whippy than homemade apple pie. More cheese fondue than Sunday roast, but he'd always considered it adequate. Didn't everyone look back at their childhoods fondly? Well, unless it had been truly ghastly, like those of children brought up on inner-city housing estates without shoes or Scalextric. Was this woman going to confess to some horrible abuse in her childhood? How mortifying. He should have known by the fact that her ears were pierced twice.

This was his second date with Martha's sister. He wasn't sure why he'd asked her to meet him for a second time; he supposed it was because he hadn't really expected her to agree. She was a beautiful girl, very beautiful. His girlfriends were usually pretty, or the type who "made the best of themselves," so being out with this beauty was an adventure. But she was a bit . . . different to the girls he usually spent his time with, and he didn't necessarily mean different in a positive sense.

"Err, so was your childhood tough?" he asked, shifting uncomfortably in his seat. He felt he had to ask although he really didn't want to know.

"Oh no, perfect really. Doting parents and grandparents. Weekends in the caravan visiting castles and stately homes, lots of pocket money to buy Sherbet Dib Dabs and Flumps with. Nothing out of the ordinary happened. That was why it was so tedious."

See. Different, thought Tom. Odd, actually.

"And do you know what the strangest thing is?"

What? Stranger than resenting an idyllic childhood?

"Now I find myself longing to reproduce that tedious childhood. I want a house where, every morning, there is a row about lost gym kits or mislaid homework. I want children who clean the car to earn pocket money. I want to go to Legoland."

Quite mad. Tom decided to skip pudding and coffee, just get safely home as soon as possible.

Eliza wasn't sure why she'd agreed to the second date with Tom, either. She supposed it was because she couldn't bear the idea of spending Valentine's evening in alone, or, worse yet, babysitting for Martha, knowing absolutely that Martha was having her brains shagged out.

The Embassy was a very cool club. Eliza, naturally, had membership but she didn't eat there often, just came for a drink on a Wednesday (the new Friday, Thursday was so over). Dining there was far too expensive for someone who was an amoeba on the food chain of the music-video industry, so it would have been mad to turn him down.

Their first date had been at the V&A. Tom had wanted to see an exhibition about glass-blowing, Eliza had agreed because she thought it was new street talk for an exhibition on the history of drugs; it had to be, didn't it? When the exhibition had turned out really to be about glass-blowing, Eliza had laughed so much that

Tom had demanded to know why. When she explained, he'd laughed at the confusion too, which Eliza had liked about him. So here they were at the Embassy, eating oysters and drinking champagne, and it was pleasant enough.

And pleasant enough shouldn't be shunned, thought Eliza, as she stifled a yawn.

Eliza did not fancy Tom. Eliza could not imagine a universe or time zone in which she would fancy Tom. His hair parted in a funny way, and when he laughed he wrinkled up his nose, which made her think of a hamster. But she hadn't fancied anyone for so long that she was beginning to think that Martha was putting bromide in her cornflakes. Still, the oysters were nice.

She searched her mind for something to say. "Did you get any cards?"

"Cards?"

"Valentine cards."

"No." Tom thought that this was a peculiar question for his date to put to him, but politeness forced him to reciprocate. "Err, and you?"

"No, not really. Well, yours, and one from Mathew, my nephew, but no, not really." Eliza sighed, her disappointment at not receiving something else was enormous. So enormous that she didn't quite grasp just how rude she was being to Tom.

She remembered how last year Greg had taken her on a picnic. As it was February, he hosted the picnic in their front room, but it was a genuine picnic. He'd bought a stack of flowers from New Covent Garden and put them in every available vessel around the flat. He'd painted a huge sun on the wall. It was still there; the landlord would be furious and unlikely ever to give Greg his deposit back. He'd spread a rug on the floor; there was a hamper with crusty loaves, ripe cheeses, black olives, hummus and KitKats (Eliza's favourite chocolate). He'd insisted on wearing beach shorts, and playing a stupid game where he blew imaginary sand off the food and took his clothes off because the imaginary sand had got caught in his shorts. He kept moving the rug because the imaginary tide was coming in. Eventually they shuffled into the bedroom, which had been Greg's plan all along.

Then there'd been the Valentine's before last, which was possibly even more fabulous. They flew to Venice to watch the carnival. It was sensational, a riot of colour and noise and smells (some of which were pretty unpleasant, but most were food-related and lovely). They travelled on a budget airline and stayed at the local Youth Hostel. They didn't have much money, but they had a lot of imagination and a really good time. The whole trip probably cost the price of tonight's dinner.

Eliza was wrenched back to the present. "Oh my God, I don't believe it."

"What?"

"Look. It's him."

"Who?" Tom started to crane his neck in the direction that Eliza was staring.

"Don't look!" she squealed.

Tom immediately snapped his head back to face Eliza. He did it with such speed that he'd have to visit his chiropractor asap. He probably had whiplash.

"*Who* is he with? Do you know?" demanded Eliza.

"Have I got permission to look now?" asked Tom reasonably.

"S'pose. Who is she?"

Tom carefully turned and looked in the direction of Eliza's outraged glares. He shook his head indicating that he didn't know who Michael was with.

Michael leant across the table to hand something to the woman. Eliza couldn't see what was in the envelope. Tickets maybe. To a concert or show? Perhaps flight tickets? Poor, poor Martha. The woman leant across the table and kissed Michael.

She was definitely showing more cleavage than necessary, and she definitely let that kiss linger longer than necessary.

Eliza suddenly went off the idea of a champagne sorbet.

# 40

"Great gift," marvelled Eliza.

Martha was surprised that her approval was so robust, but she was grateful. She'd had a fantastic night at the Sanderson; she didn't want Eliza's predictions of doom to dampen the afterglow. "Yeah, I haven't had anything so unique bought for me since 1994."

"What was that?"

"Michael bought me a purple suede mini-skirt. It was about the width of a belt. I didn't really have the legs to carry it off, but I let him part with the forty-five notes—which was an enormous amount of money back then—because I was so flattered that he thought it would suit me."

"Did you ever wear it?"

"Only in the bedroom," Martha giggled. When had Michael stopped thinking of her that way? Martha remembered making love to Michael on sofas and tables and chairs, right at the beginning. But then as beds became more freely available they only ever made love in bed, and eventually they stopped doing much of that. Except for Fridays. The odd thing was, whenever they did make love they'd ask themselves, and each other, why they didn't do it more often. Michael and Martha knew each other's body inside out. Michael hit the spot with frightening intensity every time. Martha knew exactly how fast, how hard, how long it took to arouse Michael. So when had the intimacy dissolved into laziness?

With Jack Martha performed. She felt beautiful, interesting, undiscovered. She was a paradise, not a paradise lost. Suddenly Martha froze. It was possible that one day Jack would buy her shoes from Dr. Scholl the way Michael had started to buy her below-the-knee skirts. It was possible, but not probable. Martha would not think like that; it was not inevitable that a paradise known had to be a paradise lost.

"What about you? How did you fare?" She changed the subject.

Eliza hesitated. The most significant event of her Valentine's evening was the fact that she'd seen Michael. Should she tell Martha? Would Martha get any consolation from the fact that Michael's spotting of Eliza had almost certainly ruined his evening?

Luckily, Martha was so pumped with lust that she wasn't really capable of thinking about anyone other than herself and Jack for any length of time. "I almost feel guilty about how happy I am," trilled Martha. "Surely I should feel more miserable, not quite so thrilled at the prospect of life? But I am thrilled. It is thrilling. There's so much more out there than a man that doesn't care about me."

"Do you really think that?" asked Eliza. God, Jack really must be a magician in the sack.

"I do."

"Good, because I think there's something you should know. What I mean is, I think I'd want to know, if I were you."

Martha already knew that she didn't want to know but that she probably needed to.

"I saw Michael, last night."

"Where?"

"At the Embassy."

It was Valentine's night. Martha didn't need to ask if he was alone. "What's she like?"

"Blonde, young, tall." Martha sighed at the predictability of the situation. Michael had turned her into a cliché. "Not as slim as you," added Eliza hopefully.

That was supposed to help.

"Do you know who she was?"

"Well, I embarrassed him into an introduction."

Martha was almost amused. She'd have liked to see Michael's expression when faced with feisty Eliza.

"I didn't make a scene, Martha, because I knew you'd kill me, although I wanted to pour his soup into his lap."

He'd chosen soup. It must have been French onion, which was the only soup Michael would eat. "So what was her name?"

"Eleanor."

Martha stopped breathing. It didn't mean anything to her. That was better—or was that worse?

"I said all along that he was having an affair," continued Eliza.

"A Valentine's date does not mean he was having an affair. *I* was on a date."

"Martha, it's obvious."

"Is it?"

"Men never leave unless they have another home to go to. Another woman is always the reason they leave."

Martha flicked a dishcloth over the kitchen surfaces. She refused to meet Eliza's eye. "Don't you see? I can't believe that about the man I loved. If you're right, I've been a fool, and on top of everything else, I can't admit to being a fool. What would you like for supper? We've got quiche, and I could do some jacket potatoes or perhaps pasta," suggested Martha, and in this way she made it clear that the conversation was closed.

•     •     •

"Were you going to tell me that you were seeing someone else?"

"Yes."

"When?" Michael sighed and Martha could hear his frustration through the miles of telephone cable. She knew that her late-night call was annoying him intensely; she also wished she'd been able to stop herself making it. But she hadn't been able to. "When were you going to tell me?" she repeated.

"When the time was right. Soon," he added. It was clear that this call was making Michael uncomfortable. "Look, Martha, I knew you'd be hurt. I didn't know how to tell you."

"When did you meet her?"

"Does it matter?"

"Yes, it does. To me, it matters." Martha was indignant. Of course it fucking matters, you moron, was left unsaid.

"I've known her for . . . I'm not sure," he stalled. "Over a year."

"So you *have* been having an affair." Martha managed to make her inquiry sound matter-of-fact, as though she was discovering nothing more sinister than the fact that someone had been on a diet: so you have been using skimmed milk.

"No. She was just a friend." He sounded angry, insulted.

Martha had little patience, she owned the monopoly on feeling insulted. She lay in bed and wondered what she ought to ask next. She wondered if it mattered and whether he'd tell her the truth anyway. "Why haven't I heard you mention her name if she was a friend?"

"She was a friend of a friend. She's Karen's friend. She wasn't a very close friend."

"She's clearly that now. How long have you been seeing her?"

"A few weeks."

"How many weeks?"

"I don't know, I don't keep count."

"Two, three?"

"More than that."

"Before Christmas, after?"

"Before, maybe. Stop this, Martha." Michael sounded confused. He didn't like being confused, that was when things were said, things later to be regretted. "I don't owe you any answers. You're sleeping with Jack," he argued, in an effort to recover some composure.

"I've never lied to you about Jack. Why did you lie to me about this Eleanor woman?"

"Because you kept going on and on about an affair. I knew you wouldn't believe me if I said I'd known her for ages but just started slee—seeing her."

"And lying to me was supposed to help me trust you, was it?" snapped Martha; then she hung up.

Still, she wanted to believe him.

And she nearly did.

Martha lay awake and stared at the ceiling. She wished that Jack were there in bed with her so that he could wrap his lovely taut body around hers. His skin was clean, cool, firm.

It was easiest not to think about the possibility that the man she had loved for ten years was sleeping with someone else.

She still didn't want to believe it was an affair, however many people insisted that there was no other explanation. It might have started after he'd left Martha, the way it had with her and Jack.

Why wasn't that much of a comfort?

He'd said he thought he could be happier living in a different way. He'd said he'd be happier alone than he was with her. God, that had hurt. An exquisite white hot fork of lightning pierced her entire body every time she replayed those words in her head or understood their consequences in her heart.

But it didn't hurt as much as admitting that someone else was making him happier.

It was death by a thousand cuts.

How did this woman make Michael happy? Did she laugh at

his jokes? Assuming, of course, that he was telling jokes again. He'd stopped telling Martha jokes long ago. Did she cook better than Martha? Did she dress better? Think more logically? Would she be able to bear him more beautiful children? That thought slapped Martha like a bucket of freezing water. She looked at the photo of Mathew and Maisie that stood on her bedside table. She stretched out and caressed their faces beneath the shiny glass; she could feel their warmth and wonder beneath her fingertips. Mathew's curly, blond hair and chubby cheeks must have been especially designed to melt her heart. She leaned forward and kissed his cherry lips. Maisie's smile spread from ear to ear; the chocolate smudges did not distract from her radiance. Children were beautiful. Her children were amazing. Spectacular. Martha smiled to herself. None of it mattered. However this woman made Michael happy was all right by her, because Martha was all right by Martha. Martha believed Jack was right and Michael was mistaken. She *was* a fabulous person. The most fabulous was possibly a stretch, but she was pretty, good, kind, honest, even funny when she had the time. She cooked well, dressed well, thought well; her children were unsurpassable.

What Martha wanted now, more than anything, was to talk to Jack. She looked at the clock; it was very late, after midnight. If she called and he was grumpy because of the late hour she'd be wounded. Or if she called him and he wasn't alone she'd be devastated. Inconsolable. But Martha didn't think he would be grumpy, and she did think he'd be alone. She believed it would be OK. She trusted him.

"Do you think I'm a fool to believe in loyalty, wonder, fidelity? Still believe in it?" she asked without bothering with any conventional introductions and health inquiries.

"No, Babe, not at all," replied Jack. There was absolutely nothing in his tone that suggested Martha's inquiry was off the wall. She loved him for that.

Well, not really *loved*—that was just a turn of phrase. She wasn't saying she *loved* Jack. Was she? Jack struggled in the dark to look at his alarm clock. Eleven minutes past twelve. Poor Little Miss E., obviously a bit stressed about something. He absent-mindedly started to tickle his cats, who always slept with him, and thought hard how he could make things better for her.

"But do you think I'm stupid, gullible even, for still believing that he hasn't been having an affair?" she asked.

"Babe, you wouldn't be as cool as you are if you were a cynical old cow. And you are cool," he reassured.

"It's just that I don't want to stop caring despite the statistics, I don't want to stop searching for, well—"

"Love."

"Yes, despite the logistics."

"Hey, Martha, you're a poet and—"

"I don't know it." Martha was beginning to feel a bit better.

"Oh glum feminine angst!"

"What?"

"Oh glum feminine angst! It's an—"

"Anagram, of 'something meaningful,'" guessed Martha.

"Correct."

Martha smiled to herself. "My fingers are cold," she muttered down the telephone line.

"Should I come over? I could rub them between my hands and keep them warm," he offered.

"Yeah, do that." Martha beamed. That was exactly what she'd hoped he'd say although she hadn't known it until she'd heard the words. The odd thing was, it felt as though he was offering much, much more. More than "I'll love you forever."

# March

# 41

"Mathew, have you seen the lid to Maisie's beaker?" asked Eliza.

Mathew didn't reply; it was possible that he hadn't even heard the question, so firmly was he ensconced in his own world, inhabited solely by *Teletubbies*.

Eliza repeated the question three more times. Each time, her demand became more irate as she battled against Maisie's screams and the volume of Mathew's video. Eliza stomped towards the television set and hit the power button, nuking the *Teletubbies*. However, this did not create the desired effect. Instead of getting Mathew's attention, Eliza's actions were the catalyst for the most enormous tantrum.

"It's not fair," sobbed Mathew, "I didn't loo- loo- lose the beak- beak- beaker lid." He could hardly get his words out between sobs. He threw himself backward, bashing his head on the floor. Eliza winced and the cries exploded with renewed force. She was relieved when he rolled over on to his stomach and banged his tiny fists into the carpet, thus proving he wasn't seriously hurt, although he was giving the impression that he'd be psychologically damaged forever.

Whilst Eliza didn't really think that the tantrum was proportionate to the level of her transgression (she'd only wanted to get his attention, she wasn't going to censor *Teletubbies* for the entire duration of Martha's holiday), but she had to admit he had a point. He had not lost the beaker lid, Eliza had. And the lack of a beaker lid meant that Eliza could not give Maisie her morning milk, and so she was screaming too. There were at least five beakers in the house, but three were missing. They'd gone AWOL, along with Laa-Laa, an indispensable tool to lull Mathew to sleep, the Calpol essential for relief during teething—particularly relief for Eliza—three socks, the rain cover for the pushchair, and oh so many other essential bits and bobs that Eliza had lost count. One other beaker was in the dishwasher, and the final one was in Eliza's hand—but that was the one with the offending missing lid. Eliza should have put the dishwasher on last night. She opened it up and the smell of yesterday's supper (fish curry) hit her in a nauseating tidal wave. Eliza slammed the dishwasher closed again without retrieving the beaker.

Eliza checked the calendar. Three days down, four more to go.

Why, oh why, had she agreed to babysit for an entire week while Martha and Jack went to New York? What had possessed her? True, Martha needed a break, deserved a holiday, but chances were Eliza would have a breakdown before her sister returned, and what an indescribably terrible way to use her own precious holiday allowance. Today, Eliza had read to the children, she'd played picture dominos with Mathew, she'd participated in an endless game of chase and a mindless game of taking clothes pegs out of one jar and hiding them down the back of the settee (the clothes pegs were at hand because Eliza was using them as her first line of defence against the horrible nappies). She'd dressed both children, successfully fed Mathew his breakfast and was currently working on Maisie's. It was still only ten to eight.

The phone started to ring. Eliza knew that it would be Mrs. Evergreen offering to help. Eliza would have loved to accept Mrs. Evergreen's offer; in fact she'd have been more than happy to move out and allow her parents to move in and take over all responsibilities. They were, after all, grandparents, they probably enjoyed changing nappies. However, she knew that she would assure her mother that "everything was under control" as she had yesterday (when in reality everything was underwater or at least her mobile phone was—Maisie had dropped it in the bath). It was a matter of pride. Eliza snatched up the phone.

"I'm fine," she snapped.

"Oh good, glad to hear it."

"Martha?"

"Yes."

"I wasn't expecting it to be you. I thought it'd be Mum. How's New York?"

"Sensational, Eliza. I don't know where to start."

"My God, Martha, what time is it there, isn't it the middle of the night?"

"Yeah, we're between clubs, but I thought I'd catch you before you took Mathew to playgroup."

Eliza was so stunned by the throwaway comment "between clubs" that she nearly missed the reference to Mathew's playgroup. Nearly. She tucked the phone under her ear and walked towards the timetable that detailed her niece and nephew's extremely hectic schedules. Shit, she was supposed to be at Bunnies and Bears in twenty-five minutes. It was a foregone conclusion that she was going to be late. She surrendered herself to the inevitability of a black mark from the nursery teacher and demanded, "Spill. Are you having a glorious time?"

"Oh, the best, Eliza, I can't tell you how good."

Jack had some business in New York and had almost insisted that Martha go along with him. Apparently, he was expecting to have plenty of free time between meetings and he'd taken an extra few days' holiday so they could do the sights.

"How are the children?" asked Martha. She'd rung from Heathrow and JFK airports to ask the same. She'd rung the moment they'd arrived at the hotel, and she'd rung every morning.

"Perfect. Brilliant. Angels, both of them."

"Really?"

"Really." Eliza crossed her fingers behind her back. She didn't need to bother Martha.

"Are they eating well?"

In so much as they were eating plenty of sweets and ice cream, and none of the organic chicken and vegetable casserole or similar lovingly prepared meals that Martha had precooked and then frozen, then, yes, they were eating well. "Fine."

"And sleeping?"

"Oh yes, they're sleeping fine." In Eliza's bed, rather than in their room was more information than Eliza felt she was required to give. Instead, she tried to change the subject. "Stop worrying, they're great. We're all great. What have you done so far?"

Satisfied and happily deceived, Martha moved on to her news. "Well, Jack's been meeting people for the last two days so I've amused myself. I've done all the touristy things. I've been up to the top of the Empire State Building; it's just like it was in *Sleepless in Seattle*—well, except for about a million other sightseers. I've seen the Statue of Liberty, Times Square, and Grand Central Station. I've been to MOMA." (Martha enjoyed using the acronym.) The excitement in Martha's voice momentarily drowned out Mathew's wails. Eliza knew she'd done the right thing in offering to babysit. "I sat in the studio audience for some terrible confessions programme. I even participated by asking a question."

"You didn't!"

"I did. I'm going to be on national TV. And better yet, I started it with, 'Hey, sister.'"

"Martha!"

"I know. I have no shame. Jack's free now until Friday, so tomorrow we're going to shop until we drop."

"Fifth Avenue?"

"No, I think we'll go to the villages. The clothes are so much more hip in Greenwich and Soho."

"Right." Eliza spotted the beaker lid under the table. She bent down to retrieve it, stood up too quickly and banged her head on the underneath of the table. There should be danger money in this job; she'd sustained multiple injuries in the last three days. Scratches from Maisie (before she found the nail clippers and even then she'd had to wait until Maisie was asleep before she could cut the nails), and Mathew had hit her on the head, knee and ankle with Dizzy, Bob the Builder's cement mixer. All three incidents were accidents but, all the same, Eliza wondered if she could sue someone, perhaps the maker of the toy, or the toyshop that had sold it to her without the appropriate warnings. She doubted that the contents of Mathew's moneybox would amount to much.

"My feet are killing me. I've walked and walked," related Martha. Eliza actively coveted an injury such as blisters on her feet; it would at least mean she had new shoes, or that she'd managed to get out of the house. As yet, Eliza hadn't managed to muster the degree of military precision and organization necessary to tackle the operation of getting both children further afield than the back garden.

"Didn't you just say you were between clubs?"

"Well, there's always energy for dancing. There's always room for Jell-O, as Jack says."

"Is that from a film?"

"Probably."

"Aren't you worried that he doesn't have an original thought?"

"No, he's a man, I'd be more worried if he did," giggled Martha. "Look, I have to go. Give the kids big kisses from me."

"I will."

The line went dead. The sound of a disconnected phone was never a comforting one. Eliza wondered exactly when she and her sister had body-swapped.

And was it an irreversible transaction?

Eliza put the TV on again, but Mathew was too crafty to be palmed off that easily; he demanded compensation in the form of a Milky Way. Eliza tried to tell herself it was OK as long as she got him to clean his teeth afterwards. She gave Maisie her beaker of milk, thus snatching five minutes of relative calm.

What had she been thinking of? How had she ever imagined that this life would suit her? There were some women who were cut out to be wives and mothers and run homes with clockwork precision. Just as there were some women who were indeed suited to hosting sensational dinner parties and managed to do so on a regular basis without so much as breaking a nail, let alone requiring the intervention of the fire brigade. She wasn't one of them. She was a fantastic music-video editor (well, assistant; one day she *would* be a fantastic music-video editor). She was creative, responsive, tactful and organized at work, but she simply could not transfer those skills to running a home and a family.

She'd lived with Martha for six months now, and it had been a fruitful and interesting experiment. A change rather than a rest, but now all she wanted to do was get back to her own life. The life where she could spend her tiny wage on whatever she liked. Silly things, clothes, glittery nail varnish or fake tattoos. Last time she'd bought a fake tattoo, Martha had assumed it was a toy for Mathew. Eliza had felt too stupid and too old to use it after that. Eliza wanted the life back where she didn't have to ring to explain that she was working late and wouldn't be home for dinner. She understood that Martha required this information to run an efficient household, but Eliza simply didn't want to be part of an efficient household. Eliza longed to come home loud and drunk and not have to worry about waking the children. She was finding it hard to constantly have to worry about spelling out expletives rather than saying them. When she dropped a jar of extremely expensive Estée Lauder hand cream she'd had to shout S, H, one, T, B, U, double G, E, R, I, N, G, S, H, one, T, which simply didn't offer the same therapeutic relief as just screaming out swear words. Eliza longed to eat a pot of yogurt without having to share it. It wasn't that she was greedy, it was simply that yogurt tended to be less appetizing if it had baby snot and saliva in it, and just about everything in this house had baby snot and saliva in or on it. Dog appeared positively sanitary by comparison. Eliza missed Dog.

And she missed Greg.

God, she missed him. It was a relief admitting as much. Eliza knew she'd missed him almost from the moment that she'd closed the door of their flat behind her, but she hadn't wanted to admit as much, least of all to herself. She'd missed him at every dinner table she'd sat at since, munching her way through delicious food and tedious conversation. She'd missed him every time she'd let someone else kiss her, run their fingers through her hair. She definitely missed him when she'd endured Charlie's duff shag. She'd missed him every time she made a joke that she had to explain because no one got her sense of humour the way he did. She'd missed him when she bought a new CD, watched a new film, set the alarm clock.

Eliza sighed. She wanted to go home, but she couldn't, she didn't have a home any more. Greg was home. Their scruffy, tiny rented flat, full of mess and noise and love, was home. But it hadn't been their flat for a long time.

# 42

"'Ello, stranger. Signora Bianchi! Signora Bianchi! Look 'oo iz 'ere!" Signor Bianchi wore a smile that tickled both his ears and, surprisingly, even managed to drown his vast moustache. He was collecting coffee cups from the bar when Eliza pushed the huge double buggy up towards the door. He abandoned his task and rushed forward to help her. "Let me 'elp you with dat. Signora Bianchi!" he yelled over his shoulder with a tone that was excitement, but could have been mistaken as impatience.

Signora Bianchi emerged from the back of the shop, the area that was used as a mini kitchen. When she saw Eliza she threw her arms in the air and her fat flesh shuddered with excitement. "Our little girl!" Her beam, which was broad, flashed and then instantly disappeared as she snapped, "Where you bin, eh? We bin worried about you." Not able to maintain her anger, she enveloped Eliza in a huge hug and pulled her into the enormous bosom. Eliza thought she might suffocate, but she couldn't think of a better way to die. She choked back her tears. Signora Bianchi had emerged from behind the counter. Eliza felt honoured. "And who are de bambinos?"

"My sister's children. Mathew and Maisie. I'm looking after them whilst she's on holiday."

"You are?" asked Signora with surprise. She immediately recovered herself. "You are, of course, you are a good girl. Greg, he tell us about de 'usband." She lowered her voice. "Bastardo. Come on, bella bambina, out of the pram, let Mama Bianchi see what she can find for you." Neither child had ever visited Caffè Bianchi before, but Mathew was shrewd enough to know that "let me see what I can find for you" was code for the offer of a treat. Sweets or ice cream were imminent.

The huge double buggy wouldn't fit conveniently anywhere in the narrow café. Eliza thought she might scream with frustration. She firmly believed that buggies, car seats, stair gates, etc. were all designed by mean, childless men whose main aim in life was to add to the stress levels of hassled mums. Signor Bianchi silently took charge. He carefully collapsed the buggy and took it out the back to store. He ushered Eliza on to a stool, and Signora Bianchi proceeded to make her a very milky cappuccino. She firmly believed Eliza needed the protein, she didn't look well. Eliza smiled gratefully, and graciously accepted their help. The children were suddenly behaving like angels as they fell under the spell of Signora Bianchi's home cooking. She handed them gooey, creamy pastries.

"It's difficult, eh, bein' a mama?" asked the Signora with a knowing wink.

Eliza mutely nodded her head. "Don't get me wrong, I adore them. But visiting, even visiting frequently, is quite different to living with them. I used to think Martha exaggerated how hard it was being a full-time mum, but it's impossible to exaggerate. I'm not sure I'm cut out to be a mum."

"Not everyone is," smiled Signora kindly. "It's no shame. You are an important, creative executive with biiiiiiiggggg job in the West End." Signora Bianchi waved her arms majestically to demonstrate just how big Eliza's job was. Eliza shifted uncomfortably; she wasn't sure if the Signora's description of her job was strictly accurate. Although, thinking about it, the job was important, it was important to Eliza. "You work too 'ard, you look tired. You eatin' properly?" demanded the Signora.

Eliza smiled weakly. It was wonderful to be quizzed as to whether she was eating properly or not. Of course she was, she was dining at the finest restaurants in London a couple of times a week and Martha was never going to let her starve. But it was fantastic to be asked, it was a thrill that someone cared enough to worry about her. It felt more normal: Eliza was used to being a worry to everyone. She hadn't realized what a strain it had become being the one who was less of a concern to her parents.

The problem was obvious. Whilst Eliza had thought she'd win everyone's respect by leaving Greg and looking for a life a little more akin to Martha's, she hadn't realized that, in fact, she'd stunned her family by trying to squeeze herself into a life that she was patently unsuited to. They knew for sure that Eliza would not make a good wife to the captain of a golf club or a board director, although as the girlfriend to a struggling musician she was unsurpassable. Eliza was Greg's muse, his inspiration, his manager, and his PalmPilot when necessary. Besides which, she was his love. And he hers. Or rather, he had been.

The Evergreens had thought it a shame that Eliza had undervalued her own choices so much that she'd decided to swap tack mid-course, but they had also known enough about her character not to comment. They believed that, ultimately, she would find her own way again and they simply hoped that it wouldn't take her too long, or be that awful thing that everyone dreaded—too late.

It had taken six months, countless dates and several badly designed baby accessories for Eliza to realize that a man with a pension policy and health-care insurance wasn't necessarily the answer to her dreams. A wedding ring was not a lifebelt.

She admitted that a dishwasher was a useful accessory, but not as important to her as cable TV. She believed that supermarket shopping was better value for money and offered more choice than her local garage shop, but it wasn't where she wanted to spend her Saturday afternoons. She'd like to own a car that could transport her from A to B without trailing petrol, but her dream car was still a pink Mustang, not a dark five-door saloon.

Eliza took a long slurp of her cappuccino; it tasted delicious. The Bianchis looked on with approval. "I've made a terrible mistake," announced Eliza.

Signor Bianchi looked at the tiled floor; Signora Bianchi continued to stare at Eliza with her huge chocolate-brown eyes, slowly nodding her head up and down. "We know," tutted the Signora, "everyone know."

"I don't want the things I thought I wanted. I want . . .

I . . . I . . ." Eliza stumbled on her words, swallowing her pride was choking her. "I want Greg."

She wanted scruffy, sexy, smiley Greg. Because Greg cared about words and thoughts and music and the things she cared about. He didn't give a monkey's arse if Siberian-goose feathers were a better filler than Hungarian-duck down for a quilt. He wasn't fussed that he could have made a killing on some posh wine or other, if only he'd taken the ferry to France and filled up his car. So what if he should have invested in health in 1999 and not technology? They were unlikely ever to have enough money to buy any type of shares. She now knew what it was like to mix with people who bemoaned the lack of a good cleaner—mind-blowingly dull. These things may well be important, but not to her, not to Greg. The interest charged by the West on debts carried by the Third World *was* important, and Greg had once attended a rally demonstrating against that debt. Her sister's happiness *was* important, and hadn't Greg visited and called to try to cheer up Martha?

"Does he still come in here?" asked Eliza.

"Yes, every day," smiled Signora Bianchi, and then suddenly her smile vanished. "Ohhh," she said, pulling her mouth into an oval with such ferocity that it looked as though she was in serious danger of swallowing her several chins.

"Has he been in today?" begged Eliza with barely contained excitement. If he hadn't, she might see him and then she could explain that she'd been wrong, that she'd made a mistake, that she was really sorry, and that she didn't mind about pizza boxes.

"Yes, he bin today already," Signora Bianchi confirmed. She turned away from Eliza and started to wipe the bar surface.

"What?" demanded Eliza. Signora wouldn't answer; Eliza looked to the Signor but suddenly he was preoccupied with the children. "What is it? Tell me."

"He come in every day and recently, the last week or maybe two weeks, he sometimes brings in a lady."

Eliza felt desolate. The welcoming café suddenly felt like a cold, damp hell.

# 43

The weather was rudely cold and inhospitable. Martha had imagined that New York, New York—so good they say it twice—would only ever have sunny pavements; except of course when the snow settled for Christmas Eve, Christmas Day and Boxing Day, as per all the films she'd ever seen set in the Big Apple. She'd packed in accordance with her imagination, and without consulting the weather forecasts on the Internet. The rain bounced off the pavement and back up their trouser legs—she didn't care. They'd taken shelter in a Starbucks coffee house and were trying to pretend that there weren't any branches of Starbucks in London, when in reality there was one on every street corner. They'd made the necessary jokes about living in a global village and the world becoming a smaller place. Still, whilst Martha admitted that the menu, branding and staff uniforms were identical to those in the Starbucks back home, she thought that the experience was entirely different.

Martha threw herself into a large, squishy leather armchair and put her feet on the coffee table in front of her. Slobbing out this way always brought to mind the shrill questioning of her teachers at primary school: "Would you put your feet like that on your furniture at home?" No, categorically no; that was why sitting like this in a café was so liberating, and why Martha was prepared to pay three dollars per coffee for the experience. Martha watched the floor show (the other customers) as she waited for Jack to come back with their drinks.

There was a beautifully preserved woman in her sixties who was reading Anais Nin and had, contrary to popular belief about the habits of U.S. citizens, decided to grow old gracefully rather than hand her savings to a surgeon who would scoop up her jawline. There was a homeless guy who spoke with a heavy Irish accent, although Martha couldn't tell if it was real or put on for the benefit of tourists. He played the harmonica badly and so everyone gave him a dollar just for him to go away. There were a number of cool and clever-looking couples. Kids reading books or playing with GameBoys. They wore beanie hats, sweats with slogans and baggy jeans.

Martha realized that if any of the other customers were gazing around the coffee house, she'd look like she fitted in. Which was a good thing, because she felt as though she should fit in here—a coffee house full of fun, trendy people and women destined to grow old with no regrets. Martha was wearing a denim hat, a tight red T-shirt with the words "Drunknmunky" emblazoned across the place where her boobs would be if she had any, and tight Diesel pants. She looked funky. Hot. Damn hot. Martha tapped her finger in time with Nina Simone crooning in the background.

She smiled to herself. That morning, Martha had been flicking through her diary and realized that she and her husband had split up half a year ago. Half a year seemed a long time, and as a percentage of, say, Maisie's life, it was a long time. Mathew had now accepted he had two homes (like a prince). Maisie would never know what living with her father was like. She'd think her parents living apart was the norm.

For Martha, being married seemed like a lifetime ago; it also seemed like yesterday. She liked her bare fingers tapping in time to Nina Simone. She had nice hands and they suited nudity; she rarely felt for her rings now. She adored her twenty-dollar tops and forty-dollar trousers from Urban Outfitters that sat in bags beside her. She was pleased with the jacket she'd bought, too. They seemed to be full of possibility. There was so much more tomorrow, so much more promise in them than anything she'd ever worn before.

Jack came back to their table, bearing a tall, skinny latte and a fruit juice. He too collapsed into a squishy chair. He smiled and asked, "Tired?"

"Totally bushed. How far do you think we've walked today?"

"Miles. I'm shagged too."

Martha smiled to herself. She was bushed, he was shagged; the vocabulary was so different, but they were the same. When she'd met him, she'd talked about chaps, he'd talked about dudes. Now they met on middle ground and talked about guys. There were more similarities than disparities.

"Shall we ring Eliza and see how the kids are?" he asked.

Jack had brought a Tri-band mobile with him to the States, as he knew that Martha's phone wouldn't work on this continent. Every morning, even before breakfast, Jack asked, "Do you want to ring the kids?" One day, Martha had slept in and by the time she woke up, at 11 a.m. U.S. time, Jack had already called and could report that Mathew had been to playgroup and had drawn a picture of a racing car, and that Maisie had said "cat" very clearly when she spotted the neighbour's cat. He was clearly, ridiculously, excited by this news, which Martha loved him for.

She did.

Love him.

She was sure. Jack was . . . No, she really didn't want to say this, not even to herself. Well, she did. On one level she really wanted to say this and nothing other than this. It was possible that Jack was . . . She did still believe in it. Hope for it. Jack was . . .

The One.

Sex with a Soul.

This was what it was about. This was what all the books and magazines and chat shows and Hollywood aspired to.

It was lucky that they'd found each other.

It was just a question of learning to trust.

She couldn't identify the exact moment when she'd fallen in love with him. It could have been when he bent down to put on his ice skates. Despite his wide shoulders, he looked vulnerable as he skated around the rink at the Rockefeller Centre. He'd never skated before but he was prepared to risk life and limb because Martha had wanted to skate there since she'd seen it on an episode of *Friends*.

She might have realized she loved him yesterday when he made her a paper airplane as she sat crying over her breakfast in the diner. They'd been in New York for three days and Martha had called Eliza. Eliza sounded so in control, so sorted. She'd said that the children were "Perfect. Brilliant. Angels, both of them." She'd said that they were eating "well" and sleeping "fine." Her family sounded as though they were operating seamlessly without her.

Which was of course what she wanted.

So why when she'd put the phone down had she decided that she didn't want to go on to the comedy club after all, and that she'd rather just go back to the hotel to sleep? The next morning she'd woken up feeling miserable and even the breakfast of French toast with fresh strawberries and honey at their local diner had failed to raise a smile.

"You're missing them, aren't you?" Jack had asked.

Martha didn't even think of disguising the truth. "So much, it hurts."

She didn't want to appear ungrateful. She was having a fabulous time, but she felt bereft. He made her a paper airplane from

a drinks coaster and then took her to FAO Schwarz toystore to
buy holiday gifts and something special for Mathew's birthday,
which would be soon. She wandered around and only just managed to stop herself swooping down on every little boy and girl
and smothering them with kisses. Instead, she had to make do
with beating her Amex card to death buying gifts.

She could have fallen in love with him when he helped her
pick out a nail varnish for Eliza, or when he stopped at the window of a handbag shop and said, "I think your mum would like
that." It might have been when they were playing pool on the
purple pool table in the trendy Hudson Hotel. Or when he patiently handed her garment after garment over the top of her
changing-room door as she tried to find something new to wear
to go dancing in, although she'd brought a heaving suitcase with
her.

Or, of course, she might have fallen in love with him in the
Salsa club last December. She wasn't sure.

Michael and Martha had been planners, now she was learning
to live in the present, never forecasting, just relishing. But she
could no longer explain this relationship simply in terms of a
need for experience. She would not be that much of a sham. She
could only say it was to do with egotism, beauty, appetite and
feeling complete. Alive. Irresistible.

That seemed like love to Martha.

Still, Martha was confused. How had she managed to get to
the age of thirty-two and still be so entirely ignorant as to how
men's brains worked? She considered buying *Men Are from Mars,
Women Are from Venus,* but she thought that that was the ultimate defeat. What was he thinking? Did he love her passionately?
He'd picked her up in the street today and swung her around. It
seemed so free, so positive. Did he do that with all his women?
Did it matter? She didn't want to torture herself.

She couldn't do anything but.

When he made love to her he was a silent and conscientious lover. A sexual Ninja, he called himself, and Martha grinned at the recollection. "Highly skilled in deadly arts, strike without warning, don't see them coming."

Mad as they come.

He clearly wanted to please her; in fact, it appeared that he wanted that more than anything. All he seemed to want to do, both in and out of bed, was make her happy.

At that moment Jack leant forward and gently but firmly clasped Martha's neck and held her steady whilst he moved his full, rose-pink lips towards hers. She felt the kiss inside her ribcage and between her legs. Was he kissing her in that way because he knew she would dissolve (she was) or because he was rapt? It was so difficult to tell. How could she ask? When would she know? Did it matter? She was so proud of him. So bloody, bloody proud of the pair of them. Peas in a pod, he'd called them. And when they made love she never ever had to imagine Robbie Williams or Jude Law or that bloke from the Calvin Klein adverts. Wow.

He constantly asked what she wanted to do, where she wanted to go, which film she wanted to see, what type of food she wanted to eat. But he wasn't sycophantic or excessive the way doting men could be; he came up with wacky choices and interesting options. Martha had never come across that before.

She watched him drink his juice. He nodded his head in time with the tune, then he flicked his gum out of his mouth on the end of his tongue and in a flash the gum disappeared again. His every move made her melt as though she were snow in sunshine. Pounding his thumb on the side of his glass, in time to music, threw her into a near-frenzy. Jesus, she was thirty-two and he made her feel fourteen. Uncontrollable, uncontrolled.

Jack caught Martha's eye and grinned. His eyes glistened with tears of laughter as if he were recovering from something hilarious Martha had said. She wondered, could he love her? Was he waiting for the correct moment to declare his undying love and tell her that she was super-special?

It seemed unlikely.

Everyone had assumed that the difficult thing about coming out of a marriage was believing you'd fall in love again, but that had been easy for Martha. The tricky thing was believing someone would fall in love with her.

And it wasn't just her, was it? Why would he choose them? Why wouldn't he take all his chances with a single, childless woman? A blank slate. Why would he bother taking on someone else's children, wife and life, and have to put in an enormous amount of effort in the hope of making them his own?

It was a lot to ask.

Even if he did declare undying love, how could she believe him? Martha realized that she shouldn't make comparisons, but it was difficult not to. If she compared Jack to Michael when she'd first met Michael, there were some similarities, although Jack was nothing like the Michael she'd been waking up to over the last few years. It was the similarity that scared her. Even if he meant it now, it didn't follow that he'd always mean it. She'd heard the "I love you forever" line once too often.

It was even possible that he feared her. Was he wary of that terrible moment when she would declare her undying love to him? When she would let down her guard and tell him that, actually, it wouldn't be so bad lying in bed and reading the Sunday papers with him for the rest of her life.

Probably.

He could be somewhere in between. But where?

"I don't think I could walk another step," said Martha.

Jack looked at the day's booty. They each had several huge bags crammed full of clothes, CDs and pressies. "Let's grab a cab," he suggested.

They returned to the hotel. Their room was very small, not

much bigger than a caravan, and now it seemed minute as they filled it with their shopping. They stretched out on the bed, flicked through the cable-TV channels, raided the mini bar, and decided to eat the M&Ms anyway, even though they cost four times the amount they'd pay in a store. They used Martha's stomach as a plate, and then they made love.

# 44

After they'd made love, Jack fell asleep, but Martha didn't. Instead she lay awake, listening to the dustcarts collecting rubbish and watching car headlights making patterns on the ceiling of their room. They'd had so much fun that day. They'd bought doughnuts and ice cream. They'd shared them, actually fed them to one another, the way people do in films. And they'd tasted so good, better than anything she'd ever tasted before. In her past, she'd visited some of the finest restaurants in the major cities of the world, and yet nothing had ever sated her as well as those mini doughnuts. What was it? Did Jack simply know how to live life better than most? He certainly met all the boxes on the boyfriend wish list. Way more than Michael had ever met. Jack was chatty, better-looking, a better lover, had a larger penis, was a better dancer.

She loved him.

It should have been enough. But it wasn't.

Jack didn't want her in an all-consuming way.

Jack had other naked friends.

What did men want? More, always more. Why couldn't they trust and love one woman? Why wasn't that enough? What had this world allowed itself to become? There was always more choice, more variety.

Too much choice, too much variety.

Why hadn't Michael been happy with her, his beautiful children and home? Wasn't it enough that they had fun friends, lovely holidays and good health? Had he given all that up because someone younger, more obliging, had caught his eye? And what was Jack looking for? Another pair of tits, a slimmer set of hips? The next pretty blonde or brunette or redhead, or shaved head or pink head or just plain good head? One woman was no longer enough. Sometimes one at a time wasn't even enough, even if it was a new one every night for a month. Threesomes left Martha cold. Some men wanted to visit prostitutes or sleep with strippers; others went so far as to draw a distinction between strippers and lap-dancers and wanted to tick off both on their list. Martha was no longer prudish—she was having far too good a time in the sack to be prudish—but she was still a realist; she knew no woman could be all of these things. It wasn't possible to be the current one and the next one.

All Martha wanted was to be someone's number one.

She deserved it. As Martha listened to the sirens of police cars, she decided that if he wanted to sleep with other people he could, but he was no longer going to sleep with her. She'd done a pretty good job at ignoring the naked friends right up until the moment that she'd admitted to having fallen in love with him, and then she couldn't ignore them for a second longer. Suddenly they were everywhere. They noisily demanded that Martha take notice of them. They ordered an espresso when she ordered a latte. They looked out of the mirror in the bathroom when she took her make-up off. They climbed into bed with her when she climbed into bed with him. It wasn't to do with jealousy. Although she was jealous. Jealous of the breasts he'd touched. The shape of their muffs. The waists he'd known. The tone of their groans. But it wasn't to do with jealousy.

Martha knew that she wanted Jack, God she wanted him so much. Despite everything. Despite knowing that loving anyone was a risk. Despite the fact that she still grieved for Michael. Despite knowing that Jack *was* dangerous, that he noticed other women and they noticed him. There would always be an endless trail of possibilities. Still, she wanted him.

Martha pulled the duvet tighter around her body. She was cold. She glanced at the clock. At 3:05 a.m. she decided that she wanted him, but only if he wanted her, and only her. It was the best and the worst moment in many extremely good and criminally bad moments.

Jack was good and kind and handsome and sexy, but if his soul didn't burn for her, then the essential ingredient that Martha was demanding was missing. Martha knew her dizzy passion could easily spiral into something more permanent, but she was convinced that he didn't feel the same.

It was annoying, but she'd become very good at recognizing when men weren't in love with her.

Martha woke up feeling sad. She remembered that when she was with Michael she'd often felt sad. Or tense, or stressed, or exhausted. She'd been used to the horrible dull ache in the pit of her stomach, the ache that told her she'd forgotten, or failed, or ruined something somehow, even though she was always trying her best. She'd been so used to carrying around a sense of personal disappointment that she didn't even have to try to ignore it. She'd worn it like a pair of old spectacles. But things were different now. Martha wished she could ignore her sadness or resign herself to getting used to it, but she knew that was no longer possible. She was now far more honest with herself.

"All right, cutie?" Jack asked casually and cheerfully.

Martha had lain awake most of the night. She loved Jack, she was sure of that. Did she really want to burst his balloon? No, she didn't. But there was no alternative. It had taken quite some time, but Martha finally knew that she would not be able to love Jack to the best of her ability, unless she loved herself first. "Yeah, I'm OK, although I was going to fly home, in the middle of the night."

Jack froze. He stared at the ceiling as he tried to gather the courage to turn to her and ask the necessary "why?" He was utterly clueless.

"Because you're like all other men. You're incapable of being faithful or single-minded—but because you told me in advance that this was the case, I have to put up with it. Bastard." Martha could feel the tears welling in her eyes and her nose itched. *Don't cry,* she willed and then commanded herself.

"Why do you think I'm a bastard?" asked Jack.

"I don't understand you, Jack. I'm sorry, I don't get the naked-friend-versus-girlfriend distinction. I haven't caught up with the morals, or rather lack of them, that this century seems to advocate." She waited, hoping he'd interrupt her. That way she'd reduce her chances of saying something she'd regret. He didn't interrupt. "I'm still stuck way back in the early part of the nineteenth century. I'd actually like to be wearing a long hooped skirt if that meant I'd be protected from the disruption and disillusion that a divorce causes. I don't want to be back in the game, as you put it, but if I must be, then I at least want to understand the rules—and I don't. Your naked-friend thing seems to me to simply be a get-out-of-jail-free card. Now this may help you keep any nagging spells of conscience at bay, but to be frank, the fact that you're shagging around is not made any more acceptable just because you tell me you're shagging around. In fact, it's possibly worse."

"Whoa, wait, slow down, Martha." Jack sat bolt upright in bed and put his hands on Martha's shoulders. "I've never lied to you, or given you any false impression. Or at least I sincerely hope I haven't. I've always tried to be very honest with you."

Martha shook his hands off, not least because they were centimetres away from the rise of her breast and if Jack went anywhere near her tits her defences would be completely annihilated. "It's a fucking loophole," she yelled.

Jack stared at the floor. Bloody hell, it goes to show they're all the same in the end. This woman had told him that all she was looking for was a bit of fun. He'd thought, hoped, that she wasn't going to turn out to be hysterical and demanding. Or hurt. He definitely hadn't wanted to hurt her. Why did they tell you they could handle things that they blatantly couldn't?

"My hole isn't just a loophole. People deserve more respect. 'I love you forever' should mean forever. 'Until death do us part' should mean just that. Or shut the fuck up. Sex is more than just fun. It may not have to be about making babies every time, but it can lead to making babies and that's special, isn't it? That has to mean something, doesn't it? I don't have any of the answers. I'm not sure why I married in church besides the fact that it made pretty photos, but I did mean forever." Martha stopped raving but only so that she could breathe.

"So this isn't about us at all, it's another row about Michael," said Jack.

Martha glared at him. She held tightly to the quilt cover, her knuckles white with strain and tension. Didn't he see she couldn't separate the two things in her mind as easily as that? Men compartmentalized, women bled.

"Martha, I've never been anything other than fair with you. I've always tried to be absolutely clear. To be honest, it's easy to be good to you, you deserve it."

"Yes, you're so damn fair and nice and honorable. I don't dispute your honesty. But didn't you know that that would simply make me expect . . . hope for more?"

"Are you suggesting I should have lied and treated you badly?"

"Well, at least I would have known where I stood."

"Martha, that is the most ridiculous thing I've ever heard."

"And there's something else."

"What?"

"I love you. I want to distract myself from this truth, but I can't. I know I should be cooler and I know I should wait and I know all the sensible stuff, but the thing is, I love you, Jack. I really do. I love you."

This was his cue to say he loved her too.

He didn't.

Martha cursed the day she was a twinkle in her father's eye. But it was too late. The words were out of her mouth and into their life. She'd told him she loved him.

Three times.

Shit.

She decided that her only chance was to fake some bravado and, like a visit to the dentist, remind herself that this would all soon be over. "What?" she demanded.

Jack stayed silent and stared at the duvet cover.

His silence forced her to fill in the space. "And I know we agreed that this was just a bit of fun, but you never can tell, sometimes the unexpected happens and sometimes the unexpected is damn good and we are. I know that you care for me too."

"I do."

"You make love with me, you don't fuck me."

"I know."

Then he went silent again. Martha felt miserable. Obviously, if he loved her, now was the moment to tell her. Or even if he wasn't sure he loved her yet, but thought that he might love her one day, then this was the moment to tell her. He stayed silent.

# 45

Eliza had passed another hour with the Bianchis. But she was only there in body. Her mind was elsewhere, and her heart had stopped. She was the most stupid chick on the entire planet. Timing had never been her strong point. Why hadn't she told Greg how she felt that time she saw him when they were Christmas shopping? It would have been easy, she could have just said, "I'm sick of dating pricks, will you loaf with me forever?" But she hadn't, she'd whinged about credit-card bills and forgotten birthdays. She could have said something on Christmas Day; that was another great opportunity. OK, she couldn't exactly drag him under the mistletoe, that would have been very uncool, but she could have given him some encouragement. The nicest thing she said to him was, "You look stupid in red paper hat, here, have my blue one." Oh God, oh was there ever such an arrogant arse?

The clichés were horribly accurate. You don't know what you until it's gone. What was this other woman like? She wanted to ask the Bianchis. They weren't known for their tact. If the bitch was a five-foot-nine beauty, with flawless skin, a big inheritance of millions and a contract with the Elite agency, the Bianchis would probably make the mistake of telling that Eliza would want to know that. Did this woman share their bed? Well, of course she bloody did. Eliza wondered whether if she stood in the middle of the street in her nightie and actually kicked herself anyone would think this odd behaviour. She doubted it; they'd probably think she was a community-care patient and, in fact, she was a

The silence stretched between them for what seemed like an eternity. Certainly a long time. Too long. Martha felt the humiliation creep up through her toes. It clung and stained like tar, and then settled in a heavy lump in her stomach as though she'd swallowed enough to resurface the M1.

"Oh, forget I ever said anything, Jack," she spat. "You're all the same in the end."

"Who are?"

"You know."

"Say it, Martha. Articulate that ridiculous sexist, bizarre, scientific thought."

"Men. Men are all the same in the end."

"All bastards?"

"All bastards."

"Michael really has won, Martha." With that, out of bed and walked into the bathroom. "I c now, I'm going to be late for my meeting."

They ignored each other as Jack showered dressed. He picked up his wallet, phone ar at the door he said, "Will you meet me la

Martha kept her head under the du see she was crying. He'd think she v that she'd totally disgraced herself, cause she was angry and frustrate

And because she cared that

"I'll be at that café on U Monday night. I'll be th opened the door.

"Jack," called Ma

"I recognize than himself.

"No, Jack, it

a
C
cou
beer
agen
in th
God, v
All
you have
hadn't wa
tact. If the
personal in
Modelling A
take of think
woman sleep
wondered whe
Shepherd's Bush
it was strange be
that she was a co

damn sight less correct in the head. Would this girl stroke Dog? Take him for walks? Drink out of Eliza's glasses, the ones she'd bought in Habitat? Yes, yes, yes. This girl's toothbrush was probably nuzzling up against Greg's toothbrush at this very minute.

Eliza was not the type of girl to cry; she was more of a doer than that. She turned the buggy round and headed away from the Tube station and towards Greg's flat.

She hammered on the door. No reply, although some of the paintwork did crumble and fall to the floor. She hammered louder, loud enough to wake someone having a little nap in Sydney, Australia. She did not give space to the possibility that Greg might be out. He wouldn't be out; her will was stronger than that.

"OK, coming," yelled Greg from behind the wooden door. "Hiya." As he opened the door he smiled a wide, genuine smile.

Eliza didn't notice, she stomped past him into the flat, abandoning the children in the doorway. Eliza strode into the sitting room—it was empty. She took another couple of large paces and she was in the kitchen—uninhabited. She turned and strutted into the hall, held her breath, threw open the bedroom door—deserted. There was only the bathroom left; Eliza hesitated, she didn't like the bathroom at the best of times, but needs must. She confidently flung open the door—all clear.

"Looking for something?" asked Greg. He sounded amused.

"An earring," muttered Eliza. Then she paused and faced him.

Greg was smiling. Of course he was, he rarely did anything other than smile. He'd taken Mathew and Maisie out of the buggy. He was holding Maisie in his arms; she was nuzzling up against his goatee (facial hair that was the result of Greg not having yet made it to the bathroom that day, rather than a fashion statement); Mathew was looking for Dog. He found him asleep under the table in the kitchen, and he and Eliza swooped to pet Dog together.

"What type of earring?" asked Greg; he didn't bother to hide his amusement, but he was polite enough to play along with Eliza's charade as long as necessary.

Eliza glared at him; she knew she'd been rumbled, so she didn't bother to elaborate further on her excuse. "I've just been to see the Bianchis," she said by way of explanation.

"About time, they're always asking after you."

"They seemed well. Unchanged."

"Nothing much changes around here, Liza."

"That's not what they said," countered Eliza, cryptically. She carried on glaring at Greg and waited for his defence. He met her gaze but didn't seem in the least bit fazed or embarrassed. Eliza thought about this for a moment. Of course he wasn't fazed or embarrassed, why should he be? So he had a new girlfriend. What did she expect? She could hardly be fired with indignation and outrage. She had dumped him, unceremoniously, unexpectedly, and from a great height. She'd done this six months ago, what did she think he was going to do? Behave like a monk for the rest of his life? Besides which, she'd dated, almost non-stop, for all the good it had done her. She'd even had sex. The memory made her shiver. So her hunt for Mr. Perfect had been unsuccessful, of course it had. It was doomed from the start. Her Mr. Perfect was never going to be a man whose biggest passion was rugby or fly-fishing. She'd never find a true spiritual partner amongst men whose only interest in spirits was how woody a particular malt was. Her Mr. Perfect would not wear a tie. He would not drive a saloon car and however disappointing it was for Eliza to admit it, it was unlikely that her Mr. Perfect would have started a pension policy aged twenty-one. That level of organization would simply turn her off.

Her Mr. Perfect was more likely to be creative, relaxed, witty and, therefore, on occasion, a bit lazy and messy.

Greg.

Greg was her Mr. Perfect.

"Fancy a cuppa?" asked Greg as though she'd been popping in to see him every week for months, and there was nothing unusual about her sudden arrival, nothing peculiar in the fact that she'd searched his home as if she was looking for the definitive answer to "What is love?"—and, in a way, she had been.

"Yeah, that'd be nice."

Greg put Maisie on the floor and she scrambled towards Dog, thrilled with the opportunity to torture him alongside her brother. Eliza was just about to object—she could only imagine what filth the children would be crawling in—when she noticed that the carpet was clean. There were no dog hairs, no can rings, no empty, crushed cigarette packs. Eliza took a moment to have another look around. It wasn't just the carpet that was clean. There was no fog of smoke, there was no stale, lingering smell of Dog sweat. In fact, the windows were open, allowing fresh air into the flat (or at least air as fresh as air ever gets in a huge city with over seven million inhabitants). There were no empty coffee cups; there weren't even any sticky rings showing where the coffee cups had once rested. There were no pizza boxes; there weren't even any flyers offering to take your credit card details in return for the service of delivering a curry to your settee.

Eliza bit her lip to cork the scream that wanted to erupt. She turned on her heel once again and rushed into the kitchen. Where were the towering stacks of dirty dishes? Why wasn't the lino sticky? Oh God, the oven had been cleaned. She rushed through to the bedroom. The purpose of her last search had been to unearth "the New Woman"; Eliza had expected to catch Greg and "the New Woman" *in flagrante delicto*—not that she'd thought through what she'd do if she had caught them in such a predicament.

However, in her haste to uncover what she'd expected, she'd failed to see the unexpected. The flat was clean. The bed was made; there were no sweaty socks or sticky undies on the floor.

There was a smell of soap in the bathroom, aftershave in the bedroom, and Mr. Muscle in the kitchen. Eliza was used to the flat smelling worse than a locker room.

Eliza dropped into the settee and leant forward, holding her head in her hands. This was worse than finding "the New Woman," in a negligee, swinging from the lampshade. Not only did he have a New Woman but the New Woman had succeeded where Eliza had failed. The New Woman had persuaded Greg to clean up. Eliza started to cry. Silent tears slid down her cheeks, scalding her.

"Hey, what's up?" asked Greg kindly as he returned to the sitting room with their cups of tea. He sat down next to Eliza and slipped his hand around her back. His warmth and kindness just made her want to howl.

"Oh, it's nothing," assured Eliza, wiping her tears and snotty nose on the back of her jacket sleeve. Greg leapt up for a box of tissues, but as he offered it to Eliza she started to sob again. Tissues! Proof positive of a woman's intervention. There is no way on this earth that Greg would ever buy tissues. Eliza had her pride. That was all she had. She didn't have a boyfriend, or a flat, or even a plan, but she did have her pride. She was *not* going to tell him what was the matter. "Martha's away, I'm babysitting. The children woke up early today, well, every day actually, and I'm tired. Silly, I know. This childcare lark is harder than it looks, and I'm not very good at it."

"Looks like you're doing a pretty good job to me."

Eliza smiled, pleased to receive any praise, however little evidence it was based upon. "What makes you say that?" she asked, fishing for further compliments.

Greg looked at the children; Eliza followed his gaze. Mathew was eating Dog's chocolate drops, and Maisie had fallen asleep in his basket. Eliza knew for a fact that Martha would not approve. Hardly nutritional, hardly sanitary.

"Well," Greg said, and hesitated. "Both their shoes are on the right feet."

Eliza grinned. "How are you?" she asked, remembering her manners but hoping that he wouldn't tell her. She really didn't need the details on just how wonderfully sexed up and loved up he was right now.

"Not bad at all." He smiled but didn't elaborate.

Eliza was grateful for his sensitivity. They both fell silent, not that it was uncomfortable.

"What are your plans for the rest of the day?" asked Greg suddenly.

"To get through it without the loss of a limb or incurring any other serious injuries such as concussion or a fracture."

Greg smiled. "We could take them to the zoo."

"We?"

"Yes. You and me. I'm not doing anything better, and you're not. I've missed the kids. But if you don't want to—"

"Great. No. Yes. I mean, yes, I want to, that's a great idea. Two sets of hands are always better than one."

And I'd like to rip your clothes off and take you on the futon, thought Eliza. But she didn't say so; it didn't seem like the right moment.

# 46

She wasn't going to go. Why should she? She'd been made a fool of once, and once was once too often. It had been nice. Fun. But it was better all round if she just left it where it was. Hadn't she begged Michael to stay, humiliated herself completely? Surely she should learn from that experience and then at least something would have come out of this whole sorry mess. She wasn't going to waste a moment longer on a man who didn't love her and only her. Naked friends had been all very well when she was in her—what did Eliza call it?—her recovery stage. And, yes, she was very grateful that her recovery stage had been spent with Jack. A Sex God with a good heart. But she'd recovered now. And the recovered Martha deserved more than a timeshare. The relationship had been a beautiful, amazing rebound relationship. That was all. Eliza had been right. Martha had been wrong, but she was grateful that she'd been wrong. If she'd listened to Eliza, she would have missed out on the best three months of her life.

True, he'd never lied to her, or hurt her, or let her down, and that was good of him. He'd recognized how vulnerable she was and he hadn't abused her trust. But, then, he'd got a good deal too: Jack got unlimited, astonishing sex with a grateful, rampant divorcee. And she got, well, unlimited, rampant sex with an Adonis. The deal between her and Michael had been a little more prosaic, more sock-washing and bread-earning, less foreplay; but the principle had been the same. And as for her and Jack's sharing doughnuts, laughing, chatting, reading, playing with the kids together, well, that had been a bonus. And as for that next bit, the bit that she found difficult to describe . . . The bit where she was sure that she was in love with him, that they were alike despite the outward appearances, were peas in a pod, well, she'd have to forgo all of that too if he didn't love her.

Because she did deserve to be loved.

Martha's cheeks burnt at the recollection of what she'd said. She'd told him she loved him and he'd ignored her. He hadn't made any comment at all. She might just as well have said, "Funny weather we're having, aren't we? Strange the way there's intermittent showers and then beautiful bright skies." Martha took little comfort in the fact that what she'd said was true.

So there was absolutely no point in meeting him at Union Square. The sensible thing for her to do now was get on a plane and go home to her children, her family, her friends, and get started on her real life. Which, thanks to Jack, would no longer be limited to jam-making and cake-decorating; she'd also include a little hip clothes-buying and DVD-watching. What would be the point of meeting him? Everything that could be said had been said, and more. Martha thought all this as she boarded the Subway. She took the R line, which did pass through Union Square—but she told herself she didn't have to get off there, she could stay on and go to Soho and do a little more shopping before she left for JFK.

Yet again, she'd been deceived into thinking it was a warm day. It amazed her how her optimism won over experience, time after time, after time. The sky had been blue and bright for the ten minutes it had taken her to choose her outfit this morning. It was now bitingly cold. People in the carriage sat hunched in their own coldness. Of course, like London, no one struck up a conversation, preferring instead to read the third-rate adverts on the posters. Martha wondered what it would be like to live in a world where people talked to one another on the Tube, actually smiled at the buskers, even sung along. But she knew it was another romantic notion of hers, not unlike falling in love and hoping to be loved in return. Ridiculous, unrealistic.

When Martha got off the train at Union Square, passed her token through the machine and pushed through the turnstile, she told herself that she didn't have to go to the café where they'd spent a hilarious evening the other night, she could shop. She looked at her watch. It was four forty-five. He'd said that he'd be there from four and that he'd wait for her. He hadn't said how long he'd wait, although the implication was that he'd wait for quite some time. She was curious to know if he'd wait for forty-five minutes. She doubted it. But it would be easy to check. She could just pop by the café and see if he was there, which was un-likely. Martha walked up to the door; she could see through the window. It wasn't very busy, but she could not see Jack. The dis-appointment turned her knees to wet newspaper. She was too sad and shocked to cry. Although she was convinced there was noth-ing more to say (she, for one, had said more than enough) and al-though their relationship was inadequate and ill-defined, it had at times seemed heavenly. A tiny little bit of her thought he might have thought so too and therefore found something else to say.

Martha needed a sweet, hot drink. She was shaking so much it looked as though she was breakdancing, and if she didn't get off the street quickly someone would probably try to force a dol-lar on her.

She pushed open the café door. No one turned and stared at her, which surprised Martha as she was sure that, besides her strange hue, there must be a huge comedy arrow above her head pointing at her and saying "disappointed, again!" She went to the bar and ordered a caffè latte, full fat, four sugars.

The waitress assumed that she'd just witnessed a horrific acci-dent or had been a victim of a mugging at the very least, because Martha looked so traumatized. "Hey, Girlfriend, you OK?"

Martha moved her head a fraction. It wasn't clear if she was trying to nod or shake.

"You look cold. Why don't you go through to the back of the café? There's a fire there and it's real restful."

Martha followed the suggestion as though it were an order. She hadn't known that there was another part to the café. The back room was empty, all but for two people. A woman, by the window, reading the *New York Times*.

And Jack.

Jack was sitting by the fire.

"Martha, fantastic, you came. I wasn't sure you would." He

jumped to his feet. "Can I get you a drink? No, you've got one, err, me too." In fact there were three empty juice glasses on the table in front of Jack. Martha stared at them. "I got here early," he said, by way of explanation, "just in case."

He leant forward to kiss Martha but she ducked. She knew if he kissed her she'd be without resources. She'd cry out, "Forget all that stuff I said this morning. Forget the demand for exclusivity, and forget that I said I loved you. Let's just go back to the way we were. Just be with me. Don't leave me." Which wouldn't be very dignified. She pressed her lips together in an effort to restrain herself from backtracking.

He took hold of her hand and held it tightly for a moment. He tried to look into her eyes but she wouldn't meet his. She stared at the floor miserably. He lifted her hand to his lips and kissed it. The kisses branded her, embossed his signature. She was sure she'd be ruined for life. No other man could possibly be this unique combination of sunshine and sexiness. She didn't really believe in this one.

Jack sat down and waited for Martha to sit opposite him. But she stayed resolutely on her feet. She didn't feel comfortable, and she didn't want him to feel comfortable either. A little bit of her wanted to punish him for not loving her, and whilst she realized that making him stretch to reach her hand wasn't exactly the same as putting him on the rack in the Tower, it was all she had available to her at that exact moment.

Jack waited a second, realized that Martha wasn't going to sit down and then stood up again. He still held on to her hand. "God, I've had the most bizarre day," he said.

Martha stared at him with disbelief. Was he taking the piss? Hers hadn't been exactly run-of-the-mill, either. It wasn't every day that you told someone you loved them and (this was possibly the most salient point) the person you'd said "I love you" to ignored you.

Jack beamed at Martha.

Oh my God, he did love her, he was going to tell her now. Suddenly Martha could see such warmth and hope and excitement in his eyes. Why hadn't she looked closer this morning? Then she would have seen it all, and saved herself this horrific day of worry. Martha allowed her body to relax as though it were sinking into a huge warm bath full of bubbles. She felt her dreams envelop her and then buoy her up. She waited for the words.

"I've got a new job," said Jack.

"What?" demanded Martha. Had she misheard?

"A job. That's why I'm here—for a job interview—and today they told me I've got it."

"What?"

"Isn't it fabulous, Martha?" Why had he started calling her Martha? Where had "Little Miss E." gone? Was she to be buried with their history? "I'm going to be running the New York branch, I'm going to be MD, Martha."

"Congratulations. I'm very happy for you," said Martha as she collapsed into the nearest chair. She sat down before shock could slam her over. Jack took this as a good sign and sat down again too. And the odd thing was, a bit of Martha was actually happy for Jack. It sounded like a good position, and he was obviously thrilled; she loved him, she wanted him to be happy. That's what a bit of her thought. The rest of her thought that he was the most obnoxious, cruel, tactless bastard to be so obviously delighted at the prospect of leaving her but, hey, as he'd said all along, he wasn't in this game to find a girlfriend, he still had too much he wanted to do.

"Well, I'd love to stay and chat over the details of your new contract, etcetera," said Martha, not doing such a brilliant job of hiding her pain, "but I have to get back to the hotel, I have a plane to catch."

"A plane? But why? Are the kids OK?" asked Jack, suddenly anxious.

"Yes, they're fine. I just don't want to be here with you any longer. I don't see the point." Martha made to stand up. She wondered if her reserve would last at least until she got out of the café. Then she could sob or scream or do whatever struck her as most appropriate.

"I don't understand," said Jack. He did look genuinely bewildered. "You said you loved me."

Martha glared at Jack. How could he be so insensitive as to bring that up? He really had no idea. "I was drunk," she said.

"You couldn't have been drunk. It was in the morning."

Martha considered telling him she'd changed her mind. But what would the point be? She couldn't salvage any self-respect by telling a lie. She considered demanding "Love me. Love me. I'm a good person, and a pretty person, and a funny person. I have so much love to give." But she feared it would fall on deaf ears.

Again.

So instead she said, "I do love you, Jack." Funnily enough, she didn't feel the humiliation that was surely due when she said this. She supposed the difference was that this time she didn't have any expectations at all. She was just stating a fact. "I hope you're very happy in your new job. And country," she added significantly. "But I've never been a fan of long-distance relationships, and I make a lousy pen pal. I'm sure it won't take you too long at all to surround yourself with a posse of new naked friends."

Jack looked sad, disappointed. What had he been expecting? That she'd keep her bed warm for him to pop back over the ocean now and again, to come back for a bit of London action between the sheets?

"Martha, I know you've gone through quite a bit—"

"Some would say that."

Jack chose to ignore her tone and pushed on, "And I know

you're hurting, but, well, maybe I could be there for you."

"I don't suppose you'll have time to stay friends, what with servicing all your new naked friends."

"Right," said Jack slowly. He dropped his head into his hands and used the heels of his palms to rub his eyes. "There are no other naked friends."

"Well, you haven't been in New York long," said Martha. "Don't worry, I'm sure you'll—" She stopped mid-sentence. "What do you mean?"

"There are no other naked friends. Here or at home."

"But . . ." Martha left the word hanging in the air. Jack was gorgeous; she'd always been sure that he must be spending his every waking moment beating women off with a stick or, worse still, not beating them off. What was he saying?

"There haven't been any other naked friends since I met you. Since the Salsa club."

Martha didn't want to make another mistake. "Why?"

"Because there wasn't any need. I didn't want to be with any other woman."

Martha shook her head and gently and surreptitiously pinched the skin on her forearm; she wanted to check that she was awake. "So why did you let me think that there were other women?" How could he have put her through such misery and uncertainty? Not that she had been all that miserable. Mostly she'd managed to blank out the possibility of other naked friends. But Eliza had been very uncertain and had done her level best to make Martha miserable.

"I didn't really think that you'd think there were others. Besides not wanting others, when would I have found the time, and where would I have found the energy, considering the amount of shagging we do?"

Martha wished he'd stuck to his first answer; it was far more romantic.

"Besides which, there were the children," continued Jack.

"Well?"

"And the marriage."

"But everyone has a history. You do."

"I was never sure which way it would resolve itself. You were barely out of a marriage. In fact, technically, you aren't out of your marriage. I didn't want to put pressure on you."

"I *feel* divorced. And soon I really will be. It feels true, and I don't know if there is any other measure. It doesn't feel as though Michael is mine any more or that I am his, despite the names on the mortgage deed and the pension policies. He's gone. He's vacated my home and my heart." Martha really hoped she didn't sound as though she were begging.

"And, in all honesty, I wasn't sure if I could take it all on, if I was up to the job of being a . . . a . . . what's the word?"

"Boyfriend," suggested Martha.

Jack glared. "A family man."

"Oh, I see, and now it's OK to tell me that you don't have any other naked friends because you're leaving anyway, and that's my consolation prize." Martha was almost proud of how indignant she sounded.

"No, Martha, that's not it. I love you. Martha, you are the most fabulous person I have ever known, I've told you that. I love you so much. I think I've loved you for a while, and I was just waiting for the right moment to tell you. Today I actually ached for you. Can you believe that?" Jack was laughing. "Today I knew that the only thing that could make a perfect day even better was seeing you. I want you to come with me. This job is the job of a lifetime. I'll be earning three times my current salary. I can give you and the kids a really great standard of living. It's proved easier than I thought it would be, the unknown, being around children. They're great. Noisy, smelly, but great. The company will pay for our home and the kids' education; we can be a real family. A happy family. Me devoted to you, hanging on your every word." He was laughing and joking, but he meant it too. "I didn't say anything to you this morning because I wanted to know exactly what I was offering you." Jack was smiling a wider smile than Martha had ever seen before. It shone through his eyes, his pores; even his hair seemed to glisten with happiness. He'd worked it all out. He had a solution. He was able to offer Martha the Happily-ever-after she wanted and she deserved. He'd never been happier.

"I can't live here, Jack."

"No, not straight away. You'll have to pack up the house."

"Michael."

The word punched Jack. It knocked him to the ground more certainly than if Lennox Lewis had landed a blow.

"He'd never agree to it. He'd have a court order slapped on me quicker than you could say 'Green Card.'"

"We'd fight it," said Jack. He stood up, panicked, and ran his fingers through his hair. Almost instantly he fell back into his chair again. "We'll fight it." But Jack already knew that Martha would never be able to join him. His words drifted, without gravitas, like feathers in the air on a very windy day.

"I can't take his children away from him."

"They're your children."

"And his."

The lovers sat in a silence that deafened them. Martha watched her sweet coffee go cold, and she wondered how brave she was expected to be. Surely the call for heroes and martyrs had long been extinct. Apparently not.

"I don't know what to do," sighed Jack. He looked at Martha with desperation and she knew what he wanted her to say.

"Take the job, Jack." Martha was thinking, If you love something let it go, if it comes back it's yours. If it doesn't, it never was. And she hated the fact that the most important things in her life could always be distilled down to a message on a twee Hall-mark card. "When do they want you to start?"

"End of April."

"We should get a drink and celebrate. You can have orange juice but I need something a bit stronger."

"I signed the contract. I didn't think." His tone was apologetic.

Martha would have felt sorry for him, but she felt so sorry for herself that she didn't have the capacity to feel pity for anyone else, not even Jack. "No." Of course not. Why should he? He wasn't married to her; they weren't his children.

For the last three years, in every waking moment, Martha had thought about her children and what was best for them; she was used to it, it was automatic. Jack didn't have the same responsibility, he wasn't there. He could break the contract, there would be a get-out clause—they both knew that—but neither of them suggested that he do so.

# 47

The visit to the zoo was less of a success than Eliza had hoped. From the second Greg had offered to take them there she had indulged in *visions*. Visions, such as him pushing the double buggy (in a manly way), freeing her up to concentrate on humorous stories of how she'd filled the last few months. Of course, she also planned that these anecdotes would be tightly edited and generously embellished so as to paint her in as strong a light as possible. There would be no point in admitting that most of her dates had been mind-

numbing, cheap or tedious—that would not cause her ex to sizzle with jealousy, and she wanted him to sizzle. Think bacon in
a pan. She imagined that the children would suddenly trans-
form from small demons to more celestial characters, so as to
give the impression that she was in control after all. She hadn't
visited London Zoo, or indeed any zoo, since the age of eight.
Her dim recollection was that the place was full of cute furry
animals.

Greg tried to push the buggy, but he wasn't good at turning
corners, got a bit frustrated, then heavy-handed, and bent one of
the axles in temper. Eliza was so worried about what Martha
would say when she saw her precious Maclaren buggy that she
was rendered speechless for a good few minutes.

When she finally did say something it was all very derogatory.
"Bloody hell, Greg. How can you be so cack-handed? Or rather
cack-footed. Martha'll go mad, you total arse."

"Total arse," repeated Mathew as clear as a church bell, stopping Eliza from continuing her tirade.

"Jesus, Eliza, it's a pram, not a kidney machine, it doesn't matter. I'll bang that axle out with a hammer when I get home.
Chill. Since when have you been so hyper?" scowled Greg.

Eliza doubted Greg's ability to fix the buggy. He wasn't particularly handy with a toolbox, but she decided to bite her tongue.
Which meant it was impossible to entertain him with anecdotes
of her disastrous dates. She did try, but the stories didn't sound at
all amusing—which shouldn't have surprised her, as they hadn't
been funny to live through. The children felt far too comfortable
with Greg to improve their behaviour one iota. They continued
to be picky, sticky and tricky. The animals were not cute. They
were sad and smelly.

It was not a roaring success.

Despite all this, Eliza felt happier than she'd felt in months.
Even when it started to drizzle, she comforted herself with the

fact that although she was in hell on earth, she was at least doing her time in damnation with Greg.

Which made it acceptable. Despite the overwhelming smell of camel faeces clogging her nostrils.

He didn't have a pension policy. He didn't have private health care or a monthly salary. He had no hope of ever struggling into the higher tax bracket, and yet he was everything she wanted. He always had been, even when she hadn't known it.

Eliza felt overwhelmed with remorse and regret. Greg might not have a fitted kitchen, or even a juicer, but these were surmountable problems. He did have a girlfriend, and this obstruction would be less easily overcome. The Bianchis had told her that he seemed very happy, that he was "always laughing" with this new woman. And he was clearly into her in a big way, because why else would he have cleaned up his flat? Oh God, how could she have been so stupid and careless as to muddle it all up so completely?

It was mortifying to admit, but she *had* left Greg on a whim. They'd had a dull couple of months, he hadn't had any work, and was actually subsidizing his gigs with the money he earned from selling hats. It was ridiculous. And whilst Eliza loved her job, she didn't earn a fortune, or at least not enough for two. Because money was tight they rarely went out or did *anything*. By contrast, all of their friends had suddenly started to grow up: everyone else seemed to be getting engaged or buying houses or getting promoted, and Greg didn't show any inclination to do any of this. His idea of planning was to think about what he wanted for tea before 5 p.m. And for a while all of this had seemed to be insuperable.

But she'd muddled it up. She'd lost sight of what was important. And how a person made you feel was very important. She should have talked to him.

Eliza was glad it was raining; perhaps that way Greg wouldn't notice the bastard tears that had sprung from nowhere. At the moment she was safe enough, they were hovering in her eyes. She just looked as though she had an awful cold, but they were threatening overspill any second now.

"This is boring," whinged Mathew. He made a half-hearted attempt to escape his captivity by bouncing around in the buggy; the movement woke Maisie, who let out an almighty howl of objection. Eliza envied her this freedom of expression.

"Let's give this up, no one's enjoying it very much," said Greg.

Eliza was about to grumble "Best bloody idea you've had all day," when she looked at him. He seemed so disappointed; after all, the zoo had been his suggestion. Eliza would put her last pound on the fact that this wasn't what he'd imagined, either. There he stood in the grim zoo, with her grim niece and nephew, in the grim rain. He didn't even have a jacket with a hood.

Yet he was still smiling. Well, at least, the corners of his mouth weren't actually turned down.

He took her breath away. He was all the romance of jazz songs in smoky bars, blooming roses, crooning voices and spectacular musicals. This was as delightful as floaty dresses, red wine, hazy memories, bright dreams, small waists and even those kisses where he takes your chin in his hands and tilts your face up to his.

Problem was, this scene also had a hint of that other type of romantic—the tragi-romantic: a host of missed opportunities, maybes, should-have-beens and what-ifs.

Eliza wasn't going to accept that. She may have been impulsive and at times confused, mistaken or rash, but she was, above all things, a very determined woman.

"No, look, it's just a bit of rain, I'm having a great time," she lied.

"Eliza, remember who you're talking to."

"OK, it is a bit crap," she admitted. But she didn't want it to be over. All her senses were being assaulted. It was almost impossible to see the animals for the drizzle, or have a conversation that would drown out Maisie's screams. Eliza was so cold she couldn't feel her fingers. And she couldn't smell anything other than animal shit. But the worst thing would be for them to go home now, for Greg to leave her with nothing but the taste of regret. "How about we go and get something to eat? It's getting late. The children are probably crabby because they're starving."

"And because they're children," Greg added.

"Oh yeah, and because of that. How about lunch? My treat." Eliza hoped she sounded nonchalant. Because desperate has never been an aphrodisiac. Say yes. Please say yes. Please.

"OK, if you're paying," said Greg, but he was smiling and Eliza had the feeling that he'd have come anyway; it wasn't just the promise of a free chicken-and-chips that was luring him.

They found a burger bar where the management didn't sigh and huff and puff at the sight of the buggy.

They took off their damp coats and draped them over the backs of chairs to steam. The children were given fizzy drinks and a pot of crayons, Greg and Eliza asked for a half-bottle of red wine and the mood distinctly brightened. They placed their order (everyone chose something with chips, and Eliza didn't have the energy to argue for vegetables). The service was speedy, the food was tasty, and as the damp clothes dried off everyone slipped back into their more sunny personalities.

"Shall we order the other half?" asked Greg, pointing to the empty bottle.

God, where had that gone? wondered Eliza. Mostly down her throat, a little on her T-shirt, and a bit down Greg's throat was the answer. She looked at the kids. Mathew was taking an impromptu nap, and Maisie, rather surprisingly, was sitting quietly amusing herself (admittedly, this was by ripping up menus but, hell, she was happy). Eliza agreed to another half-bottle. "Go on then."

"Only if you promise to tell me another date horror story."

"Easy, I've hundreds of them," laughed Eliza. She'd been selective so far. She hadn't told him about the list of criteria, or the horrible shag. But she did tell him about having tea with Rupert Bear, and about all the men who were in love with Martha. When he laughed at her stories the experiences seemed less horrible. "I mean, you have to ask yourself how is it that these men ever get a chance to reproduce. They must have evolved in some way, but who sleeps with these men? And why?" asked Eliza.

Greg was laughing as though she were the funniest woman on earth. Eliza thought he must be a bit drunk.

He caught the waitress's eye. Eliza wasn't thrilled to note that the waitress clearly fancied Greg. Eliza had used to enjoy the fact that other women found her boyfriend attractive. It was less amusing when he was your ex-boyfriend. Greg was flirting shamelessly. The poor flustered girl could hardly concentrate on pouring the wine, and she'd brought sparkling water when they'd asked for still. Eliza let it go, she was having too good a time to fuss about something so small.

They hadn't talked about their new status quo. They'd never said "let's be friends" the way some couples did when they ceased to be couples. Greg was just being Greg—fun, easygoing. Eliza didn't really want to be his friend—"just good friends" was the death knell as far as she was concerned—but better friends than enemies, or nothing at all. So she chattered pleasantly about what she'd been doing with her time. Her successes at work, her failures on dates.

"You've certainly kept yourself busy," said Greg as he lit up a cigarette. He immediately stubbed it out again. "Sorry, I didn't think about the children."

Eliza wanted to kiss him. In truth, she'd wanted to kiss him from the moment that she'd set eyes on him that morning, but she definitely wanted to kiss him now. How considerate. "You're like a different person," she said thoughtfully.

"Good."

"Why do you say that?"

"Well, you didn't like the old me much, did you?" said Greg. Eliza blushed. "I wouldn't say that."

"Oh, but you did. Repeatedly."

For the first time that afternoon there was an awkward silence. Eliza knew what she should do. "Sorry," she mumbled.

"Oh, that's OK. You only broke my heart." Greg was grinning with everything on his face except for his eyes. His eyes showed hurt.

"I *am* sorry," said Eliza, more clearly this time. "Still, it's all worked out for the best, hasn't it?"

"Right," said Greg, nodding. Then he stopped nodding and asked, "How exactly?"

Eliza was stumped. "Well, you look great, you're obviously very happy."

"Right." More nodding. Greg started to play with his cigarette packet; he was clearly desperate for a fag. "I feel like shit, actually."

"Don't joke with me. This new girlfriend of yours no doubt makes you very happy, and she's obviously a great influence. You look fantastic, the flat's clean, even Dog looks wonderful." Eliza hated the bitch with a passion.

"New girlfriend?"

"You don't have to try to protect me. The Bianchis told me. You know how it is with them. Couldn't keep a secret if their lives depended on it. They said she was lovely." Obviously Eliza didn't want to be nice about this hellcat, this usurping witch, but she had no other option; she didn't want to alienate Greg.

"There is no girlfriend; I have no idea what you're on about," said Greg.

"No girlfriend?"

"No."

"You're not going out with anyone?"

"No. Nor have I since we split up."

"You haven't been out with anyone?" asked Eliza. She was fighting the euphoria that threatened to explode in her head and heart.

"No, not so much as shared a bag of chips."

"But the flat is clean."

"You said you didn't like the mess. I thought about it and decided maybe you had a point about that."

Eliza basked in the glory of these victories. She felt as though she had just swept the board at the MTV video awards. She was carrying the trophies for all the categories: Hiphop, Pop, Indie, Rock, R&B, Dance, Garage and even Breakbeat. She was a winner! He'd tidied his flat for *her,* and he hadn't shared chips with anyone since she left. Then she asked, "Have you slept with anyone?"

"Yes, I am flesh and blood."

They both knew that the question wasn't a polite enquiry.

"How many?"

Greg had a choice. He could tell the truth, and risk losing her all over again, because if he'd read this situation clearly, then Eliza was still interested in him—despite everything she'd done to try to prove otherwise. He could tell her that he'd slept with five women, and that none of them had meant anything at all, which was the truth. Or he could find a less offensive (but still realistic) number. Would she believe . . . ? "Two, but not at the same time."

"Well, that's a relief," she said sarcastically.

Two, two, Eliza fumed. He hasn't been out with anyone but had scored twice, whilst she'd dated almost constantly and had had only one very run-of-the-mill fumble. There was no justice.

Bastard.

Just two. Two. Greg had groupies. OK, low-key groupies. Not on the Gallagher-brothers scale, but one or two cute-looking chicks who served in the Lamb and Flag where he played were clearly gagging for it. And there was a couple of girlies from North London who followed him to every gig. Besides, he was lovely. He could have slept with lots more than two.

Sweetstuff.

"They were both just sex. Ignoble, I know, but I made that clear before anything kicked off. The truth is, Eliza, they were pretty disappointing shags anyway."

"Both of them?"

"Yes."

"You're sure?"

Greg paused. He was clearly having to think about it, which made Eliza want to eat her tongue. She swore to herself that she'd never again ask a question unless she already knew the answer.

"Technically, they were fine." This was another lie. Technically, they'd all but one been great, but Greg thought that was more information than Eliza required. "But I couldn't get into it."

"Why?" asked Eliza, and this time she did know the answer—she just wanted to hear it said out loud.

"Neither girl was you, Liza. There didn't seem much point in it. Because—erm—at the risk of sounding like a twat, you're the one for me."

# April

# 48

Martha and Jack had decided to enjoy their last month together to the full. They agreed to have no whinging, no crying and no tantrums—the same rules that they set out for Mathew. They now realized what the toddler was up against. Jack was given leave from his responsibilities in the London office so that he could put his affairs in order before emigrating. In fact, he spent most of his free time playing with Martha, Mathew and Maisie. He decided he wanted to see all the sights of London before he left. As he'd lived in London all his life he, naturally, had failed to visit the Tower, Madame Tussaud's, or ride the Eye. So they set about rectifying the situation by dragging the kids around the tourist traps. They ate burgers out of cardboard boxes and bought overpriced, poorly made key rings from souvenirs shops. They got caught in the rain and forgot their umbrellas, they lost their way and patience on the Tube—it was exactly like being a proper family.

They went for a ride on a tourist open-roofed double-decker bus. Martha wanted to stand up, snatch the microphone from the guide and yell out to London about the unfairness of finding Jack at this time in her life. She remembered a time when all she'd wanted was to fit in; ideally, to disappear. Now she wasn't afraid of standing out. However, she didn't yell out her grievances to London; no one would have heard her above the traffic. Instead, she asked Jack how his application for his Green Card was progressing. She tried not to stamp her feet when he said that it had been approved without any hiccups.

Martha took a suitable interest in the quotes Jack got for selling his car, transporting his furniture, and renting out his flat. They packed up his pictures, his computer and his DVDs into boxes to be shipped to his new flat—which they would not be making their home. Martha battled with a terrible sense of déjà vu; she didn't know where she found the energy to do this all over again. She repeatedly told him that she was OK with the decision for him to leave. She repeatedly listed the reasons why it would be impossible for him to stay.

"We could see each other at weekends—it's only a seven-hour flight," said Jack hopefully and unrealistically.

"That costs hundreds. How would we afford to pop backwards and forwards? We're hardly Madonna and Guy Ritchie. Besides, I only have every other weekend free. How could we sustain any kind of relationship?"

"People do."

"It would be unsettling for the children. I have to concentrate on the kids."

"Well, maybe I'll take the job for a few years and then come back."

"Maybe, but I can't count on it, and I can't spend the next few years imagining what you're getting up to and with whom. It wouldn't work. It was hard enough for a few months. And before you say anything, you would be meeting other people." This was a euphemism, but Martha couldn't bring herself to say anything more explicit. There would always be the endless trail of possibilities.

"I could stay. There are other jobs."

"You love New York, and it's a great job. It might be years before you're offered something as big in the London office. Besides, if you turned it down your firm would think you lacked ambition. They'd sideline you. You can't cut your career off at such an early stage."

"I could—if you asked me to."

Martha didn't reply. She couldn't ask that. She couldn't control or dictate. That wasn't love. One day he'd wake up and resent that he was bringing up someone else's children, that his Saturday nights were ruled by unreliable, hormonal babysitters.

Eliza thought this was Martha's joker card and that her sister should hike up the emotional pressure. Eliza insisted, "I've seen him with the kids. He adores them. You could play the 'they've lost one father already card.'"

"Very honorable," muttered Martha sarcastically. "Besides which, they haven't lost their father; Michael lives only five minutes away." Martha was infuriated with her sister, but what angered her most was that she knew Eliza was right. Jack probably could be persuaded to stay. He was a very loving and worthy man. This—combined with his filthiness in the sack—had left her nearly helpless.

If he woke up to find her crying silently into her pillow, she wouldn't say that it was reality that was letting her down; she'd tell him she'd had a bad dream.

"Did you, Baby? What about?"

This threw her. She wasn't counting on that level of interest. "Daleks," she lied.

Jack kissed her eyelids and held her close until she went back to sleep. His body folded into hers and their sweat sat, muddled, in the crease at the back of her knees. She'd miss his warmth. Martha knew that, besides their mingling sweat, she'd miss many other things about Jack. She'd miss his affection. Jack was always kissing her. He kissed her nose. He kissed her fingertips. He kissed her in the street. He kissed her in shops. He kissed her on the Tube. He kissed her whenever she turned to him and said "Kiss me." Which was indecently frequently.

He was a beautiful world.

She'd miss his ability to see the best in people and situations. She'd miss his cheerful unflappability. The kids would miss his energy, particularly his ability to carry them endlessly around on his shoulders. She'd miss his eyes that flooded with emotion. She'd miss his cock moving inside her. She'd miss his sense of humour, the way he continually recalled silly facts. She'd even miss his stupid film quotes.

She felt the loss already.

They both talked about keeping in touch. They made elaborate plans about what they'd do when Martha and the children visited. But they both doubted that their plans would ever be more than comforting pipe dreams. How would Martha be able to stand by and watch Jack build a new life entirely separate to hers? More fundamentally, how would either of them be able to build a new life if they stood on each other's sidelines, haunting each other's memories? A clean break would be essential.

Martha began to concentrate on how she would fill the void when Jack left. She didn't want a repeat of the loneliness that she'd felt on Michael's departure. Coffee mornings held little allure, but a night out with the girls at the local pizza parlour, enjoying a carafe or two of house white, well, that would be fun. The void would be filled with making her own decisions regarding childcare, buying a new sofa, putting some more shelves up in the children's rooms, taking the car to be serviced. She planned to read her AA manual before she went to the garage. Whilst she had little hope of completely understanding what the mechanic was saying, she would at least like to give a good enough impression of doing so, in order to avoid being totally ripped off. She applied for a part-time job, as an office administrator, at the local primary school. She was well aware that she wasn't charging up the corporate ladder with such a position, but the school had a crèche that Mathew and Maisie would be able to attend, she'd have long holidays and she liked the teaching staff.

Eliza moved out of Martha's home and back in with Greg. This wasn't a surprise to anyone other than Eliza. Martha knew that she'd miss her sister's bossy but friendly presence. Living on her own wasn't going to be easy, but it was time she stood on her own two feet again. In fact, it might be the first time she'd ever stood on her own two feet, but she felt ready. Besides, it was worth it just to see how totally blissed out Eliza and Greg were. Martha was pleased that her Christmas sixpence wish hadn't been wasted.

Martha planned to fill the void by pushing on with the divorce.

Martha waited until both children were safely, peacefully asleep. Jack was in the sitting room, clearing away the kids' toys whilst half-watching cable TV. He flicked through the channels, finding entertainment when most would only be bored. He yelled through to Martha occasionally: "Come see Halle Berry; doesn't she look different with long hair?" or "Have you ever seen a polar bear fishing? Quickly come and see." Martha stood in the doorway and marvelled that he was tidying her children's toys and that he wanted to share everything with her, everything from bathing the children to his opinion on which supermodel was most likely to go like a train. Moments like these made her sure that, however many AA manuals she read, she wasn't going to avoid missing him.

She downed her glass of wine along with the whiny "Why me? Why me" voice that had of late persistently screeched from her heart. She picked up a colouring book of Mathew's and roughly tore out three or four pages. Next she sought out a pen—not an easy task in these days of electronic communication. There weren't any on the desk, the desk that she still thought of as Michael's. The ones in the jam jar on the kitchen windowsill had dried up, and there were only pencils in the vase on the telephone table. Martha went upstairs to the bedroom and began to rummage through her knicker drawer. She had a vague memory that . . . Yes, she was right. A pen from Tiffany's, a present for her thirtieth birthday. It had stayed in its box ever since, eternally awaiting the "special occasion," hoping to avoid being left on someone's desk or on a shop counter. Well, this was pretty bloody special. The perfect pen for the task. Martha began to scribble.

# 49

**"You're late, Michael,"** said Martha as she opened the door.

"Don't start, Martha, I've had a hard day at the office."

"Look, I've had a hard day too. I've been to the dentist and had a tooth drilled whilst Maisie balanced on my stomach and Mathew attacked the nurse. I've rowed over the phone with some NHS bureaucrat, for forty minutes, and all I wanted to do was change the time of Maisie's appointment for her hearing test. And I've had a job interview. Just because my tools are jars of pasta and packets of crayons, instead of laptops and PowerPoint presentations, it does not automatically follow that my life lacks significance. My life is still as enormous as yours is," said Martha.

"Right," said Michael, somewhat taken aback. He was quite unused to this new Martha that he'd encountered of late. He wondered if she'd attended some sort of assertiveness course in New York, or whether over there they pumped out aggression-inducing chemicals through their air-conditioning systems. He didn't dare ask. The odd thing was he rather liked this confident, unabashed Martha. She reminded him of the girl he'd married.

Michael looked around the kitchen, where they now stood, and craned his neck as he tried to see into the living room. Martha knew that he was looking for Jack, who had gone out for the evening. Jack didn't like the idea of meeting Michael, and so far had avoided it at all costs. He knew that the middle-class, modern way was to shake hands, have a chat, behave in a civilized manner towards your girlfriend's ex, but he wouldn't do it. He wasn't jealous of Michael, but he didn't like him. He couldn't forgive Michael for not loving Martha. He couldn't forgive him for having the chance that he'd never have, the freedom to love Martha without any boundaries, restrictions or problems with immigration.

"Jack's not here," Martha said defiantly. "He's gone out for the evening, but he'll be back later tonight." She wanted to make it clear to Michael that she had no reason to hide Jack, and that he wasn't secretly stowed upstairs. "There's so much to discuss, we thought it better if he went out and left me to it." Martha adored saying "we" to Michael and meaning her and someone else. A little bit of Martha would have liked Michael to meet Jack because she was sure that he would die of jealousy then. Not because Jack put his hands all over Martha's body on a regular basis, but because Jack had amazing pecs and abs.

Martha made Michael a cup of coffee and then they sat facing each other across the kitchen table. The decree nisi sat between them; they were meeting to discuss the final practicalities of the divorce. They were days away from the date when Martha could apply for the decree absolute. Then that would be it.

Over.

"I've made a list," she said, "of the things we need to discuss. I've divided the issues into groups according to priority."

"Priority?" asked Michael in a voice that betrayed a blend of amusement, astonishment and a dash of anxiety.

"Yes, priority," insisted Martha, without giving away the fact that her stomach had jumped into her mouth and then sunk straight back down into the depths of her toes.

"The children are our priority, surely," said Michael smugly.

Martha took a deep breath. Of course she knew the children were their priority. They'd always been *her* fucking priority. The seemingly endless nights when she'd sat up listening to them cry. Fed them, changed them, winded them, held them, played with them and still, sometimes, they wouldn't sleep. They were her priority when she took them to the swimming baths even though she hated swimming herself, found it quite scary. They'd been her priority when she'd given up her job and her body. They were her priority when she took them for their injections and cried on the inside as the cold, sharp needle sank into their lovely, chubby baby legs. They were her priority when she rowed with them every morning because they wanted chocolate for breakfast and they had to clean their teeth. They'd been her priority when her life had become a constant round of cleaning and wiping and comforting and disciplining. A battle against an intricate network of confounding equipment: highchairs that were always filthy, buggies that refused to fold, non-spill cups that did spill, building bricks that always found their way into the video recorder. They were always her priority.

But they'd never really been his. Not if she was honest with herself. He'd never once got up in the night to comfort a crying child. Even now he had to ask where the nappies were kept, and he didn't know what size Maisie took. He didn't buy shoes or coats or vests, or any of their day-to-day needs. (Could any mother imagine walking past BabyGap and not yearning for the latest collection? Even if you can't afford it, you want it. Apparently, that was a gene that Michael had missed out on.) The children had been her priority when she'd said no to starting a fabulous new life in New York. Because even if she could have fought for the legal right to take them abroad, she knew that the best thing for her babies was to have a relationship with both parents.

Martha thought she might explode with indignation that Michael should even hint that she ever had any other priority, but instead she took a deep breath and resisted. She wanted to concentrate on the list. If she managed to think of the list as an agenda at a business meeting and if she managed to think of Michael as a colleague, with whom she shared a joint project, they might just get through this evening without a row.

Which would be a good thing.

Martha was exhausted with rows. She thought she'd had enough rows with Michael to last them a lifetime.

Her list wasn't demanding or unreasonable, but she had decided what she wanted to save from the embers of their marriage. "I don't want to have to leave the house, if at all possible," she said.

"I agree; it'll be better for the children if they stay here."

Martha looked at Michael and tried to hide her astonishment. She hadn't expected him to concede quite so easily. "I've been looking at ways that I can take over the mortgage and increase it so that I can buy you out of your share. I'm not expecting any maintenance from you for me, but for—"

"The children, absolutely. What do you suggest?"

Martha named a figure. It was the percentage of salary that the divorce Website had recommended as reasonable maintenance.

Michael said he thought it was a lot of money.

"Not especially. That's what the courts recommend," said Martha firmly.

Michael agreed to it.

"I'm going to get a job," Martha said quietly. She wasn't sure what Michael's response would be. While they'd been married he'd been very opposed to her working. He said that it wasn't good for the children, besides which, it would mess up his tax returns.

"Yes, you mentioned that you'd had an interview today. I think a job is a good idea, it'll give you some independence."

Had anyone ever been so patronizing? But Martha held her tongue. After all, Michael was agreeing to everything that she was suggesting; she could hardly moan because she didn't like the way he was agreeing. She waited to see if he'd ask what her job was to be. He didn't. Martha sighed. Why should she be surprised at how little interest he had in her life?

They slowly worked through Martha's list. Dividing pension policies, shares, responsibilities for loans and the mortgage. It seemed inextricably complicated unthreading their lives. Luckily, their mortgage was reasonable because Martha had benefited from a big pay-off when she'd taken voluntary redundancy after finding out that she was pregnant with Mathew. That had been a piece of luck. The lump of cash had been used to reduce their mortgage. Martha had done her sums: she'd have to be careful, cut a few corners, but they'd manage. She'd sell the Range Rover, give half the money back to Michael, and still be able to afford a smaller, more economical car. She might even convert the attic and rent it out to a foreign student. It was a lovely room; it even had an en-suite bathroom. Besides, it would be nice to have the company and good for the children to be exposed to someone from another country and culture. She and the kids would be fine, no danger of starving.

They came to the end of the list and both Martha and Michael sighed audibly. They'd managed to iron out the final details of their divorce without a row. It had taken a great amount of restraint on both sides, but they had done it. They looked at one another and smiled.

"Silly to be proud of not rowing, isn't it?" said Martha, articulating what they were both thinking.

Michael smiled and half-laughed. Martha was surprised to see evidence of her husband, the old Michael, flare up in this man's face—the man she'd come to think of as a stranger. She breathed in and thought she might drown in the intimacy. The feeling lasted for a nano-second, then her husband disappeared again, leaving Martha feeling oddly bereft, leaving her wondering if she'd imagined him.

"Would you like a glass of wine?" she offered. She'd kept well away from the alcohol until all the potentially inflammatory money-talk was over, but now she fancied a glass. She wasn't sure if the drink was celebratory, or in commiseration.

"That would be lovely," smiled Michael. He loosened his tie and threw it over the back of the chair, as he always used to. The gesture was disconcertingly familiar. "Did you have fun in New York?" he asked.

Martha knew he was trying to be friendly. "It's amazing," she beamed.

"Isn't it?" agreed Michael.

"I can't think why I hadn't been there before. I should have joined you on one of your many business trips."

"Maybe you should have."

Martha was embarrassed. Michael had never invited her on any of his business trips. She hadn't wanted to sound critical or regretful. It was just hard to find neutral territory.

"Are you happy with Jack?" And that certainly wasn't neutral territory.

"Yes," she admitted.

"You didn't waste much time in replacing me," commented Michael.

Martha thought about his comment. "I don't see it like that. Jack isn't a replacement. He's—we're—something in our own right."

"You're saying you don't compare him to me?"

The words "frequently" and "favourably" shot through Martha's head, but she resisted flicking them into their history.

She said, "I try not to," which was infinitely more conciliatory. There was enough hurt swilling around as it was. She didn't want to hurt him more than necessary. It was true that Michael had crushed her dreams, cracked her heart and stamped on her life as she knew it. But if Martha was honest with herself—a skill she had rediscovered and relished—his exit had released her. She'd swapped her husband for fake tattoos, fairy lights, deep, loving, new relationships, toned thighs, scruffy jeans and a sense of self.

They fell silent. Martha walked to the drawer to hunt for the corkscrew. She looked out of the window on to her beautiful garden. It was dark, but in the light from the kitchen Martha could just make out the spring flowers, daffodils and crocuses, were finally in bloom, the sunny yellows and sturdy lilacs danced prettily in the wind. Mathew's swing moved a fraction. The garden looked happy and peaceful.

Michael followed Martha's gaze. "Eliza told me about Jack's job in the U.S."

"Did she now." Martha was irritated but, luckily, she had her back to Michael and he wouldn't have known unless he was watching her very carefully; then he might spot the fractional rise of her shoulders, as tension shot through her spine. Martha had decided to avoid telling Michael about her choice not to take the children abroad. She didn't want him to misinterpret her actions. She hadn't done it for him; she'd done it for them.

"She told me that he asked you to go with him," continued Michael.

Martha turned to face him. She put his glass of wine down in front of him and took a huge gulp of her own. "Yes, he did."

"But you said no."

"That's right."

They sat silently facing one another. Martha couldn't think of anything she wanted to say, or anything she wanted to hear.

Conversely, Michael clearly had something he wanted to say

and something he wanted her to hear. "Martha, I may be a million miles away from target here, and if I am, I apologize, but I have to ask; does this mean there is a chance for us?"

Martha must have misheard. She didn't understand. "What do you mean?"

Michael looked directly at her and he had the bloody cheek to look at her with his shiny, smiley, deep-brown eyes. The eyes that she'd fallen in love with more than ten years ago. The eyes that Maisie had inherited.

"I didn't realize there was still an 'us,'" she said. Her voice treacherously cracked in the middle of her sentence.

"Martha, there's always been an 'us,'" implored Michael. "You, me, Mathew and Maisie."

Martha's head was spinning. She blinked ferociously in an effort to keep those bloody tears at bay (what were they about?) and to try and remain focused. "But what about Eleanor?" asked Martha. "Are you still seeing her?"

"Yes."

"Was it an affair?"

"Stop asking me that, Martha. Look, we've both made some awful mistakes in the last six months."

Had she?

"We've both said a lot of terrible things."

That was true.

"But it's clear that we *are* supposed to be together, that we *are* happier together."

Was it? Martha didn't know. Martha had waited for this declaration for so long. She'd waited from the moment that Michael closed the door behind him way back in September. Why had he chosen now? Was he being sentimental, or maybe had he and Eleanor had a row? After waiting for so long, why was it that Martha didn't want to hear this? She'd thought Michael had looked happier since he'd left her, and that made a sort of sense.

She didn't want to hear that all this pain had been for nothing.

"I thought that you didn't want me, but when I heard that you'd turned Jack down, I realized that I still had a chance."

Martha stared at Michael, uncomprehending. It was impossible for her to follow his logic. What did he mean, she didn't want him? Of course she'd wanted him. She'd begged him, literally prostrated herself, asking him to love her, not to leave her and her children. It was he who hadn't wanted her. He hadn't wanted her as she was: the housewife whose greatest ambition was having a lovely family and home, whose greatest concern was Michael and his happiness. She'd felt safe with Michael. And soon safety slipped into dependency, and then nose-dived into over-dependency. She couldn't pinpoint exactly when her personality had merged with his, had been dominated and then eradicated. She'd bored him, and now she could admit that she'd been quite bored with herself, too. Now she didn't want to be that boring person, but still she thought he was ungrateful. When he'd left she'd been faced with a huge void. She'd felt nothing. She'd had nothing. She'd been nothing.

But now she was something again.

She'd rediscovered herself. It hadn't been easy. In fact it had been bloody. Jack had helped her find herself and she was grateful. She was just Martha. Not Martha, Michael's wife; not Martha, Mathew and Maisie's mother. Not even Martha, Jack's girlfriend.

It would have been nice if Michael had wanted to help Martha rediscover the more funky, hopeful girl that he'd fallen in love with, but he hadn't.

"Jack can't know that when you get sunburnt, through flagrant abuse of the suncream manufacturer's advice, you incorrectly insist that your red-hot limbs will certainly be 'brown in the morning,'" began Michael. Martha smiled. It was true that every summer she burnt herself, and her stubborn defence always was: "It'll be brown in the morning." Michael had always nodded at this statement, indulging her, pretending to be convinced.

Jack did know.

"He doesn't know that it's funny that you always drop the soap in the shower," continued Michael. He was referring to the fact that Martha had tiny hands, and every single time she took a shower she would drop the slippery soap. Michael used to think her little doll-like hands were attractive and her dropping the soap made him smile. "Only the two of us know the mess in our home is made by Little Goblin," said Michael enthusiastically. Martha nodded and didn't bother correcting him. Before the children were born, Michael and Martha had had an imaginary character that reportedly lived in the shoe cupboard: the Little Goblin. He was blamed for all mess, breakages and loss of keys. The truth was, nowadays the mess, breakages and loss of keys were likely to have been created by much more human "Little Goblins"; Michael didn't know this.

It was nice to share the old jokes. Over the last few months they'd been so angry with one another and themselves, humiliated by their failure, disillusioned and disappointed, that it had been impossible to spend any time together relaxing like this. Michael sat facing her, smiling gently, as was his way. He had been such a gentle man when she'd first met him.

His smile acted like a key, turning slowly in a lock and allowing a door to be prised open. Suddenly, Martha was submerged in memories that she thought she'd buried. Their first holiday together: a terrible, cheap package holiday, because in those days they both earned peanuts. They'd walked miles each day to find a quiet beach and to avoid the lager-lout, tabloid-reading tourists. Martha's new sandals rubbed, causing blisters, and walking hurt, but she didn't tell him—she'd wanted to appear fitter, braver, and more adept than she was. They'd eaten in a *tapas* bar—the same one every night, because the entire island was overrun with appalling anglicized restaurants offering "genuine English breakfast with white-sliced, and fish and chips." They'd avoided the purple liqueurs as well, and noisy, packed clubs; they'd just wanted to be alone. They'd gone back to the hotel early and made love. They'd been to a water theme park and taken photos of each other bombing down slides, photos Martha had ripped up last autumn, though the images were still with her.

They had loved each other. Very much. He proposed on a beach in the Bahamas; he'd worked out where they'd watch the sunset from. They'd once looked at stars through a telescope together. He'd held her hair and hand when she had food poisoning. They'd painted the children's nursery. They'd danced. They'd watched the fireworks welcome in the new millenium from London Bridge, and then they'd walked home. It had taken them until four in the morning. There were so many memories. Ten years.

Michael must have been thinking along the same lines because he interrupted her thoughts. "Do you really want to start all over again on memories?"

Martha didn't say "We've already started." Nor did she say "But we can never catch up." These were the two thoughts that surged into her head almost simultaneously. Then again, Martha firmly believed in quality, not quantity.

Michael and Martha had walked down the aisle together. That would always be important, vital. They had loved each other. Martha wanted to remember these things. She still loved him.

In a way.

But was it enough?

One day she'd tell Maisie and Mathew. She'd say "We did love each other."

Jack didn't know about Little Goblin, but he had already learnt that Martha was never simply hungry—she was always starving—never cold—but always freezing—never warm—but boiling. Her dash from one extreme to another made him laugh. Better yet, they'd found their own space. Their own sayings. One time, Martha had wanted to emphatically tell Jack that he was "so not just a pretty face," but she'd muddled her words and instead she'd said "you are just so not a pretty face." It had become a catch phrase between them, and always induced a disproportionate amount of laughter. He knew what her favourite book was. He brought her a glass of water to bed every night as she had a slight allergy to her pillows and always woke up coughing. It didn't matter if she woke him because they would reassure each other that "it was not the cough that carried her off but the coffin they carried her off in." It didn't sound like much, but it was *their* familiarity. When she made love with Jack, she not only tasted his cock but his thoughts too. He kissed her eyelids and could see her clearly, all of her. He moved her ground, gave her especially good thoughts and memories. He was quickly becoming her universe. He'd even cut back on his mildly annoying habit of constantly quoting from films that she'd never heard of.

But Jack was leaving.

And she'd be alone again.

She thought all this as she drank her glass of wine and Michael waited. They were drinking out of wineglasses that Martha had bought to replace the ones he'd taken, but earlier on they'd been drinking out of coffee mugs that they'd bought together. It was all so confusing. Much messier than she'd ever wanted her life to be.

"I miss the kids, Martha."

"I'm sure you do," nodded Martha sadly, and the surprise was that she didn't have to fight the urge to yell *"Well, whose bloody fault is that?"* She just felt sorry for Michael. "What happened, Michael? Why did you leave?"

Michael looked pained. It was clear she was putting him on

the spot, but she had to understand. It had been months now and she still didn't get it. She was probably being dense. It was probably simple to him. The way in mathematics some people think that quadratic equations are pure and beautiful, while others are blinded by them and shake and cry at the very thought. To move on it was necessary for her to totally understand when they'd taken the wrong road.

"You know how we used to comment on couples in restaurants who ate together but didn't say a word to one another throughout the whole meal?" Michael started.

"Yes."

"I was scared we were becoming like them."

Martha nodded. It was true. Her life had been like the children's goldfish (unimaginatively called Goldie—although, more amusingly, Jack called it Horn). It, too, simply spent its days, pointlessly circling around and around, forgetting that it had just visited the same place only seconds before. It gawked at life, other people's lives, but didn't comment, let alone participate. Martha had felt like that goldfish. "You could have said. We could have fixed it."

"Maybe."

"Certainly," said Martha confidently. "Sometimes I'm rummaging through a drawer and I come across something that you bought me, earrings or a scarf, thoughtful gifts that remind me that you loved me."

"I did, Martha. I do."

"And I want to scream that things have changed so much. What we had was bona fide."

Michael no longer recognized his wife's language, but he did recognize her mind. She was saying it was too late. She was sorry, but he'd left it too late.

Martha wished it wasn't. She wished that this hadn't happened, and that she and Michael could have been in love forever.

She wished it so much she wanted to curl up in a ball and never have to stand up again.

"It doesn't have to be too late," said Michael.

Martha started to cry. She was surprised that there were any tears left in her. Where did they come from? Martha had spent years and years believing that everything Michael said was gospel. She'd thought he was right about where they should live, what she should wear, even what wines she should drink, so she thought it was the ultimate irony that she couldn't believe him now. However much she wanted to.

"You broke my heart, Michael. Accept some responsibility."

# 50

"**A**nd you're happy with that decision, are you?" demanded Eliza.

Martha moved the phone away from her ear and glared at it indignantly, sticking her tongue out, which was very immature, but made her feel a lot better. "Are you saying you think I made the wrong decision?"

"No."

"Good."

"Not necessarily."

"Not necessarily? Since when have you been a big fan of Michael's?"

"I'm not, necessarily. It's just—"

"What?"

"Well, you've managed to give two men the big heave-ho in almost as many weeks. D'you think that's a considered decision?"

"What century are you living in, Eliza?"

"I'm not saying women can't manage without men—"

"Good." God, was there anything more annoying than a newly engaged woman? Eliza believed that the answer to everybody's problems was finding the love of your life. She was evangelical.

The worst of it was, Martha agreed with her.

Providing of course that he didn't bugger off to the other side of the globe, which actually hurt a lot and caused problems rather than solved them.

"Look, Mar, I'm just saying that . . . oh, I don't know. I'm just saying I'm sorry that it's all so complicated."

"Yeah, I am too."

"It's not going to be an easy day for you today, is it?"

"No, not really."

Jack was catching the 19:50 flight to New York. Martha had decided that she wasn't going to go to the airport with him. Her mum and dad and Eliza and Greg and even Michael had all offered to look after the children so that she could go and wave him off, but she'd declined. Martha hated goodbyes and however much she practised, she could never think fondly of them. Goodbyes were cruel. They were sad. She didn't want to stand in the terminal and cry.

What was there left to say?

Over the last few weeks Jack had said some of the sweetest things to Martha, he'd given her plenty of pure and strong memories to look back on. Enough, but not too many. She was not going to live a life of regret and recollection. She was going to live a full life. Jack had never judged or categorized Martha. He hadn't looked at her and thought "failed marriage" or "single mum" or "bored housewife." He only saw Little Miss E., sexy, feisty, funny Little Miss E. who should be in clubs and bars and flagship fashion stores just as often as she should be at the local park or sitting through an NCT meeting. Jack had made her feel beautiful and strong and important, and the best thing was that she didn't think she needed him to keep up the belief. She could do it on her own.

She had to.

"Mum and Dad mentioned they might pop over to yours today," said Eliza.

"Did they now?" Their intentions were transparent. Martha felt mildly guilty that she was such a worry to them but, mostly, she was just happy that they would be popping by. She wanted to be consumed by their unconditional love. She thought it would be more bearable watching the clock nudge around to ten to eight if her parents were with her and she had to pretend that she wasn't watching the clock.

"Greg and I aren't up to much, either. There's not a lot to do on a Friday night, is there?" said Eliza. "So we thought we'd swing by, too. Maybe bring a takeaway over for everyone."

Martha was grateful. She knew Eliza had a thousand more interesting alternatives on a Friday night. "Thanks, Eliza, that would be lovely."

"What do you fancy: Indian, Thai?"

"Bring Thai."

"Right."

"Right."

Martha allowed the children to stay up later than normal. The excuse she used to them and herself was that their grandparents and aunt and uncle were coming to visit. The truth was, she didn't want to be alone, not even for half an hour. Besides, she had no energy to fight with them about cleaning their teeth. The children realized that this was as good as it got, if you were three and under (staying downstairs after 7 p.m.) and therefore were behaving impeccably. Mathew was patiently helping Maisie to put plastic shapes into the

correct holes, and he told her the names of the shapes she was playing with. It probably didn't matter that so far he'd told her a trian-
gle, a star and a square were all "rounds." Martha put a couple of
bottles of wine in the fridge but resisted opening one; she could
wait until the others arrived. She surveyed her home. She was very
grateful that she wouldn't have to move. It felt like a happy home.
Not at that exact moment, perhaps, but mostly.

The early evening sunset filled the kitchen with orange light.
Martha stretched to see the skyline; her view was mostly of
houses and flats but, undaunted, a little bit of sunset forced its
way through the congested London sky and promised 7 million
people that summer would arrive eventually. Martha saw a plane
overhead. She checked her watch. Of course it wasn't Jack's plane,
it was far too early, she was being melodramatic. But she wondered who was on that plane, and who was being taken away
from their loved ones.

Or perhaps towards. Because Martha still did believe that—
somehow—everything turned out OK. Maybe her OK wasn't
just yet. But she did believe in it, she had to.

Martha had spent the afternoon tidying up. She was no
longer obsessive about cleanliness or neatness. She didn't waste
time mopping her cream carpets with bleach, or washing the inside of vegetables, or alphabetically arranging her cookbooks but,
because her mum was coming to visit, she'd pushed the vacuum
around and cleared away the plates from the children's tea. It
hadn't taken long. She'd also had calls from Claire and Dawn.
Claire had carefully not alluded to the fact that Jack was leaving,
but had frequently repeated an invitation for Martha and the
kids to join her family for Sunday lunch, an invite Martha intended to take up. Dawn was more forthright, and asked Martha
if she felt like shit; then she'd said, "Don't answer that, of course
you do." Martha had also gone on line and paid a couple of bills,
but still the afternoon had dragged.

Martha picked up a magazine and started to flick through the glossy pages. She no longer had to sit and count on her fingers the blessings in her life; instead, she was imbued with a general sense that she was surrounded by good things. The same good things—her children, her family, her friends. She was grateful for her time with Michael. It hadn't worked for them, but it didn't mean that what they'd had was meaningless. Their time together had meant a lot to her. It was still a mystery as to why it hadn't worked; both of them had wanted it to, albeit at different times. But would the benefit of hindsight or time travel have put her in a different place? She doubted it, because she felt as though she was in a place where she belonged. She felt strong and brave in her new place, a place she would have liked to share with Jack.

She had no idea how she would fill the time until her family visited. She had no idea how she'd spend the rest of her life.

Martha wondered what she'd do with all the time she used to spend with Jack, the time that they'd filled with play and prattle. He'd told her about over- and under-steering on cars, pixels in TV screens, how engines worked; and she'd told him about hyperbole, the conventions of Greek Tragedy and that cabbage is good for cracked nipples. Together they'd played I-Spy. They'd divided all their friends and families into types according to the world of Winnie-the-Pooh (because it was true that everyone in the end can be boiled down to Pooh, Tigger, Eeyore, Piglet, Kanga or Roo; there might be Owls too, but Martha hadn't met any). They'd talked about which Superhero they would want to be (Jack wanted to be Superman. Martha opted out; she thought it was a lonely life being a Superhero).

The truth was, Jack and Martha weren't the sort of people who could change the world in any profound sense. If they could have, they would have found the cure for killer diseases and written a five-point plan for world peace. But they were just ordinary people. The best they could hope for was to avoid heart disease and obesity by eating sensibly, and to take some of the menace out of the school playground by bringing up at least two children with a set of values that prioritized love, honesty and respect.

Martha thought it was enough. Her life was important enough.

"We let ourselves in, darling," said her mum. Suddenly Martha was aware that Eliza was putting food in the microwave. Greg was opening wine, Mrs. Evergreen was kissing her and the children, and Mr. Evergreen was checking on the garden.

"Where are the coasters?"

"Have you been pruning?"

"Do you want a spring roll?"

"Have the children been good today?"

The chatter was constant. It was clear that there had been a tactical agreement that any direct allusion to Jack was forbidden. His name was all the more glaring for its absence. They'd all come to fill her life with their love and concern, which would no doubt mean that there would be some sort of family squabble at some point in the evening, nothing serious, something about what to watch on TV, or who should nip to the garage to buy chocolate. Little things that showed that they cared about one another, rather than the reverse. Martha brightened and realized that she was looking forward to her Thai takeaway and the evening in with her family. She was looking forward to her life.

She was going to see an Elvis impersonator. She would chat to slow old ladies in the high street who had no one else to talk to, because she'd have time to do so. She was going to put a fireplace in her bedroom. She was going to cry when her friends had their babies and not be embarrassed that she was a hysterical female and far too emotional. She was already wearing unsuitable clothes; she might take the children to Australia to visit an old school friend who'd emigrated there years ago. She was going to learn to snowboard. She was going to buy a new dining-room suite. She was going to do a flower-arranging course, no apologies. She was going to take a photo of the children every day if she felt like it, even if they were all the same. She was going to start her new job, she was going to skip meals, she was going to eat chocolate, and tomorrow she'd have fried eggs, if she felt like it.

Martha was so engrossed in her survival strategy that her father almost had to shake her to get her attention.

"Martha, 'phone for you."

Martha took the call in the hall. It was the least noisy part of the house. The children were overexcited at seeing nearly all their favourite people in one room at the same time, and so were insisting on acting like children. The adults seemed to be following their lead.

"Martha?" His voice was quilted with kindness, and now as always, Martha felt at once loved and loving, sexed and sexy.

"Yes?"

"It's me."

"Yes, you silly bugger, I know that." Martha wished he hadn't called. She'd just been starting to feel brave. She didn't want to have to go through a goodbye; she'd been very clear about that.

"I'm at the airport."

"I know that, too." Martha sniffed silently and hoped he couldn't hear her breaking heart and her screaming soul.

"Little Miss E., you know all the reasons we couldn't work?"

"Yes, I do." Her head was weary with turning them around, wishing them away, then admitting they were there to stay.

"Can you think of one reason that it might work? Just one?"

Their conversation was interrupted by an announcement from the tannoy: "This is the last call for British Airways flight BA0179 to New York."

Martha heard the announcement, so he certainly must have. He ignored it. If he wasn't careful he was going to delay the plane. She fought and fought to hold back her sobs but images swooshed into her head, damaging her resolve. She saw them dancing in the kitchen, pretending to be Adam Ant, and dancing in Fabric, pretending to be cool. She remembered the chocolate heart and the anagrams of "something meaningful." She thought about Jack making paper airplanes, bathing the kids, changing the water filter, ice-skating. The idea of letting these memories go was causing a pain so intense that her body felt it was being mangled, she thought she might scream. "Just one," she sobbed.

"What is it, Babe? What's the reason?" He sounded frantic.

"This is a call for all remaining passengers travelling on the 19:50 British Airways flight to New York, please make your way to the departure gate immediately."

Just piss off, thought Martha. She meant the tannoy announcement, rather than the love of her life.

"Baby, listen, recently you've given me lots of reasons why we won't work. Can you give me one that we will? Just one."

"I love you, Jack, I love you, and without Hope my heart will break." She was sobbing harder. God, she was such a girl. Sometimes it seemed she hadn't learnt anything in all these months.

"And I love you, Little Miss E. And your messy kids and messy life. I love them," said Jack.

Martha could tell that he was tearful too. "Do you?"

"You know I do."

This is a call for passenger Mr. Jack Hope, travelling on the 19:50 BA0179 flight to New York. Please make your way to the departure gate immediately."

"They're calling for me."

"I know."

"I gotta go."

"I know."

"But, Martha . . ."

"What?"

"I'll be back."

"Is that a line from a damn film?"

"No—well, yes, it's Arnie, but it's me, too, Babe."

Martha walked back into the sitting room. A barrage of confused questions heralded her arrival. It was clear they'd known who was on the phone, and they'd been trying, and failing, not to eavesdrop.

"What did he say?" asked Mrs. Evergreen.

"Everything all right?" asked Mr. Evergreen.

"Well?" asked Eliza and Greg.

"Was it Jack?" asked Mathew.

"He said he'd be back," smiled Martha.

"Hurrah!" Mrs. Evergreen jumped up and down on the spot, Mathew started to cheer and Maisie, who probably had little understanding of the situation but was caught up in the excitement of the moment, started to giggle and throw her head back, gurgling in a way that always made Martha want to laugh too. Martha didn't know what to do. She was laughing and crying at the same time. Even Mr. Evergreen looked relieved.

Luckily, Eliza had a grip on reality. "When? When will he be back?" she demanded.

"Leave it, Liza," said Greg gently. He reached out to put his hand on Eliza's arm as though his physical restraint could stop her tongue. But his caution came too late; her words were out and the damage was done. The mood was broken.

"He didn't say," admitted Martha.

"Surprise, sur-bloody-prise."

"But I believe him."

"Will you stop with this trusting thing! Yeah, he may come back when Mathew is graduating, or Maisie needs someone to walk her down the aisle. Or he may come back sooner than that. He may come back after he's shagged a few more women in New

York, or then again, he might not, because he might meet one that he really likes and decide to stay."

"He wouldn't do that."

"Why wouldn't he? It's not good enough saying that he'll come back at some point. You need him now. You need him to help with the kids, to do that throwing-them-in-the-air thing that makes them squeal with delight. You need him to carry heavy shopping bags. You need him to give you a good servicing—you're in your thirties, that's your sexual prime. Sorry, Dad." Eliza realized that her father was probably hoping that the ground would open and swallow him up. He hadn't heard his daughters discussing sex since their guinea pigs had had babies—Eliza had been eight at the time and fascinated. "You need him to sort out the tax on your car."

"I can do all those things. Well, except for the servicing," admitted Martha. "Sorry, Dad."

"I know you can, Martha, but I don't want you to have to do them alone." Eliza had been standing in the doorway from the kitchen to the sitting room. She now collapsed into a chair and said, "If he loves you he should be here by your side." Eliza was shaking. She was quivering with anger and indignation. She wanted more for her sister. Her sister deserved more.

"I can't make him, Eliza. I can't force him. I don't even want to. That's not love."

"But what are you going to do?" Eliza wished that there was a solution.

Martha thought there might be many. "I'm going to be OK. I have no idea how things are going to turn out, but I think I'm going to be OK."

# 51

The party lost some of its edge after Eliza's outburst. They ate the takeaway but the jollity was forced, and Mrs. Evergreen couldn't persuade anyone to eat up the last fishcake, even though the mango sauce was delicious. She turned her attention to tidying the kitchen. Mr. Evergreen shuffled off to the garage to buy some chocolate bars in the hope of restoring good humour. Eliza tried to make amends by reading a story to the children and putting them to bed. Which just left Greg and Martha. They watched a repeat episode of *One Foot in the Grave* in silence, until Martha could stand the silence no longer and demanded, "Do you think she's right?"

"Oh, always, about everything," joked Greg. "At least in public. Which bit do you mean in particular?"

"About him shagging *other* women? About the fact that he'd be by my side now if he really loved me."

Greg shrugged. He was distinctly uncomfortable. He might be engaged now. He might have managed to spit out a fairly decent proposal to Eliza, but that didn't mean he was capable of talking about love and stuff to other women. He liked Jack. He'd seemed like a laugh. And Greg liked Martha, she had a good heart; he liked her especially since her groovy clothes now matched her groovy personality. But he didn't really want to get embroiled in a "do you think he loves me?" conversation. In his experience this type of conversation was rarely satisfactory.

He was grateful to be saved by the bell. Mr. Evergreen had probably forgotten the keys. Martha let Greg answer the door. Well, he'd seemed keen to do so; he'd leapt up out of the settee.

She hadn't seen him move so quickly since Brazil scored that second goal in the World Cup semi-finals—then he'd jumped up and down for ages, fired with fury and disappointment.

"D'you know what, Martha?" yelled Greg as he opened the door. "I think Eliza was right."

"Do you?"

"Yeah, girl, if he really loved you he would want to be by your side *now.*"

"Right," mumbled Martha, and she sank deeper into a depression that wasn't just induced by Victor Meldrew's miserable tones.

"Hey, Babe, budge over, I don't think I've seen this one."

And it was Jack.

Jack sat down next to her on her settee. Martha gawped, unable to say anything.

Greg was clearly much more in charge of his faculties. He acted like the perfect host and passed Jack a can of Carling. Immediately, he took it away. "Oh, right, yours is an orange juice, isn't it? I'll go and get one from the kitchen."

Martha still found it impossible to speak. Bloody hell, who'd turned her tap on? Once again she was crying. Would she ever stop?

"Hey, Babe, what's up?" said Jack. He tenderly leant in and kissed away the tears that were streaming down her face. "Didn't I tell you I'd be back?" His eyes were an exotic and erotic mix of passion and love. Deep, deep love. She believed in it. She was wise and foolish enough to believe in it. She was brave enough to say it. Optimistic enough to hope for it. In love enough to know it.

He loved her.

# Up Close and Personal with the Author

BOTH MARTHA AND ELIZA ARE ENVIOUS OF THE OTHER'S LIFESTYLE. IT SEEMS THE GRASS IS OFTEN GREENER ON THE OTHER SIDE FOR MANY OF US THESE DAYS. WHY DO YOU THINK THIS MIGHT BE?

I'm not sure that envy is a *recent* phenomenon: if it was then Moses wouldn't have included the commandment "Thou shalt not covet thy neighbours wife" on his stone tablet all those years ago. But it might be that we are especially prone to envy nowadays because we have much more choice and instead of this making us feel more content we constantly worry that we've chosen the wrong route and that we could have done better if we'd married someone else, taken different subjects at school, bought a property in a different part of town, and so forth. Personally, I don't understand envy: it's a waste of energy. I'd rather improve my own lot than worry that someone else's grass is greener.

BEFORE THE BREAK-UP OF HER MARRIAGE, MARTHA SEEMED TO HAVE TURNED INTO THE PROVERBIAL DOWNTRODDEN HOUSEWIFE. CAN YOU RELATE TO THIS AT ALL?

I don't think Martha was ever the proverbial downtrodden housewife. After all, she's affluent, she has healthy children, a lovely home stacked with an array of mod cons and her husband's not cruel, drunken, or abusive. Just because she's a devoted homemaker and wife doesn't mean she's downtrodden. But she does suffer from a lack of self-confidence and I think those who work in the home are sometimes prone to this.

LIKE MARTHA, THE BREAK-UP OF YOUR OWN MARRIAGE WAS VERY SUDDEN. HOW DID YOU COPE WITH BEING BOTH SINGLE AND A SINGLE MOTHER SO SUDDENLY?

Admirably. Much like Martha. I'm very proud of that. It's worked, in so much as four years after the event my ex-husband and I have managed to stay friends.

AFTER THE BREAK-UP WITH MICHAEL, MARTHA FINDS IT DIFFICULT TO TALK TO HER FRIENDS ABOUT WHAT HAS HAPPENED. WHY DO YOU THINK IT CAN BE DIFFICULT FOR WOMEN TO TALK ABOUT MARITAL BREAKDOWNS?

I don't know about other women but the reason I found it difficult was that initially I was in shock, then denial, and then I felt an overwhelming sense of shame and failure. Besides, I had a terribly old-fashioned, inherited view that life as a single mum was not only very difficult but also undignified. I'm over all that nonsense now. Talking did help. Knowing when to shut up is useful too!

HOW DO YOU FEEL THE EXPERIENCE OF DIVORCE HAS CHANGED YOU AS A PERSON?

I'm happier, stronger, kinder, and more confident. I absolutely reject the idea that a divorce is the end of the world. Don't get me wrong—I was raw and devastated for a long time. Divorce is a terrible thing that I wouldn't wish on my worst enemy but I believe that what doesn't kill you makes you stronger.

## YOU HAVE A NEW PARTNER NOW. ARE THERE ANY SIMILARITIES BETWEEN HIM AND MARTHA'S NEW PARTNER JACK?

I've re-married and Jack Hope is an accurate portrait of Jim Pride, my husband. The book is very autobiographical in that sense. When Jim came into my life, I was struck by his name (and other things!) and I really believed "fate" was giving me back some pride. I trust that, in some small way, the character Jack Hope gives hope to lots of women in a similar position to the one I was in.

## HOW DOES IT FEEL TO FIND NEW LOVE AFTER A LONG-TERM RELATIONSHIP HAS ENDED?

Sensational. I'm really lucky that someone so wonderful and incredibly special came into my life.

## AFTER A FRUITLESS SEARCH FOR THE PERFECT MAN, ELIZA FINDS HER SOUL MATE WAS RIGHT THERE ALL THE TIME—IN HER LESS-THAN-PERFECT BOYFRIEND GREG. DO YOU THINK MANY WOMEN HAVE UNREALISTIC IDEALS OF WHAT RELATIONSHIPS SHOULD BE?

Absolutely. I get a bit bored of hearing women complain that there are no men out there and then in the next breath they produce a list of what they want from a man that's longer than a six-year-old's list to Father Christmas. *Of course* we should have standards and *of course* we all have deal breakers: I think women should be choosy when it comes to assessing their potential mate for decency, wit, morality, humour, and even sex appeal. But I get extremely cross when girlfriends specify a certain income bracket, brand of clothes, type of car, or postcode that they are looking for in their perfect boyfriend. Shallow, shallow, shallow! I've heard of guys being dumped because he sleeps on the wrong side of the bed, the colour of his duvet, his like/dislike of cartoons, or his fondness for smash potato. But then men are just as bad and are often more demanding with regard to potential partner's personal appearance. It's enough to make you despair for the human race. Except I don't despair, it's not my style.

# Want it ALL?

Want to **read books about stuff *you* care about**?
Want to **meet authors**?
Heck, want to write stuff you care about,
want to *be* **an author**?

Want to **dish the dirt**? Sound off? Spread love?
Punk your boss? Out your mate?

Want to **know what's hot**? Want to *be* **what's hot**?
Want **free stuff**?
Want to do it **all at once, all in one place**?

**18-34 year olds**, there's only one stop… one spot.

# SimonSaysTheSPOT.com

Visit us at http://www.simonsaysTheSPOT.com

# There's nothing better than the perfect bag...

# Unless it's the perfect book.

Good girls go to heaven...

# Naughty Girls go Downtown.